THE HUNTER CHRONICLES

Return to Exile

SIMON & SCHUSTER BOOKS FOR YOUNG READERS
NEW YORK • LONDON • TORONTO • SYDNEY

THE HUNTER CHRONICLES • SNARE 1
Return to Exile
E. J. Patten
ILLUSTRATED BY John Rocco

SIMON & SCHUSTER BOOKS FOR YOUNG READERS
An imprint of Simon & Schuster Children's Publishing Division
1230 Avenue of the Americas, New York, New York 10020

Book design by Laurent Linn
The text for this book is set in Minister Std Light.
The illustrations for this book are rendered digitally.
Manufactured in the United States of America • 0711 FFG
2 4 6 8 10 9 7 5 3 1
Library of Congress Cataloging-in-Publication Data
Patten, E. J., 1974-
Return to exile / E.J. Patten ; illustrated by John Rocco.—1st ed.
p. cm.— (The hunter chronicles)
Summary: On the eve of his twelfth birthday, Sky, who has studied traps, puzzles, science, and the secret lore of the Hunters of Legend, realizes his destiny as a monster hunter.
ISBN 978-1-4424-2032-8
ISBN 978-1-4424-2034-2 (eBook)
[1. Identity—Fiction. 2. Hunters—Fiction. 3. Monsters—Fiction.
4. Supernatural—Fiction.] I. Rocco, John, ill. II. Title.
PZ7.P2759Re 2011
[Fic]—dc22
2010053480

For Katie: Drops of light, like rain, you fill me up.

CONTENTS

PROLOGUE
Shiny Baubles and All

Phineas T. Pimiscule was not what you'd call an "attractive" man. He wasn't "desirable" or "appealing." He didn't like "things" or do "stuff" or "wash" himself. He was not the kind of guy to "put" "quotation" "marks" around "words" or to say things in an unassuming or assuming way.

He *was* the kind of guy who wore a monocle.

He had also been known to fraternize with unsavory characters—a necessity of the job, and possibly a result of monocle-wearing. He traveled the world, seeing the worst of it—places with grotesque names like The-Twelve-Levels-of-Hidden-Terror, Devil's Hill, and Wyoming.

His wasn't a glamorous life, but it was a necessary one . . . more necessary than anyone realized.

But tonight—on the third night of the Hunter's Moon—the necessities of such a life had caught up to him. And after all these many long years, Phineas could finally feel his time drawing near, and he almost welcomed it. Almost.

Cradling a crying infant in his arms, he raced along the lonely path that led from his property to the sleepy, unknowing town beyond. Decaying trees towered over him like a big tower towers over smaller, *less-big* towers.

Dead leaves crunched beneath his feet like sharp teeth on bones, and the moon cast blue-black shadows all around that looked like monstrous figures eating unspeakable living buffets.

His antiquated frock coat hung from him in tatters, ripped by claws, fangs, and worse, and Phineas, mumbling and cursing, did his best to ignore the pain that shot through his body with each jarring step.

At the bottom of a long and lonely hill, Phineas collapsed gratefully against a fallen tree.

"Shhh . . . no more monsters, Sky. Cross my heart," Phineas promised, bouncing Sky gently in his arms, "You're safe now. Uncle Phineas is here. No more of that nasty business. Shhh . . ."

Glancing down, Phineas grimaced as he noticed dark blood trickling from a black mark on Sky's small hand. Phineas sopped at it with a dirty handkerchief, revealing two crescent moons running vertically on Sky's palm, from his fingers to his wrist, with the moons pressed together at the tips like a giant eye. Another mark, pale and white, sat within that dark eye, smaller, and with horizontal moons.

Phineas pressed his handkerchief against the trickle of blood, and no matter how hard he tried, he couldn't seem to stop tears—his *own* tears—from coming.

"I'm so sorry, Sky. I'm so, so sorry. Your mother was right. I couldn't protect you. And now look what I've done."

Sky quieted as he watched Phineas weep, the infant's

forgiving eyes as big and blue as the ocean. And then, with eager hands, Sky reached for Phineas's monocle.

"You like that, do you?" said Phineas, using the dirty handkerchief to wipe his eyes and nose before returning the cloth to Sky's hand. "I suppose you would—shiny bauble and all."

Phineas pulled the strange monocle from his eye and dangled it in front of Sky, swinging it back and forth like a pendulum.

There was a noise above—the fluttering of wings. Looking up, Phineas spotted dozens of oversize black and white crows landing on the branches around them.

"Piebalds," said Phineas, narrowing his eyes at the strangely intelligent black-and-white birds, "there's plenty to eat back at the manor!"

Phineas glared. He'd never cared for the things: Never trust a creature whose brain is smaller than a pea.

"CAW!" cawed the largest of the Piebalds.

"What do you mean you've become vegetarians?" Phineas replied suspiciously. "Since when?"

"Neat trick," said a voice from the shadows.

Phineas spun, a gun slipping into his palm from up his sleeve.

"Hold on, hold on! I'm not armed! Not even a hunter anymore—remember? You booted me out yourself!" The man stepped out of the shadows covered in grime and gore, hands raised. He was unshaven, his skin rough and tanned like toffee left in the sun, and a faint smile played on his lips like a sun waiting to shine—if only there weren't so many clouds.

"Beau?" said Phineas. He shifted his leg, cringing at the pain. "Your timing is impeccable, as always. Though, next time you attempt to sneak up on me, try not to smell like entrails."

"*Attempt* to sneak up on you?" Beau scoffed. "You seemed pretty surprised to me."

"All for show," said Phineas. "I like for my former students to have a healthy sense of self-worth."

"So," said Beau, taking a few steps closer, "you really *are* Phineas, then?"

"At your trial three years ago," said Phineas, holding the gun steady on Beau as the man took another step closer. "I gave you a book, but for the life of me, I can't seem to recall the title."

Beau stopped a few feet away. "The book was *Twenty Things You Didn't Know About Women and Wish You Could Forget Now That You Do*. It doubled as a wedding gift."

"Sorry," said Phineas, lowering the gun. "I didn't mean to dredge up the past."

"Don't apologize," said Beau. "At least we know we're both *us*."

Phineas snorted. "I knew I was me *long* before you showed up. . . . Though, come to think of it, I have been suspicious of late." Phineas dusted his monocle with the dirty handkerchief and returned it to his eye. "So, Malvidia couldn't be bothered to come herself, then? She's usually so hands-on when it comes to traitors."

Phineas pushed himself to his feet with a huff while Sky sat cradled snugly in his arms, watching the Piebalds.

"I think she knew you wouldn't kill me, and maybe she thought I could talk some sense into you," said Beau as they began walking down the path together.

"It's hardly the time for sense, I should think, since *nonsense* has been serving us so well," said Phineas, sounding annoyed, and frustrated, and terribly tired all at once.

"So, you're really running, then?" asked Beau. "You're going to let Malvidia take over what's left of the hunters and just hide from it all? What will the Hunters of Legend think of that?"

"The Hunters of Legend rejected me long ago, and good riddance to bad rubbish, I say," said Phineas. "Besides, they have their own problems at the moment."

"Namely *you*," said Beau. "I know you want to protect Sky, but do you really know this boy anymore? Can you vouch for him—that he's really what we think he is? With that black mark on his hand, are you really so sure he won't become what we all fear?"

The air between them grew silent and heavy. Even the Piebalds stopped their constant cawing.

Finally Phineas spoke, his forehead creased with thoughtful lines.

"Ah, '*fear*'—a funny word, that," said Phineas. "Did you know you can't have '*fear*' without an '*ear*'? Imagine if we used a nose instead of an ear. Do you suppose people would fnose a nose as much as they fear an ear? I don't suppose I know . . . s."

Beau almost smiled. "You always knew how to ruin a moment. But just because you're not afraid doesn't mean others aren't. The hunters are the weakest they've been in centuries—since the days of Bedlam Falls! What are we supposed to do when the Arkhon's prison fails like the others? You and Nikola are the only ones who understand how it works, and Nikola's now insane!"

"There are fail-safes to buy us time if it fails," said Phineas.

"And those are?" asked Beau.

"Something I'd rather not talk about, lest prying ears overhear," said Phineas, glancing at the Piebalds flying overhead. "But I'll be watching. When the time comes, I'll return more openly. Maybe then I will have enough leverage to ensure Sky's safety."

"And if you die before then?" asked Beau.

"I won't leave you *clueless*," said Phineas, smiling.

Beau sighed. Phineas knew Beau hated puzzles, but that just made Phineas smile all the more.

Up above, the Piebalds flapped off into the night, cawing and thinking about what they'd heard. They flew north toward red, blue, and black clouds full of strangely colored lightning and unnatural thunder—toward a terrible storm raging like unholy titans above a sprawling, dreadful manor.

Lightning struck the manor and the grounds around it again and again, illuminating a gargantuan glowing wall several football fields away from the manor itself, and hundreds of dark figures of all shapes and sizes (some human, some less so) locked in a horrifying struggle.

As the Piebalds sailed higher, they noticed countless bodies—so many bodies scattered everywhere.

A funnel cloud of furious lightning and color formed over the manor. Great rushing wind rose up, drawing the Piebalds closer. They banked left, racing to escape the funnel's pull.

The dark figures below broke, racing for the glowing wall.

Thunder cracked. A gruesome wave of light and darkness exploded out of the manor, crashing through everything.

And then . . .

Nothing more.

CHAPTER 1

A Trap, Like a Good Story

A good trap is like a good story: hidden and leading toward one inevitable conclusion," muttered Sky, checking his vines with a practiced delectation.

He dropped to the ground to get a closer look, his dirty black hair dragging through the dirt.

"Rule number two," whispered Sky, brushing leaves over the vine, trying to make the pattern look random. "A good trap, like a good story, has to arise naturally from the environment. It has to be seamless. If the prey suspects what's coming, they'll bolt."

Standing but still partially crouched, Sky shimmied behind the closest tree. He peeked out, surveying the forest for signs of life. Traces of fading sunlight slipped through the canopy above, moving across the earth like matadors with threadbare capes teasing and taunting the night onward. And the night—*stupid thing that it was*—kept taking the bait.

Just like Sky.

His stomach growled at the thought of bait. He'd eat some right now if he had any. The problem was, he'd already eaten it. He pressed his back against the tree, holding his stomach.

Didn't his uncle know there were child labor laws to protect kids from this kind of thing? He must have set up a bazillion traps today, and still nothing. He was only eleven, for crying out loud! No, not eleven—twelve, actually. It was his birthday, after all, and an awful one at that. And yet nobody seemed to care. He'd been wandering the woods all day, hungry, alone, and with nothing to look forward to, except for yet another horrible move.

He was getting tired of it. He pulled out his yo-yo and practiced a few tricks: pinwheel, double or nothing, rock the baby. Just as he was slipping into a Ferris wheel, he heard it—

SNAP. "AARGH!"

He flipped his yo-yo into his pocket and raced west toward the sound.

"Yes, yes, yes, yes, YES!" He ran into the broad clearing and saw Uncle Phineas hanging by his ankle on the clearing's edge. "HA! Goulash for you!"

His uncle smiled down at him.

"Yes, yes, well played. I get goulash for your birthday party tonight, and you get leftover pizza. Bully for you. Now, if you wouldn't mind cutting me down?" said Phineas.

Sky walked toward the tree that served as the linchpin of the trap, laughing. "You mess with the best, you hang like Aunt Tess."

"That was your great-great-aunt Tess, and she wasn't hung. She was drawn and quartered," said Phineas.

"Same dif," said Sky, searching through the jumble of vines to find the primary link.

"Only in that your bowels void in both situations. Though I assure you one is much messier than the other," said Phineas.

"Really? Which one?"

"I'll leave that for your overactive imagination to puzzle out," said Phineas as he swung back and forth, back and forth.

"That's the third rule of trap building, right? A trap," said Sky, trying to imitate his uncle's not-quite-British I've-been-in-America-too-long accent. (Clear throat.) "A trap, like a good story, needs to hint at greater things without revealing them until the prey is snared."

"Spot on, though your imitation could use some work," said Phineas.

"You can add vocal coaching to my curriculum right after botany," said Sky, "since you seem intent on boring me to death."

Sky found the main vine and started tracing it through the jumble. This was a particularly complex trap that used all the fundamentals of trap building: direct and misdirect, attract and repel, lure and snare—all the things his uncle had taught him over the years.

"Botany could well save your life one day, you know," said Phineas, "if you'd only read all the books I gave you and not just the ones you like."

"Pshaw," said Sky. "If the day ever comes that I need botany, I'll eat the goulash—a whole pot of it."

"I don't think goulash is healthy for a body in the throws of rigor mortis. . . . Actually, I think goulash may cause rigor mortis, but if you promise to eat it, I'll see to it that you have some in your hour of need," Phineas replied. "It might make a good side dish to your *words*."

"Ha, ha. Eat my words. I get it. It's a word puzzle, like an acrostic or an anagram, but not as clever," said Sky sarcastically as he gave up on the vine he'd been working on and started tracing another.

Phineas smiled. "It was very clever of *you,* Sky, using a triple trolley—or the troll snatcher, as Sir Alexander Drake used to call it before he was brutally murdered."

"You don't have to call it the 'troll snatcher,' Uncle Phineas; I'm twelve now, all grown up. I know there are no trolls to snatch," said Sky.

"Which reminds me . . . ," said Phineas, wiggling around like a prize marlin. A small wrapped box fell from his tattered frock coat. "Happy birthday."

Sky let go of the vine he'd been playing with and crossed the open space between them to pick up the box.

"Well, go on! Open it!" said Phineas, smiling down at him, his strange monocle fastidiously clinging to his face despite all the laws of physics. He'd worn the monocle for as long as Sky could remember. It was dark, strange and thick, like a jeweler's monocle, with retractable hooks that fit over the nose and ear.

Sky shook the box.

"But . . . aren't you going to be at my party tonight?" asked Sky, suddenly worried.

"Of course. I know I haven't been around as much of late, but I've never missed it before, have I?" replied Phineas. Sky felt measurably better. He couldn't imagine a party without Phineas.

"I'm giving this to you now because this is one gift best given in private," Phineas supplied, answering Sky's next question before he could ask it. "Well, go on!"

Grinning, Sky ripped off the wrapping paper and opened the box. Inside he found an antique pocket watch, similar in style to the monocle his uncle wore, but lighter, sort of grayish.

"Your watch?" said Sky, surprised. He flipped it open, watching as the numerous dials ticked and the moon made its way around the edge like a peddler looking for a place to push his wares. Phineas had tried to show him how to read it once, but he'd never figured it out.

After a moment the dials settled down and the moon took its place in the night, full and heavy—just like the moon overhead. "It's amazing! Thank you."

"She's old, but she keeps good time," said Phineas. "The great monster hunter Solomon Rose and I once argued over whether or not the moon ran by her or the other way around. You share a birthday with him, you know, both born under the Hunter's Moon."

"Solomon Rose? The greatest monster hunter of all time? Died more than four hundred years ago—and you claim he argued with you over this watch? I find that hard to believe," said Sky.

"I argued with him, actually. And just because you find it hard to believe doesn't mean it's not worth believing," said Phineas. "Sometimes the hardest things to believe are the only things worth believing at all."

Sky closed the watch and started to put it away. He paused, noticing an etching on the back: a white eye, like two crescent moons pressed at the tips, set deep into the metal. He raised his left hand, comparing the etching to the birthmark on his palm; they were identical.

His white birthmark had always felt so strange to him, like paper held too close to a candle, not yet burning, but destined for ash. Another mark, black and gruesome, surrounded the first with the two crescent moons running vertically from fingers to wrist. He called this second mark his cicatrix, or just "trix" for short, because it reminded him of an unhealed wound. Whereas the birthmark felt hot, the trix felt cold, shifting, and sometimes brittle, like it might burst open at any moment.

The watch didn't have the trix, but there was no mistaking the birthmark.

"You did this?" asked Sky, showing Phineas the etching on the watch.

"Not me. That etching was done a long, long time ago. Centuries ago, in fact," said Phineas.

Sky smirked. "Yeah. Uh-huh."

"It's true, Sky! Your birthmark—it's special. It's the Hunter's Mark, not seen since Solomon Rose himself."

"Really?" said Sky, not taking Phineas seriously, but wanting to. "So where's the trix, then? I assume it's special too?"

"Not particularly," said Phineas, his expression unreadable.

Something in the back of Sky's mind seemed to growl as if upset—a peculiar sensation that usually ended with him in trouble. Over the years, he'd come to call this unpredictable sensation his "little monster." His sister assured him it was *completely* abnormal, and probably terminal—perhaps an incurable disease eating away at his brain or, even worse, early onset puberty (if there was, in fact, a difference between the two).

He didn't think it was abnormal, but having never been inside a normal person's head, he couldn't be certain.

The sensation didn't really bother him—in fact, quite often it was the only friend he had—but sometimes it could get on his nerves.

Feeling uneasy, though he couldn't explain why, he ignored the sensation and grabbed the next vine.

"Sky, do you remember the poem from *The Evil Echo of Solomon Rose*?" asked Phineas, swinging, his face turning as red as a turnip as blood continued rushing to his head.

"Er . . . not particularly," said Sky. "Something about evil echoes and gloaming? I'm not really sure." *The Evil Echo of Solomon Rose* was his favorite story. He knew the poem, though perhaps not as well as he should. He tended to skip poems when he read, but what was he supposed to do when so many of them droned on endlessly and made no sense whatsoever?

Besides, it'd been almost a year since he'd read it. . . . Well, since he'd read anything, really.

"You should know this poem backward and forward by now, for how many times you've read it," rebuked Phineas. "I've seen the book. It's all ragged and abused."

"I know, I know," said Sky, "but maybe you should tell me the poem to help me remember."

Sky preferred hearing Phineas recite the poems anyway. His accent and old-world charm—magnified by the frock coat and monocle—gave the poems a portentous air. Plus, Phineas was hanging upside down and looked like a beet; in Sky's opinion, it didn't get much funnier.

"All right, then—but just this once!" said Phineas.

Just this once had happened many times before.

Phineas began:

> The evil echo came, a gloaming in the dark,
> 'pon belly bowering and crawing for the Mark,
> to Solomon Rose the same, who sang the
>   names of yore,
> and with it brought his evil forth, a gibbering
>   from the moor.

My branches shook and writhed, and standing
did I shriek,
"Why callest thou me, thou thawing thorn?
What sorrows dost thou seek?"
Old Solomon shook and shivered, but
dreaming of Lenore,
'pon his evil he shed his mind, and cast it in
the gore.
"I'm Solomon," he said, "and my servants you
shall be,
till earth and sky begin to shake,
and the sieves of time begin to seep."
Then he found us, and bound us,
and sent us off to dream,
till finally watchful waiting, our senses fading,
his evil echo slithered off to sleep.

Phineas finished, and the grove filled with a weighty silence.

Sky knew all about the Echo. They weren't popular like vampires and werewolves, monsters that—according to his uncle—had been a little *too* popular and had been hunted to extinction as a result.

Phineas claimed (and Sky doubted) that dozens of different kinds of monsters, like the Echo, survived still—monsters that were far cleverer, far better at hiding, far stronger, and far more terrifying than vampires and werewolves.

The Evil Echo of Solomon Rose described the various Echo as vaguely treelike, with large black leathery wings that folded out of their trunk-ish bodies. Their branchy arms could be as inflexible as iron one moment, and as slithery as tentacles the next, and when the wings spread out, the branches swept downward into a rickety protective shell. Or, if the Echo chose, the wings spread outward like writhing spears to flay and terrify those below. A tree one instant, a nightmare with wings the next.

Great pupil-less white eyes ran half the length of the trunk—eyes that Solomon Rose gouged out, one by one, when the Echo refused to follow him against a monster he claimed would destroy the world. Robbed of their sight, the Echo began to "see" through highly sensitive organs in their branches and mouths—tasting the scents, sights, and emotions around them.

Echo kept to themselves, hiding in the old, dark forests of the world. Tangled roots spread deep, deep beneath them, clinging to the roots of other Echo like children holding hands, and they spent days and nights lost in a haunting sort of collective dream.

According to the Echo narrator of *The Evil Echo of Solomon Rose*, breaking an Echo from its roots ended the dream, effectively exiling the Echo, and was one of the cruelest things that could happen; it was also one of the best, because a rooted Echo couldn't fly, and flying, as the narrator claimed, was a dream worth waking up for.

"The Mark in the poem is the Hunter's Mark," said Phineas.

"Are you sure about that?" Sky appreciated his uncle's efforts to tell a good story, but honestly . . . "Are you sure it isn't just a terrible paper cut? Or maybe a stick caught Solomon in that moor—left a nasty mark on his cheek—big red welts all swollen and puffy . . . just horrible."

"I know the kind," said Phineas. "I suspect I may have one just like it around my ankle."

"I am here to serve." Sky swooshed a tangled vine in front

of him and bowed mockingly from his knees, like an actor taking full credit for a mediocre performance. "And I'm twelve now. I can do without all the lessons."

"I think I may still have a lesson for you," said Phineas. "A grape might become a raisin, and taste the sweeter for it, but even a raisin will rot on the vine, if you do nothing for it."

"You just rhymed 'for it' with 'for it,'" said Sky.

"So?"

"That's atrocious—just dreadful really," said Sky, mimicking his uncle; maybe he couldn't mimic his uncle's accent very well, but the words were easy enough. "You could've just said you wanted down. You didn't have to bore me with a poem."

"Ah, but can't a poem have more than one meaning?" asked Phineas. "Perhaps I was making the important points obvious to illustrate a *point*."

Sky followed one of the vines across the ground, pulling it from the earth. "Hold on. I almost have it." It seemed to be leading him toward the next tree, but for some strange reason he couldn't remember laying it. Of course, he'd laid so many today it was hard to keep track.

"You know," said Phineas, "the triple trolley really was brilliant. The only thing I can think of to top it would be the quadruple quandary—"

Sky stopped suddenly, the vine taut in his hands.

"No—" But he didn't get any further. The coil under him snapped closed around his ankle, dragging him into the air. Uncle Phineas started laughing and clapping his hands together.

As Sky rose upward, Phineas gently descended to the

ground. Phineas undid the coil around his ankle and crossed to stare up at Sky.

"How do you like my poetry now?" asked Phineas.

"You meant 'for' as in 'four' . . . as in quadruple—as in quadruple quandary," said Sky. "You were giving me a clue."

"Quite so," said Phineas. "You really should pay more attention to poems."

"You tricked me," accused Sky as he swung in the air.

"Of course I did. If I didn't trick you, it wouldn't be a trap," said Phineas. "Use your heart. *Understand*. Learn to see things in the now, not as they were or will be, or as they might or should be, but as they are, right now, in this moment. The heart sees the now; the mind only sees the next. If you can't learn to see the now, you'll never see what's truly there, and then where will you be?"

"Trapped," said Sky.

"Precisely. But if you take care of the now, the future will work out as it should. Rule number four: A trap, like a good story, pretends to be something it's not until the very end." Phineas turned and started walking away.

"But that's the same as rule number one!" Sky exclaimed.

"Maybe if I say it twice, you'll remember," Phineas called over his shoulder.

"Where are you going?" cried Sky, beginning to feel nervous.

"You're moving to Exile tonight, remember?" Phineas prodded. "Some of us don't have time to *hang out*."

Sky groaned. The pun was bad enough, but did he have to bring up moving?

"Wait," said Sky, suddenly realizing something. "Aren't you coming with us?"

"If things turn out as I hope, we'll finally be neighbors!" chirped Phineas, sounding more excited than he'd sounded in a long time. "See you back at the house for your party—and goulash! Happy birthday, Sky!"

Phineas laughed, quickening his pace. But when he reached the far edge of the clearing, Sky saw him slow down, and then stop. For a second he wondered if Phineas would let him down after all, but Phineas just stood there staring into the far woods, as silent as the approaching night.

Phineas turned around, and Sky could see his face in the half-light. Phineas's smile had disappeared, and he looked grim, almost frightened. He removed his monocle, dusting it with a handkerchief before returning it to his eye, and then he spun around and ran off into the gathering darkness.

For a moment it almost seemed to Sky as if the deepening shadows followed after him, terrible and menacing. Something long and silvery flashed in Phineas's hand, and then he was gone.

Sky shook himself. Too much blood in his head—that was the problem. Couldn't see straight. He'd thought Phineas might come back for him, but then . . .

Well, not coming back after all. It was just like him. Always disappearing when Sky needed him.

Sky swung slowly back and forth, back and forth. He was hungry, alone, and he had nothing to look forward to except goulash and a move. And now he was trapped. This was definitely, hands down, bar none his *worst birthday ever*.

CHAPTER 2

Exile

Sky's birthday wasn't over, and what was worse, it wasn't getting any better.

He pressed his fingers against the car window, feeling the cold with one hand while he twisted a Rubik's Cube with the other. He lined up a side without even looking.

Sky was good at puzzles. He'd broken free of the quadruple quandary in less than fifteen minutes. It was a good trap, but if you swung in just the right way and jerked just so . . . Well, give him something with missing pieces—or something where things just didn't fit together right—and he could figure it out. Puzzles, he could understand.

His family was a different matter entirely.

They had moved six times in as many months, and before that, for as long as he could remember, they'd moved almost as much. His parents had never really explained why they moved all the time. Oh, they'd certainly tried—lost jobs, bad schools, poor air quality, too many beaver dams—but Sky knew none of it was true.

Especially the beaver dams. Honestly, it was like his parents weren't even trying to come up with good excuses anymore.

The fact was, his family was a mystery, a puzzle with missing pieces. And he was beginning to think that, unlike traps and Rubik's Cubes, this was one puzzle he'd never figure out.

"I still don't understand. You're saying he never came back? Not even for goulash?" asked Sky. He pulled out the pocket watch Phineas had given him and started fiddling with the dials. The watch didn't make any more sense to him now than it had before, but he needed a distraction.

He felt uneasy. Something was wrong, and he couldn't put his finger on it. Even his little monster seemed on edge.

"He'll be fine, Sky," Mom consoled, her latest knitting project in her hands. Mom's hands were always moving—twiddling needles, moving dirt, strangling innocent sponges, writing letters to government officials to let them know her opinions on the state of the world, and the way things are, and the outrageous price of gasoline and milk and milk-based products. Mom's hands moved almost independently of her, as if they had a mind of their own.

"Just because the man chose to flee like a coward rather than eat my goulash doesn't mean something happened to him," Mom continued. "You shouldn't let his stories get to you like this. What was it today? Harrow Wights and Harrow Knights? Edgewalkers? Wargarous, maybe?"

"Echo," said Sky.

Mom harrumphed. "Well, don't let it bother you. Phineas promised he'd meet us in Exile, and that's where he'll be."

"And if he's not?" asked Sky for the three-hundredth time.

"He promised he'd be at my party. He's never missed my birthday party before!"

Mom sighed, turning back to her knitting without another word.

Sky slumped down in his seat. Something was wrong. He could feel it. . . . The way Phineas had stopped, and how frightened he'd looked, and then how he'd just run off into the woods . . . it wasn't like him. Uncle Phineas wasn't the kind of guy to leave without goulash; he was the kind of guy to make others eat goulash with him, or perhaps *instead* of him. So why hadn't he come back to the house?

"Dad, Sky's looking at me again!" said Hannah, his sister. She looked up from her magazine, *Cheerleader's Quarterly*, obviously annoyed. She had long blond hair, eyelashes like spiderwebs, and lips like rubies. At fifteen, almost sixteen, she excelled in every sport, captained any team she joined, and was always the most popular girl in the room.

She was everything Sky wasn't.

"I wasn't looking at *you*," Sky retorted. "I thought I saw something out your window."

"Yeah, it's called corn," Hannah responded sarcastically, "or, as the Indians called it, 'maize.'"

When Sky moved, he left nothing behind—no friends, no teams, not even a forwarding address for bulk mail, which was the only kind of mail he ever got. But when Hannah moved . . . when *Hannah* moved, *that* was different.

"Hannah, there's no need to pull the Indians into this!" Dad chided from the driver's seat. "They've had enough problems as it is."

Sky's Dad, Herman—or Mr. Weathers, as his friends called him—peered at Sky in the rearview mirror, the corners of his mouth perked up in a perpetual smile. There were rumors that Dad had frowned once back in '69 when he'd learned of the hippie movement, but that was before Sky's time, and he had his doubts.

"Hey, this isn't about me, Dad. Learn to control your offspring!" said Hannah.

"I'm not offspring," said Sky, checking his armpits to see if he smelled. He showered nearly every day, except when he didn't, so the thought of Hannah questioning his hygiene was highly offensive.

"That's *Irish Spring*, you dolt! I called you offspring!"

"Same dif," defended Sky.

"If you *were* Irish Spring, you'd smell good like soap—not like rotten cabbage! And since you brought it up, would it kill you to take a shower? Just once a month maybe? If you won't do it for us, *please*, Sky, will you *do it for the children*?" Hannah put her hands together, putting on a show of pleading. "Just think of *the children*!"

"Would you two knock it off!" Mom reprimanded. "Sky's smell is perfectly normal. It's the scent of youth." Mom spoke in his defense, but Sky almost wished she wouldn't.

"More like the stench of youth. And I don't care what it is! He should use deodorant or something," said Hannah. "Even Europeans have that much courtesy."

"You've never even been to Europe," said Sky.

"I don't have to go. I can smell it from here!" said Hannah. "At least during those blessed moments when *you're* not around."

"Just a little longer now, kids. That's all. Please just try to get along." Mom closed a loop and moved on to the next layer of yarn-web.

Sky slumped back in his seat.

Worst. Birthday. Ever.

The car behind them flashed its lights, and Dad rolled down his window to wave them on.

"A 1957 Cadillac Eldorado Brougham," said Dad, whistling as the car passed. "You don't see those around anymore."

"Gee, Dad, I wonder why," said Hannah, rolling her eyes.

From within the Cadillac's murky depths, Sky could just make out two dark shadows watching from the front seat. His little monster growled in the back of his mind, surprising him.

Over the last few years, Sky had learned to ignore his little monster. He didn't let it push him to get in fights at school or to argue with teachers or to sneak out at night and wander. . . . Well, not as much as he used to, anyway.

More often than not it pushed him into trouble. But sometimes it warned him of trouble too.

As the old car disappeared into the darkness ahead, Sky could almost hear the little monster's whisper. *"Beware."*

Beware of what? An old car?

Five minutes later they reached Exile. Most the town was invisible, hiding respectfully in the trees, but plenty of old buildings hunched together along Main Street, like hobos around a campfire trying to warm their socks.

Sky had been born here, he knew, but he couldn't remember anything. His parents seldom spoke about why they'd left, and what little they said was seldom worth saying at all.

They'd lived in a house here. Sky had gathered that much. Not an apartment, not a duplex or motel, not a run-down rental, but a house they'd actually owned.

Even Uncle Phineas had a home here—a large estate, by all accounts—that he'd left behind. Sky had never known

Phineas to live anywhere, let alone on an estate; even the word sounded important.

Uncle Phineas traveled the world selling old books, and on those rare occasions when he did visit, he didn't stay long. Sky couldn't imagine Phineas staying in one place long enough to own it.

As they slipped through the quiet streets, Sky's thoughts jumped back to Phineas.

"But what if he's not there?" asked Sky for the three-hundred-and-*first* time.

"Sky, your uncle loves you very much. I know he doesn't visit like he used to—it can't be helped—but that doesn't change things. He'd give anything for you—for all of us, for that matter." Mom sighed, shaking her head, as if there were more to say but she wasn't willing to say it. "For all his faults, he's a greater man than you realize. If Phineas said he'd meet us in Exile, *he'll meet us in Exile*."

"But—"

"Drop it, Sky," said Mom, cutting him off. "I know you're nervous. I know you don't like moving—none of us like it—but this move is . . . It's . . . different."

"That's what you always say," said Hannah, peeking over the top of *Cheerleader's Quarterly*.

"Yes," said Dad, smiling, "but this time we mean it."

Hannah snorted, and Mom rolled her eyes.

"Very delicately handled, Herman," said Mom.

Dad grinned.

At that moment they turned onto a cracked blacktop road that wove its way through an old neighborhood before coming to a dead end at a rusted wrought iron fence.

Beyond the fence—far, far away—Sky could just make out

the black pinnacles of what must have been a very large church or house.

"That's not it, is it?" asked Sky.

"What's not it?" said Mom.

"That," said Sky, watching the pinnacles disappear behind red and orange fall leaves. "Up on the hill over there. With the pinnacles and all."

Dad cast a strange glance at Mom. "You can see that from here? In the dark?"

Sky had forgotten it was dark out, but as he realized it, everything seemed to fade away—or maybe he just wanted it to. "Er . . . not anymore. Now that you mention it, it is kind of dark out."

"Little freak," said Hannah without looking up from her magazine.

"Hannah!"

"What, Mom? He is!"

"To answer your question," said Dad, ignoring Hannah's unpleasantness, "no. That's not our house. That's Phineas's house."

"*That's* Pimiscule Manor?" Sky exclaimed, trying to get a better look.

"Everything on that side of the fence is his," said Mom, staring at the rusted fence, her jaw clenched, eyes distant. "The estate goes on for miles. Cass and I never did find the northern boundary."

Mom had mentioned Cass before—a friend that, by the way Mom talked about her, must've died—but Sky knew she wouldn't say anything more.

"Uncle Phineas never mentioned it was so . . . er . . . ," started Sky.

"Ugly?" offered Hannah.

"No."

"Repulsive?"

"No."

"Repellent? Abhorrent? Freakish?"

"No!" exclaimed Sky. "I was going to say 'big'—and you didn't even see it!"

"I don't have to see it. I've seen the way Phineas dresses," said Hannah. "I mean, really—a frock coat? His house must be *ghastly*."

"I want you two to stay away from there," said Mom. "You especially, Sky. No nighttime forays."

"Why?" asked Sky, confused. "How am I supposed to see Uncle Phineas if I have to stay away?"

"It's likely," said Dad, "that if Phineas *is* able to stay in Exile—"

"Which isn't certain," added Mom.

"Right. Not certain at all," continued Dad. "But if he does stay, then he won't be staying at the manor. Nobody has lived there for a very long time. It's certainly not safe—broken stairs, vandalism, glass everywhere. Termites have likely eaten the place to rot. Best to stay away. Besides, Phineas may stay with us for a time, but it's hard to say."

Staying with them? Sky felt elated. As embarrassing as it was to admit, he considered Uncle Phineas his best friend. Well, his only friend, really. Moving as often as he did made it hard for Sky to make friends.

Plus, he was a bit odd. How many kids spent their birthdays talking about monsters and trying to trap their uncle in the woods?

But of all the people he'd ever met, he felt certain Phineas understood him best.

"Ah, this is our place," said Dad. They rolled to a stop at the last house on the right, just next to the fence separating Pimiscule Grounds from the rest of the neighborhood.

The house sagged like an old woman carrying a bag of groceries. Cracked wood—as dry as a desert—peeked out from faded paint. Tall weeds covered the lawn and poked through a broken walkway that led to a porch, which (given the slightest provocation) might fall right off.

"It's a hole," said Hannah, scowling at the run-down house. "It's like a giant pigeon pooped on the grass and that's where we're going to live."

Everyone exited the car, and Dad moved around, looking at the house from different angles, as if that could improve the sight. Reaching up, Dad adjusted a sagging shutter. His shirtsleeve snagged as he pulled away, and the shutter broke right off and dangled from his arm. He jerked his arm around to shake it loose; the shutter fell, but it took half his shirt with it. Dad wasn't known for his grace and elegance. In fact, he'd once broken his leg while playing the banjo. Admittedly, it had been a tough song to play, but even so.

"I never thought I'd be back here again," said Mom, her eyes unfocused as she stared off into the night. With a heavy sigh she started to unpack the car, leaving Sky to wonder whether she was happy to be back or horrified. From the look on her face, Sky suspected it was probably a bit of both.

But why come back, then?

"Listen to Mom for once," said Hannah. "Just . . . just try to be normal, okay? Just promise me? Stay away from the house, no wandering around at night, no building traps, or hiding in your room fiddling with puzzles all day listening to voices in your head, or talking about hunters and monsters all the time. No being . . . being . . ."

"Me?" Sky offered.

"Right," said Hannah. "Try to be someone else. Someone cool. You could have friends here, a real life. Don't you want that?"

Sky did want that. He wanted it quite a bit.

"All right. I promise I'll try," said Sky. "Is that good enough for you?"

She looked him over once, frowned, and then nodded.

Walking to the end of the driveway, Sky looked up the empty road.

"Where is he?" wondered Sky.

He heard the gate to Pimiscule Grounds open, and he turned, hoping to find Phineas trudging through in a worn frock coat and monocle.

Instead he found a bright-eyed brown-haired girl stuffing something into her backpack as she exited Phineas's property. She looked to be about Sky's age, and her clothes were black, somewhat frumpy, and *very* baggy, like hand-me-downs that had been first worn and then trod upon by elephants.

She seemed to sense his eyes upon her, because she stopped suddenly and looked right at him. She frowned.

Sky politely looked away so she wouldn't think he was staring. He'd never been good with people.

When he looked back, the girl was gone.

"Disappointed?" Dad stepped up next to him.

"What? No. . . . I mean, I don't even know her," said Sky.

Dad stared at him, a strange expression on his face. "I

meant about Uncle Phineas. But if you'd rather talk about the lady love you left behind . . ."

Sky turned bright red, and Dad laughed.

"No, Sky. I know. The only lady love for you is the night, and she seems to be with us wherever we go." Dad put his arm around Sky. "It could be different here, you know—better. It was for me."

"Then, why did you leave?"

Dad didn't say anything for a moment, thinking.

"Sometimes," said Dad, "we have to give up what we *love* for what we love *best*." He pulled Sky close in a one-arm hug, and then he patted him on the back, turned, and walked away.

Love best? What did *that* mean? It almost sounded as if Dad had left Exile because of Sky, but what did Sky have to do with any of it?

His family was a puzzle with missing pieces, and the more Sky learned about them, the more pieces he found missing.

And the biggest puzzle right now, the one that bothered him most of all, was Phineas. Where was he? Had something happened?

Sky turned to follow Dad, glancing up the road one last time. At the end of the street, a faded-red 1957 Cadillac Eldorado Brougham slowly drove past. From within the car's shadowy depths, he could almost see two sets of sinister eyes watching him.

And then the car was gone.

CHAPTER 3

Feckless Shadows

An old truck drove down an empty street lined with abandoned houses and rolled to a stop just shy of a wrought iron fence that seemed somehow familiar, though Sky couldn't remember why.

He watched from the shadows, slowly creeping closer and closer, though why he did, he didn't know. It just seemed like the thing to do.

His trix ached from cold, though it wasn't terribly cold out. Looking down, he saw a tiny rip on the trix, and a stream of black blood dripped onto the Hunter's Mark. He wiped his hand against his pants, feeling odd. He couldn't remember having black blood before. Of course, he couldn't remember his trix bleeding before either. Come to think of it, he couldn't remember much of anything.

He turned back to the truck. He could see Uncle Phineas in the driver's seat scribbling furiously on some papers propped against the dash. Uncle Phineas. . . . He felt like he should remember something about his uncle, but he couldn't remember what it was.

A moment later he heard a rumbling engine, and a faded-red 1957 Cadillac Eldorado Brougham pulled up, stopping just up the road.

Sky narrowed his eyes, a feeling of wrongness stealing over him. Where had he seen that car before? He could almost remember, just like he could almost remember how he'd gotten here.

A man stepped out of the car. Darkness tipped with fire writhed about him like worms in the dirt, and Sky nearly screamed. He couldn't see the man's face or clothes.

He squinted his eyes to pierce the unnatural murk, but the flames flashed brightly, blinding him!

Sky stumbled forward, blinking away the flashes and tears until his vision returned.

The old truck door creaked, and Phineas stepped out, the papers he'd been scribbling on conspicuously absent. His frock coat was ripped and his hair was disheveled. A long cut ran down his cheek, caked with fresh blood.

"Bat! It's been a long time!" said Phineas, in good spirits despite his appearance. "You seem . . . different. Is that a new cravat?"

New cravat? What in the world was a cravat? Couldn't Phineas see the darkness and blinding flames?

Sky tried to scream a warning, but his tongue kept slipping away from him.

As the man strolled toward Phineas, a woman stepped out of the car. She had piercing blue eyes. Small wrinkles lined her forehead, and wisps of gray hair wrestled with brown, but she didn't look terribly old.

"Give us the keys, Phineas," said the woman.

"Well . . . Ambrosia," said Phineas, narrowing his eyes. "What a surprise. You followed me, then? I suppose that means you're not really Bat, after all. A pity, really. He was a good man once." Phineas turned to regard the man. "You'd be the Wargarou, then? From Whimple?" Phineas's voice went cold.

The darkness around the man who was not Bat seemed to smile a confirmation.

"Ah," said Phineas. "I guess that explains the cravat."

Before Sky could blink, Phineas pulled a long, glittering knife from his frock coat; in the same motion his shoulder jerked, and a gun dropped into his other hand.

The two figures pounced, their bodies writhing unnaturally—distorting and shifting. Worms of fire-tipped darkness lashed at Phineas, bursting from the Wargarou's body.

Sky screamed, helpless, but Phineas couldn't hear.

Five dark shadows, like wolves, burst from the abandoned houses and rushed Phineas. He moved like wind among them, twisting and diving, weaving and cutting. But there were just too many.

"You've almost found me, Sky!" said a voice—his *own* voice—inside his head.

He felt a push, and then he was flying.

"Phineas!" Sky screamed, opening his eyes. He bolted upright in his bed, safe and sound in his new home.

He took a deep breath to calm himself and wiped the sweat from his forehead.

He shivered. Another nightmare to add to his collection; would they ever stop? But this one seemed so much more real.

Moonlight trickled through his window, casting feckless

shadows across unpacked boxes and the random bits of furniture they'd found hidden away in the attic after they'd arrived. An old desk and gas lamp, a plastic ficus tree with missing leaves, and a dresser with a mirror on top, against which he'd laid his least-favorite, and only, tuba. (Mom claimed it built character; Sky claimed it built more determined enemies.)

The only other possession he could claim as his own, aside from the pocket watch, Rubik's Cube, and yo-yo that sat on the desk, was a small collection of old books—journals from supposed "monster hunters," myths, folk stories, narratives, encyclopedias, botany and metallurgy guides, science books, bestiaries, and maps, some hundreds of years old.

Uncle Phineas had given him the collection when he was five. Up until a few years ago, he'd been slowly working his way through it—a few journals, a myth or two, and most of the stories: *The Shadow Wargs of Whimple, Reaper Keeper, Demon Wraiths of Windsor, The Hogsnatcher King, The Tourmaline of Foresight,* and, of course, *The Evil Echo of Solomon Rose*.

He'd always planned to read the other books. When he was younger, he'd loved the stories, and the maps, and guides, and science stuff, and bestiaries. He'd loved all of it. As he'd gotten older, he'd grown less interested in the more boring stuff, but he still loved talking about the stories with Uncle Phineas, even if he didn't quite believe them anymore. But in the last year or two, after Uncle Phineas had stopped visiting as often, he hadn't seen the point. Why read the books when Phineas wasn't around to improve on them? He'd never talked to anyone else that had even *heard* of the stories or monsters before. And so, the collection was still packed away, like it usually was, resting next to his tuba.

As his eyes drifted across the darkened room, he realized

that he could hear murmuring. At first he thought it was coming through the vents, a low, metallic *scratch . . . scratch . . . scratch*, but as he stood, he realized the sound came from outside.

Tap, tap, tap.

Sky sat still. What was *that*?

Tap, tap, tap.

Slipping from his bed, he padded to the window.

A large black-and-white crow sat on the windowsill, pecking at his window.

Tap, tap, tap.

Sky slid the window open. The crow flew back to the tree and sat on a branch, staring at him. Sky looked closer and noticed dozens of black-and-white crows watching him.

"Er," said Sky, not sure what to say to a crow that had, for some inexplicable reason, decided to wake him up in the middle of the night. They looked larger than other crows he'd seen, maybe half again as big, and the Piebald markings—the black-and-white pattern—gave them an almost eerie glow.

"CAW," cawed the crow.

"Er," said Sky, starting to get a creepy feeling. The crows seemed somehow familiar, but Sky couldn't see how that was possible. They were *birds*. Admittedly, they were strange birds, but birds nonetheless.

As he watched them, he heard voices. To his right, just beyond the large tree outside his window—by the fence separating their property from the trail leading to Pimiscule Manor—he could see his parents.

Sky grabbed his pocket watch off the desk and checked the time. Nearly midnight.

"CAW!" cawed the crow.

"Shhh!" Sky hissed.

He stuck his head out farther, straining to hear.

". . . Jack could get you, you know," said Mom, voice full of worry. "You're not exactly in practice. And what if he's not even there? Sky's right. Phineas wouldn't have left without saying good-bye. And he most *definitely* would've met us here. What if he's been duped like Beau was? Or has disappeared like Cassandra?"

"I'll be fine," said Dad, "and Phineas probably just didn't want to draw attention to us."

"Not likely. You know how he dotes on Sky," said Mom. "He would have met us. Nothing would've stopped him, and something that could . . . That scares me more than anything. What else is hiding in this town, Herman? What could possibly have taken someone like Phineas?"

"Helen, if Phineas *is* missing—it's more important than ever that I check things out. Ursula may know something, and no matter what she did to Beau or anyone else, if she has information as she claims, we need to find out what it is. If Phineas is gone, it falls to us. You know why we came out of hiding. A fail-safe has been thrown. Nikola's wall has returned under a full moon! We have to do something. We have to try!"

"Don't go up there tonight, Herman. *Please*. Malvidia has set a trap for us, no matter what she's promised . . . and her promise *never* extended to Phineas."

"But if we can meet with the Hunters of Legend tonight in Phineas's place, to explain—" started Dad, but Mom cut him off.

"I seriously doubt *one* meeting with the Hunters of Legend is going to get them to side with Phineas. If Phineas can't convince Malvidia and what's left of her hunter riffraff that he's not a traitor by protecting Sky, how is he ever going to convince the Hunters of Legend? And how could we? It's a trap, Herman. Malvidia has trapped us by letting us return, but she's trapped Phineas most of all. Phineas is getting old, and I'm not just talking physically. The loneliness, the isolation. To be hunted like he is—forced away from everything he's ever known and loved, and then to be forced again to distance himself from the very person he's sacrificed everything to protect! He's worn down . . . after all these years, and just when we need him most. We can't afford to lose him, Herman. We just can't!"

"That's why I *have* to do this!" said Dad. "Even if Phineas isn't there, he must have left us clues, some kind of instructions."

"But—"

Sky watched as Dad wrapped Mom in his arms, pulling her close. They stood that way, silent for a time.

"It has to be me," said Dad tenderly. "You've always been the better of us, in all things. That's why you have to stay. Because if I fail—"

"Don't—"

Dad pressed his fingers against Mom's lips, silencing her.

"Because if I fail," Dad continued, "we'll need the best to protect our children."

Sky could hear Mom crying. He'd never heard Dad talk like this. Ever. The words were dark, like an unlit candle in a lonely cave.

"If I don't come home tonight, take the children and run. Get as far away as you can as fast as you can. *Use every asset at your disposal* to hide yourselves, no matter the cost. Will you do that for me?" asked Dad.

Sky didn't hear her say yes, but she must've, because Dad

let her go. He held her at arm's length, and they stared into each other's eyes.

They gave each other a final kiss, and then Dad walked through the arch gate leading to Pimiscule Manor. He gave a parting wave to his wife and then disappeared up the trail.

Sky stood at the window watching Mom. Time slipped by unnoticed. He waited for her to return to the house, but she didn't. She just kept standing there, as silent as the stars.

"CAW!"

Mom spun at the sound, and Sky fell back into his room, crashing loudly to the hardwood floor.

"CAW!" The crow landed on his windowsill.

"Go away!" whispered Sky, waving his hands. He jumped to his feet, shut the window, and dove into bed.

A moment later he heard footsteps coming up the stairs.

His door opened and a ray of light slid over him. *I'm asleep, I'm asleep, I'm asleep,* Sky thought frantically. *I didn't hear anything. Just me and the crows sleeping peacefully.*

The light hovered over him like a wrecking ball . . . swinging . . . swinging . . . and then it drifted away as the door closed. He listened to Mom's footsteps on the creaky floor until they trailed off down the hall, followed a moment later by the distinct cardboardy sound of boxes being unpacked.

He lay for a moment, thinking, *breathing*. Whatever Phineas had been preparing him for all these years with his strange books and games seemed to have arrived, and like a well-placed trap, it had captured them all in a snare.

Who would want to take Phineas? Phineas had always been odd, nearly as odd as Sky, which might explain a few things, with his stories and his frock coats and his traps and his puzzles and his claims of monsters and hunters and his monocle-wearing. But he wouldn't hurt a soul. He was harmless, wasn't he?

And to hear his parents talk about Phineas . . . Sky knew he traveled a lot. His life was similar to Sky's in that way, but "forced away from everything he's ever loved?" Isolation and loneliness? Being *hunted*?

Had something really happened to Phineas?

Sky's nightmare returned to him in vivid detail—the creeping, the hiding, the dead end street, strangely like his own, ending in the same wrought iron fence, the abandoned houses, and . . .

The Wargarou, five shadowy wolves—Shadow Wargs, he knew from his books—and some unknown shifter named Ambrosia. Each of them were shifters of one kind or another. Not simply "shape" shifters that could only change their shape, but *true* shifters, as Phineas called them, capable of changing colors, weights, identities, and even their own elemental makeup.

Sky had read about Wargarous and Shadow Wargs in *The Shadow Wargs of Whimple*. Wargarous were much larger and more terrible than Shadow Wargs; Wargarous were the *real* monsters in the stories, the pack leaders. They created Shadow Wargs by binding willing power-hungry people to them in blood and darkness. But *The Shadow Wargs of Whimple* dealt more with Shadow Wargs than Wargarous. Another book, *Wicked, Wicked Wargarou*, discussed Wargarous in far more detail, but he hadn't read it in some time. He thought about finding it but feared the noise would draw Mom's attention.

Fortunately, he did remember something about Shadow

Wargs. Wolflike and horse-size, they started as people. But when they chose, they could shift into Shadow Wargs, creatures made of darkness that could slip between shadows without being seen. And almost nothing could harm them.

Almost nothing. . . . But, if he remembered correctly, Shadow Wargs did have weaknesses like . . . like . . . well, like *something*.

The Shadow Wargs of Whimple tells the story of a penniless shoe salesman who outwits a pack of Shadow Wargs by exploiting their weaknesses, whatever they are, only to marry the mayor's daughter and discover when he lifts the veil that *she's* the Wargarou. The story doesn't end well; the shoe salesman gets away in the end with the mayor's real daughter (the Wargarou ate her sister, not her), but the town is slaughtered. Uncle Phineas had given him the book with a customary cryptic warning: "Sometimes it's best to leave the veil *down*."

Of course, it was all bunk, just a story.

Shadow Wargs and Wargarous were no more real than any other monster, and the idea that Uncle Phineas was some kind of monster hunter was laughable. But if it was really just a story, and the dream was just a dream, then why did Sky feel so on edge?

"Sometimes the hardest things to believe are the only things worth believing at all," Sky muttered, remembering what Phineas had said while hanging upside down only hours before. "And sometimes," Sky continued, "they *aren't*. And sometimes 'for it' rhymes with 'for it' and I'm trapped whether I want to be or not. And sometimes I should stop talking to myself or myself might think I'm crazy."

The fact was, he didn't believe it—monsters, hunters, his

dream being more than a dream—but he was certain of one thing now: Phineas was definitely missing, and he needed to do something about it.

He heard Hannah's door open. A moment later Mom's door opened at the end of the hall. Sky tried to calm his breathing.

His little monster came and went unpredictably, but lately it seemed to be with him more and more. And right now it pushed at his mind, tugged on his emotions, stronger than ever, whispering, "*Don't go,*" "*Stay safe,*" "*Dad will take care of it,*" "*Please don't die!*" It was exactly the opposite of what he'd expected. Normally it would have been egging him on.

His trix burned with cold, and a small trickle of black blood oozed from the dark eye. Just like it had in his dream. It had never done that before.

Sky gritted his teeth.

"What's going on?" asked Hannah. "I thought I heard a door shut."

"It's nothing," said Mom. "Go back to bed."

"Did Sky wander off again?" asked Hannah, trying to make the question sound idle, but beneath it he could hear worry in her voice.

"It was your Dad. He ran to the store to get some stuff for tomorrow; it's nothing to worry about," said Mom, lying outright.

"Are you sure that's all?" said Hannah, sounding almost anxious. "Sky didn't maybe slip out while you weren't looking?"

Sky listened intently to the sudden silence in the hall.

"Hannah, Sky is sleeping soundly in his bed. If there's something you should be telling me . . ."

"No, no! Nothing like that. It's just . . . it's just this *place*, you know?" said Hannah.

"Hannah, listen to me. It's just your imagination . . . just the shadows," said Mom gently, "There's nothing to be afraid of."

"I know, I know," said Hannah. "You're sure he's there?"

"Sure as sure," said Mom.

"All right. Good night, then," said Hannah.

"Good night, then," said Mom.

Sky heard Hannah's door shut. A moment later his door opened again, as he knew it would.

As soon as the door closed, he slipped out of his bed, pulled on his shoes and coat, propped open the window with his tuba, and climbed onto a tree branch just outside his window.

Thankfully, the crows had flown.

CHAPTER 4

The Arkhon

His legs ached with cold as the wind whipped through his plaid flannel pajamas, and he wished he'd brought a flashlight, mainly so he'd have something to occupy his hands—his left hand especially, which still hurt, though it had finally stopped bleeding. His little monster grumbled but, it seemed, had finally given up.

This wasn't Sky's first nighttime foray into deep, dark, and scary woods, even if it had been a while. And he could see *freakishly* well, as Hannah liked to point out, so the dark wasn't really a problem. Some of his earliest memories involved wandering through dark places without a light, searching for something he couldn't find—something that called to him, begging for him to keep searching, the little monster pushing him on.

His parents had caught him the first couple of times he'd slipped away, but as he'd grown older, he'd grown savvier. In the early days, even up until a few years ago, he'd dragged Hannah along more often than not. She'd loved the adventure as much as him, but then she'd "grown up," as she'd put it none too delicately.

Now if he went at all, he went alone.

He felt a twinge of guilt as he thought about the promise he'd made to Hannah to stay away from Phineas's run-down manor, but in his mind *she* was the one who'd abandoned *him*. She was always trying to get him to fit in and be normal—and he tried. Oh, how he tried. But deep inside he knew he wasn't normal, and he felt it now more than ever in these dense, dark woods.

He knelt down, studying the ground. It had rained a few nights before, and the ground was still soft like molding clay. Clearing the leaves, he noticed several shoe prints.

Saltine crackers sat about beneath the leaves, some whole, some crunched to bits.

"CAW!"

He looked up; the crows had returned. They sat in the trees all around him, watching.

"You're not helping," said Sky.

"CAW!"

He threw a handful of crackers into the air, and the crows swooped down, snatching them up.

Wiping his hands on his pants, he continued up the path, trying to keep his fears at bay.

"Fear takes imagination," Uncle Phineas had once told him. "It's never about what's really out there—what your eyes or your ears or your nose is telling you. It's about what's in your brain. The more you *can* imagine, the more afraid you'll *be*."

"But don't worry," Phineas had continued, "things are never as scary as they first appear. Usually they're *much, much* scarier. There are things on this earth that no amount of imagination can properly fear, things so horrible that neither tomb of earth, nor vault of sky, nor depth of sea can contain them. And when they come forth, they'll make you long for the days when all you had to worry about were two leafy green vegetables resting on an otherwise empty plate. Now . . . *eat* your brussels sprouts."

They were strange, encouraging words, and since then Sky had done his best to master his fears (and eat brussels sprouts), but sometimes it was very, very hard (especially eating the brussels sprouts).

The trees became sparser as he moved up the hill, eventually opening into patches of open fields and broad clearings swarming with wildflowers and plants, some of which he recognized because Mom grew them in the house, along with everything else. The others were probably mentioned in the boring botany books Uncle Phineas had given him.

Ahead, still in the distance, he saw the spires rising from Pimiscule Manor, glinting in the moonlight. They looked eerie beneath the dappled shadows of the passing clouds, like giant pawns in an inhuman chess game.

The spires drifted behind the trees again as Sky reached a crossroads.

Kneeling down, he checked for tracks, but the ground was hard and rocky. To his left, farther away, the trail disappeared into a forest, and beyond he heard running water, a small stream of some sort, far away. To his right the trail looked like it simply ended twenty yards away, but on further inspection he noticed broad stone steps that trailed off into the darkness below, and he realized that he'd been walking along a steep ledge for some time.

Ahead the path continued on toward the manor.

He thought back over the conversation he'd overheard—missing uncle, lots of names he didn't remember, some vague allusions to terrible things, but nothing about where Dad was actually *going*.

Feeling anxious, Sky picked the path to the manor and kept walking.

The trail twisted and turned, moving north through patches of trees and brush, up a switchback, and then, eventually, east to connect with a broader cobblestone road coming up from the southeast that led from, Sky guessed, the main gates to Pimiscule Manor itself.

As the manor rolled into view, and the top of the manor peeked over the hill he was climbing, the first thing he noticed was a stained-glass dome bubbling from the top. The spires that he'd taken for pawns earlier, he could see now, were not pawns at all but bishops wearing their pointy hats, ready to move diagonally at a moment's notice.

As he got closer still, he spotted a thick stained-glass wall, similar to the dome, sweeping high into the air. The glass wall surrounded Pimiscule Manor like the arms of a street urchin clutching a loaf of bread, the manor several football fields within.

As strange as Sky found the glass wall, he found what was within the wall itself even stranger. Within the thick panels of different-colored glass, he saw liquids the color of night before dawn and odd mists, like breath captured on a cold morning. He saw peculiar cylinders and chambers arranged in peculiar patterns, connected by sparsely scattered tubes and bizarre mechanisms.

Upon the wall above him, he saw . . .

"Monsters." He stared up at the dozens of lifelike monster

statues spread out along the top of the wall. "This isn't real. It *can't* be. Who would build this?"

Statues, and yet they looked so real! Their faces snarling, screaming—terrifying. As if time had simply overtaken them, enfolding them forever in her arms. He'd seen realistic wax statues in museums, but this seemed beyond that.

Through the distorted colored glass, he caught glimpses of the grounds on the other side, covered in thick copses of trees, decaying gardens, ditches, and cornfields—the manor silent under the full moon, bathed in blood by a section of red stained glass, and then frozen by blue glass, sickly in green.

He saw even more of the grotesque statues mixed in the fields, hiding in the trees and cornfields, and hanging from traps.

His eyes slid across the trees and back again, locking on a horror more fearsome than the rest, a monstrosity as black as the night and as tall as the surrounding linden trees for which he'd almost mistaken it. It had unfurled leathery wings and tentacular arms, like fall branches somehow unmoving yet writhing and gripping and seething in madness at the same time. For a moment it almost seemed alive, staring at him with spiteful, pupil-less white eyes.

Something clicked in Sky's mind, and he suddenly recognized the monster. "*The Evil Echo of Solomon Rose*. It's an Echo!"

The white eyes, the wings, the branches like tentacles . . . it had to be!

The Evil Echo of Solomon Rose was the first book Phineas had ever given him. Sky had been three at the time, before he'd gotten his big collection, and he hadn't been able to read a word of it. But it was his favorite, not only because it was the first book Phineas had given him, but also because it was one of the only books Sky had that told the story from the monster's side of things.

Phineas had explained that the book's title was a play on words. "Evil" described *Solomon's* echo—the results of his actions—not the monsters themselves.

Had Phineas collected all these statues on the other side of the strange wall? Were these the inspiration for all the stories Sky had read?

He had a new piece to the puzzle that was his family.

Sky left the Echo statue behind and continued taking in the sights as he walked along the wall, until he reached a large crystalline gate with innards like a giant disassembled watch.

"It's not often we get visitors up here, especially on the first night of the Hunter's Moon," said a woman behind him.

His heart leapt into his throat, and he spun around ready to bolt.

A young woman, maybe twenty-five years old (though something in her manner made her seem far older), stepped out of the trees, ignoring his distress. She had long, flowing blond hair that cascaded down her back like stardust, and eyes as deep and blue as ocean ice. She wore blue jeans, a T-shirt, and a long black trench coat.

She was absolutely, in every sense of the word, beautiful.

"Personally," continued the woman, "I like it up here, under the full moon. I come here every night it appears. I find it . . . peaceful—though not nearly as peaceful as it was before all *this* started to appear." She gestured at the wall, taking it all in with a flip of the hand.

"Who are you?" asked Sky, backing away nervously. Could he outrun her?

"You might be better off asking *yourself* that question, Sky," said the woman. "Who, exactly, are *you*?"

Sky frowned. He wasn't sure how to respond to *that*. But what was even more disturbing . . .

"How do you know my name?" asked Sky suspiciously, feeling *very* uneasy. Did this woman know Phineas? Did she have something to do with his disappearance?

The other possibility was that she was some kind of monster or witch intent on baking Sky in an oven—buried under a light, flaky crust—and eating him with a side of cranberry and a bit of sorbet to cleanse the palette of boy juice, but Sky pushed the ridiculous thought aside. A weird manor and a weird woman did not mean that monsters were real.

"You may not believe this," said the woman, "but we've met before. My name is Ursula."

Sky didn't believe it. He would've remembered, especially someone with a name like Ursula.

"You wouldn't remember me," continued Ursula, stepping closer. "The meeting was brief and I looked different at the time. But, Sky, even if I hadn't met you, I'd know who you are. Many *things* know who you are, even if you don't."

Sky didn't like the way she'd said "things."

"Why would anybody know me?" asked Sky.

"You're asking the wrong question, Sky. The right question is, why don't you know yourself? Who you *really* are?"

"I know who I am," said Sky defensively.

"Do you? They told you, then, about the Arkhon? About the night you were taken? About the mark on your hand?"

He glanced at his Hunter's Mark in the middle of his trix. But then, was she talking about the Hunter's Mark or the trix?

And what did she mean he'd been "taken"? And *what in the world was an Arkhon*?

"What? This old thing?" said Sky, laughing nervously as he showed her his palm. "I picked it up at a secondhand store—got a really good deal too. I can give you the address if you'd like."

Ursula stepped closer to the gate, her eyes drifting from Sky to the manor beyond. "A horror is coming, Sky. Something so monstrous that neither vault of sky nor depth of sea can contain it."

He shivered. He'd heard those words before. From Phineas.

"He's coming, Sky," said Ursula, shaking her head as she stared up at the moon, "He's coming as sure as the moon is full, and when he comes, he'll bring the night with him and wash the world in a sea of blood."

"Who's he?" asked Sky.

"*He* is the Terror of the Night, the Bringer of the Dark, the One of Three, the Immortal, the Blood Thief, the Wasting Hunger, the Shifting Horror, the Moon Goblin. . . . He's one of the most evil monsters that's ever lived. He's the Arkhon, and Pimiscule Manor is his prison."

"I don't understand," said Sky, feeling uncomfortable. Was she actually saying that monsters were real? Was everyone around him going mad?

"Neither do I. That's the problem. Something terrible is happening before our very eyes, and I haven't the slightest idea how to stop it," said Ursula.

He looked back at Pimiscule Manor, while keeping one eye on Ursula. He still didn't trust her, but she almost sounded like Phineas, which made him almost want to trust her.

But how could he believe what she said? If he accepted that monsters were real—that *these* monsters were real—he'd also have to accept that Phineas had been serious all these years, that he really had been training Sky to be a hunter.

Which meant that his parents had been lying by dismissing Phineas's stories. But hadn't Mom lied to Hannah earlier about where Dad had gone? Hadn't Mom and Dad talked about hunters as if they believed they were real? The missing puzzle pieces in his family . . . Could this really be it?

"These monsters, this wall—none of this should be here," continued Ursula, "The Arkhon—he's waking up. I know your uncle very well, Sky. He's a great man—a *careful* man, and careful men don't take careless risks. He would never have come back here, would never have brought your family here—*never*—unless he knew something that could stop this from happening."

Was this why they'd come back? To stop a monster he'd never even heard of from breaking free of its prison? And if the Arkhon was so important, why hadn't Phineas mentioned it before? It was all so insane!

"I'm dreaming, aren't I?" said Sky, remembering his earlier nightmare.

Ursula shook her head.

"But if this *were* a dream, you'd deny it was a dream whether it was or not, wouldn't you?" asked Sky.

"If your dreams are all like this," said Ursula, a smile playing on her lips, "I'd fear more for your sanity."

"I've thought of that," said Sky, "but if I were crazy, I probably wouldn't know it. I mean, every lunatic is sane in their own mind, aren't they?"

"True. Perhaps you should consider yourself insane. Then,

whether you are or not, at least you'll enjoy yourself," said Ursula.

Sky nodded at the wisdom of her words.

"So. Uncle Phineas? You think he knows how to stop this? We're talking about Phineas T. Pimiscule, right? Old guy, wrinkled face, wears frock coats and a monocle? Likes botany and goulash?"

Ursula smiled. "That's the guy."

"You're wondering if I know where he is," said Sky, finally realizing why Ursula had told him all these things.

Which meant *she* didn't know.

Ursula nodded. "He was supposed to meet me here tonight. When I saw you . . . Well, let's just say I was surprised. I thought maybe he already knew what I had to tell him."

"Wait a minute," said Sky, remembering the conversation he'd overheard between his parents. "My parents talked about you."

"Did they?" asked Ursula, taken aback.

"Not to me," said Sky, wondering why that had surprised her. "I, er, overheard them, maybe. Anyway, I remember hearing your name, now that I think of it. Dad said if Phineas was really missing, then something fell to him. I think they were hoping to find Phineas here talking to you. That's why I followed him."

"Herman's here? On the grounds?" asked Ursula, sounding concerned as she began scanning the trees.

"Yeah," said Sky, beginning to feel nervous again. "Why? Is that a problem?" He remembered how concerned Mom had been when Dad had left—as if he might not come back. But what could be so dangerous? And, come to think of it, where was Dad? Shouldn't he have beat Sky here?

Sky glanced up at the snarling faces on the wall above him and shivered.

"It shouldn't be, but—" Ursula stopped suddenly, raising her nose to the air. She sniffed. Sniffed again. "No, that can't be. Not here. That would mean . . ."

Her eyes flipped to Sky, and she looked worried.

"It's not safe anymore, Sky," said Ursula, ushering him abruptly back along the wall and down the winding cobblestone path.

"Not safe? What are you talking about? What about my dad?"

"Did your uncle say anything to you? Anything at all?" asked Ursula, sounding frantic. "Did he tell you where to find the keys?"

"Keys? What keys?" asked Sky, confused. And then something popped into his head, a memory half remembered, almost like a dream.

Or a nightmare.

Ambrosia had asked Phineas for the keys.

But what did it mean? The dream couldn't have been a metaphor or his sleeping mind solving a puzzle, as he'd supposed, since he hadn't heard anyone mention keys before the dream.

Once again he had to wonder, could it have been real? Had he really seen Phineas get attacked, captured, possibly even killed? The thought horrified him.

Sky thought about telling Ursula, but he held back. Could he really trust her? This woman he'd just met? He couldn't remember everything his parents had said about her, but he remembered how worried they'd been, how they'd sounded almost scared as they talked about her.

Ursula's story, as implausible as it seemed, was almost believable. But if he believed her, if he believed monsters were real, he also had to acknowledge the possibility that she might not be all she seemed.

Ambrosia wanted keys too. And she was an unknown *shifter*.

"If you find anything," said Ursula, sounding disappointed, rushed, and frightened, "or he contacts you, leave me a note in the box by the main gate. Be careful who you trust. Not everyone's as they seem."

Something howled off in the distance, deep and low—almost like a wolf, but darker somehow, almost sinister. Ursula cocked her head, listening as another howl answered, and another. She started moving faster, rushing Sky toward the trail that broke off from the cobblestone road.

A chill ran down Sky's spine. His mind filled with images of sharp teeth and swirling night. But it was just shadows, wasn't it? That's what his parents had always told him. It's just the shadows. Just your imagination.

There was another howl, closer this time, coming from the northeast.

"What is that?" asked Sky, his voice trembling.

They reached the trail, and Ursula pointed.

"Go that way. Run as fast as you can and don't stop until you get home," said Ursula, shoving him toward the trail as she turned and headed southeast. In the distance, lower down the hill, Sky could see a cemetery. Why did Phineas have a cemetery on his property?

"Wait!" yelled Sky, fighting off the adrenaline rushing into his system. It was stupid, but he had to do something. If this was all real, if this woman was really Ambrosia, a shifter pretending to be someone else, she might kill him.

But why would she come to meet Phineas tonight if she already had him? Could she be the Hunter of Legend who, according to his parents, Phineas had had to convince that he wasn't a traitor so he could stay in Exile?

"I saw Phineas tonight!" Sky blurted.

Ursula turned around, narrowing her eyes.

"In a dream," Sky continued, uncomfortable. A dream. Was he really *saying this*? "He was attacked by a Wargarou and his pack." He paused, taking a deep breath. "And a woman was there—another shifter, but not like the others. Phineas called her Ambrosia."

Ursula hissed, a frightening sound that scared Sky down to his toes.

"Ambrosia," Ursula spat. "Are you *certain*?"

Sky nodded. In the moonlight he could see Ursula grinding her teeth.

"Phineas isn't a traitor!" Sky declared, feeling bolder than he had any right to. "If you're not just putting me on, then, whatever he did, he didn't do it! You need to help him!"

Ursula quirked her head. "I know," she said. She looked away, unable to meet his eyes. "But there's nothing I can do."

"B-but," spluttered Sky, "if you know he's innocent, if this is all real—you're a Hunter of Legend! The oldest and wisest and most powerful! You've probably lived for centuries and can do all kinds of things normal hunters can't do! You have to help him!"

"A Hunter of Legend?" Ursula laughed. "Whatever gave you that idea?"

"But, then," Sky muttered, more confused than ever, "if you're not a Hunter of Legend, what are you?"

Before she could answer, a shadow moved through the trees on the other side of the cobblestone road. At first Sky mistook it for the shadow of a passing cloud, but then the shadow opened two red *sinister* eyes.

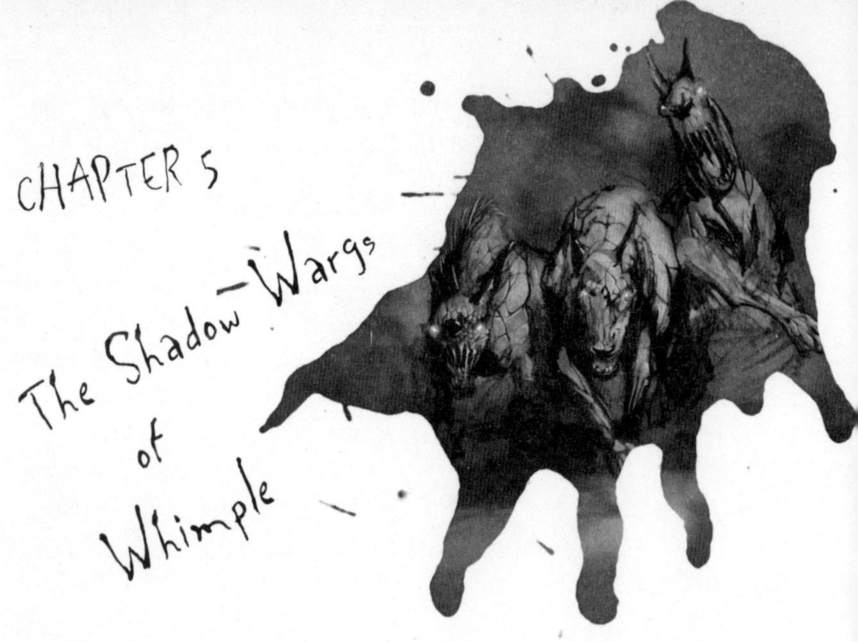

CHAPTER 5

The Shadow-Wargs of Whimple

Sky inhaled sharply as the monster seeped out of the darkness, flowing like velvet. Thick black fur mottled its larger-than-a-horse-size body. Spittle dripped from elongated, slavering jaws, and it let out a slow, rumbling growl that shook Sky like a very small rock in a very big landslide.

This was no statue. *This* wasn't his imagination.

Monsters, hunters, his dream, Phineas . . . *everything*. It was all true!

"Sh-Shadow Warg," Sky mumbled in terror, recognizing one of the shadowy monsters he'd seen attack Phineas in his dream.

"Run!" yelled Ursula.

She drew an old revolver from her coat. The silver casing flickered blue in the moonlight and fire spilled from the tip.

The Shadow Warg yelped as the bullet hit—its body sliding back into the silky darkness like melting butter—and the bullet dropped to the ground, useless.

Two more Shadow Wargs appeared, rushing in before Ursula could get another shot off.

Sky's feet felt like glue. He couldn't get his mind to work right. His little monster screamed at him to run!

"It's all real," he muttered, dumbfounded. "All of it."

A Shadow Warg rammed into Ursula, knocking her down. The second, the smaller of the two, grabbed her gun arm. Sky heard a crunching sound, Ursula gasped in pain, and the gun fell a few yards away.

Sky stared at it.

"Sky!" Ursula shrieked, the Shadow Wargs tearing her apart. "RUN!"

Something finally clicked in Sky's head.

He ran for the gun.

Three more Shadow Wargs stepped out of the shadows—the original that Ursula had shot, and two reinforcements—joining the two already here.

Five of them total, just like in his dream. But no Wargarou and no Ambrosia. Where had they gone?

He didn't take time to wonder. He dove for the gun, coming up with it just as the three new monsters joined the other two and tore into Ursula. He aimed at the most vicious, the one that'd crushed Ursula's arm.

He pulled the trigger.

For all his supposed training, Phineas had never taught Sky how to shoot—a glaring omission, Sky now realized.

The bullet shot out of the muzzle in slow motion, crossed the distance between Sky and Vicious (as he now thought of it), and *thunked* into the Shadow Warg's side.

Unfortunately, it was the *wrong* Shadow Warg.

The Shadow Warg—the one Ursula had shot, which Sky

now dubbed Bullet—slipped into the shadows, and the bullet dropped to the ground.

Still, at least he'd hit something.

Vicious spun around, baring fangs.

Sky backed away.

"NO!" Ursula screamed.

She grabbed the monster's leg . . .

And *bit it*.

Vicious howled in agony. Sky covered his ears.

Ursula's body suddenly began to bubble and burble, flowing around her like a cape in the wind. Her skin turned black and sprouted thick hair. Her head stretched, along with her teeth and nose, and her body grew until Sky found himself looking at *another* Shadow Warg.

He stared in astonishment. A shifter—a *monster*!

Had she been playing him all along? Could Ursula really be Ambrosia? But, then, why had the other Shadow Wargs attacked her? Why would she defend Sky?

With her teeth still locked around the Shadow Warg's leg, Ursula jerked back, knocking the monster to the ground. She lashed out, snapping at the neck of one, then ramming her head into another.

The Shadow Wargs tried to regroup, and Ursula turned her eyes on Sky, narrowing them in an all too human way.

He got the message. Dropping Ursula's gun, he turned and ran.

Behind him he could hear Shadow Wargs circling and yowling as they closed on Ursula.

He sprinted down the trail, struggling to remember weaknesses. How had the shoe salesman in *The Shadow Wargs of Whimple* beaten them? Why had he stopped reading those books!

Glancing over his shoulder, he spotted two Shadow Wargs closing in on him fast, their bodies leaping and swirling from one shadow to the next. Vicious led, followed by Big, the biggest of the Shadow Wargs.

Great.

Sky cleared the trees and raced for the crossroads. The two Shadow Wargs broke through a moment later, and a third Shadow Warg appeared beside them. *Bullet*—the smallest of the pack, the Shadow Warg that kept getting shot.

Vicious, Big, and Bullet. Three new friends he'd rather not play with.

Sky's mind raced. Shadow Wargs had three weaknesses . . . *silver*, which could temporarily drive them back to the shadows—probably what Ursula used for her bullets. *Fire*, which could actually hurt them, and . . . and . . . *wolfsbane*! That's it! That's how the salesman had beaten them! He'd planted wolfsbane everywhere, and they wouldn't go near it!

Sky lifted his head and looked across the moon-drenched landscape, along the steep ridge on his left that ran part of the trail's length. There in the distance, beyond the crossroads just ahead, he'd seen wolfsbane . . . he was sure of it!

If he could just get there . . .

He felt breath on the back of his neck. He dove to the side, but not fast enough.

Vicious slammed into him!

Sky flew through the air, crashing against stone steps before tumbling down, head over heels, along the crossroad's leftmost fork, along the dark steps that cut through the ridge—finally coming to a stop far below where he'd started.

He lay dazed, his little monster raging in his mind, urging him to get up!

Climbing to his feet, he limped toward a great black wall in the distance, a towering hedge rising into the night sky and stretching as far as he could see in both directions.

A break in the hedge opened in front of him less than thirty yards away. He pushed toward it.

His ankle ached and he bled from cuts on his arms and face.

He longed for sleep. A nice bed. A Band-Aid or four. Maybe some warm milk.

He thought of Dad, wandering about the grounds, blissfully unaware, barely able to put one foot in front of the other without falling over himself. If Shadow Wargs found him before Sky did . . .

He couldn't let that happen. The opening in the hedge, the promise of escape, beckoned him onward. Twenty yards. Ten yards . . .

Bullet crashed into him like a mallet, driving him to the ground. The Shadow Warg leaned over him, spittle dripping from its ravenous jaws as they opened . . . opened . . . white teeth in a cavern of night.

Sky grabbed a rock and threw!

The rock sailed up, up, and through the monster, landing with a clatter in the darkness beyond.

That's when fear took him—pure fear, mindless and primal. It started in his toes, moving through his body like wildfire. It smashed into the trix on his left hand, raced through his Hunter's Mark, and exploded outward in swirling currents of shadowy light.

He grabbed Bullet by the head, trying to push the Shadow Warg away. A peculiar vertigo took hold, and it seemed as if he were standing in two places at once. He looked over and saw himself smiling toothily back at him, and then something hit his chest and he was suddenly back on the ground again, Bullet's huge head lying on him, eyes closed.

He crawled out from under it. What'd happened? Had he killed it?

His hand ached. Dark blood, like syrup, dripped from the black trix on his palm, mingling with a thick, shadowy light spilling from the Hunter's Mark within the trix.

He looked back at Bullet. The Shadow Warg lay on the ground, its chest rising and falling, up and down, up and down, slowly, like the beat of a metronome.

Sky scrambled toward the hedge opening, his hope of saving Dad and Phineas fading like tears on a coffin as Vicious and Big advanced. Five yards. Three . . .

Vicious grabbed him by the shoe and yanked, dragging Sky away.

Sky jerked back and slipped free of his shoe. He crabwalked backward—hips in the air, hands and feet on the ground, eyes locked on Vicious—until the gargantuan, thorny hedge wall pressed painfully against his back, sticking in his hands and neck.

Thorns.

He jerked away, and it seemed as if the whole hedge followed him. He scrambled away from it. A slow itch started in his neck and hands. Tingling warmth spread through him like sugar, and then he was tired. *Oh, so* tired.

He slumped forward.

Vicious dropped Sky's shoe. The Shadow Warg turned to Big, growling.

The shadows danced around Vicious, and in that dance—in that growling—Sky could almost make out words, as if the shadows themselves talked.

"Tastes like sock," Vicious seemed to say. *"But this kill's for my mother."*

Sky's mouth dropped open. Had he really just heard that?

His little monster raged in his head, yelling at him to run, and his hand burned. Black trix blood flowed freely across his palm. As Sky watched, the shadowy light that had burst from his Hunter's Mark—now covered in blood—faded, faded, and winked out.

Vicious turned back.

Tired and battered, waiting for death, Sky looked up to meet the Shadow Warg's terrible red eyes —

And saw something move on the ridge twenty yards away. A black-cloaked figure—hood up, face hidden—raised some kind of weapon and fired.

A huge silvery-blue glob of gelatinous goo splashed into Vicious. The impact sent the Shadow Warg tumbling.

A hunter had come!

Another hunter appeared beside the first.

The newcomer raised his hand. A long shaft of wood popped out of his sleeve, a pistol grip landing in his palm. Rods flipped out from the grip, locking into a bow.

The hunter raised the crossbow, and two metallic suction cups shot out of his sleeve, first one, then the other, sliding into the bow cradle.

The hunter fired.

Suction cups flew at Vicious. Two trailing wires, sparking with arcs of electricity, streamed from the suction cups like it was some kind of demented medieval Taser.

The cups glommed on to Vicious with a *clomp*, sticking to the thick goo like fingers in frosting. Electricity crackled down the wires, enveloping the goo and the Shadow Warg in blue lightning. Vicious rolled once, and then froze solid as the goo turned to ice.

Sky's mouth fell open—whether out of shock, numbness, or sheer slobbering madness, he couldn't tell.

In Phineas's stories hunters fought with fire, stakes, knives, traps, and pistols—with occasional herbs or vegetables thrown in for good measure. Sky had never heard of anything like these weapons before.

"This can't be happening," mumbled Sky sleepily, "I've gone insane, and I'm not enjoying it at all."

He tried to move his hand, but ended up falling on his face. He rolled to his back, fighting to keep his eyes open. He couldn't move his arms, couldn't get up. He watched, helpless, as Big galloped toward him, dodging flying watery globs of goo along the way.

Desperate, Sky looked to the cliff for help. He knew the hunters were too far away, but it didn't stop him from looking and hoping.

In his dying moments he didn't want his last thought to be, *Oh, my. What big teeth you have.* Secretly he'd always wanted his last thought to be *So that's what poisoned chocolate tastes like!* But that didn't seem very likely at the moment. Even if he'd had some, he didn't think he could put it in his mouth.

So instead he watched the thing he'd spent a good portion of his life reading about, never believing in but secretly wanting to be—a monster hunter.

In the fading, gibbering corners of his mind, he wondered who these hunters were and why they'd chosen to help him and what they'd say in his eulogy. Probably something like "Here lies Sky Weathers. He was never really good at much, but at least he didn't soil himself in the end."

He wondered if it'd be true.

In the midst of his scrambled thoughts, he watched the two hunters slap their chests. Steam billowed suddenly from beneath their robes. They crouched, and then leapt, sailing up, up, up, and off the ridge.

Big stepped in front of him, filling his view with fangs . . . mouth open . . . head dropping—

Blue lightning flashed!

Big yelped and tumbled out of view as the hunters fell from the darkness above like cannonballs and crashed into the Shadow Warg's back and side, their robes shining in a blue nimbus as they collapsed to the ground and continued rolling.

The nimbus fell away and the two hunters lay on the ground, unmoving. Silent.

Big climbed to its feet and stalked toward the fallen hunters.

Sky couldn't let this happen.

Calling up every ounce of strength he had, Sky rolled to his stomach and clawed his way toward the two hunters that had tried to save him.

"Hey! Big! HEY!" yelled Sky, exhausted. Raising his hand, he *willed* the Hunter's Mark to light up again. Phineas had told him it was special. He'd put Bullet to sleep, hadn't he? Knocked it out somehow? Could he do the same to Big?

Sky concentrated, his trix numbed by cold, ripping wider, the little monster screaming to run, black blood dripping. . . .

Nothing happened.

The Hunter's Mark felt as cold as his trix.

The last of his strength spent, he tumbled to the ground. Warmth spread through his body, promising him sleep, rest . . . *peace*. He fought it back, forcing himself to watch Big close on the unmoving hunters.

"Please," Sky begged. "They were just trying to help me."

The Shadow Warg looked at him, its head cocked to the side. Big growled, and the shadows danced around it, but this time Sky couldn't understand a word.

But the eyes . . . Big's eyes looked apologetic—pleading, even.

The Shadow Warg stood over the fallen hunters. Then it lunged at the closer of the two.

A third hunter raced past Sky, ramming Big in the side.

Big rolled, coming to its feet snarling. The Shadow Warg charged.

The hunter, nearly as big as Big, leapt over his two friends, crashing into Big. He grabbed the Shadow Warg by the jaws with two silvery gloves and forced the monster backward, step by slow step.

Twisting the Shadow Warg's head, the hunter stepped back, and sent Big tumbling.

The hunter dove on top of Big. The two wrestled on the stony earth, punching and biting and kicking.

Big bucked, and the hunter flew off. A blue light shimmered around the hunter as he hit the ground. He rolled to his feet, arms up, legs spread, ready to take the hit from the rushing Shadow Warg.

Darkness swirled around Big, and then *poof*—the Shadow Warg slipped through the shadow of the moonlit hedge to the hunter's own shadow, reappearing right behind him.

"NO!" Sky screamed.

Thoomp.

A ball of goo struck the Shadow Warg, knocking it over.

The big hunter spun around, obviously confused.

Sky saw the goo cannon drop from the first hunter's hand as the hunter flopped back to the ground. The weapon looked odd close up, like it had been welded together out of old cans.

Something sparkled in the moonlight. On the fallen hunter's wrist, Sky saw a slim bracelet with a pendant made of intertwined silver wire that looked like half a strand of DNA.

The third hunter grabbed Big by the tail. Electricity shot out of the hunter's silvery gloves, running through the goo in a lightning storm, but Big slipped through his hands into the shadows, leaving behind an empty, icy cocoon.

This time the Shadow Warg didn't reappear.

Sky was safe. The hunters knew about the Shadow Wargs.

They could protect Dad.

Slowly, delectably, Sky let his heavy eyelids drop shut.

A moment later he heard footsteps coming from the hedge.

"Sky?" said a voice that sounded very familiar, though he couldn't figure out why.

His eyes fluttered open and he tried to lift his head, but it fell back to the ground. Lifting his eyes, he saw a pair of penny loafers and faded slacks. Further up he saw a trench coat, and finally, Dad's face staring down at him.

Dad wasn't smiling.

"Sky," said Dad, his voice strangely detached, "you weren't supposed to be here tonight."

Sky tried to warn Dad about the Shadow Wargs, but he couldn't get his lips to move.

Kneeling down, Dad scooped Sky up in his arms and started jogging for the steps that led back to the top of the ridge. As Dad ran, Sky looked around lazily, trying to spot the three black-cloaked hunters who'd saved him, but there was no sign of them, or anything else. Just the tall, dark hedge.

"It's okay, Sky. You've been pricked by Dovetail," said Dad.

Sky tried to say "Dovetail?" but it came out "Wshaaa."

"It's the hedge. Very poisonous. It can cause sleepiness, paralysis, hallucinations, even . . . even worse things," said Dad, unable to say more.

"Haalllasha?" said Sky.

"It's very common. You could see things, smell things, even *hear* things that aren't really there—sometimes *horrible* things," said Dad. "You didn't go into the Dovetail, did you?"

Sky tried to respond, but his lips felt like molasses.

"Hold on, Sky. We're almost there," said Dad as he rounded a bend and the arch gate came into view. Beyond it Sky could see the warm glow of the town lights beckoning to him like ice cream on a hot day.

And then everything went dark.

CHAPTER 6

Foibles of Youth

The sun peeked over the horizon, doing its best to drive away the cold that lingered from the night before, but in Exile the cold was like an unwelcome guest that never seemed to pick up on subtle hints to leave.

The house shook and groaned, waking Sky, who groaned even louder than the house. He rolled over in his bed to turn off the nonexistent alarm clock. He batted at the air a few times before he overreached and tumbled to the floor.

He stood up and looked around the room, wondering where the horrible grinding sounds were coming from. They seemed to fill the whole house, shaking it like a passing train. Fear washed through him as he remembered the night before. He patted himself, checking for injuries. His wrist and ankle were tender, but he'd had worse.

It all seemed so unreal in the light of day. Had he dreamed it? Hallucinated it? Was it an effect supposedly brought on by the thorny Dovetail, as he knew his parents would claim?

He couldn't believe that.

The grinding started up again, shaking the floor.

Holding his hands over his ears, he headed for the window, popped it open, and looked out to see if the house had miraculously moved next to an expressway while he'd slept.

Now that the sun was shining, he could clearly see NO TRESPASSING signs on the fence surrounding Phineas's estate. A sign above the arch gate read PIMISCULE ESTATE. VISITORS UNWELCOME.

As bad as last night had been, the grounds looked a lot less menacing in the morning light.

"Water's on!" Dad yelled.

Looking down, Sky saw Dad standing hip deep in a pool of murky brown water next to the house. He held a bent wrench in one hand and a rusted hammer in the other and he was dripping with foulness from hair to hip.

Despite the fact that Dad was an engineer, he was not the handiest of men. It still astounded Sky that Dad had picked engineering as a career.

What astounded him more was the fact that Dad had just *successfully* turned the water on. It was the first time he'd managed to do it . . . ever, and he'd had *plenty* of tries over the years at the different places where they'd lived.

"How you feeling, Sky?" asked Dad as the grinding abated.

So it hadn't been a dream. At least Dad acknowledged that much.

"Fine, considering," said Sky.

Dad nodded and turned his attention back to the murky water, sifting his hands through it like a prospector searching for gold.

"You remember anything?" asked Dad.

"Sort of," said Sky. "It all seems a little fuzzy."

"Dovetail can do that to you. I'd suggest you stay away from it in the future," said Dad. "Do I make myself clear?"

"Perfectly," said Sky.

"Good. Your mother would like to talk to you when you get a moment," said Dad without looking up.

At that point Sky knew he wasn't going to discover anything more from Dad. Of course, he'd likely get an earful from Mom as soon as he saw her.

The house shuddered and let out another loud groan.

"Is it supposed to sound like that, Dad?" yelled Sky above the noise.

The old pipes belched and sputtered. Neighbors were starting to come out of their houses, strolling casually to get their papers, but he knew they were really there to investigate the ruckus.

"It's fine! Nothing to worry about!" yelled Dad. He waved his wrench at Sky, took a deep breath, and dove back into the water.

A moment later the groaning subsided, ending with a high-pitched shriek as the house shook one final time.

Sky shut the window with a sigh. Despite the fact that he really wanted this move to work out (mainly so he wouldn't have to move again), it wasn't starting on the best foot.

He picked up his pocket watch, thinking of Phineas. Was he hurt, dying somewhere? Had Ambrosia and the Wargarou taken him prisoner? Was he even still alive?

Sky wouldn't give up hope. Phineas *had* to be alive. Sky just couldn't imagine a world without him, and he knew Phineas wouldn't have allowed himself to be trapped. He would've had a backup plan, his own trap—a quadruple quandary. All Sky had to do was find it and spring it.

Almost an hour until school started. It was a record; he'd actually be able to shower this morning. Plus, if he moved fast, he could sneak in some extracurricular activities and still make it to school on time.

Grabbing his school clothes (and avoiding Mom), he headed for the bathroom. He already knew what Mom would say. She'd give him the same old story—it was just the shadows, just your imagination, you didn't see what you think you saw.

He needed to see Pimiscule Manor again. The wall, the monsters . . .

He needed to clear his head, and he thought a good stroll past the manor before searching for Uncle Phineas's truck would be just the thing. In his nightmare he'd seen where the truck was parked. He knew Ambrosia, the Wargarou, and the Shadow Wargs had ambushed Phineas on a dead end street near the manor. If Sky followed the fence long enough, he knew he'd find the place.

And then, maybe *then*, after he'd gotten some fresh air to clear his head *and* seen the manor *and* searched his Uncle's truck *and* gone to school . . . maybe *then* he'd talk to Mom.

The bathroom door creaked as he pushed it open, and the medicine cabinet creaked again as he pulled out his toothbrush and toothpaste. He closed the cabinet and starred at his reflection in the dirty, chipped mirror.

Large ears poked out from beneath black hair, which was getting long enough now that it spent as much time in his eyes as on his head. His eyes were brown and boring, and his nose was pinched at the top, rounding into a little nub at the bottom that looked like a turnip. His face was oval and pale, like he'd had all the blood leeched out of him.

He was skinny, but not horribly so. Hannah liked to compare him to an onion, not because he resembled an onion in any way, or because he was particularly complex. No, she liked to compare him to an onion because onions stank, and sometimes she was just not very nice.

He stared at his reflection, looking at the small scratches and cuts he'd collected during his wild run.

Raising his toothbrush, he began to scrub at his teeth in smooth, even strokes. He spit into the brown-stained sink, washed the toothbrush in slightly brown water, and returned it to the medicine cabinet. He smiled in the mirror, but his teeth didn't seem to be any cleaner than before.

Looking down, he expected to see black trix blood covering his hand, but his parents must've cleaned it up. The trix had never bled before last night. Before his dream.

All his life his parents had assured him that the trix and birthmark were perfectly normal, but now he was certain they weren't. They were anything *but* perfect, and far from normal.

The trix bled black blood, and the birthmark—the Hunter's Mark—glowed. How was that normal?

Somehow he'd put a Shadow Warg to sleep, and for a moment he'd been able to understand the monsters. At least he thought he'd been able to.

He furrowed his brow, squinted his eyes, swung his hand around in the air to make it light up. . . . Nothing.

"You can't wave your deformity away, stupid," said Hannah from behind him.

He lowered his hand, *feeling* stupid.

"I know that," said Sky, grabbing a hand towel. "I was just trying to be environmentally friendly. Save the planet, air dry your hands. You should try it sometime."

Hannah rolled her eyes. It was sort of her signature move.

"I'll make sure and do that," she said, grabbing her toothbrush. "You're going to be late, you know."

"What do you mean? I've still got, like, forty-five minutes," said Sky, checking his pocket watch again.

"Your watch is off; maybe you should buy something that's been built in the last century. You've got *fifteen* minutes," said Hannah, showing Sky the time on her cell phone.

"This watch is never off," said Sky, confused. Uncle Phineas had carried the watch for as long as Sky could remember. It had never been off before. Had Sky somehow damaged it?

"Well, there's a first for everything," said Hannah.

Sky shook the watch, listened to it. Nothing rattled—a good sign. He put it back into his pocket.

"Fifteen minutes," said Sky, looking at the shower with a sense of remorse, "it looks like the children are going to suffer and Europe gets another day of stench-screen."

"It could be worse," said Hannah, smirking. "What if we actually stay here long enough that people realize you're my brother? Just think of the impact that could have on my social life."

"That *would* be horrible," said Sky, matching her smile. "I guess the world's bad enough without me making it worse, right?"

"You're not so bad," said Hannah, tussling Sky's hair, "when you're not all freaky."

"You're not so bad either," said Sky, smiling back, "when you're not all witchy."

Hannah made a grab for Sky, but he ducked under her arms and disappeared down the hall. "Better hurry up, Sis," Sky yelled over his shoulder. "Wouldn't want to miss cheerleading tryouts!"

"As if they'd start without me," Hannah called back through a mouthful of toothbrush.

Of course they'd wait for her. She was the only one trying out. Years ago Hannah refused to move unless Mom called ahead to set up tryouts with the cheerleading coach the moment they arrived. Mom strove to make their lives as stable as possible, but she'd thought Hannah's request was unrealistic. Hannah had persisted.

"I need the semblance of a normal life," Hannah had complained to Mom. "There's a dreadful orphanage just up the road that's offered to take me in. The drapes are awful, and all they serve are bits of bread crumbs and cold soup for meals—and the beds are made of recycled tacks and small pins—but I'm sure the mistresses there will be very gentle with their beatings. . . ."

Mom had given in. Hannah had gotten her way like she always did. Now cheerleading coaches met her whenever they moved, and she always made the team, usually taking over as captain by the end of the first week.

Sky stopped at the top of the stairs, listening for Mom. He could smell thick, buttery pancakes cooking and cinnamon hot chocolate percolating in the cocoa machine. His stomach rumbled. The last thing he needed this morning was a lecture, but the smells called out to him, promising that any torture he had to endure would be worth it, if he would but succumb to their scrumptious flavors.

He reached the front door, still torn. He stepped toward the kitchen, back toward the door. Finally he reached for the door handle.

"There's always school lunch," he mumbled, thinking of the greasy pizza and stale rolls they'd served at his last school. His stomach growled at him.

"You weren't thinking of leaving without saying good-bye, were you?"

Sky stopped midturn and spun to face Mom.

"No, of course not! I was . . . er . . . just going to help Dad with the . . . er . . . plumbing thingy," said Sky, kicking himself for his inability to lie.

"Plumbing thingy? And were you going to fix it with your guilty conscience?" said Mom.

"Mom, I—"

"You are *grounded,* Skyler. Three weeks!"

"Three weeks! Come on! It wasn't like I went up there *alone*," prodded Sky.

"Your father had a perfectly good reason for being there," snapped Mom.

"Which was . . . ?"

"Don't change the subject! Do you want another three weeks added to the first? I can make it six weeks!"

"I'm just saying," said Sky, "don't you think the moral outrage of my own conscience is punishment enough? Can't we just chalk it up to the foibles of youth?"

"Foibles of youth? You nearly got yourself killed! Dovetail is *incredibly* dangerous. Why you felt you had to sneak out in the middle of the night and follow your father, I'll never know," said Mom. "What were you thinking?"

"I—"

"I want you home right after school! No friends, no playing around! If you're not on that bus, I'll find you and drag you home if I have to! You're just lucky I had Crow's Feet, mister, or you would have been in *big* trouble."

Sky didn't even have to ask why she had Crow's Feet (apparently the antidote for Dovetail) lying around the house.

Mom had *every* kind of plant lying around the house, and most of them were antidotes for one thing or another. Every time the family moved, she stayed up all night unpacking so that by morning everything would seem "normal"—and the plants were always the first to come out.

Some had come in the car, but this time around more had come from the attic of their new home—dried herbs and flowers, hearty green plants, yellow plants, and red plants, dead brown plants that crumbled at the touch, and light gray plants covered with thistles. Their house was like a greenhouse, their pantry like a plant graveyard, filled with powders and seeds and dead stuff, and it was the same wherever they moved to. Hannah got her tryouts, Mom got her plants . . . and all Sky got was a plastic ficus tree.

"Well, Skyler, what do you have to say for yourself?"

"I—," started Sky, but at that moment the front door burst open. Dad walked through, forcing Sky to jump out of the way to avoid getting smashed.

"Herman!" yelled Mom. "You know I've asked you to use the mudroom!"

"Oh, right. Sorry," said Dad as he stepped into the entryway. Dad was covered in green-brown gunk from his head to his feet.

Hannah appeared at the top of the stairs. "Ewww, Dad. Gross!"

"It's just mud, Hannah. Deal with it," said Mom.

"And maybe some sewage," said Dad, "I think I hit a pipe out there."

"Ewwwww!" Hannah squealed.

"Well, don't just stand there dripping on my floor!" Mom reprimanded.

"Right," said Dad, shuffling his way toward the kitchen, the floorboards creaking loudly with each of his shimmying steps.

"Gee, Dad. Maybe you should cut back on the pork pie lunches," taunted Hannah.

Sky smiled. The floorboards did seem to be bowing under Dad more than they had the night before. How much sewage had he gotten into?

"Mudroom's the other way, Herman!" prompted Mom.

"Right." Dad spun around toward the mudroom, accidentally flinging a clump of gunk onto Hannah's shoe as she descended the stairs.

"Ooohhhwww! Mom!"

"Deal with it, Hannah," said Mom. "It's too late to change."

Hannah stormed past them and out the front door.

"Lived here for *years* before we moved. You'd think the man could find the mudroom," said Mom.

Sky slipped past, quick-stepping after Hannah before Mom could return to her tirade.

"We're not finished, Skyler!" Mom yelled after him.

"Sorry. Bus and all! Can't be late!" said Sky, rushing for the door.

"You're still grounded!" yelled Mom. "I want you home right after school—no excuses!"

"Excuses," muttered Sky, upset that Mom had grounded him without ever explaining why Dad had gone to the manor in the first place. "At least I *offer* them."

"What was that?" snapped Mom.

"After school, then," said Sky, shutting the door. Three weeks; what was he going to do locked inside for three weeks!

CHAPTER 7

Broken Promises

Sky found Hannah just outside wiping the sludge off her shoe with a pile of leaves. "I know these are just going to be ruined."

He snagged the crossword puzzle page from the newspaper on the doorstep and shoved it into his backpack. Most of the time, teachers ignored him in class, giving him plenty of time to use his mind.

"Maybe you should try *dealing* with it," Sky prodded.

Hannah rolled her eyes. "If I have to hear her say that one more time . . ." She shook her head in exasperation, pushing even harder with the leaves.

He looked up and noticed that the tree above them was filled with giant black-and-white crows. They seemed to be staring at him.

"No more crackers," muttered Sky, waving his hands. "Shoo . . . shoo!"

The birds stared at him, looking offended.

"What was that?" asked Hannah as she stood up.

"Er," said Sky. "I said you're never going to get that off your shoe."

"No duh, Sky. I already said they were ruined."

They started walking toward the bus stop. Sky glanced back at the house every few yards until he finally saw the living room curtain drop; Mom, apparently finished with her spying to make certain Sky made it to the bus, had finally gone back to the kitchen.

Sky spun around and started walking toward the arch gate.

"Bus stop's over there, dummy," said Hannah, pointing toward the corner where several kids stood, including a bright-eyed girl who kept watching them.

Sky glanced at the girl, looked away, and then glanced again; it was the same girl he'd seen exiting Pimiscule Grounds the night before. She was trying to act like she wasn't watching them, but he knew she was. He'd used the same awkward I-wish-I-knew-how-to-be-cool glance on her last night.

He turned back to Hannah. "I'm walking to school. You up for it?"

"I don't *walk*. Besides, I know what you're doing. You just want to get a closer look at Phineas's house, even though you know you're not supposed to, and you're inviting me along so I won't tell on you."

"Maybe Phineas's house wants to get a closer look at me," said Sky mysteriously.

"That doesn't even make sense," said Hannah.

He smiled, but she wasn't biting.

"I'm not letting you drag me into this, Sky. You remember the time you convinced me there was gold in Mr. Peabody's outhouse? I stunk for a week!"

"We just needed a smaller sieve! And look, this isn't like that; it's just a walk," said Sky.

"Yeah, right. And I'm *just* a cheerleader," said Hannah, flipping her golden blond hair. She turned her back on him and continued toward the bus stop.

He looked back and forth between the arch gate and Hannah. She wouldn't tell on him, would she?

Sighing, he ran to catch up to Hannah.

"Don't you even care that Mom and Dad lied to you last night?" asked Sky, committed to giving it one last try. "I heard Mom tell you that Dad went to the grocery store, but you know he didn't."

"Maybe he was going to go to the store afterward," said Hannah, sounding like she couldn't care less.

"Maybe. But why did he go to Pimiscule Grounds in the first place? And where's Uncle Phineas? Don't you think it's strange he missed my birthday party? That he didn't meet us here?" asked Sky.

Hannah shook her head. "It doesn't matter, Sky. It's only been one night. So Uncle Phineas didn't show up to your birthday—big deal! Your party wasn't that great anyway! Mom's nasty goulash, leftover pizza, frozen pie? Really? And on a move day no less! That's just poor planning."

"That's not my fault," said Sky. "How can I help when I was born?"

"It's never your fault, is it? That's the problem," Hannah retorted.

Sky didn't know what had gotten into her. "You're not even a little curious?" he pressed.

"Not at all," said Hannah.

"But—"

"Just take the bus, Sky. You've already broken enough promises for one day, haven't you?" Hannah chided.

He felt the sting. Hannah wasn't disinterested; she was upset! He'd promised her that he'd try to be normal, and then he'd snuck out at night and gone to Pimiscule Manor anyway.

She'd actually expected him to keep his promise to her! Didn't she know him better than that? Even weirder, she was worried about him.

"You're mad that I went to Phineas's manor, aren't you? That I broke my promise? Honestly, Hannah—"

"I don't want to talk about it," said Hannah, cutting him off. "Look, Sky, can't you just let it go for once? Let someone else get in trouble for a change! Go to school. Stay on Mom and Dad's good side. Let them take care of it! This is your chance to be normal—to have friends and not be so lonely all the time. Do you really want to mess that up?"

Up ahead the school bus pulled around the corner. Several kids, maybe fifteen in all, of all different ages—from elementary to high school—milled around talking to one another as they waited. One of the stranger things about Exile was that most everybody went to the same school. His parents claimed it had always been that way.

Sky looked over his shoulder at the arch gate and back at the bus. Lonely. Hannah knew him better than he'd thought.

"Sorry, Hannah. I've got to do this," said Sky, stopping a short distance from the bus. "Promise you won't tell?"

Hannah turned around. She pursed her lips, looking worried. The bus honked.

Sky glanced at the driver, who waved his hand for them to

hurry. The girl he'd seen exiting Pimiscule Grounds the night before hadn't gotten on the bus either. She just stood there, watching them.

Hannah sighed. "Fine, Sky. I won't tell this time, but you'd better hurry. If you're late to school, Mom will find out about it. You know she will!"

"Thanks, Sis. I owe you one!" He turned and ran toward the arch gate. "And I really am sorry!"

"No, you're not," Hannah snapped, heading for the bus, "but you *will be*."

Shadow Wargs might have been horrifying, but he didn't have to live with *them*.

Sky raced for the arch gate, hoping that what he found beyond, in the light of day, would give him the clues he needed to find his uncle and perhaps stop one of the most evil monsters who'd ever lived.

CHAPTER 8
What the Sun Brings

Sky rubbed his fingers together, massaging the fine powder on the crackers. Not salt . . . not sugar. Finer than either. He sniffed the powder but it had no smell. Who had put it here? And why?

"Weird." He dropped the cracker back to the ground by the gate, where it was rapidly snatched up by a hungry crow.

"CAW!"

He looked up and noticed several more crows watching him from the trees. As he left, he kicked up the leaves, revealing more crackers.

"Enjoy."

He followed the trail east, passing through the field with the flowers and wolfsbane. He came to the ridge and, following it north to the crossroads and the steps he'd fallen down, looked over the shallow valley thirty feet below that housed the towering Dovetail hedge.

The Dovetail had looked so black at night, but the sun brought out an entirely different effect. White leaves, like feathers, covered thick black branches, and red and black budding flowers seemed, to Sky, strangely inviting.

Of course, there were the *poisonous thorns* to consider.

The unnatural hedge rose nearly as high as the ridge itself, higher in the middle with a sprawling, barely visible thick green canopy in the center. It stretched for almost a mile across barren red earth that seemed very out of place. Every plant, every tree, every bush in the red valley looked either dead or dying . . . except for the Dovetail. How could something that big thrive on soil like that?

In spots he could see openings in the Dovetail, twisting and turning like a giant maze, and, looking closer, Sky noticed that the ground beneath the Dovetail was actually green and luscious, not red at all.

"What an odd plant," said Sky, staring, wishing for the first time in his life that he'd studied more botany. "Leave it up to Phineas to plant a maze in the middle of nowhere."

Why someone would plant such a thing, he hadn't a clue. And why Dad had gone in there was even more confusing, but Sky was sure Dad must've gone in, since Sky had heard him approach from that direction. Of course, Sky supposed he could've been hallucinating, as Dad claimed, but the only thing the Dovetail had made Sky was sleepy. Had Dad simply lied about the hallucinations to explain away what'd happened? Sky suspected as much. Dad had seemed a little too anxious when he'd related Dovetail's hallucinatory effects. Sky knew his parents wanted to protect him, and they'd keep lying to do it. The only way he could get them to be honest was to confront them with undeniable evidence. Unfortunately, he didn't have any at the moment.

Sky left the Dovetail behind, following the trail farther north, through the trees, and then east again until he arrived at the main cobblestone road.

In the distance, beyond the cemetery he'd noticed the night before, he could just make out the school—Arkhon Academy—hiding to the east at the base of the hill.

Who would name a school after, according to Ursula, one of the most evil monsters that has ever lived?

He pulled out his pocket watch and checked the time. He had maybe ten minutes.

"You're going to be late," said a voice behind him.

He practically jumped out of his sneakers. He turned and saw the girl from the bus stop.

"Why do people keep doing that?" demanded Sky, breathing heavily as he tried to slow his racing heart.

The girl quirked her head and stared at him with a raised eyebrow.

"You should have ridden the bus," said the girl matter-of-factly. "Maybe then you wouldn't be late. Nobody's *making* you late, you know."

She sounded almost offended.

"Not the *late* part—the *sneaking up* part," said Sky, beginning to feel foolish, though he didn't know why. She was the one sneaking up on *him*!

The girl stood shorter than him, but not by much. She had a freckled round face and brown eyes, and messy red-brown hair. She wore a black faded T-shirt and a pair of hole-ridden, too-big blue jeans rolled up at the cuff and cinched at the waist with a tattered faux-leather belt. A large backpack, also thread-worn, hung from her shoulders, ready to burst. If he hadn't known any better, he'd have said it was almost the same outfit she'd had on last night.

Hannah would have been outraged.

She glared at him like he was a wayward child throwing smashed peas at the wall.

"Why are you here?" asked the girl. "You realize there are NO TRESPASSING signs all over the fences, right? That usually indicates that you *shouldn't go in*."

He might have even said she was cute, if she hadn't been glaring at him and chastising him like his mom.

"This is my uncle's place," said Sky. "So as you can see, *I'm* not trespassing."

"Your uncle? Nobody lives here. Nobody's *ever* lived here," said the girl, narrowing her eyes. "Who exactly are you?"

He sighed. "Why does everyone keep asking me that?"

He'd already lost a few precious minutes to this girl's interrogation. He needed to get moving.

She opened her mouth again, but he cut her off.

"Sorry to be rude," said Sky rudely as he turned and began walking toward the manor, avoiding the girl's glare, "but I'm in a bit of a hurry."

"What're you doing?" asked the girl, scrambling to catch up. "You really shouldn't just wander around this place."

"Why not?" asked Sky.

"Because . . . you just shouldn't," said the girl.

"Oh. Okay, then. I guess *that* makes sense," said Sky sarcastically. He'd definitely been spending too much time with Hannah. She was starting to rub off on him—everything but the popularity and looks.

"This whole place is honeycombed with mine shafts. You could fall and break your leg, and nobody would ever find you," said the girl.

"That's funny; I haven't noticed any shafts. And you seem awfully concerned about me considering we don't even know each other," said Sky.

"Fine. I'm Crystal. Pleased to meet you. Charmed, I'm sure. Can we go to school now?" said Crystal.

"I'm not stopping you," said Sky.

"But you're not helping me either. What's your name anyway?" asked Crystal.

"It's Sky."

"Well, Sky, it's not safe to be up here alone," said Crystal.

"Yeah. You mentioned that. The mine shafts, right?"

He rounded the copse of trees, watching the manor slowly drift into view. Something wasn't right about it. Where was the wall? Maybe he just had to get closer.

"Don't worry. I just want to see the glass wall and the sleeping monsters. Then I'll run along to school, okay?" said Sky, biting at her more than he'd intended.

"What sleeping monsters?"

"*Those* sleeping monsters—" said Sky, stopping midstride.

There were no sleeping monsters. No glass wall; no wall whatsoever! Just the run-down old manor in the distance.

"No, no, no, no, NO! Where did they go?" yelled Sky. "They were right here! The monsters, the glass wall, *Ursula*! I didn't hallucinate it! I didn't dream it! It was *real*!"

He'd been so sure.

"Nobody lives here, Sky. Nobody's *ever* lived here. That's what I've been trying to tell you," said Crystal. "And if we don't leave now, we're going to be late for class, and Miss Hagfish—"

"My uncle Phineas *does* live here," said Sky angrily, cutting her off again. "Well, er . . . he used to anyway. He might again."

"Phineas?" said Crystal, frowning. She looked up at the decrepit manor.

"Yeah. Phineas T. *Pimiscule*," said Sky, "as in *Pimiscule Manor*! Ah! I'm so stupid! Hannah was right. I should've taken the bus!" He kicked a tree.

"Come on," said Crystal. "We'd better get going. You really don't want to make Miss Hagfish angry."

She turned and started walking. Sky started to follow, but then he noticed something . . . a slim bracelet hanging from her wrist, with a silver pendant that looked like half a strand of DNA.

But, no. She couldn't be, could she?

"So, you've never seen Phineas around? Old guy, wears frock coats and a monocle?" asked Sky, scanning the woods around them.

"Why? Should I have?" asked Crystal.

"You just seem like the kind of person who knows stuff like that—where the mine shafts are, which creepy manors have never been lived in, who my *teacher* is, even when I don't."

"Your mom called ahead," said Crystal, "I overheard Principal Lem telling Miss Hagfish."

"Do you spy on your teachers a lot?" asked Sky.

"Do you have a *point*?" Crystal countered.

"You still haven't answered my question," said Sky.

Crystal looked at him, her eyes measuring. "Look, there's this guy—Phineas *Smith*, the groundskeeper. Okay, he used to come around, but he doesn't anymore, hasn't for years."

"So you haven't seen him? Recently, I mean?" asked Sky.

"I . . . No, not recently. I wish I had," said Crystal,

sounding almost bitter. "Why? Is he missing? Do you think he's here somewhere?" She looked around anxiously, as if Phineas might pop out of a tree.

"That's a nice bracelet," Sky said accusingly.

"Hmm?"

"Your bracelet," said Sky, "it's very distinctive."

Crystal covered the bracelet with her hand.

"My uncle gave me something like that once," Sky continued. "It was a puzzle, though, not a bracelet like yours. Two metal pieces locked together, each like half a strand of DNA. You had to put pressure at just the right points to break it apart. Very hard. The trick is in the pairings. It took me forever to solve. That's why, when I saw it last night, I knew I'd remember."

"What are you talking about?" asked Crystal nervously.

"You're a hunter, aren't you? You were there last night," Sky continued, "by the Dovetail! You saved me from the Shadow Wargs!"

"Don't be silly. I was home in bed. You saw me exit the grounds," said Crystal, putting her hands in her oversize pockets—apparently, Sky suspected, to hide the bracelet.

"But you came back. Later. You followed me somehow."

"You're being ridiculous," said Crystal.

"Those crackers, the powder—those are yours, aren't they?" said Sky. "Do you use it to track people? Sniff it out with dogs or something?"

"It's phosphorescent," said a booming voice behind him, sending Sky out of his sneakers again. "Lights up under a black light. Makes it way easier to find things. Crows eat it up after a few days and we have to replace it, but it works."

Sky turned and saw a giant step out of the trees—not

a *literal* giant, of course, just a very big kid. The newcomer looked just a little older than him, but he was bigger . . . much bigger. He stood nearly as tall as a Shadow Warg and looked to weigh nearly as much. He had mocha skin, like an islander, and he wore a Bahamas' button-down, brown leather sandals, and Bermuda shorts, despite the cool weather.

"Of course, the crackers have done some strange things to the crows," said the giant.

"I was handling it, T-Bone," snapped Crystal as the giant casually strolled toward them.

Sky looked back at her, trying to keep one eye on her and one eye on T-Bone. He had a hard time believing these two *kids* were two of the hunters he'd seen last night. But T-Bone was about the right size as the hunter who'd wrestled the Shadow Warg Big.

And then there was the bracelet. Crystal's bracelet was unmistakable. She was the first hunter he'd seen, the one who'd shot Vicious with the goo cannon. But if these two were here, where was the other one?

"*That* was handling it? I told you it wouldn't work," said T-Bone. "You should've just left him alone. Now he knows who we are!"

"It would have worked if you'd just butted out," said Crystal. "It's not safe up here. He shouldn't be wandering."

"He wasn't buying it. He *knows*," said T-Bone. "Besides, we're late for school. Let's kill him and get on with things."

"Er," muttered Sky, suddenly terrified.

"He's *kidding*," said Crystal.

T-Bone smiled. Sky looked at those teeth, wondering.

"Andrew, make a note that Crystal needs to leave her jewelry behind on future outings," said T-Bone.

A kid, stick-figure thin, emerged from behind a pile of rocks farther along the cobblestone road. On his head he had a cowlick called the "double crown" by haunted hairstylists the world over. He wore a white dress shirt—unbuttoned at the top—glossy black slacks, and thick spectacles that clearly labeled him as a member of the "out" crowd.

Another kid his age? How was that even possible? Sky would have thought maybe at least this hunter, Andrew, would've been an adult—maybe a real hunter training the other two . . . but this? So who had trained them? Were there more?

"Note to self," said Andrew, holding up his hand while pretending to write on it with an invisible pen. "Hold . . . T-Bone's . . . calls . . . will . . . be . . . out to lunch . . . indefinitely . . . due . . . to . . . stupidity . . . and . . . an . . . overactive . . . bladder. There. Got it."

T-Bone leaned over to Sky, whispering conspiratorially, but loud enough for everyone to hear, "He gets prickly when he doesn't get to bed by eight."

"And when monsters try to eat him," added another boy, appearing from a trail to Sky's left. They'd nearly reached the cemetery. "I'm just sorry I missed out on the fun."

"Took you long enough, Hands," said T-Bone.

Hands looked a year or two older than Sky and a few inches taller, though not as tall as T-Bone. But where Sky was neither athletic nor flabby, Hands was most decidedly athletic. Hands stood, cool and confident, in a designer polo, expensive shoes, and banged-up jeans, but where the holes in Crystal's jeans looked earned over many long years of wear by much bigger people, the holes in Hands's jeans looked purchased.

"You're nuts, Hands," said Andrew. "Only you would call getting nearly eaten by monsters *fun*."

"Can we please walk while we belittle one another? You know how Miss Hagfish gets," said Crystal as she started walking along the cemetery trail Hands had just come from.

Sky was flabbergasted. These were the hunters who'd saved him last night? Well, not Hands, but he was obviously one of them.

Sky followed after them, thinking. Could there be someone else behind these so-called hunters? Their weapons seemed far too advanced for them to have built themselves. And who had trained them? Were they part of a larger group? Sky remembered his parents mentioning someone named Malvidia leading what was left of the "hunter riffraff." Was he looking at them now? If so, the hunters must have been desperate indeed.

Of course, his parents—Mom especially—had seemed to suspect Malvidia of setting a trap for Phineas. Could these monster hunters in front of him be part of her trap? Did they know something about Phineas?

He knew it wasn't the subtlest approach, but he was running out of time.

"All right. So is someone going to tell me what's going on? For starters, where's my uncle and how did you move the glass wall and the sleeping monsters?" asked Sky.

"No idea what you're talking about," said T-Bone.

Sky began to object, but Crystal cut him off. "He's telling the truth, Sky. You're right. We saved you from those wolf things last night, but we've never seen a glass wall here or any sleeping monsters. It *always* looks like that."

"That's not possible," said Sky, shaking his head. "I *saw* it. And if the Shadow Wargs were real, then so was the Wargarou and Ambrosia and the sleeping monsters and Ursula—and that means my uncle is missing, maybe even dead."

"Shadow Wargs . . . that's what you call those Clydesdale-size wolves?" said Andrew.

"Yeah. Shadow Wargs. From *The Shadow Wargs of Whimple*," said Sky.

"Is that some kind of book?" asked Hands.

"My uncle gave it to me," said Sky, suspicious. How could they not have heard of *The Shadow Wargs of Whimple*? How could they not even realize what they'd been fighting? "So you've never heard of it? Malvidia never made you read it?"

"Who?" asked Andrew, sounding genuinely confused.

"Nobody makes us read anything," said T-Bone.

"But *The Shadow Wargs of Whimple*! It's a classic!" said Sky, dumbfounded. How could they be *monster* hunters and not know about *monsters*? "The story's about a penniless shoe salesman who bests a pack of Shadow Wargs by planting wolfsbane in the town, but when the Wargarou finds out, he kills everyone," said Sky.

"Well, that's a delightful story," said Crystal. "Any others to brighten our day?"

"What's a Wargarou?" asked Hands.

They really didn't know.

"Wargarou—the Shadow Warg pack leader? Made of fiery darkness and horror? How can you not know any of this?" exclaimed Sky. "You're *hunters*!"

"And you know a lot of stories like that?" asked Hands, looking at the others. "Names, weaknesses, that sort of thing?"

"Some," Sky admitted hesitantly. "Uncle Phineas gave me a small collection of books about monsters and the like."

"Phineas Smith?" asked Andrew, sounding excited. Sky noticed that Hands and T-Bone also seemed to perk up at the name.

"You know him?" Crystal asked them, before Sky could.

"Uh . . . he used to be the groundskeeper, right?" said Andrew.

"Have you seen him?" prodded Sky. "Recently?"

"No. Why, is he here?"

Sky sighed. "You *are* monster hunters, aren't you? Here to fight the Arkhon if he escapes?"

Crystal looked at the others, then back at Sky. "Sky, we don't know anything about any of that. Call us what you like. It's just the four of us. We've never heard of the Arkhon or any of this, unless you're talking about the school. And nobody besides *you* knows about us."

"Including our parents," added Andrew.

"Sky, you shouldn't know this. About us. It's not safe for you," said Crystal.

"Oh? And I was safe before?" said Sky.

"You would be if you'd stay out of places you're not supposed to go," snapped Crystal.

"You're telling me if someone you loved was missing, you'd just sit around and do nothing?" Sky snapped back.

Crystal stopped walking, and he nearly knocked her down. She turned on him, her mouth tightened into a thin, hard line. The others stopped too, casually forming a small circle around him. And suddenly everyone was glaring. He glanced around uneasily. What had he said?

"Er, Crystal?" said Sky.

Crystal narrowed her eyes, opened her mouth to speak, decided against it, and finally turned and walked away. Sky started to follow, but T-Bone stepped forward, blocking his path.

"Sky," said T-Bone, placing his massive hand on Sky's

shoulder, "all of us know what you're going through. Believe me. We *do*. But what you know about us—what you've figured out—you can't share that with anyone. Nobody. Not your parents, not your sister, not your uncle, or your best friend, or your best friend's dog. No one. If people find out, it could be very dangerous for us, our families . . . for *you*. If you tell anyone about us—and I want you to listen carefully. If you tell *anyone* about us, we'll make sure you don't tell anyone else again. *Ever*. Do you understand what I'm saying?" said T-Bone.

Sky looked around at their solemn faces. Andrew and Hands avoided eye contact, and Crystal had disappeared down the trail, but T-Bone stared directly at him, unflinching.

Sky knew what they were saying. He knew exactly what they were saying.

"All right?" said T-Bone.

Sky nodded, unable to speak.

"Good man," said T-Bone, patting him on the shoulder. "I think we have an understanding."

T-Bone, Andrew, and Hands, turned and followed after Crystal.

Sky watched them go. What had just happened?

"Tonight, Sky!" yelled T-Bone over his shoulder. "You show your cards and we'll show ours. If you really want to know what's going on in this town, meet us at the crossroads at sunset!"

Sky watched them disappear down the trail toward the school. His life seemed to be getting increasingly complicated—a missing, possibly dead, uncle; lying parents; monsters; nightmares; and now monster hunters who were more clueless than he was! Things were shaping up to get very interesting. Very interesting indeed.

CHAPTER 9

"Enot Od Naba Ban Do Fone"

Instead of following T-Bone and the others to school, and knowing Mom would kill him if she found out, Sky detoured south, through the cemetery and along the cobbled driveway toward the front gate. He knew if he just followed the wall long enough, he'd find Phineas's truck, and he wasn't disappointed. He found it three blocks east of the main entrance by an ivy-covered gate on a dead-end road lined with run-down and abandoned houses, just as he'd dreamed.

He eyed the houses warily as he approached, remembering the Shadow Wargs that had burst out and attacked Uncle Phineas.

There was no sign of the Cadillac.

Sky searched the asphalt around the truck for signs of attack—blood, loose hairs, notes saying "I kidnapped your uncle. Please find me *here*."

He found bits of dried blood leading toward the gate and

Pimiscule Grounds. Had Phineas really gotten away? Was he hiding somewhere on Pimiscule Grounds?

Something had kicked up the leaves around the gate, but Sky couldn't find any tracks, blood drops, or bits of cracker. The neighborhood didn't look like the kind of area the fearless, though clueless, monster hunters would bother protecting.

Sky left the gate, heading back for Phineas's beat-up old truck. Sky and Phineas had restored it years before in Dunwitch when Sky was eight.

They'd spent hours upon hours in the garage, poring over detailed specifications and then acquiring and laying out the parts like the pieces of a giant puzzle—exhaust deflectors, vent shades, gas tank, converter hub, intake manifolds, fenders. They'd worked over the truck like it was Silly Putty, and slowly something shiny had emerged from the rusted debris.

And then Phineas had banged it all up again. Sky shook his head in disappointment. Uncle Phineas was harmless except when it came to his truck. Of course, after what Sky had seen in his dream, he could see why the truck might look the way it did.

Sky cracked the unlocked door and slipped inside the musty cab. He clearly remembered seeing Phineas write on some papers, but Phineas hadn't had the papers with him when he'd stepped out of the truck.

Which meant they were probably still here, and if they were here, he knew precisely where to look—a special place Phineas had insisted on adding even though it had taken hours of work and had made Sky question his uncle's sanity.

Reaching down, he felt along the frame of the passenger door under the glove box until he found the spot.

He punched it, and the passenger floor flipped up, revealing a secret compartment and, at the bottom, a few folded pieces of paper. Sky removed the papers, closed the compartment, and sat back to read:

Property of Phineas T. Pimiscule, Hunter's Journal Addendum

(If you're not Phineas T. Pimiscule, then get your HANDS OFF!)

Ambrosia and the Wargarou caught up with me outside Skull Valley before I could find Cass, and it was all I could do to get away. Somehow they must've tailed me to Herman and Helen's afterward—as if dodging hunters all these years hasn't been bad enough!

I hated to run off before Sky's party—Helen's goulash notwithstanding—but I couldn't let them find Sky. I had to lead them away.

The Wargarou I've tangled with before, and lived, but Ambrosia presents more of a challenge. There are so few Whisper left, and it's been so long. I'd almost forgotten how viciously devious they can be! Of all the Arkhon's shifters, they are the worst. I'd lose hope in the lot if it weren't for Ursula, and even she strains credulity to the point of breaking. Poor Beau. I don't know if he'll ever be the same. He won't be if he ever finds out she's here.

I have a deep foreboding that I won't like what Ursula has to tell me later tonight. I think I already know. After all these years of searching for answers, to finally find them now is almost too hard to believe.

But it may already be too late. The Arkhon is coming, and there's no more time for searching and remorse.

I fear for Sky and what it all might mean.

By my estimates, the prison will collapse completely before the third night of the Hunter's Moon two days from now—and even before then if Ambrosia has her way. I have to stop it. If Nikola were still sane, maybe he could fix the prison and I wouldn't have to, but in the face of insanity, sometimes the only course left is more insanity!

The Arkhon's impending escape—and the keys I alone hold to stop it—has given me the bargaining power to bring Sky back to Exile. After eleven years of constant moves and endless hiding to keep Sky alive, it seems ironic that fear of one of the most evil creatures of all would be the thing to finally bring us home. . . . Well, everyone but me, that is. Malvidia . . . that woman! I know her invitation is a trap, but there's nothing for it. Malvidia has given her word that the hunters won't kill Sky unless the Arkhon escapes or Sky shows signs of abnormality. (And with Sky, how would we ever know?) But right now, with things as dangerous as they are, that promise is the best we can hope for.

As much as I hate it, my only recourse is Bat and the Hunters of Legend, and quite frankly, I'm shocked that he agreed to a meeting (a meeting that, in all likelihood, Malvidia knows nothing about). Malvidia forfeited her claims when she sided with me and came to Exile, which makes Bat the senior member of the Hunters of Legend in Exile. Malvidia may lead the Arkhon Hunters in Exile, but she would never go against the will of the Hunters of Legend if they promised me safety (a conceit I cling to despite its seeming impossibility). Playing this card against Malvidia tears me apart inside—she has defied the odds and kept the hunters alive when I abandoned them—but she has left me little choice. If I can get Bat to commit to my safety at the meeting tonight, I can fix the prison, return to Exile permanently, and finally start training Sky in earnest rather than spending my days hunting his shadows!

Sky's time is coming faster than I'd imagined, and I fear he's not ready. He's given up on me, it seems.

⊡ ⊡ ⊡

Sky stared at the paper with a sinking feeling. It made him feel sick to his stomach. His uncle thought he'd given up on him? And what did all this mean? Had they really moved because of him? Why would Malvidia and the hunters want to kill him? He was nobody! Were they threatening Sky to force Phineas into something? Or was it something else?

Sky flipped through the remaining pages to see if he could find anything to make sense of what he'd just read, but the other pages were just sketches, some maps, fact sheets on a few cities, and, finally, some research.

Sky skimmed through the research for information on Whisper, reading quietly:

"'Changelings, unlike Whisper, are not born; they are made. Blood is exchanged between two creatures, typically a hunter and a monster, under the birth moon of one or the other, until the Change is complete. A Changeling could start life as a Whisper, or any number of creatures, but at least one of the creatures must be a shifter with "old blood." If the Change happens under the birth moon of the hunter, then both become Changeling hunters; if under the birth moon of the monster, both become Changeling monsters, at which point they are usually, but not always, swapped, one for the other. From then on, no matter what they were before, both are Changelings thereafter, becoming alike in every way at the moment of Change, and permanently linked from then on. The Change is complete and total in a way that no other shifter, no matter how powerful, can ever achieve, which is why it was so favored by hunters before the ban. To Change again, and link with another, a Changeling must kill its counterpart. Blood must return to blood, and the murder must be by its own hand. . . ."

Changelings didn't sound very pleasant, but they clearly weren't the same as Whisper.

He found another reference to Whisper on the next page, dated three hundred years earlier.

"It can be argued that Whisper are, after the Arkhon, the most powerful shifters alive, becoming more powerful with age as their body density, and therefore weight, increases, allowing them to shift into larger, heavier creatures. They have but two natural weaknesses: (1) Most Whisper must have fresh blood (or other biological sample such as skin, nasal discharge, saliva, urine, or excrement) from the intended victim to perform a shift (though older shifters can change minor features without a sample). What's more, Whisper can store only a few samples at a time, and only until the end of the next full moon—at which time Whisper become their most lethal. Experienced hunters will never engage a Whisper during a full moon. (2) Based on interrogations of captured Whisper, we have discovered that they experience a powerful driving urge to change form all the time. However, to do so at any time other than the three days of the full moon leads to madness and the eventual fall of the Whisper. At the end of the full moon, a Whisper must either return to their normal humanlike form or stay in the last form they assumed until the next full moon. Hunters, exploit this weakness at your own peril."

Sky looked through the remaining notes, but didn't find anything too helpful.

The Whisper looked even more powerful than the Wargarou, if that was possible, and there were *two* of them in Exile: Ambrosia, who'd attacked Uncle Phineas with the Wargarou, and Ursula, who'd protected Sky from the Shadow Wargs.

One bad. One good.

Phineas's journal page had implied Ursula was trustworthy, though just barely. But even if Ursula had escaped the Shadow Wargs—and Sky suspected she had—she'd already said she couldn't help find Phineas.

At some point in his search for Phineas, he was bound to cross paths with Ambrosia, and since Ursula wouldn't help, Sky would have to face her alone. What would he do then? The notes hadn't listed any real weaknesses—nothing he could use in the moment.

Don't fight over the three days of the full moon, and if you fight at any other time, do it at your own peril. Great. Very helpful. It was *already* a full moon.

Sky had begun to fold up the papers when a small wrinkle on the last page caught his eye. He stared at it for a moment. . . . Yes, it was worth a shot.

Uncle Phineas had taught him everything he knew about encryption techniques. A wrinkle was a sign of sloppiness, but maybe Phineas had *wanted* someone to notice.

Heat. That's what he needed. Heat could sometimes draw words to the surface.

Sky raised the paper to his mouth and blew on the wrinkle. Nothing. He set the paper on the dashboard and began rubbing it with his hand, but the friction didn't produce enough heat. Either that or it really *was* just a wrinkle.

Luckily, he'd helped rebuild the truck and he'd learned a great deal about its inner workings, including how to start it without a key.

The engine roared, belching out a cloud of black smoke. Sky flipped on the heater and held the paper against it. After a few seconds words began to appear around the wrinkle.

"That's it!" exclaimed Sky. "It actually worked!"

He wasn't sure which was more amazing—the fact that it had worked, or the words he found.

He read:

ENOF OD NABA BAN DO FONE

One key to set the time,
Two to see it right,
Three keys you wouldn't suspect,
To lock the prison tight.
Two, you wouldn't find
Without looking.
One you wouldn't find
Without watching.
With all three,
On the pendulum bend,
You might get lucky
And lock the prison
Up again.
But then again, maybe,
Just maybe,
You'll kill everyone
You've ever loved
And find a pain-filled end.

It was obviously a clue to the hiding place of the keys to the Arkhon's prison. Sky just had no idea what it *meant*. But neither would Ambrosia and the Wargarou if they'd found it. The difference was, Phineas had *trained* Sky, which meant Sky should be able to figure it out.

And then, beneath the poem, numbers appeared.

581.112

What was *that* supposed to mean? Was it coordinates? A legal code? Part of an IP address? A medical code? It could be anything. And what was the title supposed to mean? "Enof Od Naba Ban Do Fone"? It looked like gibberish.

TAP, TAP, TAP!

He jerked his head up, expecting crows. Instead he found a badge pressed against the window. The sheriff.

Perfect. Just perfect.

As the sheriff opened the door, Sky quickly shoved the marked page into his pocket, while appearing to shuffle the other pages.

"You look young for a car thief," said the sheriff as Sky slipped out of the truck.

"And you look too nice to arrest a young car thief," said Sky, "especially when he's not a car thief."

The sheriff, in actuality, didn't look that nice. He looked old, like Sky's Mom, and scruffy, like a billy goat, and his skin was rough and tanned. But Sky decided that in this situation, flattery was the best policy.

The sheriff frowned at him. "I suppose that passes as a compliment where you come from?"

Sky smiled uncomfortably.

"Kid," said the sheriff, "you're obviously new here, so I'll give you a little clue, free of charge. I'm *anything but nice*. Those were in the car?"

Sky pulled the papers out from behind his back. "Would you believe it's my homework?"

The sheriff stared hard as he took the papers from him.

"Why don't you go ahead and lean forward against the truck and put your hands behind your back," said the sheriff, taking out his handcuffs as he glanced at the papers.

"They're my uncle's," said Sky, beginning to despair as the sheriff slapped the handcuffs onto his wrists. "Honest! It's his truck! I helped him rebuild it myself! Look, you can see my initials next to his on the back bumper! If you'll just look, you'll see it!"

The sheriff's eyes suddenly widened as he looked through the papers, then he looked back at Sky in surprise, as if seeing him for the first time.

"What did you say your name was?" asked the Sheriff.

"Sky. Sky Weathers. You can see my initials on the back bumper next to my uncle Phineas's."

The sheriff looked at him, eyes full of suspicion, and then he walked to the back of the truck.

For a moment Sky felt an almost uncontrollable urge to run. The feeling came on so suddenly that he'd taken a step before he realized what he was doing. He ground his teeth, fought down the little monster—which didn't feel so little anymore—and stepped back toward the truck, his hands still cuffed behind him.

"It's there, in the middle, just under the O," said Sky, struggling to keep from running. Sweat broke out on his forehead, and his skin flushed red. His trix froze, ice rushing beneath the surface of his skin. He could feel it splitting open again, blood trickling across his palm. At the same time his mind ebbed and flowed like a great tide, pulling him out to sea . . . slowly pulling him away . . . and away . . .

"Open your hands," said the Sheriff, who had reappeared behind him.

Sky came back to himself. Without realizing it, he'd been clenching his hands into fists since the sheriff had first appeared. He opened them.

"Hmpf," grunted the sheriff. "You'll want to clean that oil up."

Oil? The sheriff must've mistaken the trix blood for oil.

A moment later the handcuffs came off. Sky turned around and found the sheriff eyeing him speculatively.

"So where are you *supposed* to be, Sky Weathers?"

Sky smiled.

CHAPTER 10
Miss Hagfish

Ten minutes later, Sheriff Beau dropped him off at school, and Sky—who was very, very late by this time—walked into what remained of his first class: English with Miss Hagfish.

"All right, *children*," said a crone at the front of the class. "Despite all the powers of logic and reason—and the combined faculties of my not unimpressive capabilities—you appear to be even stupider today than you were yesterday. How is that possible?"

The woman—Miss Hagfish, Sky presumed—was dressed in black from neck to ankle in an old-fashioned mourning dress, as if she'd just come *from*, or—even more likely—was planning to go *to* a funeral that was, in all probability, Sky's own.

"Sorry to interrupt, Miss Hagfish," said Miss Terry, escorting Sky into the classroom, "but I have a young boy here—Sky Weathers—who seems to be a little lost."

After the sheriff had dropped him off, he'd wandered into

the front office and claimed that he'd gotten lost trying to find his class. Miss Terry, the PE teacher, had volunteered to take him. He figured getting lost was the only excuse he could give that would keep Mom from meeting him in the parking lot after school with open arms.

"A little lost?" Miss Hagfish eyed him like she was sizing a rotten pumpkin. "Thank you, Miss Terry. I'll take it from here."

Miss Terry squeezed his arm, looking him in the eye. "Sky, if you ever need to talk about *anything*," said Miss Terry, glancing pointedly at Miss Hagfish, "my office is by the gym. Drop in anytime."

"Okay," said Sky, glancing uncertainly at Miss Hagfish. Was she really that bad? He glanced back at Miss Terry. He'd never gotten along with a gym teacher before—or any teacher, for that matter—and he'd *never* had one offer to help him. Usually they looked him over, frowned, and told him to get at the back of the line. Most of the gym teachers he'd met had arms as big as his head, thick mustaches, necks like telephone poles, and round, scrunched-up faces that made it look like they'd been sucking on lemons all day.

And that was just the women.

But not Miss Terry. She smiled, revealing teeth as white as lilies and eyes that sparkled like emeralds. Her face wasn't scrunched-up at all. On the contrary, it was quite unscrunched, drifting down like a feather to connect with a very normal-size neck.

Maybe she *was* different. Maybe.

"Thank you, Miss Terry. Now, if you're finished coddling this boy, I'd like to start my class again, *if you don't mind*," said Miss Hagfish.

"Of course," said Miss Terry, smiling sweetly at Miss Hagfish. She winked at Sky and was gone.

"Well, don't just stand there, boy. Are you daft?"

"Er . . . I was just—"

"Close your mouth, boy. You'll let the flies in. And don't think for a minute that you can lie to me! Lost! Hmpf. More likely you were vandalizing my car. I know your *ilk,* Mr. Weathers; I've dealt with *your kind* before. Beneath that layer of cultured bacteria and caked-on putrescent dirt that you've so painstakingly built up over years and years of carefully avoided showers and purposeful neglect, you've got trouble written all over your face. My guess is that it runs in your family. These things always do. Are your parents both still alive?"

"I—"

"Natural selection hasn't weeded them out yet?" pressed Miss Hagfish.

"Wha—"

"No matter. What's that on your hand?"

"My hand?" asked Sky, clenching his fists more tightly. There was no way she could have seen—

"Don't threaten me, boy! It was a simple question!"

"It's nothing," said Sky, feeling flustered. What was she trying to do to him? Break him in front of the class? But why? So he was a little late. So what? Did she do this with everyone who showed up late, or was this *personal*? But how could it be personal? He didn't even know her.

She stared at him in silence for a moment, her eyes appraising.

"Well, *Sky Weathers*, it doesn't take a prognosticator to see that you will fail *dismally* in this class with that attitude—

probably as dismally as you've failed in all the *other* places you've lived over your short, un-noteworthy life. But the state requires that I put in the effort regardless, and I am nothing if not a creature of duty—something your sort could never understand. Now, if you don't mind, will you please take a seat so that I can—hate-filled mercies of fate and fortune allowing—attempt to make this class less stupid and, if possible, you with it?"

Sky stared at Miss Hagfish in shock, his pulse racing. He could feel the little monster stirring inside of him, pushing him to strike out at her with his mouth, with his fists. The compulsion was almost overwhelming, driven by a monstrous rage that seemed to come from somewhere deep within. His trix ached, his hands clenched and unclenched, his mouth opened and closed like a fish gasping for air, and he suddenly found himself, once again, fighting for control of his mind and body.

"If you require assistance getting to your seat, I'm sure Crenshaw would be willing to provide it," said Miss Hagfish, unsmiling.

"I'd be happy to, Miss Hagfish," said Crenshaw, standing up from his seat at the back of the room. Crenshaw was athletic, with messy blond hair and a chiseled jaw—the kind of boy that girls swooned over.

"It looks like the kid has constipation of the mouth. It's very serious, according to my Dad—contagious even. The brain just shuts down, sometimes permanently," said Crenshaw, feigning worry. "Maybe Cordelia, Ren, and I should escort him to the nurse to see if there's something wrong with him."

Sky realized his mouth was open but no words were coming out. He closed it. Constipation of the mouth . . . Ha, ha, very funny.

Two of his new classmates stood up next to Crenshaw. The first, Cordelia, sighed as she stood, obviously not happy with being singled out. She had fiery red hair and wouldn't make eye contact when he looked at her—but whether she avoided his eyes because she was embarrassed or bored, he couldn't tell.

The second, Ren, looked younger than Crenshaw but was much larger, almost as big as T-Bone, and just as Polynesian. In fact, if Sky hadn't known any better (and he didn't know any better), he'd say that Ren and T-Bone were related. Ren cracked his knuckles as he watched, swinging his head around like he was about to enter the ring to fight for the super heavyweight championship of the world.

"Just the three of you?" asked Miss Hagfish. "What happened to Alexis?"

"Home sick," said Crenshaw.

"More's the pity. Well, that's all right Crenshaw; your visits to the nurse take far too long, and students always look worse when they come back—almost as bad as this boy does now. That nurse is just awful. I don't know what mail-order night school issued her degree, but it should be shut down, condemned, and then burned to the ground, preferably in reverse order. Sometimes I truly worry about this school's standards. Of course, your father *is* a doctor, and something does appear to be wrong with the boy."

"I'm fine," said Sky, still wrestling for control. Beads of sweat ran down his face. The anger, the seething malice—what was happening to him? He felt like his trix was about to split open. He could just imagine his classmate's looks when black blood began dripping onto the floor. He needed to sit down! Fast!

"Really, it's no problem," started Crenshaw.

"I said I'm fine," snapped Sky. "Getting beat up in the hall's not going to help me find my seat!"

The class went silent.

Crenshaw's smile fell.

Sky knew it was stupid to call out a person who was big, strong, and brimming with self-importance, but he couldn't help himself. Miss Hagfish might be purposely turning a blind eye but it was obvious to him that Crenshaw didn't have Sky's best interest at heart. Sky had dealt with bullies before, and they always wanted one of three things: your lunch money, their parents' love, or to make you hurt. His guess was that Crenshaw wanted all three.

Sky wasn't about to bleed all over the floor just so this bully could feel good about himself!

"And the real you is finally revealed," muttered Miss Hagfish. And then, more loudly, she said, "Detention after school for a week, Mr. Weathers, for casting unfounded and disparaging accusations against a fellow student."

Still fighting for control, Sky held his tongue, turned, and walked toward the nearest open seat.

"Uh, uh, uh, Mr. Weathers," said Miss Hagfish as he began to sit down. "Those seats belong to the children for whom you will work someday—if you don't die tragically before then. You sit over there with the rest of the future dropouts."

Miss Hagfish pointed to the far side of the room, where a small group of kids sat off from the rest in older, more abused desks.

"I know it's crowded, but even a person with your obvious limitations should be able to find a seat."

He crossed the room amidst muffled taunts and snickers.

As Sky passed Andrew and Crystal—who'd landed at the front of the "future dropouts" section—he noted that they didn't sit next to each other for some reason. Crystal stared straight ahead, refusing to make eye contact with him, while Andrew suddenly developed a strange fascination with his desk.

Miss Hagfish began tapping her foot, waiting for him to take his seat, like he'd put the entire world on hold and she had to pay the long-distance charges.

Clenching his fists tighter, Sky turned and headed down the last row on the far side of the classroom, passing a glassy-eyed freckled girl with an overabundance of armpit hair, who didn't seem to notice him, and a mousy, wide-eyed boy who couldn't look away.

He quickly slipped past them and took his seat in front of a blond girl who was chewing on her eraser unabashedly, studying him with a furrowed brow like he was a bug on display.

"Very good, Mr. Weathers," said Miss Hagfish like she was congratulating a two-year-old for finishing his milk. "You found a place after all! I'm sure you and your fellow future dropouts will get along just splendidly if you don't mess it up. Of course, that's not really your style, is it, Mr. Weathers? You're more of a lone wolf, aren't you? I can see it in your eye."

He stared at his desk, refusing to look at her. His little monster wrestled to get out. Sky pressed his fingers against his trix, trying to force the cold away.

After a few more moments of awkward silence, Miss Hagfish finally turned away from him.

"Now that that nuisance is taken care of, let's see what we can do with the rest of you."

Miss Hagfish began to lecture.

Now that attention was off of him, he exhaled slowly. Inhale. Exhale. Inhale. Exhale. Slowly the little monster faded away, and his mind became clear once again.

Sky shoved his hand into his pocket to wipe off the blood.

To distract himself he pulled out the crossword puzzle he'd gotten from the newspaper that morning and started filling it out while Miss Hagfish had her back turned. Phineas had told him that puzzles were the perfect way to focus his mind.

Normally it worked. But not today.

"It's okay," whispered a plump kid to his right with a nervous laugh, jerking Sky out of his reverie. "She's not always that bad."

"Yeah," whispered the girl behind him. "Sometimes she's *mean*."

The plump kid chuckled, but stopped suddenly when Miss Hagfish's eyes swept their way. A moment later her eyes returned to the board, where she was busy highlighting the joys of intransitive verbs in the works of Charles Dickens.

Sky glanced back and saw Crenshaw studying him. Crenshaw's toothy smile was like a promise. He was going to make Sky pay for his comment. He was going to make him pay soon, and he was going to make him pay dearly.

"Honestly, though, what did you do to her? I've never seen her treat anyone like that before—not that bad," said the boy. "And Crenshaw? That was a bad move, a really bad move."

"I guess I just have a way with people," said Sky, knowing it was more than that. Miss Hagfish had hit all his buttons. It was like she'd been trying to get him angry. She'd known things about him that she shouldn't have known—that he'd moved a lot, that he had a hard time with people, that he had an eye-shaped birthmark. "I can see it in your eye," she'd said.

He even suspected that the "lone wolf" comment had implications. Could she possibly know about the Shadow Wargs? And if she knew about that, what else did she know? And what was she trying to tell him by revealing that she knew?

"Look, no offense, but when I don't sit next to you again, please don't take it personally, okay?" said the plump boy.

Sky stared.

"Marcus has a way with people too," said the girl behind him. "Isn't that right, Marcus?"

The plump boy scowled at the girl.

"You can be the hunter or the hunted, Felicity. It's nothing personal," said Marcus.

"It's always personal to the hunted," said Felicity.

When the class ended, Sky slipped out quickly, trying to catch up with Crystal, but Miss Hagfish stopped him at the door. She plucked the crossword puzzle from his hands, looking it over while he waited and the class emptied.

"Hmpf," she said. He knew she was searching for something to pick at, some way to belittle him even more. Finally she looked up, tossing the crossword puzzle into the trash. "The *Exile Gazette*. Hardly the *New York Times*."

Sky ground his teeth.

"I hope you didn't find my lesson boring, Mr. Weathers."

"'Boring' isn't the word I'd use," said Sky.

"Oh? And what word would a cruciverbalist such as yourself use?"

"'Educational,'" said Sky.

"It has been that," said Miss Hagfish. "Mr. Weathers, I expect you here promptly after the last bell for your detention; be on time for once."

He started walking toward the door.

"And, Mr. Weathers . . ."

He stopped, turning back to look at Miss Hagfish.

"Take care that you stay out of trouble. I'll be watching."

He stared at her for a moment—her downturned, unyielding mouth, her serious, knowing eyes. And then, without a word, he turned and left the room.

CHAPTER 11

Tick, Lazy Eye, and Squid

Stepping forward, Sky set his tray on the counter and took his place in line, moving one slow shuffling step forward at a time. He was starving. He'd already missed breakfast, and the struggle in Miss Hagfish's class had left him famished.

He'd barely stayed awake in Mr. Sandman's pre-algebra class. If it hadn't been for a well-placed kick from Felicity—who'd sat behind him once again—he might have earned another detention. True to his word—and without Miss Hagfish's forced division—Marcus had sat elsewhere in the class . . . next to Crenshaw, in fact. He pretended to laugh at Crenshaw's jokes (of which Marcus was usually the brunt), but it was clear that his heart wasn't in it.

Sky'd looked up at several points during class to find Crenshaw watching him. And then, when class had ended, Sky had ducked out as quickly as possible—not only to get away, but to try to catch Crystal and Andrew. Unfortunately, Crystal and Andrew had left even faster than he had.

He wasn't sure what he'd done, but it must have been bad.

"Tuna," said Sky when he got to the front of the line.

"You sure?" asked the lunch lady, her lips splitting to reveal a set of horrendous bent and twisted teeth.

Sky looked over the other items—pile of green stuff, pile of yellow stuff, pile of white stuff . . . other . . . piles. The tuna sandwich was the only thing he recognized.

"Er, yes?" said Sky, suddenly unsure.

"Well, it's your body," said the lunch lady, casually slapping something onto his plate that might, once upon a time, have been a tuna sandwich. For good measure the lunch lady also slopped on a pile of white stuff.

"The veggies should offset the taste," said the lunch lady, flashing him another smile full of decaying teeth.

He smiled back nervously, took his tray, and left, wondering what kind of vegetable was white and had the consistency of barf.

Because almost every kid in town went to the same school (namely, this one), the cafeteria was packed with kids and segregated according to grade level. There weren't signs saying SIXTH GRADERS SIT HERE or NINTH GRADERS APPROACH AT YOUR OWN PERIL, but he could see that unspoken laws separated the groups.

He scanned the room, looking for Crystal or Andrew—or even T-Bone or Hands—but he didn't spot them. Giving up the search, he found an empty table and had started walking toward it when he felt a hand on his arm.

"Sky, my favorite brother!" said Hannah as she steered him through the crowds of students and trays, her eyes darting around the cafeteria, searching.

"I'm your only brother," said Sky as they passed several empty, perfectly acceptable tables.

"Even so. How are . . . things?"

Hannah found a mostly filled table among the tenth graders and plopped him down. She took the only other seat—opposite Sky—and let out a deep sigh of relief. Without pausing she started shoveling food into her mouth.

Several of the tenth graders scowled at him. He was on their turf and he knew it, but what could he do? He gave them a nervous smile, and they went back to eating.

"So who are you hiding from?" asked Sky, poking his fork at the pile of white stuff. The white stuff pushed back like Jell-O.

Hannah shrugged. "I don't know what you're talking about. Can't I just have lunch with my brother without all the questions? You should feel privileged."

"Oh, I do. I just thought—"

"Excuse me," said a burly guy wearing an Arkhon Academy letterman's jacket. He held a tray heaped with food. A mammoth-size lineman stood on either side of him. "You seem to be blocking my seat."

Hannah rolled her eyes. "He's not blocking your seat, Tick; there's no 'your seat' to block."

Hannah looked at Sky with desperate, pleading eyes.

He opened his mouth to give a witty reply and bail Hannah out, but as his eyes glided past the linemen, he spotted Crystal, sitting alone a few tables over.

"I . . . er . . . ," said Sky.

Hannah jumped in. "Can't you see I'm having lunch with my brother?"

Tick stared at her, uncomprehending. Even though Tick

was bigger and older, he didn't strike Sky as menacing, like Crenshaw. Tick seemed more oblivious than anything.

The tenth graders at the table sensed a conflict coming and left, their trays still full of food.

"There! Are you happy? There's plenty of room now," said Hannah in frustration.

Tick watched the table clear, and then sat down next to Sky, sliding his tray onto the table, his eyes locked on Hannah.

"This is Lazy Eye," said Tick, indicating one of the linemen, "and this is Squid. They're my bros."

Hannah rolled her eyes as Lazy Eye and Squid sat down next to Tick.

"You like my letterman's jacket? I'm captain of the football team," said Tick.

"I know, Tick! You told me that, like, three times today!" said Hannah.

"Oh. It's made out of wool, like from sheep."

Sky smiled. He wanted to stay to see where this would go, but he needed to catch Crystal before she left. He stood from the table. "Sorry. Gotta go."

"Sky, you don't have to," said Hannah, pleading.

"Sorry. I'll make it up to you, okay?"

"You seem to be saying that a lot lately!" Hannah yelled after him.

As Sky walked away, he heard Tick say, "So who was that? Like, your brother or something?"

"Sheesh," said Hannah.

Sky smiled again. He *really* wished he could have stayed.

He crossed the cafeteria carrying his tray of untouched food. His stomach rumbled as he looked at it, and for a moment he questioned his stomach's sanity.

Crystal didn't look up as he approached.

He set his tray across from her. "Hey," said Sky.

Crystal glanced at him.

"Sorry about, you know, earlier," said Sky.

Crystal didn't say anything.

"I guess I shouldn't have made assumptions about . . . about . . . about whatever it was that I made assumptions about," said Sky, struggling to figure out how to apologize when he didn't know what he was apologizing for.

"Look," he continued, "I know this is asking a lot, especially considering whatever it was that I did, but I need a favor. I'm sort of grounded because of last night. If you could pick me up tonight for the . . . ah . . . rendezvous—just tell my Mom it's a study group. It's the only way she'll let me out. Please?"

He knew Mom wouldn't let him out of her sight once he got home, and he couldn't afford to have her worrying about him if he didn't show. If he was going to find his uncle, he'd need help. And who knows? Even though they didn't seem to know anything, the monster hunters might still prove helpful.

Crystal stared at him for a moment, and then, without speaking, she stood from the table and left the cafeteria. He watched her go, wondering what he'd done this time.

He didn't have long to wonder, because at that moment Crenshaw and his goons walked through the door, their eyes scanning the cafeteria.

He ducked under the table. He didn't need this right now. He really didn't.

He looked back toward Hannah's table, but it was empty. Hannah had fled, and Tick and his "bros" had followed. No help there.

His best bet was to disappear through the closest door and

make a run for it. He started to scuttle away, and then stopped, eyeing his tray of uneaten food. He grabbed half of the tuna sandwich and shoved it into his pocket. Then he headed for the door.

"Are you okay, Sky?"

He flipped around, half crunched, and found Miss Terry watching him curiously, her tray full of food.

He glanced around nervously, and then stepped to the side, putting Miss Terry between Crenshaw and himself to block Crenshaw's line of sight.

"Er, fine. Why do you ask?"

Miss Terry looked over her shoulder and back at Sky. "You seem a little nervous. Is everything all right?"

He thought about telling her—she seemed nice enough—but he knew getting her involved would only make things worse.

"Everything's great," lied Sky. "Couldn't be better. How are you?"

He cringed. What a lame thing to say.

"I'm fine, Sky," said Miss Terry, smiling. "Thanks for asking."

Crenshaw had finally spotted him and was heading his way.

"If you need anything —," started Miss Terry.

"Yep, office by the gym. I'll drop in sometime, shall I?" cut in Sky as he began backing toward the door. "Well, it's been nice chatting."

Miss Terry gave him a curious look, and then she noticed part of the tuna sandwich sticking out of his pocket. "Ahh. I understand—the school tuna. Say no more. Mrs. Victual's gastronomic anomalies have been troubling this school for years."

He smiled awkwardly, holding his hands up in surrender. "You caught me."

"Well, until later, then," said Miss Terry as she walked away.

Sky took a quick look at Crenshaw, who'd gotten stuck trying to slip past some seniors, and then ran for the doors. He slipped into a side hallway, turned some corners, and then hid in an alcove as Crenshaw, Ren, Marcus, Cordelia, and two older kids he didn't recognize ran past. Did Crenshaw really think he needed all those people to take him on? He'd be flattered if he weren't so frightened.

He waited until their footsteps disappeared, and then he stepped out into the mostly empty halls.

CHAPTER 12
Bully That!

As Sky walked down the hallway, he saw Tick trying to carry Hannah's bag for her. They seemed to be fighting over it. Each one had a strap, and they were pulling in opposite directions. If he hadn't known better, he'd say that someone was getting mugged; he just wasn't sure whom.

Guilt and laughter warred within him. He should probably have done something. Sometime, he promised himself, he would.

He quick-stepped across the hall just as Hannah finally managed to wrench her bag away from Tick. He ducked his head to avoid her glare and headed for the library. It was quiet, safe, and he needed to do some research on the number he'd found in his Uncle's truck.

581.112.

He still didn't know what it meant, but he had a few ideas.

As he turned the corner—just as he was pulling out his

tuna sandwich for a quick bite—he crashed into Andrew, sending books (and his tuna sandwich) flying everywhere.

He scrambled to help Andrew pick up the books while two older girls who could have stepped straight off the cover of *Cheerleader's Quarterly* watched, their eyes full of disapproval.

"Andrew, you are *such* a klutz! I don't know why Mother and Father put up with you," said one of the girls, who was slightly taller than the other. "Isn't that right, Ermine."

"It most assuredly is, Jasmine. Why, just the other day I was saying to myself 'Self, you are so incredibly gorgeous. How is it that you could have such an ugly and ungifted brother?' And do you know what my self said, Jasmine?" said Ermine.

"No. Do tell Ermine," said Jasmine.

"My self said that a *real* brother wouldn't be so uncouth. A *real* brother would be like us—gifted and charming. It's only a brother of *step* who would be so inelegant," said Ermine.

"Undoubtedly," said Jasmine. "Your self is quite insightful, you know."

"I do know," said Ermine.

Andrew sighed. "They always talk like that after they've read Jane Austen," Andrew confided to Sky. And then, more loudly, he said, "YOU DON'T HAVE TO TALK LIKE THAT!"

"Why, did you hear something, dear sister?" asked Jasmine.

"Quite so. It sounded as if someone flatulated quite gratuitously," said Ermine.

"Quite so," said Jasmine.

"'Flatulated' is not even a real word," said Andrew.

"There it goes again," said Ermine.

"Indeed," said Jasmine.

Andrew sighed as Sky handed him the last book.

"Sorry," said Sky, meaning it.

"I believe this is yours," said Andrew, handing him his tuna sandwich, which looked a little worse for wear. "They're not really my sisters—stepcousins at best."

"Move it, delinquent servant!" said Jasmine, shoving Andrew forward with her foot while he tried to stand—nearly toppling him in the process.

"Truly, if you make us late for class, Mother will make you wash the floors with your tongue," said Ermine as all three of them vanished around the corner.

Sky dusted the sandwich and raised it to his mouth.

"There you are," said Crenshaw, grabbing the sandwich from Sky's hands while Ren slammed him against the wall. "I was afraid you'd gotten lost again."

Crenshaw took a bite of Sky's sandwich, frowned at it, and threw the rest onto the floor. Sky watched it slide away, his stomach rumbling. He really needed to make some friends, some big ones.

"Marcus, could you quiet that for me?" said Crenshaw, referring to Sky's rumbling stomach.

Marcus stepped forward. "Me?"

Crenshaw didn't say anything. He just stared at Sky.

"Sorry, Sky," said Marcus as he punched him in the stomach.

"Nothing personal, right?" said Sky, struggling for breath. He should have been madder than he was, or more afraid, but right now all he could think about was the tuna sandwich lying on the floor a few feet away.

"You pulled the punch," said Crenshaw to Marcus. "Here, let me show you how to do it."

Crenshaw punched Sky in the stomach. Hard.

At the last moment Sky twisted, and Crenshaw's hand smashed into his pocket watch.

Sky crumpled forward, and Ren dropped him to the floor. Crenshaw jumped around holding his hand.

"You broke my wrist! You little freak! You broke it!"

Sky started laughing, when he could get a breath.

"You think this is funny?" said Crenshaw, his eyes going crazy.

Sky tried to respond with some witty reply, but Crenshaw had knocked the wind out of him and it came out "Pahhhh . . . pahhh."

"Crenshaw, can we go now?" asked Cordelia, looking bored.

"No! No, we can't go! The freak broke my wrist!"

"Yeah, you mentioned that," said Cordelia.

"Ren, grab his arms," said Crenshaw.

Sky tried to slip away, but Ren grabbed him.

"Come on, Ren. What would your brother say about this?" gasped Sky, making a guess about Ren and T-Bone being brothers as he struggled against Ren.

"Dickens?" Ren's face twisted in pain, his eyes going distant as he dropped Sky.

Sky didn't know what was going on, or who Dickens was, but he made use of the opening and darted away.

"Marcus!" yelled Crenshaw.

Before he could build up any speed, Marcus tackled him.

"Sorry, Sky," said Marcus again as he pulled Sky to his feet.

"Stop apologizing!" yelled Crenshaw.

By then Ren had recovered. He grabbed Sky harshly, wrenching his arms behind him. "If you mention Dickens again, I'll kill you," said Ren quietly.

A bolt of fear shot through him. Who in the dickens was Dickens? More important, why did everyone keep threatening to kill him?

Crenshaw reached into Sky's coat pocket and pulled out the pocket watch Uncle Phineas had given him—the pocket watch Crenshaw had just punched.

"This here's a nice watch," said Crenshaw. "A *very* nice watch. It's so nice, in fact, that I think I'll keep it."

"Give it back," said Sky, getting angry. This wasn't just bullies picking on him anymore. It'd gone beyond a schoolboy prank. That was his watch.

He felt his little monster stir, growling protectively.

"Let's call this a payment for the rudeness you showed me earlier. Disrespect is a disease, Sky. I'm going to help you find the cure," said Crenshaw. He pulled back his fist.

Sky's trix split open. Something pure and raw swept into his mind—a pent-up anger so grotesque and powerful that Sky was nearly swept away. His body shook as he struggled to hold back the tide of adrenaline and power flooding into him.

Crenshaw's fist looked like a slug creeping forward through mud. Sky flexed his arms, jerking Ren involuntarily forward.

Sky smiled.

He could do it—break away before Crenshaw could lay a hand on him. And then he could hurt him. He didn't have to take it anymore. His little monster growled, egging him on, and Sky could feel himself giving in, the little monster feeding him strength. His body ached and shook from the effort of restraining himself. He felt that if he let go and gave in to the urge, he would do something terrible to Crenshaw, something he would never forgive himself for.

Crenshaw's punch finally connected, flipping Sky's head to the side.

Ren threw him to the ground. Sky tried to get to his feet, but couldn't get control of his body. He fell back down, his muscles clenching and unclenching spastically as he continued to fight the monster in his mind.

Without another look Ren stormed off.

Crenshaw smiled, obviously thinking he'd caused Sky's torments. He grabbed Sky by the chin, jerking Sky's head toward him as Sky writhed about, drowning in a sea of emotions—anger, fear, love, hunger, longing . . . rage. He couldn't think. He couldn't breathe. . . .

"Don't *ever* try to embarrass me again. Ever." Crenshaw dropped Sky's head to the floor, spit on him, and then walked off after Ren. Cordelia glanced at Sky, something moving behind her bored mask. Was it pity? And then she, too, was gone.

Marcus was the last to go, giving Sky a worried look. "Are you okay?"

Sky laughed, a guttural, unnatural sound, as he continued to writhe and flop upon the floor, his face twisting in horrible contortions. He tried to hold it all in, to endure the freezing and the pain and the anger. The laughing changed from guttural and unnatural to maniacal. Marcus looked frightened. "Sky, maybe I should get the nur—"

"Marcus! Get over here!" yelled Crenshaw.

Marcus looked back and forth between Sky (laughing upon the floor) and Crenshaw, who was glaring at him angrily. "Sorry, Sky," said Marcus, hesitantly shuffling off after Crenshaw. "I really am."

Sky watched Marcus go. Farther down the hall two other kids, an older boy and girl, peeled away from the shadows and joined up with Crenshaw—sentries, meant to block off the already empty halls while Crenshaw roughed Sky up.

Sky's laughs came more fitfully in bits and stints until they died off altogether, replaced by pain more terrible than anything he'd felt before.

He writhed on the ground, his blood freezing and then boiling, consuming his skin like sunlight on fog, lights bursting behind his eyes as he continued to wrestle with his little monster.

But the PAIN! He grabbed his head, closed his eyes against it, trying to shut it out—and suddenly . . .

It was gone . . .

And so was he.

CHAPTER 13
Little Monster

Sky stood up from the hardwood floor in a place very different from the school where he'd passed out. Had someone brought him home?

The trix bled profusely, leaving a black puddle on the floor. He stepped around it, moving toward a crib pushed against the wall.

This wasn't his room. This wasn't even his house!

Even so, it looked oddly familiar, like he'd been here before.

Lightning flashed outside over and over, flooding the room in eerie blue and red light that made it look cold, awash in blood.

Trees *scritch-scratched* against the window like claws.

He walked to the window, and looked out.

"CAW!" the crow screeched, sending Sky reeling back.

He stepped forward again. Thick trees blocked his view, but in the night sky above he could see red storm clouds swirling and sparkling with electricity.

Lightning flashed again. Something moved behind him, reflected in the glass. Its hair was as black as night. Its arms were long and broad. It stood, hunched over, its head brushing the ceiling. It looked old—*monstrous*—as if the bones of the earth had dragged themselves forth to haunt the world.

Sky spun from the window, but the monster was gone.

Had Crenshaw's punch knocked something loose?

"Waaah! Wa . . . wa . . . waaaah!"

The floorboards creaked like tired bones as Sky crept toward the crib. He glanced at the closed bedroom door, wondering if anyone was going to come and get the screaming baby. Was anyone else even in the house?

As he peeked into the crib, a small baby boy looked back, surrounded by stuffed animals and colored runners patterned with suns and clouds and rain and moons and stars.

He glanced at the door again, wondering who the child belonged to and if his parents had noticed he was awake. Sky could have sworn he heard voices outside the door . . . horrible howling and roaring and shrieking voices.

When he looked back, the baby had quieted. He was watching Sky, holding his little hands up expectantly.

"Me? You don't want me. I'm not very good with people; babies especially," said Sky. "You're not messy, are you?"

The baby started to cry again.

"Okay, okay! Just stop crying!" said Sky, reaching down to pick up the baby.

As he touched it, the child shot forward, its face twisting grotesquely. Black teeth jutted out from its mouth and sunk into Sky's hand, ripping the trix open even wider.

Sky jerked back, tumbling to the floor, and then he scrambled away, leaving a trail of dark blood.

He grabbed a nearby lamp, shattering it against the floor as he stood, holding the sharp-edged weapon in front of him by the shaft.

The monster pulled itself out of the crib—laughing.

"Oh, that was too good," said the monster, wiping tears from its eyes.

As it slowly crossed the room, it changed—body rippling, bones cracking horribly, face distending—until Sky found himself looking at . . . *himself* . . .

"What are you?" exclaimed Sky.

"Come on, Sky! We're good at puzzles. Figure it out," said the monster, crossing the room to sit in a recliner that appeared from out of nowhere. *"Think."*

The monster looked exactly like him, only darker somehow, with Sky's blood on his chin.

"You're . . . me?" said Sky.

"And *you* are *me*," said the monster.

"You're the little monster!" said Sky.

"Not the most endearing of names. Why don't you call me Errand," the monster said, wiping blood from his chin and then licking it off his hand.

Sky watched in disgust.

"Oh, don't look at me like that! I have to take what I can get! It hurts me too, you know," said Errand, holding up his left hand. Errand's hand looked exactly like Sky's own, with an identical Hunter's Mark and trix on the palm. What's more, the trix was ripped open and bled in the exact same way.

"See? You get hurt, I get hurt. At least for now. I'm *you,* Sky. I'm just the better part of you—the stronger part. If you'd just let me help, I could have shown you," said Errand.

"If I'd let you 'help' me," said Sky, recovering from the shock, "you would have killed them!"

"So what? What do you think they wanted to do to you?" said Errand, reclining in his chair. A comic book popped into his hands from out of nowhere, and he started flipping through it.

"They were just trying to scare me, not kill me! And how do you keep doing that?" asked Sky, gesturing at the comic book and the recliner that had miraculously popped into the room.

Errand shrugged.

Sky heard sounds coming from outside the door, moving closer. Fighting, snarling sounds and, above the sounds, a voice, yelling his name.

"Is that *Uncle Phineas*?" exclaimed Sky, heading for the door. "Phineas! Phineas! I'm in here!"

He heard another voice joining the first, a woman urging Phineas to leave.

"PHINEAS! Don't leave! I'm here! I'm right *here*!" yelled Sky, desperately pulling at the door.

"Sky, you know what we are. It's time you accepted it and stopped fighting me. *Let me help you*. I can teach you things."

"I don't know what you're talking about!" said Sky, jerking at the door handle, kicking at the wood.

"Oh? Not enough pieces of the puzzle yet?" said Errand. "Time's growing short, Sky, and you're about to wake u—"

CHAPTER 14

Bon Mot

Sky woke up.

He was lying on the ground in a pool of his own spit. The school hallway he'd passed out in was empty. How much time had passed?

The trix bled more than it ever had before. He pulled a piece of paper from his backpack and pressed it against the trix, balling the paper in his fist.

He rose from the ground feeling exhausted and shaken. What was happening to him? And what, exactly, was Errand?

He'd read about monsters that could enter people's minds, manipulate their thoughts, even enter their dreams. *The Edge of Oblivion* talked about a monster—an Edgewalker, as they were called—that could travel through people's minds, leaving their own hideous bodies behind. They were dream-stealers, gorging on a person's hopes and fears until there was nothing left—feeding a wasting hunger they could never satisfy.

In *The Edge of Oblivion* Solomon Rose led a group of hunters against the Edgewalkers. They found the Edgewalkers' wasted bodies, one by one, and killed them while they slept. This led to the monsters' complete and total extinction, if the story was to be believed.

Of course, in the story Edgewalkers didn't have the ability to change forms—to look like their victims. When they entered a mind or a dream, all they had with them was what they'd taken from the waking world: their self-image and the things on their own sleeping bodies.

Since Errand looked exactly like him, but better, he was probably *not* an Edgewalker, since Edgewalkers couldn't shift, but Sky couldn't think of anything else that fit.

Sky walked over and picked up his tuna sandwich, staring at the place where Crenshaw had taken a bite.

"Are you eating in the halls?" said Miss Hagfish, startling him as she snatched the sandwich from his hand. "And from the ground, no less. That surprises me, even coming from you, Mr. Weathers. What is that?"

Sighing, he turned toward Miss Hagfish, who was holding his sandwich in her hand like a dirty diaper. She stared in horror at the black trix blood on the floor.

"Er . . . my pen exploded," said Sky, shoving his hand into his pocket.

An older man with slicked back black hair, chalky white skin, and a square boxlike face stood next to her. He was tall and broad, wearing an expensive-looking black suit that screamed, *I'm important! You should look at me!*

"This is the troubled boy I was telling you about, Principal Lem," said Miss Hagfish as she pulled a plastic bag from her pocket and inserted the sandwich like she was performing open-heart surgery on a goldfish.

"I can see what you mean, Miss Hagfish," said Principal Lem, eyeing Sky with distaste. "Do you know what the janitor goes through to keep this school clean?"

"A lot?" ventured Sky, too tired to play games.

"A *whole* lot," said Principal Lem, taking Sky's answer seriously. "It's not an easy job. The faculty doesn't notice him, the hours are terrible, the pay is dismal . . . but do you know what the worst part is, Mr. Weathers?"

Sky shrugged; he wasn't going to get out of this, so he might as well play along and get it over with as quickly as possible. "Nobody thanks you?"

Principal Lem looked surprised. "No. Of course not!"

"Tuna sandwiches and ink on the floor," said Sky, trying again.

"No!" said Principal Lem. "It's the *poop,* Mr. Weathers—the poop! Disgusting stuff. I don't know how you children produce so much of it."

"It's because it comes out of both ends," said Miss Hagfish.

Principal Lem smiled appreciatively. "That's quite the bon mot, Miss Hagfish."

Miss Hagfish tightened her lips, apparently pleased at the compliment.

"Do you know what a 'bon mot' is?" asked Principal Lem, turning back to Sky.

Sky shook his head.

"It's French for 'I'm smarter than you,'" said Principal Lem. "Do you know what *I am*, Mr. Weathers?"

"Bon mot?" said Sky.

"Precisely. This town has gone through a lot of poop, Mr. Weathers; we don't need you going around producing more of it. All things should be done in their proper time and order by those most qualified to handle it. Am I understood?"

"Perfectly," said Sky.

"Good. Now get to a nurse to see after that cut on your face. It looks like you've had a *nasty* fall," said Principal Lem, smiling curtly before turning on his heels and heading for the library stairs. Miss Hagfish looked Sky over silently, her brow furrowed, before following the principal.

Sky watched them go for a moment, his stomach growling. He hadn't even noticed the cut on his face from where Crenshaw had hit him—or, more likely, from when he'd fallen to the floor.

He had no intention of going to the nurse. And now he couldn't go to the library—not now that Principal Lem had told him to go to the nurse. He thought about going back to the cafeteria, but something told him that, with his luck today, it'd be closed.

The only good thing that'd come from running into Miss Hagfish and Principal Lem was that now he'd likely die of hunger before food poisoning overtook him.

He just wished it would hurry.

CHAPTER 15
The Tourmaline of Foresight

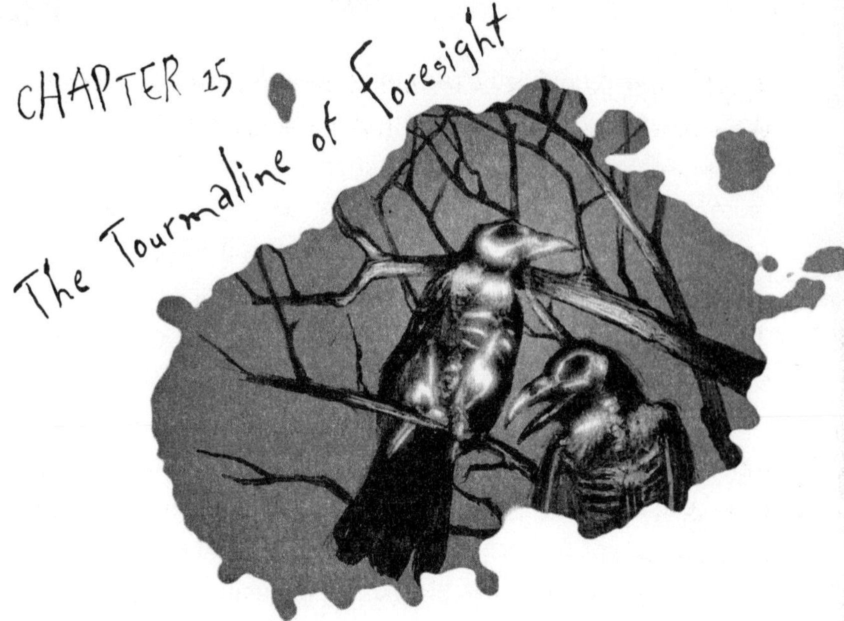

Sky stared out the window of the station wagon, resting his head against the cool surface as he watched Arkhon Academy slide away behind them.

"I didn't want to have to do that, Sky," said Mom, glancing over at him, "but you left me no other choice."

"I know, Mom," said Sky, closing his eyes, his voice weary.

When he hadn't stepped off the bus after school—because of his detention with Miss Hagfish—Mom had rushed over. She'd caught up with him as he'd walked out the front doors, and had escorted him to the car, chewing him out the whole time . . . just when all the sports teams and cheerleading squads were finishing practice and heading home. And as if that hadn't been bad enough, she'd noticed the cut on his face and had decided to fuss about him.

Nearly everyone had had the courtesy to pretend to ignore them, including Hannah, who was fleeing from Tick at the time, but Sky knew that everyone had been laughing inside.

A few had been laughing *outside* as well, including Jasmine and Ermine, who'd snickered as they'd walked past in their cheerleading outfits, Andrew trailing behind carrying their pom-poms, looking morose.

Crenshaw, still dressed in his pads from football, had simply stopped in his tracks and watched, a big smile on his face as he'd pulled Sky's pocket watch from beneath his sweaty pads and pretended to check the time. He'd also done this in gym and history, and every other time he'd happened upon Sky throughout the afternoon. (Though, admittedly, those times it had been in his less sweaty pocket.)

"You've got to learn that choices have consequences," lectured Mom. "Missing the bus has consequences. Back-talking to your teacher has consequences. Running into a wall has consequences. You should really be more careful, Sky."

He didn't say anything.

"Sky, are you listening to me?"

"Yes, Mom," said Sky.

"I'll pick you up again tomorrow, since you've managed to get a week's worth of detention on your first day," said Mom. "So be out front, or I'll come find you again. Don't make me do that, Sky."

"I won't, Mom," said Sky.

"And you can just forget about that study group with your friends! And no supper, either! I'm double grounding you!"

He stirred for the first time since he'd seen Mom walking up the school steps. "But, Mom!"

"No buts! You've made bad choices. Now you get to suffer with bad consequences! That's the way the world works. You can't stay young forever, Sky. Someday you're going to have to grow up," said Mom, looking stern.

At home she sent him to his room without supper and told him to practice his tuba.

He sat on his bed, holding the tuba on his lap as he played. He wasn't any better at the tuba than he was at anything else, but that hadn't stopped Mom from making him play.

Eventually he pulled out his Rubik's Cube and began flipping it around, blowing idly into his tuba every few minutes to keep Mom from coming up.

Over the years, Uncle Phineas had given him many puzzles—including the Rubik's Cube, Chinese finger puzzles, yo-yo puzzles (make a shape, keep it moving), lock puzzles, disentanglement puzzles (connect or disconnect various shaped rings), logic puzzles (such as chess), tour puzzles (get through the maze), word puzzles (like crosswords and anagrams), lateral thinking puzzles (guess what I'm thinking), and even the DNA puzzle he'd mentioned to Crystal. Not to mention a number of others, but Sky had left them all behind during this last move—all except for the Rubik's Cube and the yo-yo.

Those had been the first puzzles Phineas had given him, and he hadn't been able to bring himself to part with them. The rest he'd lost, broken, or grown bored of.

Now, knowing that Uncle Phineas might be dead, he wished he'd kept them all.

Shortly after five Sky heard a car, coughing and spluttering. He went to the window and watched Phineas's battered old truck pull into the driveway.

"It can't be . . ."

The front door to the house opened, and Mom crossed the yard, heading for the truck. . . .

Dad stepped out.

"Herman! You can't bring that here!" said Mom.

"Why not?" asked Dad.

"Because!" said Mom, looking around nervously. She looked up at the window and spotted Sky.

"I'd better hear that tuba, mister!" yelled Mom.

He ducked back in and shut the window. He'd hoped, truly hoped, to see Phineas. But, he knew, he'd never see his uncle again unless he found him.

The front door opened, and he could hear his parents quietly arguing in the foyer before disappearing into the kitchen for dinner, which he was *not* invited to.

He played idly on his tuba while flipping through *Wicked, Wicked Wargarou*, a story that took place after *The Shadow Wargs of Whimple* and focused on the Wargarou's efforts to find his missing pack of Shadow Wargs.

Sky skimmed the book, learning that Wargarous were vicious, vaguely wolflike, and impossible to kill. They could change shape over the three days of a full moon by eating the body of the victim they wished to change into, and they kept that shape until they ate another, or reverted to their *true* form—a terrible monster of darkness and fire. Water and cold could quench the fire, and driving off their pack could weaken them, but the only way to really harm a Wargarou, apparently, was with a hunter's blade—whatever that was.

Wargarous could flit through shadows, disappearing and reappearing like knives in a sheath. They could create Shadow Wargs and, if they found Shadow Wargs that other Wargarous had created, they could bind them. Once they bound a Shadow Warg, the Shadow Warg was bound for life, unless the Wargarou willingly freed the Shadow Warg, the Wargarou died, or the Wargarou had its pack taken from it, usually after losing a fight to another Wargarou.

Wargarous also seemed to have a love for fine things and eating small children. Usually they kept a low profile, not wanting to be disturbed, but when they changed into their fiery form, look out.

Despite his searching, Sky couldn't find any way to really defeat a Wargarou if he happened to find one.

As the sun started to set, the front door opened and Dad left, driving off in the truck.

Someone knocked on his door.

"It's open," said Sky despondently.

Hannah came in carrying a plate of food. "I'll make you a deal. You stop playing, and I'll give you this food."

"Done," said Sky, dropping his tuba to the bed as he took the plate and snarfed down the food, his stomach growling like a cornered beaver. "Aren't you hungry?"

He knew Mom would've rationed the food to stop something like this from happening.

"Big party tonight at Miss Terry's to celebrate my pending nuptials with the cheerleading squad," said Hannah.

"You made the team?" asked Sky.

"As if there were any doubt," said Hannah.

He smiled. "Still," said Sky, furrowing his brow, "kind of a weird reason to throw a party—and on a school night?"

"Who needs a reason for a party? Besides, I think you have as much to do with it as I do," said Hannah.

"Me?" said Sky, surprised.

"I'm as shocked as you are," said Hannah, "but you seem to have made an impression on her. She said she wanted to 'get to know the girl that had grown up with Sky.'"

"She said that?"

Hannah nodded. "*And* she invited you to the party."

His mouth dropped open. Nobody invited him to parties, especially the kind with other people! And *cheerleaders,* no less.

And then he remembered he was grounded. And even if he hadn't been, he had other priorities at the moment—like figuring out a way to escape so he could meet up with Crystal and convince her to help him find Phineas.

"I only wish I could go." He kicked his tuba, sending up a hollow *gonnnng*.

Hannah sat next to him. "You look terrible."

He looked at her and nearly burst into tears. He wanted to tell her about everything: the truck, the poem, the number, the nightmare, Miss Hagfish, Principal Lem, Crenshaw, the stolen watch . . . but what would she think of him? If she couldn't believe that Phineas was even missing, how would she ever believe any of the rest? And if she told Mom and Dad, who were already keeping a close eye on him . . .

"I—I'm fine. Just a rough first day. You know how it is," said Sky, trying to shrug it off.

Hannah stared at him, her eyebrow raised.

"Really, I'm fine."

She kept staring.

"I—," started Sky, but he was cut off by a knock on the front door.

Throwing down his empty plate, he leapt from the bed and ran to the window.

"She came! She's actually here!" said Sky, shoving books into his backpack as he raced for his bedroom door. "I've gotta get down there before Mom sends her away!"

"She?" said Hannah. "No wonder you don't want to go to the party."

He blushed. "It's not like that." He threw open the door

and then stopped, turning back toward Hannah. "Er, thanks for the food, Sis. I owe you one."

"Anything to stop that tuba playing. You're just awful! You know that, right?" said Hannah, smiling.

He smiled back and then ran out his door.

When he reached the top of the stairs, he heard a loud crash, like the breaking of glass.

Mom stood at the door, staring at Crystal. Glass shards littered the floor around her where she'd dropped the casserole dish she'd been drying. The dishrag hung limply from her hand.

"Mom?" said Sky.

"You look just like your mother," said Mom, her eyes locked on Crystal like she'd seen a ghost.

Mom noticed the broken dish and knelt down, picking up the pieces. "I'd drop my own hands if they weren't attached to me!"

He frowned. Mom was anything but a klutz. She had the most agile hands he'd ever seen.

"You knew my mom?" asked Crystal quizzically.

"*Your* mom? No, no, not at all! Sky, why didn't you mention your friend was coming?"

He stared at her. Was she serious? She'd double grounded him.

"But I—," started Sky.

"Well, go on," said Mom. "Don't keep the poor girl waiting!" And then, more quietly, she said, "Heaven knows she's got enough to worry about."

He looked between Mom, crawling on the floor picking up glass, and Crystal, standing silently at the door.

"Er, sure, Mom," said Sky, stepping around the glass.

As they crossed his yard, Crystal glanced at him. "Just get it over with. I know you want to ask."

"What happened to your mom?" said Sky before he could stop himself.

"It's none of your business," said Crystal without hesitation.

"Oh, right," said Sky.

She opened the gate. "Go ahead. It won't bite."

He blushed. "I'm not afraid; I was just making sure nobody was following us."

"Sky, if anyone were following us, trust me, I'd *know*," said Crystal as she followed him through the gate. "Keep to the left, just off the trail; it'll keep the fluorescent powder off you."

Several crows swooped down, staring at him expectantly.

While Crystal had her back turned, busy with the gate, he scooped up a cracker and threw it into the air. The crows snatched it up before it could hit the ground.

"It's really not good for them," said Crystal, coming up behind him.

"Er . . ."

"Watch," said Crystal.

She pulled a small flashlight from her pocket and flicked it on, pointing it at the crows. The crows' bodies lit up with a skeletal silvery-blue glow, like bones under an X-ray, making them look hideous and sinister.

"CAW!"

"Man, you weren't kidding!" exclaimed Sky.

She flicked off the black light.

"Hold it," said Sky, grabbing her hand before she could put the flashlight away. "Point it over there."

She glared at him, and he pulled his hand away.

"Uh," he muttered, feeling distinctly uncomfortable.

She flipped the flashlight back on, swinging it around to where he'd pointed. The ground was bright with powder, but there, just beyond the leaves, he saw a set of glowing footprints leading into town.

"See there? It looks like a foot, but smaller, and there are only four toes," said Sky. "And up here—these two indentations that look like knuckles? See how there's no sign of a thumb?"

Crystal nodded, watching him with a curious expression on her face.

"But the knuckle marks only appear occasionally, so it doesn't walk on them all the time," said Sky, stopping as he suddenly realized what he was looking at. "I think it's a Gnomon."

"What's that?"

"It's a monster," said Sky.

"Yeah, I kind of figured that part out," said Crystal. She looked back at the town, frowning. "Sky, I'm afraid our meeting's going to have to wait."

"What do you mean 'wait'?" asked Sky, his stomach sinking.

"We can't let that monster reach the town. Andrew and I caught something like it about a year ago," said Crystal.

"Well, that was stupid!" exclaimed Sky. "Why on earth would you do that? Gnomon are harmless!"

Crystal shook her head. "You should go home. Tell your mom the study group was canceled."

"And Phineas? He's just supposed to wait it out while you hunt some monster that doesn't even matter?" said Sky.

"Look, Sky. We never agreed to help," said Crystal. "Your uncle can take care of himself. There are people out there who can't."

"That's why you need me, even if you don't know it yet," said Sky.

"We don't need *you*," said Crystal.

"Oh, yeah? Is that why you wanted to meet tonight? Just to chat?" asked Sky. "You need what I know. How many people have you found so far?"

"What do you mean?" asked Crystal warily.

"From the school. The empty seats? People on edge? The fact that you won't even talk to the other monster hunters, or me for that matter, because you're afraid you're being watched? Kids are missing from the school, right? How many have you found so far?" repeated Sky.

Crystal blanched. "Alive? Including you? Just one."

"How many have you found—er—*not* alive?" asked Sky.

"You don't want to know. Honestly, you don't," said Crystal, her voice hard and brittle at the same time, like glass ready to break.

Turning, she started walking up the trail.

Sky gulped, and then ran to catch up.

"That's what I've been trying to tell you, Sky! There are dozens of missing children, and most of them have gone missing over the past year! We even lost one last night," said Crystal.

"Who?"

"Alexis," said Crystal. "Crenshaw claimed she was sick today, but she wasn't. T-Bone checked it out during lunch. The police were searching her house."

"That's terrible," said Sky.

Crystal nodded. "Chances are that if Phineas is gone, he's *gone*. The best we can do is stop it from happening to others. *That's what we do*. We've got to hunt this thing tonight, before someone else disappears, which means you need to go home. What we do is dangerous enough without dragging you into it. At best you're a distraction, and at worst you're a casualty."

He shook his head. "You're wasting your time hunting this thing. It didn't take the kids."

"Oh, yeah? And how would you know that?" said Crystal.

"Because *I'm* the only one who actually knows what you're hunting!" exclaimed Sky.

"So enlighten me," Crystal countered, turning to face him, arms folded.

Sky sighed. This would be a lot easier if she'd just cooperate. That's why he liked puzzles. Puzzles were nice. You moved a piece, it went where you put it. People, on the other hand . . .

"It's called a Gnomon," said Sky. "It's sort of like a garden gnome but *much* larger, with longer arms, a less pointy hat, and no opposable thumbs," said Sky.

"So, basically, it's *nothing* like a garden gnome," Crystal retorted.

"Yeah, I guess," said Sky, frowning. "Do you want to hear this or not?"

Crystal shrugged.

Sky rubbed his temples. Puzzles. Definitely easier.

He pulled off his backpack, withdrew an old leather-bound book, and began to leaf through it.

"Look, there aren't a lot of stories that talk about Gnomon. *The Journal of Alexander Drake*, *Much Ado About Gnomon*, and this one called *The Tourmaline of Foresight*, which is the only one I've got on me. It's about this guy—Nathaniel the Noteworthy—who sets out to find this jewel called the Tourmaline of Foresight because he thinks it will help him see into the future. After crossing the Ingubriate Ocean—"

"The what?" asked Crystal.

"*Ingubriate Ocean*. They used different names for everything back then. My uncle said 'Ingubriate' was another name for the 'Atlantic' Ocean," said Sky.

"Oh."

"So anyway, after crossing the ocean, Nathaniel parts ways with Rubber Duckikus the Ineffable—"

Crystal snickered.

"'And reaches the Beach of Bungled Dreams,'" said Sky, beginning to read from the book as he walked, trying to keep up with Crystal.

"'And Nathaniel hugged Rubber Duckikus the Ineffable with a mighty hug and smote upon his back with a mighty smoting. And after the hugging and the smiting and the smoting, they shared a slice of delicious toast and parted ways, each to his own fate.'"

"Toast?" said Crystal, raising an eyebrow.

"Just listen," said Sky, turning his attention back to the book. "'On the Beach of Bungled Dreams, Nathaniel found the Gibbering Pool of Unhelpful Insights and plunged into its fathomless depths. When he emerged, confused and crampy because he'd swum too soon after eating delicious toast, he discovered that his clothes had been stolen by the Four-Toed Gnomon who would have ruled the world, but for the lack of thumbs. Their marks are thus:

"Four to the foot
larger than man,
long of the arm
and not very tan,
they look like gnomes
with less-pointy hats,

and if you find one,
you better skee-dats . . . tle.'

"The story pretty much goes on like that—bad rhymes and lots of references to delicious toast," said Sky.

"So does Nathaniel the Noteworthy find the Tourmaline?" asked Crystal.

"Not really. He ends up sharing toast with Samuel the Simpleton, who's apparently like a world-class toast maker, and Samuel sort of tricks Nathaniel into taking the Carbuncle of Self-Loathing instead," said Sky.

"Oh."

"But the point is, you guys don't even know what you're hunting. I do. And you're wasting your time," said Sky. "We should be looking for Phineas."

"But that story doesn't say Gnomon aren't kidnappers," said Crystal.

"Yes, it does! They took his *clothes*, not *him*," said Sky.

Crystal shook her head. "That's pretty weak, Sky."

"It's not weak. It's a *pattern*," Sky defended. "It pops up time after time in stories that mention Gnomon. They show up, take some object, and leave. There's not a single story of them kidnapping anybody. They keep to themselves, protect their families, live underground—that sort of thing."

"Well, look, Sky. These *Gnomon*, as you call them, are monsters! Taking people is what monsters do! They kidnap and they kill and they destroy lives and break up families, and you're never the same after!" Crystal shouted. "Just ask the families of all those missing people. You think they'd care whether it was a

Gnomon, or a Shadow Warg, or a . . . a . . . whatever? They're *monsters.* That's all that matters!"

"Not all monsters are like that," said Sky, remembering the peaceful Echo before Solomon Rose, remembering the way Ursula protected him from the Shadow Wargs. "They don't all do those things. You can't just lump them all together like they're the same. The hunters in the stories—"

"We're not the hunters in your stories, Sky! We're a bunch of teenagers carrying weapons we made out of garbage!"

"But what if— Did you just say you made your weapons out of garbage?"

Crystal sighed.

"I know what you're trying to do, Sky, and I admire it. Honestly. But we've *tried* to talk to them. They grunt and they howl and they try to claw our eyes out!"

"Maybe you just have to learn how to understand them," said Sky, thinking about the brief moment he'd understood Vicious. Admittedly, it hadn't helped him, but still . . .

"And how would we do that?" asked Crystal.

"I don't know," said Sky, "but I know it's possible. At least I think I do."

Crystal stared at him, her expression unreadable.

"Look," he continued, "most of the stories I've read are about hunting monsters—what to look for, weaknesses, how to kill them, that sort of thing. And *most* of the time the monsters got exactly what was coming to them. But a few of the stories—*very* few of them—okay, just one actually—talks about a guy who could communicate with monsters, and he learned all kinds of things! Of course, he later used those things to subject them to his will."

Crystal rolled her eyes.

"But my point is that not all monsters are the same. They're not *all* bad!"

"You mean like those Shadow Wargs we saved you from last night?" said Crystal.

"Touché. But one bad apple, and all that," said Sky.

"One bad apple is all it takes! Sky, you know a lot about monsters. It's why T-Bone invited you to meet us at the crossroads tonight, but you haven't seen them like we have. You don't know what they're capable of. You haven't had to face one down over a pile of bones that you once *knew*. *We* have. There's a reason we fight these things, and it's obviously not for the pay!" Crystal gestured down at her secondhand clothing, her point clear.

"I hear what you're saying," she continued, "but monsters that seem cute and cuddly and misunderstood in stories are generally quite horrible in real life. None of us likes the idea of killing one—it's why we made our weapons the way we did—but at the same time, we wouldn't hesitate to do one in if we had to. When one's staring you in the eyes, and it's life or death, there's just not time to ask it about its motivation. Usually . . . it's pretty obvious."

He didn't say anything as they approached the crossroads. He wasn't sure what to say. Crystal was right. He hadn't fought monsters like she had. His pathetic effort to protect Ursula the night before hadn't even worked. He hadn't even been able to shoot the right Shadow Warg! And they would've killed him if the monster hunters hadn't arrived.

Crystal bent down, checking the ground. "They're not here yet—probably still checking equipment. Think you can make it back to your house without getting eaten?"

He looked out at Exile's lights, bright and twinkling

under the full moon. Crystal was right about him—he *wasn't* a hunter—but she was wrong about monsters. She'd hunted them, but she didn't know them, not like he did.

Some monsters were bad—out of control evil, horrors so terrible that neither tomb of earth, nor vault of sky, nor depth of sea could contain them.

But the Gnomon?

His knowledge about them was flimsy. The stories made Gnomon seem quirky and strange, but maybe they weren't what he thought. Maybe he wasn't seeing them clearly, the way Phineas had taught him to.

But one thing was certain. He wouldn't find Phineas on his own, not in time. He just wasn't familiar enough with the town, and after last night, he knew he wasn't equipped to deal with a monster if he ran into one. He wasn't a hunter.

The monster hunters were.

Tomorrow night, on the third night of the Hunter's Moon, the Arkhon would break free. Phineas would die.

Sky needed help.

And the only ones he trusted enough to help him were these complete strangers—the only ones he'd met who were doing the best they could even though they were clueless.

"Crystal, pleeease. I need your help," Sky begged. "If you want to hunt Gnomon, fine. Let's hunt Gnomon! I'll tell you everything I know! But afterward you've got to help me. My uncle is out there somewhere hiding to stay alive, or maybe he's been captured by a Whisper named Ambrosia and a Wargarou. Maybe he's even dead, but no matter what, I've got to find him, not only to save *him*, but because if I don't, then monsters—the bad kind—will break free tomorrow night and kill *everyone* in this town."

"Sky," started Crystal, shaking her head.

"Look!" said Sky, desperate, "I have a lead—a poem and a number—but I don't know what it means. You guys are smart! I saw those weapons you built. We can help each other! You've made it this far, hunting monsters without knowing anything about them, really, but it won't last. I *know* things about them. I've spent my entire life studying them! The monsters, the disappearances at the school . . . I think we're after the same thing. Something's behind all this, and I can help you figure out what it is! But in exchange *you've* got to help *me*."

Crystal stared at him, frowning. The silence lengthened.

"All right, Sky."

He sighed in relief.

"But only if everyone agrees to it," finished Crystal.

"Fine," said Sky. And then, more quietly, he muttered, "Thank you."

Crystal shook her head, as if she couldn't believe she was doing this, and then she turned and started walking along the western fork leading into the forest. "The others are *not* going to like this."

CHAPTER 16
The Monster Hunters

"I don't like this," said T-Bone."The deal was that we'd meet at the crossroads. You didn't even blindfold him!"

"What's the point? He would have figured it out anyway," said Crystal.

Sky smiled as he crossed a worn-down clapper bridge, the moonlight glinting off the water in a shimmering cascade of brilliant geometries.

They'd run into T-Bone on his way to the crossroads, and he wasn't happy. Crystal then told him about the Gnomon, and about Sky accompanying them, and T-Bone was even less happy than before.

"How can you expect to keep the secret lair a secret if you keep bringing people to it?" asked T-Bone.

"It's not people; it's just him. Besides, I didn't hear you complaining when I brought you here," said Crystal.

"That's because I was an asset!" said T-Bone.

Ahead, Sky could just make out a shack of some sort,

nestled in a grove of gnarled trees. It was layered with cracked wood and rusted iron joints, and it leaned southward like an old man on a three-legged walker. Decaying grounds-keeping equipment rested on disassembled tractors surrounding the shack, and yellow grass and weeds grew in thick patches all around.

"Your secret headquarters is a gardener's shack?" Sky snorted somewhat critically.

"We prefer to call it a secret lair," said T-Bone as he opened the door, "but you can apparently drop the 'secret' part."

Sky went in, followed by Crystal, and last of all, T-Bone, who shut the door behind them, casting the room into total darkness.

Inside, the large single room was full of rusted iron picks, bent shovels, busted rakes, and dulled clippers. Ripped-apart engines lay randomly about, with pieces scattered everywhere, and gears, sprockets, and other mechanical mishmash sat on broken tables collecting dust.

Crystal flipped on an old gas lamp, blinding Sky's freakish eyes for a moment.

When his vision finally adjusted, he noticed that the flame in the lamp continued to dance back and forth, even with the door shut, and a thought occurred to him.

"Mine shafts," said Sky, walking toward the source of the breeze. "I thought you were just trying to scare me! There really are mine shafts around here! Your secret base isn't in the gardener's shack. It's under it, isn't it?"

"It's a secret *lair*," said T-Bone, ignoring Crystal's smug *I told you he'd figure it out* look. "And it's not all man-made. Most of it's a natural cave system that was expanded over the years and then filled with garbage."

"Garbage?" said Sky, remembering Crystal's reference to the garbage they'd used to make their equipment. "What kind of garbage?"

"The garbage kind," said T-Bone. "You know—made of trash."

"Who'd go through all the trouble of hollowing out a natural cave system just so they could dump trash into it?" asked Sky.

"No idea," said T-Bone. "It's on your uncle's property. Why don't you tell us?"

He supposed it was possible—even probable—that Phineas had dumped the stuff; it was his property, after all. But why would Phineas fill caves with garbage? Unless . . . Sky thought about the glass wall he'd seen around the manor. For something like that the parts had to come from somewhere, and the unused bits had to be stored somewhere afterward.

"It's technology bits, isn't it? Gears, cylinders, glass, metals, and such? That's where you get the material for your equipment," said Sky.

The only explanations for the wall and a disappearing prison were magic or technology, and Phineas had always assured him there was no such thing as magic, only natural forces misunderstood. "Of course," Phineas had always added, "there are *a lot* of misunderstood forces."

The garbage had to be technology bits, or else the prison really was magic, and the garbage really was just garbage.

"Could be," said T-Bone guardedly.

Crystal didn't comment, which he thought was strange, considering that she'd apparently found the place. He had the impression she knew more, but for whatever reason, she wasn't saying. Curious.

Crystal walked over and pulled the cord on an old lawn mower, starting it up, while T-Bone turned a key in a beat-up ignition on the other side of the room, setting yet another engine rumbling to life.

"It seems weird that someone would hollow out some caves, dump some trash, and then just walk away!" Sky yelled above the noise, watching Crystal.

"Yep!" T-Bone replied.

Crystal avoided Sky's eyes as she crossed to a table in the middle of the room, picked up a chain from the floor, and yanked on it.

Suddenly, from underneath the floor, he heard metal scraping and gears whirring, ropes snapping taught. Steam escaped from somewhere below, and then the floor lurched and began to descend.

"Okay," said Sky, glancing around as the walls of the shack slipped away above him. "That solution might have escaped me."

T-Bone smiled a smug *I told you he's not as smart as you think* smile at Crystal, who pointedly ignored him.

"So, you just found this place?" asked Sky, trying again to get some answers.

The floor lurched to a stop, and everything went quiet.

"You ask a lot of questions," said T-Bone, stepping off the platform into a corridor lit by faint blue-green lights every few feet.

"Give him a break, T-Bone. So did you," said Crystal, joining T-Bone in the corridor.

"Fair enough," said T-Bone, flicking a switch.

Gears churned, steam flooded the corridor, and the floor started to lift. Sky scrambled off, rolling into the corridor as the floor of the gardener's shack disappeared above.

He stood up, scowling, and dusted himself off.

Crystal glared at T-Bone.

"Nice reflexes, Sky," said T-Bone, smirking at Crystal. "I can see why you invited him along."

Turning, T-Bone stormed off down the corridor.

Crystal sighed. "Don't worry; he'll warm up to you. He's just concerned you might die."

"Then, we share a common concern," said Sky.

"I heard about what Ren did to you today," said Crystal as they began walking down the tunnel.

Ahh, Ren. That explained a lot. But was she really concerned about Ren, or was she concerned about what'd happened after? Sky didn't think anyone had seen him pass out, but even if they had, no one could've guessed the cause. He was probably safe.

Sky shrugged, curious to see where the conversation would lead. "They're brothers, then?"

Crystal nodded. "Not close. Not after . . . well . . ."

"Dickens?" said Sky, remembering the name that'd upset Ren. "Another brother, right?"

Crystal glanced at him. "You know?"

"Not really. I just know Ren gets a bit, er . . . *sensitive*," said Sky, trying to be delicate, "if he thinks you're talking about Dickens."

Crystal nodded. "T-Bone has a big family. Thirteen kids, all said and done."

"Thirteen!" Sky exclaimed. He couldn't imagine that many people growing to be that big, and all of them with some kind of natural hatred for Sky the first time they met him.

"Well, there *used* to be thirteen," said Crystal.

"Something took Dickens?" Sky guessed.

Crystal nodded. "About a year ago. Andrew and I were tracking this thing with too many arms and legs in the cemetery to the north—"

"To the north? I thought the cemetery was east, overlooking Arkhon Academy," said Sky.

"That's the new cemetery, built about twelve years ago," said Crystal. "The *old* cemetery is spread out in the swamps and forests north of Pimiscule Manor. Anyway, while we were following this thing south, T-Bone and Hands—whom we didn't really know at the time, outside of school and football games—were coming in from the east cemetery following Dickens's trail. You see, T-Bone's mom used to volunteer at the school in the art department. She's an amazing artist—paintings, sculptures, drawings, origami. She does it all. Crazy about it, really. Named all her kids after famous artists and writers."

"Ren? Ah, I get it. Short for 'Renoir.' And T-Bone?" asked Sky.

"Aaron Thibeaux T-Bone Walker. A musician. She's a big fan, apparently," said Crystal.

"I don't even know who that is," Sky admitted.

Crystal shrugged. "That's not the half of it. T-Bone's four oldest siblings are John, Pauline, Georgina, and Ringo. It just gets worse from there, really."

"Tragic," said Sky.

"Tell me about it. Dickens was the youngest, only three at the time. She'd bring him on volunteer days and let him finger-paint while she worked with the other kids. One day Dickens just wandered off. They closed down the school, searched the halls. Sheriff Beau even led a manhunt, but they didn't find anything. After several weeks they called off the search, but T-Bone refused to give up. He quit the football team, and so did Hands. They'd been best friends for years, and Dickens's disappearance hurt Hands as much as anyone. He doesn't have any brothers or sisters of his own, and T-Bone's family was as close as he got.

"They looked for Dickens every day before and after school," Crystal continued. "They would've quit school too if T-Bone's mom had let them. Like I said, at the time they didn't know about me and Andrew, the secret lair, or monsters, and we didn't want them to. But we watched them roaming the town day and night, and we looked for Dickens ourselves, but no luck. We knew monsters had taken him. We also knew nobody would believe us."

"You told people?" asked Sky, surprised.

"We tried. At first we sent anonymous letters to people—city council members, like Hands's mom; the mayor, the police chief—but nothing happened," said Crystal. "We considered telling our parents, but we didn't want them to know we'd been wandering around Exile in the middle of the night. We didn't want them to worry."

"And you didn't want them to stop you," said Sky, knowing what *that* was like.

"Precisely," said Crystal. "So we told the sheriff."

"Sheriff Beau? Seriously?" said Sky, remembering his encounter with the sheriff earlier in the day. The sheriff hadn't arrested him, but that was about the best he could say of the experience.

Crystal nodded. "He's mean, but he seemed like the most promising candidate since he was actually *looking* for the missing kids, and sometimes even in the right places."

"What'd he say?" asked Sky.

"Dismissed us. Told us to stop wasting his time and stay at

home or he'd tell our parents we'd been wandering around at night," said Crystal. "That's when we realized it was just us. No one else was going to protect the town."

"What about the hunters?" said Sky. "Phineas mentioned a few names in the journal pages I found. Malvidia? Bat?"

"Not ringing a bell," said Crystal.

"Probably for the best. Malvidia sounds awful, but she leads the hunters here, according to my parents, and Bat's really a Wargarou pretending to be a Hunter of Legend," said Sky.

Crystal nodded. "So you believe hunters might have Phineas?"

Sky looked at her. She hadn't even batted an eye when he'd mentioned the Hunters of Legend—the oldest, most powerful hunters alive. Assuming any really *were* alive, since most books ended with their deaths. He'd read of Hunters of Legend that lived forever, could rip up trees by their roots, and outrun bullets—hunters as tough as the monsters they fought. Most of his books were about one Hunter of Legend or another, hunters such as Alexander Drake, Portense Happenstance, Nathaniel the Noteworthy, and Solomon Rose. Did Crystal know more than she was letting on? Maybe he was just reading too much into it.

"No," said Sky, watching her, "I don't think hunters have him, though they have been hunting him."

"Maybe he did something that *deserves* hunting," said Crystal, sounding bitter.

He stared at her. "What's that supposed to mean?"

"It means maybe you're right," Crystal snapped. "Maybe there were real hunters in Exile once upon a time, but if there were, they left us to fend for ourselves."

They walked in silence, their footsteps ringing in the empty tunnels.

"So what happened to Dickens?" asked Sky, breaking the awkward silence.

Crystal glanced at him—her scowl shifting to a frown.

"A few months after Dickens disappeared, while Andrew and I were searching for the monster in the north, T-Bone, Hands, and Ren were searching for Dickens in the eastern cemetery. They'd just crossed over the bridge by the crypt of Andrew's mom—died when he was a baby," added Crystal at a questioning look from Sky, "when T-Bone heard a child laughing. To this day he swears it was Dickens. He even claims he caught a glimpse of him through the tombstones. They chased the kid, whoever it was, but he was always a step ahead. When they finally reached Pimiscule Manor . . . Well, they found what was left of his body in the library."

"That's horrible," whispered Sky, shaken.

"The monster Andrew and I had tracked found them as they tried to recover Dickens' remains. T-Bone, Ren, and Hands fought, but the monster was strong, and it kept shifting and changing, growing and splitting off body parts. It got to Ren, knocked him to the ground with an extra arm while an extra mouth went to work on his gut. Andrew and I froze the thing before it could disembowel him completely, but it was a close thing. The doctors stitched him up, and Sheriff Beau collected Dickens's remains. Later the sheriff confirmed that the DNA matched Dickens's."

Sky shook his head. He understood now why they were so obsessed with hunting monsters.

"The sheriff took a statement from Ren," continued Crystal, "but it never made it into the public records. Ren tried telling people what'd happened—his parents, officers, teachers, people on the street—but nobody believed him. Even T-Bone and Hands denied seeing anything."

"Why would they do that?" asked Sky. "They don't seem like the type to ignore something like that."

"They're not. They'd insisted on joining up with Andrew and me after they'd seen what our weapons could do. Ren was unconscious by the time we showed up, and T-Bone didn't want him involved in monster hunting. He'd lost one brother, and he wasn't about to lose another, even if it meant lying to him. Ren's never forgiven him for it."

"Wow. I had no idea," said Sky.

"Nobody does except for us. Crenshaw was the only one who believed Ren's story, though I don't think he *really* believes it. I think he just saw an opportunity to get a bodyguard. Ren's his lackey now. Ren and T-Bone have been at odds ever since," said Crystal.

A thought struck Sky. "Do you still have the monster you froze?"

"It's with the others," said Crystal. "Why?"

"Just curious," said Sky, frowning. "I don't think I've ever heard of anything quite like it before."

"That doesn't surprise me; it's the only one like it we've ever caught," said Crystal. "Come on. I'll show you."

"You really don't have to," started Sky, not wanting to delay the search for the Gnomon and, in turn, the search for his uncle, just because of his curiosity.

"Don't worry about it. Andrew and Hands are probably there already. I'll dump you with them while I help T-Bone with the gear," said Crystal.

CHAPTER 17

The Last Great Alchemist

You guys froze all these?" asked Sky, looking over the frozen monsters—maybe ten in all, scattered randomly throughout the cavern. Andrew and Hands were working on one of the Shadow Wargs—Bullet—with a long needle. Actually, as Sky looked around, he realized Bullet was the only Shadow Warg. Big had gotten away, but where was Vicious?

"No, no! Try the silver needle," said Andrew, who was watching Hands with a nervous twitch, unable to pull his eyes away.

"Don't be a backseat phlebotomist," said Hands. He pulled out the needle he was using and inserted a different one that looked, if possible, even longer than the first.

Sky cringed as it sunk in. He turned away and started walking among the monsters, looking for the one that'd killed Dickens.

"Did you say something, Sky?" asked Andrew.

"I asked if you guys froze all these," he repeated.

"Yeah, we froze them. It's Andrew's secret recipe—eleven chemicals and spices. Mmmm," said Hands.

"It's nothing special," said Andrew, "just a medley of garlic extract, ionic silver solution, a hint of sodium acetate for conductivity, some cesium to increase the nucleophilicity of the carboxylate group for supercooling . . . that sort of thing."

"Er, okay," said Sky as he came to a stop in front of a horrible-looking monster with heads, arms, and legs growing all over its body—some human, some *not*.

Sky opened his backpack and pulled out one of the books he'd brought, an old bestiary called *The Fantafstik Book of Myfical Mofnsters*. He began to flip through it.

"But before we supercool it," continued Hands, assuming Sky was still interested (which he wasn't), "we make the solution gaseous and lighter to carry, and then we store it in specially made containers—"

"Empty five-gallon ice cream buckets from the city dump," said Andrew.

"Which we then connect to the Pounder—," said Hands.

"That's the hand-cannon Crystal uses, the one we made from old sardine cans we found at the dump," said Andrew.

"She douses the monsters, and then T-Bone, Andrew, or I shock it with the Shocker, the Cross-Shocker, or the Collapser. They're the metal gloves, the Taser crossbow, and the metal staff, for the layman. The electric shock activates the solution, causing it to instantly freeze and stay frozen even at room temperature," said Hands.

Sky found in his book a drawing of a monster that looked like the one in front of him, and he began to skim. "'A Gloom . . . rolling chaos . . . takes on forms by ingesting blood . . . unable to sustain . . . unpredictable . . . hibernates in winter . . . slows in cold or cement . . . avoid at all costs . . . insane . . . a fallen Whisper, changing out of season, giving in to the consuming urge, forever lost in madness.'"

A fallen Whisper.

"It doesn't work on everything," said Andrew.

"What's that?" said Sky, distracted.

"The solution," said Andrew. "It doesn't work on everything—not yet—but we improve it with each new monster we capture."

Whisper had a driving urge to shift all the time, but to do so outside of a full moon led to madness and the fall of the Whisper. They became Glooms.

And a Gloom was captured after killing Dickens. What had it been doing in the manor at the exact moment Dickens arrived? It couldn't have been hunting Dickens; Crystal had said Dickens had come from the east cemetery, while the Gloom had come from the north. Was it just coincidence? Bad timing for Dickens? But what had taken Dickens in the first place? If it had been the Gloom, surely it would've eaten him before that night.

Sky left the Gloom behind and found the Gnomon that Crystal had mentioned. It was shorter than Sky, coming maybe to his chin. Its skin was pasty white, like dead flesh, and it wore a battered wool cap pulled over the place where ears would've been if it'd had any. The Gnomon was smaller than he'd expected, the four-toed feet and hands little more than half the size of the footprints they'd found earlier tonight.

Almost like a child's.

"How long ago did you guys capture this Gnomon again?" asked Sky.

"The what?" asked Andrew.

"The Gnomon. This four-toed monster here," said Sky. "How long ago?"

Something was bugging him, but he couldn't quite put his finger on it.

"Little over a year," said Andrew. "Crystal and I bagged that one in the east cemetery by my mom's crypt before T-Bone and Hands joined up. Why do you ask?"

Before T-Bone and Hands . . .

"Are there a lot of them around?" asked Sky.

"Not that we know of," said Andrew. "That's the only one we've ever seen, and of course there are the tracks you and Crystal found tonight."

"Got it!" yelled Hands, holding up the black-sludge-filled syringe triumphantly. Andrew held out a beaker, and Hands squirted the sludge in, capping it with a silver cork as Sky made his way back to them.

"What are you going to do with that?" asked Sky.

"Experiment," said Andrew. "You helped us find the perfect subject."

"To the lab!" Hands yelled dramatically, running from the cavern.

Andrew rolled his eyes at Sky, and then followed, with Sky close behind.

They led Sky through the twisting corridors, past bubbling lakes and steaming whirlpools, past caverns filled with ripped-apart equipment and piles of ash and technological garbage, until, after a few moments of directed wandering, they reached a cozy cavern made up of two secondhand couches that (according to Andrew) they'd picked up at the dump, a number of worktables, stools, and shelves that they'd picked up at the dump, and a large framed picture of the dump that they'd picked up at the dump. Why they had this last item, Sky didn't know, and he really didn't *want* to know.

The worktables and shelves were covered with laboratory equipment that Andrew had slung together out of junk. Old Coke bottles sat on busted camping stoves, bubbling strange liquids. Containers of various sizes, materials, and makes held gooey liquids, multicolored powders, and superdense solids, as well as a number of—thankfully—unidentifiable biological samples. Andrew's lab was part science, part alchemy, and part "What is that thing?"

"You built all this?" asked Sky, impressed.

"Mostly," said Andrew.

"What's this?" asked Sky, poking at a collection of rusted copper pots and modified lightbulbs filled with liquids.

"I wouldn't touch that," said Hands.

"Why not?"

"'Cause it'll explode," said Andrew nonchalantly as he opened a cabinet and pulled out some Cheez Whiz canisters from an overflowing bin.

Sky jerked his hand away. "You keep exploding stuff out in the open like that?"

"Science can be very dangerous," said Andrew.

"But this stuff here sort of looks like urine," said Sky, pointing at one of the lightbulbs filled with a yellowish bubbling liquid.

"That's because it *is* urine," said Hands.

"You're boiling your urine?" said Sky in disgust.

"In 1669 the last great alchemist, Hennig Brand, discovered phosphorus by boiling and purifying his own urine," said Andrew.

"That's disgusting!" Sky exclaimed, looking closer.

"And highly explosive," said Andrew, "but how else are we supposed to make the scrumptious glowing powder we put on our crackers?"

"You know you can buy that stuff, don't you?" said Sky, stepping away from the urine.

"Where's the fun in that?" asked Hands.

Sky shook his head. These guys were certifiable!

"Did you know there's absolutely no record of Hennig Brand's death or burial?" said Andrew. "True story."

Hands nodded, obviously enchanted by the idea.

"I like to think that the last great alchemist lives on still . . . somewhere . . . out there," said Hands, staring off into the half distance. "A lone man engaged in a desperate struggle to keep himself alive—to create the elixir of life before death's long shadow finds him. A lone man, huddled, afraid, bent with years, his loved ones long since departed to wander the lonely wastelands alone. . . . A lone man . . ." Hands's voice dropped to a hush. "The *Last. Great. Alchemist.* Forever burning his own urine to make the world brighter for us all."

"You really need to lay off the supernatural romances, Hands," said Andrew.

"You'd prefer that I read Jane Austen maybe?"

Andrew glared.

"So is that urine too?" asked Sky, watching as Andrew placed two glass canning jars on the table next to the Cheez Whiz canisters. One was filled with a deep blue liquid that looked like melted ice. The other was a deep red, like fruit punch. "Because if so, you might want to seek immediate medical attention."

"I'm trying to improve our two formulas—FIRE and ICE. ICE is what we call the freezing formula, and FIRE is the thawing formula. ICE plus electricity equals frozen monster. FIRE plus electricity equals angry, unfrozen monster. They're works in progress," said Andrew.

"What're the Cheez Whiz canisters for?" asked Sky.

Hands raised one, squirting the contents into his mouth.

"Oh," said Sky.

"Hands pilfers them for us from his dad's store," said Andrew. "We store liquids in them using that machine there." He pointed at a cobbled-together machine that looked like it might explode at any moment.

Hands put on some swimming goggles and filled a turkey baster with ICE while Andrew readied the microscope.

"Looks like your experiment will have to wait," T-Bone taunted as he and Crystal walked in carrying several duffel bags. T-Bone stopped when he saw Hands in his goggles. "We're the cool ones, Hands. Remember?"

"Whoever told you that?" asked Hands.

T-Bone threw a bag in front of Sky.

"What's this?" asked Sky as he unzipped the duffel bag and pulled out some odd-looking football shoulder pads, longer than normal and covered with buttons, with a waist strap attached to the bottom. He accidently hit a button as he held it up, and four rods, like inflexible fishing poles, shot out of the bottom of the pads near the waist, nearly touching the ground.

"This," said T-Bone, taking the shoulder pads from him, "is a loaner. We expect it back in one piece after tonight."

Crystal grabbed the shoulder pads from T-Bone, hit a button that retracted the rods, and proceeded to slip the pads over Sky's head. "This is the main piece of our equipment, Sky. We call it the Core. It controls everything else, helps with falls, protects our vitals from bites, that sort of thing."

"It also helps us carry all our gear, which is heavy," said Andrew.

"Speak for yourself," said Hands as he curled his bag like he was lifting a box of feathers. "Oh, I'm sorry. Am I holding something? I didn't notice."

Andrew rolled his eyes.

"Each piece of gear connects to the Core," continued Crystal.

"These are called Jumpers." Crystal hit a button, the rods shot out again, and she attached several oversize cans of whipped cream to them. "When you slap here," she said, and pointed to a button on the Core, "the Jumpers will kick in and send you into the air, kind of like a jet pack. The Jumpers should give you three or four good jumps before you need to refill them."

"And when you land," said Andrew as he connected a small round device to the front and back of Sky's Core, "remember to use the Shimmer—this button here. It combines plasma windows and superconductivity to manipulate the electromagnetic fields around you."

"Kind of like a force field," added Hands.

"Right," said Andrew, "but it works differently—more like diffusing energy through time and space."

Sky raised his eyebrows. Time and space? Was he serious?

"It's the only thing I didn't build from scratch," Andrew continued. "I used the—"

"It won't protect you completely," Crystal cut in, glaring at Andrew. Sky caught the look; she obviously didn't want to share the information.

"Especially," Crystal continued, ignoring Sky's befuddlement, "against things like fire or acid, but it should soften the landing and block claws and teeth. Each zap lasts about three seconds, so make sure you time it right or you'll break your neck. And it can run out of juice, so use it sparingly."

She pulled out a large water cannon, the Pounder, and attached it to the Core, next to his shoulder. Then Hands attached two partially flattened five-gallon ice cream buckets full of ICE to the Core's back and connected a thick hose from the buckets to the Pounder. It was lighter than he'd expected.

"You'll use the Pounder tonight," said Crystal, "like me. The ICE stays in a semi-gaseous form until you pull the trigger, making it lighter to carry. It'll be nice to not be the only one spraying."

Crystal attached a few old Cheez Whiz containers to the Core.

"This last thing here is the Fogger," started Crystal.

"No need to explain," said Hands, smiling mischievously. "He knows all about *the Whiz*. Don't you, Sky?"

Sky smiled, but before he could make a witty retort about wandering alchemists bringing a bit more light into the world, Crystal cut in.

"A *pee* joke? Honestly, Hands. I thought better of you," said Crystal.

"Why on earth would you do that?" said Hands.

"The Fogger," said Crystal, ignoring Hands's jibe, "shoots out a jet of Fog that hides us when we need to hide. It's made out of a number of chemicals that *won't* freeze. It also has a distinct smell—"

"It reeks," said Hands.

"And it hides our scent from any predators," finished Crystal.

"Last but not least," said Andrew, throwing a black hooded

cloak over Sky's head, "we cover it all with a cloak to hide our ugliness from the world."

Sky stared down at himself. He had no idea what he was doing, but at least he looked pretty cool.

"There's also a black light and some *tasty* crackers you can add to your backpack," said Hands, smiling. "You should be able to strap your pack between the ICE canisters."

"So, it's simple," said T-Bone, summarizing. "We spray it, we shock it, it freezes. If it hits back, we shimmer. If it doesn't freeze, we fog it and fall back. Got it?"

"Er," said Sky.

"He'll get it. It just takes a while," said Crystal.

T-Bone shook his head. "This is a *bad* idea."

CHAPTER 18

Right Is Right

They popped out of the sewers near the bowling alley, and Sky took a deep breath of fresh air, trying to remember a time when the night had smelled quite as good. The roads were empty, the stores along the sides of the road long closed.

"This is it," said Crystal, shining her black light at the ground to illuminate the Gnomon's footprints. The fluorescent materials had long since worn off, but it turned out that biological samples were just as visible under black light, and the Gnomon had stepped in plenty of *those* in the sewers.

They had followed it aboveground for a time until the trail had entered the sewers near Main Street. It turned out that the monster hunters spent much more time in the sewers than they'd like to admit. The lair tunnels connected at various points, and monsters occasionally used them, though mostly monsters didn't appear to like the sewers any more than they did.

"You think it's going bowling?" asked Hands, surveying the poorly lit bowling alley across the street.

"How could it?" said Andrew. "It has no opposable thumbs."

"It could hold the ball in its mouth," said Hands.

"And just swing its head back and forth like an ostrich, could it?" said Andrew.

"Guys," said Crystal, trying to get their attention.

"What? You don't think it could bowl with its mouth?" said Hands.

"Not while maintaining proper form. There *is* technique involved, you know. It'd shoot all gutter balls," said Andrew.

"What if the lane had bumpers?" said Hands. "And it was disco night?"

"Oh, well, sure. If it was disco night . . . ," said Andrew.

"GUYS!" yelled Crystal.

Andrew and Hands turned and looked at her.

"It's not going to the bowling alley," said Crystal.

"Well, that's a relief," said Hands.

"It's headed for your dad's store, Hands," said Crystal, raising the black light so that they could see the footprints making a beeline for the giant Redbrick Department Store in the distance.

"Oh, crap," said Hands, his smile fading.

The fluorescent tracks gave out about a block from the store, but Crystal assured him they were still on the trail. She claimed she could *smell* the Gnomon, though Sky wasn't sure how she could smell anything above their own stench.

As they made their way toward the store, they had to weave in and out of the shadows, hiding from random cars as they passed by.

He thought he spotted a faded-red 1957 Cadillac Eldorado Brougham at one point—and he raced for the corner—but it turned before he could get a good look.

"My dad's still here," said Hands when they finally reached the store. A shiny new Mercedes sat alone in the parking lot. "He's going to kill me."

"You sure it's in there?" asked T-Bone, glancing nervously at Hands.

"The nose never lies," said Crystal.

"All right, then. Crystal, Andrew, you're with me. Hands, take Sky around back and make sure the monster doesn't come out," said T-Bone.

Everyone except T-Bone turned to look at Crystal. She nodded once.

Sky laughed. He was beginning to see how things *really* worked around here.

T-Bone ground his teeth. "Now that we all have *permission,* let's see if we can capture this abomination."

"It's a *Gnomon,*" Sky corrected.

"It's whatever I call it," said T-Bone.

"Ease up, T-Bone," said Crystal. "We brought Sky along for a reason, remember?"

"*You* brought him along for a reason, not me. You and Andrew caught a monster like this before. We don't need him. Spray it, zap it, bag it. End of story," said T-Bone.

"Actually," said Sky, "what Crystal and Andrew captured a year ago was a Gnomon *child.*"

"What?" said Crystal, looking truly disturbed.

"A child. That's what you captured. Full-grown adults are half again as tall and many times stronger," said Sky.

"A child," said Crystal, the blood draining from her face.

Everyone looked shaken, even T-Bone.

"Why didn't you say something before?" asked Crystal.

"Because . . . I decided we needed to come here tonight," said Sky.

"*You* decided?" T-Bone bristled.

"I did, and you want to know why?" said Sky.

"I'm just dying to know," said T-Bone.

"Because that Gnomon in there—I think we should try to talk to it," said Sky.

"Talk to it? Are you nuts?" exclaimed T-Bone.

"Look," said Sky, turning to Crystal, "when you caught the Gnomon in the cemetery, it tried to run, didn't it?"

Crystal nodded.

"A Gnomon's four-toed feet and four-fingered hands are for burrowing, not fighting. I'm sure it could fight if it had to, but not when it could run," said Sky. "They hide and they scavenge and they live underground, usually near construction sites or in cemeteries where the ground is softer from constant digging—"

"And empty of people fearful of facing their own mortality," added Hands.

"Er . . . sure," said Sky.

"*And* where there are dead bodies ripe for the picking," added Andrew.

"Not so sure about that one," said Sky, "but it wouldn't surprise me if Gnomon—not people—had dug out the tunnels in your lair. And you want to know the most interesting thing about Gnomon? They're one of the few monsters that don't live alone."

"What're you saying? That they travel in packs like Shadow Warg?" said T-Bone, looking around warily.

"He's saying," said Crystal, "that they live together as families."

Sky nodded, watching as it slowly sunk in.

"Maybe we should ask it what it's doing here," said Sky.

"Is this thing dangerous?" asked T-Bone.

"I don't believe so," said Sky.

T-Bone shook his head. "So you're guessing."

"It's not a guess. It's a puzzle. It's what I'm good at," said Sky.

"Is this thing full-grown—the one we're hunting? Could it hurt people?" asked Crystal.

"It's not a child, but . . . I don't believe the Gnomon would hurt anybody," said Sky, uncertainty creeping into his voice. He was basing this all on stories he'd read. He'd had to read between the lines to figure all this out, and the lines were *very* blurry.

T-Bone shook his head. "'Believe'? Not good enough, Sky. If this thing hurts people because we . . ." His voice trailed off. "Let's just get this over with." Without looking at anybody, T-Bone spun and walked off toward the storefront, his expression grim.

Andrew followed a moment later, but Crystal lagged behind. "Sky, we're just freezing it. We're not going to kill it. We'll be gentle, okay?"

"I'm sure its family will appreciate that," said Sky.

She frowned and then followed after T-Bone and Andrew.

"Well," said Hands, "it looks like it's just the two of us."

They circled the store, moving through the thick fall trees and crackling bushes. Silently they made their way to the back. The air in the night sky was dark and heavy, like oil spilled in tepid waters. Sky couldn't believe they'd brushed him off so easily. Didn't they care that they might be harming a monster just trying to feed its family? Sure it could hurt them, like anything backed into a corner fighting to survive, and maybe the Gnomon really *was* nasty and violent, but how would they ever know? This entire night had been a waste. He should've gone back to the manor.

"So you really believe that stuff?" said Hands, breaking the silence. "About some monsters being good, I mean?"

Sky nodded. "Are you really afraid of your dad?"

"Whoa! Ease up on the personal questions there, hombre," said Hands. "You've gotta start light. Why don't you ask me about the weather."

"Okay. How's the weather?" asked Sky.

"My dad's a jerk," said Hands, "a bona fide jerk. All he cares about is money and making more of it."

"Uh," said Sky.

"And my mom's even worse. Totally power hungry. No. Really. She inherited Exile's power plant when my granddad died—privately owned, no shareholders. Now she's on the city council and bucking for mayor so she can protect her 'interests,' which don't include me, by the way," said Hands.

"I'm sorry," said Sky, not sure what else to say.

"Don't be. I'm rich. It's the American dream, and I'm living it. If I do everything my dad says—when he bothers to talk to me with his mouth, I'll get everything I want: a huge house, my spot back on the football team if I want it, video game systems, an indoor pool, and any car I want when I turn sixteen. Hmpf. Yeah. Because *that's* what I want," said Hands. "If it weren't for my grandpa Osmer—that's my dad's dad, not the dead one—

I'd probably be a complete juvenile delinquent. You ask how the weather is, Sky? It's balmy. Quite balmy, and I'm wearing a ski parka two sizes too big. How's that for personal disclosure?"

"Um . . ."

"That's what I thought. But you'd already figured me out, hadn't you?" asked Hands.

"Er . . . ," said Sky, who had, in fact, deduced only a small part of what Hands had said.

"People aren't puzzles, Sky," said Hands. "You can't figure us out."

"So none of that was true?" asked Sky, suddenly confused.

"Oh, all of it was true," said Hands as they reached the back door to the Redbrick Department Store. "So you wanna go in?"

"What about T-Bone and Crystal? They told us to wait here," said Sky, suspicious. What kind of game was Hands playing?

"Since when have I ever listened to T-Bone?" Hands pulled out a key and opened the door. Sky looked at the key and back at Hands. Hands noticed. "Lifted it from my old man. They don't call me Hands for nothin'. Coming?"

Sky hesitated. He didn't want to make T-Bone any angrier. He was already walking a fine line, and he really did need their help. On the other hand—

"We don't have a lot of time for introspection," said Hands. "If you really think this Gnomon thing's not so bad, you'd better do something about it, and fast—before the others freeze it stiff. What's right is right. It's the first rule of monster hunting. If you're going to be one of us, you've gotta learn that."

"Who said I wanted to be one of you?" asked Sky.

Hands looked over Sky's outfit and raised an eyebrow. "You've got a lot of friends banging down your door, do you?"

"All right, fine. I want to be one of you," said Sky, "but what about your dad? What if he spots you?"

"Forget my dad. He's a jerk anyway," said Hands, smiling.

"What's right is right?" said Sky.

"Always," said Hands, "except when it's not. That's the second rule. Are you ready?"

Sky slapped a button on his chest, and the Pounder—the massive hand-cannon that fired freezing ICE—shot down his sleeve and into his hand. He took a deep breath. "Ready."

Hands opened the door.

CHAPTER 19

Gnomon-clature

The storeroom was crowded with pallets of food, machine parts, books, sporting equipment, kitchenware, video games, movies, TVs, and a thousand other sundry goods, stacked on three-story metal shelves.

Sky crept through the darkness behind Hands, holding the Pounder in front of him, his arms and legs shaking like Jell-O in a very mild earthquake. Moonlight streamed through windows above, casting elongated shadows that looked like iron bars in a prison cell, and it seemed like every box twitched and every shadow danced in the deathlike silence that radiated from the warehouse void like a breathless echo.

For all Sky knew, the Gnomon could be watching them right now, licking its teeth, waiting for them to get to just the right spot before it pounced. Outside, everything had all seemed so different. It was easy to imagine a misunderstood and innocent Gnomon trying to take care of its family—and he still believed that was true—but now, *inside*, with his life on the line, what if he were wrong?

They reached the doors leading to the main floor, and Sky peeked out. Dim red-blue floodlights illuminated the aisles, and a dull hum filled the air, caused, Sky guessed, by refrigerators and cooling fans—but the store seemed otherwise silent.

Sky slipped through, and Hands pointed up at a glass window overlooking the store floors. Looking up, Sky could clearly see Hands's dad bent over a keyboard.

"He can't see us," whispered Hands. "The office light should blind him. Any ideas about what this Gnomon might be after?"

Sky shrugged. "Food, maybe? A new TV for the Gnomon hole? No idea."

"Well, let's start with food," said Hands.

They crept through aisles, sticking to the shadows, until a moment later they reached the dairy section.

Sky inched forward, peeking around the aisle corner.

On the floor he spotted a mess—several ripped-open boxes of snack cakes, splattered eggs, chunks of bread, smeared cream cheese, and spilled milk. Hovering over the mess, he saw . . .

"T-Bone," whispered Sky, pushing Hands back into the aisle so they could hide.

"Where is this thing?" T-Bone asked Crystal and Andrew.

"Beats me," said Andrew. "Maybe it ate and ran, or maybe it spilled the milk and started crying—though I don't see the point. There's no use crying over spilled milk."

"Lame, Andrew," said Crystal.

"Totally lame," agreed T-Bone.

"Well, Hands would've appreciated it if you hadn't sent him off to babysit," said Andrew.

"That was as much for his good as Sky's," said T-Bone. "You know what his dad would do to him if he caught him."

Sky glanced back up at the office window, but Hands just smirked.

"So where to next, O Fearless Leader?" said Andrew.

"We should probably check the—," started T-Bone.

"I was talking to Crystal," Andrew cut in, smiling mischievously. "What's the nose say?"

T-Bone glared at Andrew.

"I—I'm not sure," said Crystal, glancing over to where Sky and Hands were hiding. Sky ducked back. There was no way she could have known they were there! And yet . . .

"Maybe we should start in puzzles and lay out some goon stop grids," said Crystal. "I've got a good feeling about *puzzles*."

"What's a goon stop grid?" asked T-Bone.

"I don't know. Maybe we'll figure it out when we get to puzzles," said Crystal.

T-Bone rolled his eyes.

"As good a plan as any," said Andrew.

Sky waited until they wandered off, and then he turned to Hands, a big grin on his face.

"Why are you smiling? They're about to freeze your pen pal," said Hands. "Crystal's nose never lies."

"No," said Sky, "I'll bet it doesn't, but the Gnomon's not in puzzles."

"How do you know that?" said Hands.

"Because 'goon stop grids' *is* a puzzle. It's an anagram, and not a very good one. She knew I was here. She was sending a message," said Sky.

"An anagram? You mean the letters are out of order? What's the message?" asked Hands.

"Do you have a pen?" asked Sky.

"That's a lame message," said Hands.

"No, I'm asking: Do you have a pen?"

"Uh-uh," said Hands, shaking his head, "still not getting it."

Sky sighed.

"Just messin' with you," said Hands, grinning. He hit a button on his chest, and a pen shot into his hand. He disconnected it from the holding wire and handed it to Sky. Sky stared back at Hands, sincerely wondering if he was crazy.

"What? You never know when you'll need a good pen," said Hands defensively.

Sky took the pen and picked up a box of cheese crackers. "May I?"

"Be my guest," said Hands. "Defile the whole store for all I care."

He turned over the box and started scribbling out words, trying to decode the anagram.

"Dings goo ports. No. Grid togs snoop. Probably not. Ah . . . wait . . . There it is! Thank you, thank you, hold the applause!" said Sky, mock bowing.

"Don't get too full of yourself. You only decoded it. Crystal put it together in her head," said Hands.

"You really know how to kill a buzz. You know that, Hands?" said Sky.

Hands smiled. "So are you going to tell me what it is, or should I pat you on the back some more?"

"Sporting goods," said Sky. "The Gnomon's in sporting goods."

They crossed the store, staying clear of the toys section, where T-Bone and Andrew were tearing apart the nets from the bouncy ball containers and stringing them across the ends of the aisles, scattering the balls around the floors as they built their "goon stop grids."

Sky almost laughed; Crystal was making them build an actual trap! Hopefully the trap would keep T-Bone and Andrew occupied long enough for Sky to talk to the Gnomon. Crystal was on his side, and if he could win her over, he could win over T-Bone. Of course, if he didn't find Phineas by tomorrow night, it wouldn't matter anyway.

"So, what are you planning to do once we find this thing?" asked Hands after they'd passed toys and entered school supplies.

"I don't know," said Sky. "I hadn't really thought that far ahead. Maybe I could just talk to it, tell it to leave quietly or something, ask it what it's looking for, ask if it has seen my uncle or eaten any of Arkhon Academy's students recently."

"Let me know how that works out for you," said Hands.

"You don't think it'll work?" said Sky.

"Think about it. You're a scared monster outside your home turf and some kid in a funny robe leaps out at you and wants to 'talk.' Even if it doesn't rip your head off—"

"It runs," finished Sky. "No matter how friendly I seem."

"And if the Gnomon runs . . . ," said Hands.

"The jig is up," said Sky. "Crystal and T-Bone will have to stop it."

"Spray it, zap it, bag it. End of story," said Hands.

"And talking to a frozen Gnomon would be significantly harder," said Sky. "So you have a better plan?"

"Me? No. I'm the impulsive guy. I have no plans," said Hands, "but Crystal does."

Sky quirked an eyebrow, wondering what Hands was talking about.

And then he got it.

"Goon stop grids—a puzzle and a plan all in the same sentence," said Sky, shaking his head at Crystal's feat. "It's not just busywork. She really means for us to use the trap. Crystal's a genius!"

"Tell me about it," said Hands. "You go high, I'll go low. Try not to let it see you. And try not to get killed, okay? The others would never let me live it down."

"You sound like Hannah," said Sky.

"Your sister? I'm insulted. My voice is much more masculine than that," said Hands. "But maybe you could hook us up sometime just so we could compare—purely for curiosity's sake, of course."

"You really don't want that," said Sky. "Trust me. You're better off with the monsters."

A small metal tube shot into Hands's gauntlets, expanding into a full-size staff. "Maybe you're right. Her heart does seem to be set on someone else."

Sky smirked. "He is captain of the football team, you know."

"I know; I was on the football team. I hear his letterman's jacket is made out of wool. You know, from, like, sheep and stuff?" said Hands, doing a perfect imitation of Tick.

Sky laughed, covering his mouth to garble the sound.

Hands tapped his staff against his head and pointed it at Sky. "Fair thee well, young monster hunter! I go to drive the beast to the pit! But first I must stop in yonder aisle to make the world a little bit brighter for all." And then he disappeared around the corner, no doubt to make good on his promise.

Still grinning, Sky headed for the back of the store, holding his Pounder hand-cannon at his side.

As he rounded the corner, moving from automotive to sporting goods, he spotted the Gnomon.

Sky's heart leapt into his throat.

It was hunched over, its long arms pressed to the ground as it meandered forward like an orangutan. It was much larger than he'd expected, standing taller than the shelves even when hunched over, and its back and legs and arms were bulging with taut strings of ropy muscle that connected together in odd, inhuman ways like lines of licorice wrapped around a decaying oak.

Fear raced through him. Sky took a step back. The Gnomon was so *monstrous*. How could he face something like that with its white, nearly translucent skin, popping with red and blue and black veins, and its four claw-tipped fingers like pieces of a broken shovel?

His muscles contracted, driving him another step back.

Nobody would blame him if he ran. Phineas was still out there somewhere. Phineas needed him. If Sky died here today, who would find Phineas? Who would stop the Arkhon from waking up and breaking out of his prison? Who else knew about the poem and the number he'd found? Sky *needed* to run. Too many lives depended on him.

Grinding his teeth, he stepped forward. *People depended on him here*.

Phineas would never condone abandoning the immediate

few to save the future many, even if it meant sacrificing himself to stay.

See the now, take care of it, and the future will work out as it should. That's what Phineas had taught him.

Sky calmed his breathing, tried to focus his mind on what was happening around him, to cut out the distractions, to see things as they truly were.

The first thing he noticed was that the trix on his palm had split open again. He clenched his hand into a fist to stop the bleeding.

He turned his attention back to the Gnomon. It lingered near the tennis rackets, banging one against its four-fingered hand, almost like it was playing with it.

The monster looked over its shoulder, and Sky inhaled. The large, black eyes; the nose-less wrinkled face; pale, white-gray skin like mush with those pulsing red and blue and black veins, a red cap pulled over its head, lipless mouth full of razor-sharp teeth ready to grind him like rock—

The now slipped away.

"It won't talk to you," said a voice behind him.

Sky's stomach lurched, and he almost cried out, but he covered his mouth and jerked back before the Gnomon could spot him. The Gnomon stopped for a moment, its flesh shifting to a pale ocean blue as it listened.

Blue as it stills, black as it flies, red as it kills. The words from *Much Ado About Gnomon* rolled through his mind eerily, haunting him as he waited, breath held. Finally the Gnomon went back to pounding at the tennis racket, its skin returning to translucent white, before Sky spun to face Errand.

"What are you doing here?" whispered Sky, pinching himself to see if he'd fallen asleep again.

"You're not asleep, so stop pinching yourself. It kind of *hurts*," said Errand loudly.

"Shhh! It'll hear you!" whispered Sky, glancing nervously back at the Gnomon as it set down the tennis racket and moved on to the baseball equipment. It picked up an umpire chest protector and slid it over its head, pounding its fist against it before adding an umpire's mask.

"You're such a killjoy," said Errand. "It can't hear me. Only you can."

"You mean you're not really here?" said Sky, turning his attention back to Errand. "You're just in my head or something?"

"Where else would I be?" asked Errand. "I already told you. I'm you and you're me. I'm your 'little monster,' as you so affectionately refer to me."

"I'm going nuts," said Sky, "completely insane, and I didn't even realize it'd happened, which means I *must* be." Convinced he must be going insane, Sky looked back to see if the Gnomon had suddenly changed into a wombat.

Fortunately, the Gnomon was still a Gnomon, which meant he probably wasn't insane, though he might have *preferred* a wombat.

He watched the Gnomon pick up a baseball bat, stare at it for a moment, and then put it in its bag. The Gnomon picked out a few more pieces of protective gear, some baseballs, some bases, some mitts and other miscellaneous equipment, shoving it all into a large bag it dragged behind it.

He wasn't insane, but maybe he really *was* dreaming. He pinched himself again.

"OW! Would you stop that!" exclaimed Errand.

"What do you want, Errand? Why are you trying to make me run away?" said Sky.

"Don't blame me for your fear," said Errand, "But now that you mention it, I would like it if you'd leave. After all, if you die, I die."

"I'm not leaving just yet," said Sky.

"I noticed," said Errand. "It's not going to talk to you, Sky. And even if it did, you wouldn't understand it in your currently pathetic condition anyway. No offense."

"No, of course not. How could I give offense when I'm only offending myself?" said Sky.

He was really beginning to question the whole "I'm you" bit, but whatever Errand was—hallucination, Edgewalker, or otherwise—it was probably best to just play along for the moment.

"You need to get out of here before something terrible happens. I can't afford to have you die," said Errand.

"Look, either help me or get out of the way," said Sky. "You can't keep trying to make me afraid or angry just to get what you want. You do it at the wrong time, and you'll end up getting us both killed."

Sky glanced at the Gnomon. When he looked back, Errand was gone.

In the ominous silence of the store, broken by the occasional whisper and hiss from the Gnomon—like dozens of horrible voices hissing in the dark—Sky began to wish Errand had hung around.

The more he looked at the Gnomon, the more he realized how crazy it all was. The monster was twice his size and capable of digging through granite and throwing rocks the size of a couch. What had made him think he could do this?

He wasn't a hunter. He wasn't Solomon Rose.

Solomon had gouged out the Echo's eyes out of spite,

and here Sky stood quivering in his boots and wanting to *talk*. Maybe he just didn't have what it took to be a hunter.

Maybe that's why Phineas had never taken him on a real hunt before, or taught him how to shoot and fight. Maybe he saw what Sky really was, when Sky couldn't see it himself.

Something clattered near the front of the store, drawing his attention back to the moment.

He watched the Gnomon's head jerk up, and wondered what must be running through its mind. Was it intelligent? Could it think?

It looked around warily, its flesh shifting blue as it stilled. Sky ducked back, but as he did, he threw a tube of tennis balls so that it landed, rattling, behind the Gnomon.

Without hesitating the Gnomon took a step and leapt over the shelf into the next aisle with its bag, its flesh shifting black as it fled for the front of the store, where Hands was waiting to drive it back toward Sky.

Sky scrambled down the aisles, trying to keep up without being seen as the now frantic Gnomon veered back and forth, looking for an escape.

Sky threw an air filter, a bottle of SAE 30 oil, a box of pencils, a frying pan. He didn't want to hit it so much as scare it toward the trap.

As Sky crossed the next aisle—grabbing a baby monitor as he passed, ready to throw—he suddenly slipped, sliding across the floor in a pool of motor oil that had erupted from a thrown bottle. His Pounder hand-cannon flew from his grasp, even as he clung to the baby monitor.

He crashed into a display of hand sanitizer, knocking it to the ground with a thump.

He wrestled his way out from under, and came face-to-face

with the Gnomon. It stood up on its back legs, raised its arms in the air, and let out a hideous shriek that pierced the silence of the store like a wartime raid siren, its flesh turning thick and as red as blood as it readied to *kill*.

As Sky stared into that gaping mouth full of jagged teeth, all thoughts of talking fled. He didn't remember he had a weapon a few feet away. He didn't remember all the stories he'd concocted of misunderstood Gnomon and misunderstanding hunters.

He spun, and he ran in terror, his Pounder hand-cannon dragging forgotten behind him, pulled along by a wire jutting from his sleeve.

And above the sounds of the clattering Pounder, he could hear the Gnomon with its strange multi-voiced hissing as it jumped after him.

He saw Hands pop into the aisle ahead, his eyes going big. And beyond Hands he saw Andrew on top of a shelf, raising his Taser-like Cross-Shocker with its electrified prongs.

A sudden noise behind Sky drew his attention. Over his shoulder he spotted T-Bone rounding a corner with sizzling metal gloves, crashing into the Gnomon, and he heard Crystal yelling.

He knew he should turn and help—that's what a real hunter would do—but all he could do was run, his cowardly feet moving as fast as he could make them.

T-Bone let out a muffled scream from behind, and the Gnomon threw him!

Sky watched T-Bone sail over his head and slam into Hands, and they both tumbled into a shelf, which crashed to the ground from the impact.

Andrew, who'd been perched on top of the shelf, tumbled

with it—his shot going wide and low, flying toward Sky with uncanny accuracy.

Sky dropped to the ground, avoiding the serrated suction cups by inches as they shot into a board game. Electricity raged down the wires connecting the Cross-Shocker to the prongs, and the board game promptly burst into flames, sending out a rancid plume of burned plastic and ash.

The fire spread.

Sprinklers kicked on, dousing him in water. He scrambled back to his feet and kept running, his legs carrying him forward even though his mind had long since fled.

Over his shoulder he saw the Gnomon rear back onto its feet, shrieking at the falling water, its translucent red flesh distorted, hideous, and twisted.

Sky leapt over the fallen shelf, which had dominoed into the next and the next. He hit his Jumpers, remembering the jet-pack-like device at the last possible moment.

The Jumpers carried him up . . . up . . .

He was going to make it! He was going to escape the Gnomon!

But as he sailed through the air toward safety and sanity, he passed over Andrew, T-Bone, and Hands desperately struggling to get out of the wreckage of the shelves below as the Gnomon closed in.

It was the only thing that could've pulled him back from the brink of madness. His friends—the people who'd risked their lives to save him just the night before, and again today—lying helpless upon the ground, fighting for their lives.

He couldn't let them die.

Shelves tumbled in front of him, below him. He flew over the falling shelves, almost ahead of the wave.

The Pounder hand-cannon dangled uselessly from his sleeve. He didn't have time to retract it and get a shot off.

But then he realized that he still had the baby monitor he'd picked up!

He spun in the air, hurling the monitor at the Gnomon. His aim was off and the monitor clattered against a shelf a few feet away, but he'd gotten the Gnomon's attention. It knew who'd been tormenting it.

With a shriek it leapt after him, breaking through the shelves, shouldering them aside, and hurdling clean over them.

Looking ahead again, Sky saw the ceiling rushing toward him. He flipped off his Jumpers, but the dying thrust and momentum rammed him into the ceiling, knocking down tiles, sheets of metal, lights, and Formica.

"Shimmer, you idiot!" Errand screamed in his head as he fell toward the nets and balls of the goon stop grids trap Andrew and T-Bone had built.

Shimmer. . . . Shimmer. . . . Right! The time-space force field thingy!

Sky slapped his chest as he hit the trap, the ground knocking him senseless through the shimmering blue light that suddenly surrounded him.

Before he could stand, the Gnomon jumped on him, clawing and biting, its blows blocked by the protective nimbus of the rapidly fading Shimmer.

In frustration the Gnomon hit Sky in his stomach. Hard.

Sky flew backward and smashed into a row of action figures, which tipped and fell to the ground with a loud bang. Caps from toy guns exploded and popped like firecrackers.

The goon stop grids trap finally triggered, and nets, balls, and stuffed animals rained down from above, encasing Sky and the Gnomon in a soft and comfortably fluffy tomb.

As the nets fell from the ceiling, Sky scrambled free from the edge of the trap, emerging just as the monster hunters arrived.

"Don't shoot it!" screamed Sky.

Everyone stared at the thrashing Gnomon in silence as the store alarms blared, red lights flashed, and the sprinklers rained water upon them.

The Gnomon moaned and shrieked and cried in pitiful and horrifying tones, trying in vain to escape Crystal's well-constructed trap.

"Whatever you're planning to do, Sky, you'd better hurry," said Hands, nursing a split lip.

Sirens blared in the distance. Emergency services would arrive any minute. Sky stared at his hand, at the pale white Hunter's Mark, at the trix surrounding it with a small tear down one side dripping black blood. Last night he'd understood Vicious, the Shadow Warg. He didn't know how, but he suspected Errand did.

Whether Errand was an Edgewalker or something else, he knew how to edgewalk. He'd been there during the nightmare when Phineas had been attacked. He'd been there to put Bullet, the Shadow Warg, to sleep by the Dovetail hedge. He'd been there in the school, drinking Sky's dream blood and making him strong. And each time he appeared, the trix seemed to split wider. Each time, Errand seemed to be more powerful than before.

Sky didn't know how to put a monster to sleep, edgewalk into its dreams, and talk to it where it felt safe . . . but Errand *did*.

It was time to force Errand's hand, to see how badly he really wanted Sky to live.

Slowly Sky began to walk toward the struggling Gnomon.

Errand appeared at his side. "What're you doing, Sky?"

"I'm going to talk to that Gnomon," said Sky, trying to sound confident, when inside all he wanted to do was run.

"You mean that struggling, flailing, hideously strong monster there? The one that could easily kill you with an accidental flick of its four-fingered hand? The one that you have *no idea* how to communicate with?" said Errand.

"That's the one," said Sky without slowing his pace.

"I just wanted to be sure, " said Errand, frowning.

"I'm going to put it to sleep, edgewalk into its dreams where it feels safe, and talk to it," said Sky, "and you're going to help me."

Errand scoffed. "And why would I do that?"

"Sky," said Crystal, sounding worried, "who are you talking to?"

"You have about ten seconds to decide, Errand," said Sky.

"I don't know what you want from me," said Errand.

"Six . . . five . . ."

"Sky, what are you doing?" asked Hands. "This doesn't look like *talking*."

"Seriously," said Errand, "you need to get out of here! You can't get caught!"

"Three . . ."

"He's even more certifiable than *we are*!" Sky heard Andrew say.

"Two—"

"All right, all right!" said Errand.

Sky stopped a pace away from the Gnomon's flailing arms.

"You don't know what you're asking for," said Errand.

Sky could hear sirens approaching, getting close. "You'd better hurry," he said.

"You want this? Fine. Raise your left hand and repeat after me—*exactly* as I say," said Errand. "I am a fellow monster; I mean you no harm."

Sky raised his hand, feeling sick. "I—am a fellow—*monster*." He looked at the monster hunters, their expressions falling. "I mean you no harm."

Nothing happened. Errand busted up laughing.

"What's so funny?" asked Sky.

"You! I never thought you'd actually say it!" Errand said, laughing some more.

"What! You mean I didn't—"

Errand grabbed Sky's arm and threw him at the Gnomon.

And the world fell apart around him.

CHAPTER 20
Edgewalking

Sky's mind lurched.

Madness took hold of him as he was sucked forward and spun, like water circling a drain, his mind everywhere and nowhere at once.

He struggled for breath with no lungs, hunger with no stomach, desire with no yearning. He grew and shrank, woke and slept, cried and laughed, all carried on a wave of insanity, until he flopped to the rocks, cold and uncomprehending, and tried to remember who he was and why he was laying on rocks in a sprawling underground cavern full of faded and washed-out colors that jumped and swirled like ink in water.

He climbed to his feet, breathing in the musty cavern air. Slowly memories returned—his family, Exile, the hunt in the Redbrick Department Store, his missing uncle . . . the Gnomon.

He was inside the Gnomon's head.

Leaning over, he vomited.

"Vomit? Really? I take you out edgewalking, maybe a nice

meal afterward, and that's the thanks I get?" Errand chided, looking as shaky as Sky did. "I can't take you anywhere nice, can I?"

Sky still had his monster hunters' equipment, his clothes, and his yo-yo. "At least I didn't vomit on you," he snapped.

He hit a button on his Core chest plate, launching the Pounder hand-cannon into his palm as he crept forward.

Wading through puddles and streams and darkness, he worked his way toward a tunnel at the far end of the cavern that seemed to take them upward. He wasn't sure what good the Pounder would do here—or if the ICE would do any good without the zap it needed to freeze—but he was sure of one thing: he felt more comfortable with the Pounder than without it.

"You're still mad that I embarrassed you in front of your friends, aren't you?" said Errand.

"Embarrassed me? You made me say I was a monster! We'll be lucky if they don't freeze us while we're in here!" exclaimed Sky.

"Unlikely—they probably won't even have moved. Time doesn't really have much of a hold on *dreams*," said Errand, sounding wistful.

Sky rolled his eyes. "Look, the plan is, we find the Gnomon, talk to it while it feels all safe and warm and snuggly in his own dreams, let it know we're not enemies, find out what it knows, and then go home. After that you stop bugging me. Forever."

For a moment he thought he saw sincere pain on Errand's face, but it was gone as quickly as it had appeared.

"You want me to stop bugging you? Fine. You get us out of here and you'll never see me again," said Errand. "By the way, the Gnomon's a she, not a he."

"How can you tell? And what do you mean, if I get us out of here? Can't you just send us back when I'm done?" asked Sky. "Like you did when you pulled me into that dream at school?"

"Males are bluer. And that was your own head, stupid. Well, or mine anyway, and it wasn't really a dream, and you woke up on your own. But my point is, this is the Gnomon's dream. We don't have any power here," said Errand.

"You mean you can't summon a chair or change your hands into claws or anything? How could you do that before if you can't do it here?" asked Sky.

"You and I have a unique relationship that allows for some unique interactions. I might not be you, but that doesn't mean I'm *not* you."

"Oh. Well, that makes sense," said Sky sarcastically.

"Look, Sky. You know how this works. You read *The Edge of Oblivion*. All we have is what we brought with us and what we can find here," said Errand. "Of course, what you probably don't know is that because the Gnomon knows we're in its head, there are only three ways out: One, you convince the Gnomon to let us go. Two, we drive it insane until it doesn't know up from down."

"I'm not going to do that," said Sky. He'd come here to talk, not make things worse.

"Always the noble one," said Errand, smirking.

"What's the third option?" asked Sky.

"We die," Errand stated.

"Die?" said Sky, beginning to feel nervous. "Don't you think that's being a little melodramatic? It's just a dream!"

"You asked," Errand pointed out.

They reached the end of the tunnel. Sky glanced back at

the shifting dark. Something had followed them up from the cavern below.

"So . . . you're serious?" Sky asked. "If something catches us in here—a memory, a nightmare, the Gnomon itself . . ."

"We die," said Errand. "Or, on the bright side, it could keep us alive and just torture us for eternity."

Sky frowned. Not the brightest prospect he'd ever faced.

"Your cuddly Gnomon doesn't seem quite as cuddly anymore, does it?" said Errand, sounding smug.

With a final look over his shoulder, Sky lifted aside a stone tile above him and clambered through. He popped out behind a granite bed in a small, windowless room. A sliver of moonlight seeped through a crack in the door.

With a start he realized the room wasn't a room at all but a *mausoleum*, and the granite bed . . . It was a *coffin*. He shivered, trying to figure out why the Gnomon would have a mausoleum in her head. These places must have been significant to her in some way.

"It's her home!" Sky realized. "She lives under the graveyard. And if I'm right . . ."

He circled the coffin, letting the moonlight shine onto the characters etched in the stone.

"I was right! 'Emaline Livingstone, beloved wife, beloved mother of Andrew. May she rest in peace. Born January 7, 1-76.'" Someone had scratched out what looked like a seven in her birth date and had written a nine next to it. "Died . . . eleven years ago," finished Sky.

He bent down, noticing a place where Andrew had carved into the rock "With Love Forever, ANL."

"I was right. *Crystal* was right," said Sky, hardly able to believe it. "I think the Gnomon might really have taken them."

Silence.

"Errand?" Sky whispered.

The large stone door ground and scraped across the floor like carpenter's nails on a chalkboard as something pushed the door open.

Moonlight flooded the room.

Sky ducked down. *Pad, scrape, pad, scrape*. Knuckles and sharpened claws, four-toed feet and four-fingered hands.

"I can feeeel you in here, hhhunterrr," said hundreds of rasping out of sync voices as the Gnomon inhaled, breathing in the putrid crypt air. "Ahhhh. . . . You smell of feeeear and blooood. . . . I . . . somethiiingg is wrong. . . . Yoou are diffffer-ent. . . . You are not welcommme heeere."

Sky moved around the coffin as the Gnomon circled. He peeked out, spotting the open door. Where was Errand? Had he already run?

"But . . . tooo late. . . . You cannot essscaaape from Rauschtlot, hhhhunterrr," said Rauschtlot, pausing on the other side of the coffin.

Sky took a deep breath, getting ready to run for the door.

Suddenly Rauschtlot leapt upon the coffin, shrieking.

Sky fell back, dropping his Pounder as he saw the horror. The monster grabbed his leg. Saliva dripped from Rauschtlot's mouth. Her flesh was translucent red, like blood, and pulled tight like paper. Her eyes were large and black, pupil-less. Her fingers and toes were long and spiked with nails warping into malformed claws that, when clicked together, resembled a shovel, but when separate, resembled a quick death.

Here, in her dream, she looked even worse, more nightmarish.

Her lipless mouth opened, revealing sharp rock-eating

teeth, and on her head, where a hat normally rested, were hundreds of tiny, pulsating mouths opening and closing, opening and closing as they talked and laughed in discordant tones.

Rauschtlot shrieked from her mouths in triumph, dragging him closer . . . closer . . .

He couldn't get his body to respond. He wanted to scream, to run in terror and madness, but he couldn't.

Rauschtlot smiled, her fangs dripping . . . dripping. . . . So close . . .

"Errand! Help! I'm sorry! I want you around! Pleeease!" yelled Sky. But Errand didn't respond.

"Calling for your tamed mohhhnssssster," hissed Rauschtlot. "Not all mohhnsters are so taaame."

"I want to help you!" screamed Sky. "Please! I can help you!"

"There is nooo hellp from the niiight hhhunterrr. . . . You're sooo small . . . like . . . Nackles . . ." Rauschtlot trailed off, her eyes going distant.

When her eyes came back into focus, she seemed sadly resolute. "Rauschtlot will maaake it faaast . . . like hhhunterrr pack did for Nacklesss . . ."

"Nackles? Your—your daughter?"

Rauschtlot opened her mouth, yanking him toward her. "A merrrcccy to ssspare you frommm the niiight—"

"No, wait! Nackles is still alive! She's alive!" cried Sky desperately.

Rauschtlot hesitated. "Aliiive?"

Sky nodded furiously. "She's alive. She's just frozen! I can bring her to you!"

"A liiie. Hhhunnterrs killll. Hhhunnterrs alllwaysss killll. A mmmercy I giiive yooou . . ."

Rauschtlot's mouth opened even wider, as if she could swallow him whole.

He screamed, jerked, pulled against her.

And then he remembered. *The Tourmaline of Foresight*—the four-fingered Gnomon who would have ruled the world, but for the lack of thumbs.

The thumbs!

For millennia hunters survived not because of greater wit or strength than monsters, but because of one little digit that allowed them to create and *hold* weapons and tools—the opposable thumb!

Instead of pulling against her, he rotated inward, breaking her thumbless grip and catching her by surprise.

He dove, and came up with the Pounder cannon. "Don't make me do this!"

Rauschtlot leapt at him, and he fired. A globe of jellylike liquid launched from the tip, the force propelling him backward, toward the open door.

His shot went wide, and the freezing ICE goo—made of nasty stuff monsters didn't like—caught Rauschtlot in the leg, knocking her from the coffin. She writhed on the ground shrieking as her leg smoked.

He caught movement out of the corner of his eye. Errand popping his head out of the hole Sky had climbed through earlier.

"Sky! Lead her away!" yelled Errand.

"What? Are you CRAZY?" yelled Sky.

"Just do it!" yelled Errand, disappearing back down the hole as Rauschtlot regained her feet, howling in rage.

Sky turned and ran.

The night sky was bright with stars, and a blood-red full

moon shone down on the bent trees and cracked headstones like the eye of some behemoth, as he shot out of Emaline Livingstone's mausoleum into the murky red light.

He dodged a broken gargoyle and jumped a fallen branch, heading northwest toward the manor. Rauschtlot shrieked behind him. He crossed a small stream, stumbling in the current.

Rauschtlot shrieked again, closer, gaining.

"This was such a bad idea," he mumbled to himself. He crossed a trail, pausing to get his bearings. A thin mist hung low near the ground.

"Mist. *Mist*!" Sky screeched, a way out coming to him in a flash.

He turned, just as Rauschtlot loped into view. She bit at the air as she charged, hundreds of teeth clacking in the night.

Reaching up, he slapped his chest and held his breath as rancid, sulfuric Fog billowed out of his cloak, exiting the Cheez Whiz canisters where it was stored. This wasn't fog. This was *Fog*, a concoction of the monster hunters meant to utterly blind the senses of everything within it while the hunters fled.

Rauschtlot charged, raking with her claws.

Sky stepped to the side at the last moment, and Rauschtlot ran past, blinded by the Fog. But as she passed, she caught him with a flailing arm, sending him to the ground. He rolled, and then came to his feet. On shaky legs he ran back toward the mausoleum, shutting off the Fog as he went.

He sprinted across the uneven ground, his robes bogged down with water from the stream.

As the mausoleum came into sight, he thought about all the many torturous things he was going to do to Errand if he ever got out of this.

And then something stepped out of the mausoleum. He stopped in his tracks. . . . It was another Gnomon! This Gnomon was smaller than Rauschtlot, about half as tall, and it looked familiar.

Errand stepped out from behind the Gnomon, smiling.

"I talked her into coming up for a look around," said Errand.

"Is that . . . *Nackles*?" asked Sky, bewildered.

"Don't get too excited. Nackles is still a Gnomon Popsicle back at the monster hunters' secret lair, courtesy of your hunter friends. This one's just a memory, but she may be enough to get us out of here," said Errand.

"You're going to drive her insane," said Sky, realizing what Errand was planning, "You're going to threaten her daughter."

"I'm going to ask her politely to let us go," said Errand. "If she interprets more than that, it's her business."

Nackles dove for the door, and Errand wrestled her back.

"I'm not going to let you hurt her," said Sky, stepping forward.

Before Errand could respond, Rauschtlot loped into view, slowing when she spotted them.

Nackles stopped fighting.

"Mmmmotherrr."

"Nnnacklesss," said Rauschtlot, holding out her arms, her face full of longing and forgotten pain. Nackles tried to run to her mother, but Errand held her tight. Rauschtlot's arms slowly dropped.

"We want out of here," said Errand. "You let us out, you get your daughter. You don't, and I put her back where I found her, but maybe not in the same *condition*."

Sky frowned at Errand. "We need her trust, Errand—not her rancor."

"We tried it your way, Sky," said Errand. "It's my turn."

"You invaaade my dreeeamsss, edgewalkers," said Rauschtlot, looking back and forth between him and Errand. "Yooou have no powerrr heeere."

"Just because we can edgewalk doesn't mean we're Edgewalkers. You know what we are," said Errand. "Are you sure you want to bet that we don't have power here?"

Rauschtlot hissed, turning to Sky. "You promisssed. . . . You promisssed to help meee."

Sky frowned. "I did promise her, Errand. Give her Nackles. She'll let us go. Won't you, Rauschtlot?"

Rauschtlot bobbed up and down energetically.

"See?" said Sky.

Errand shook his head. "You're naïve, Sky. You don't know the first thing about monsters. You give her Nackles, and she'll kill us both." Errand turned back to Rauschtlot. "Isn't that right, Rauschtlot?"

Rauschtlot didn't say anything.

"She's too afraid. She can't let us go. If her master finds out, she'll find Nackles and kill her while Rauschtlot watches, and then she'll torture and kill Rauschtlot for good measure," said Errand.

"What do you mean, if her master finds out? Who's her master?" said Sky.

"Sheee will find the keysss before you. Sheee will uuuse them to freee the niiight. All will diiie."

"Her master is Ambrosia," said Errand.

"Ambrosia! She's the Whisper that attacked Phineas!" Sky exclaimed.

Errand nodded. "I know. I showed you that, remember?"

"The niiight will take what is hisss," hissed Rauschtlot, "jussst as you took what is oursss."

"The Night? You mean the Arkhon, don't you? Look, you don't have to help Ambrosia," said Sky. "I'm going to stop her. I can get your child back for you—your *real* child. Crystal and Andrew didn't know what they were doing when they took her. Just let us go and promise not to hurt anyone! I'll make sure nobody hunts you. We can do an exchange. What *they* took for what *you* took."

Rauschtlot stared at Sky, and the moment seemed to drag.

"I'm right, aren't I?"

Rauschtlot hissed.

"Errand, give her Nackles," said Sky.

"Bad idea."

"Just do it, okay?"

Errand sighed and let Nackles go. She ran to her mother and hugged her.

"I have a plan to stop the Arkhon in case I can't find the keys and the prison opens, but I need your help. Can I count on you?" said Sky.

Rauschtlot hugged Nackles, and then nodded.

"Good. I'll keep my promise," said Sky. "I need you to keep yours."

CHAPTER 21
The Wisdom of Ignorance

Help me take this off her," said Sky as he struggled with the net. "She's promised not to hurt anybody."

Sirens blared in front of the store, and Sky heard a door slam open back in the warehouse—Hands's dad on the move.

The monster hunters stared at Sky. He didn't know what he'd looked like while he'd been gone, or how much time had passed, but he guessed it couldn't have been more than a few seconds, by the look of things.

He reached for his pocket watch before he remembered that Crenshaw had it. He glanced at his hand, noting the black blood dripping from his trix.

"Please. I know this looks bad—," started Sky.

"Looks?" growled T-Bone.

Hands edged past T-Bone and started helping with the net. Crystal followed and grabbed a different corner. Andrew gave a shrug and began throwing bouncing balls out of the way.

T-Bone looked around, and then turned and walked off.

For a moment Sky feared T-Bone had left them to their fates, but then Sky heard a crashing sound as T-Bone pushed over a shelf in electronics, drawing attention away from them.

Sky stepped next to Crystal to help with the net. "Thank you," he muttered, not sure what else to say.

"As soon as we free this monster, it's *over,* Sky. You're on your own," replied Crystal without looking at him.

"Her name's Rauschtlot," said Sky, but Crystal had already moved off.

He threw the last of the net off and stood back.

Rauschtlot crawled to her feet, her flesh still red and dangerous. She looked at each of them, her face unreadable.

"Keep your promissse," hissed Rauschtlot.

And then she leapt twenty feet into the air, through a glass window in the ceiling, her red flesh rippling to black as she vanished into the night.

"Those hisses and pops. It almost sounded like it was trying to speak," said Andrew, watching Rauschtlot disappear.

Sky glanced at Andrew. Was he being serious? Of course she'd just spoken!

"My dad is going to kill me," said Hands, shaking his head as he looked around at the mess they'd made.

"Only if he finds out it was you," said Andrew.

"Good point," said Hands. He stepped forward, hit his Jumpers, the oversize whipped cream canisters shot out some steam, and he sailed through the same window as Rauschtlot. Andrew followed a moment later.

Crystal stepped under the window. "I went out on a limb

for you tonight, Sky. I trusted you. If that monster harms anyone . . ."

"You can still trust me," said Sky. "She won't hurt anyone."

Crystal stared at him for a moment, and then shook her head. "We'll need that equipment back, so . . . be careful on the jump out."

He felt like she'd just slugged him in the gut. No, it was worse than that. Not even Crenshaw's punch measured up to this. He'd never officially joined the monster hunters, and now she was kicking him out for good.

"All right," said Sky, choking on the words.

Crystal gave him one last glance and then jumped through the window in the ceiling.

He stepped forward and hit his chest so he could follow . . .

Nothing happened.

He hit it again.

Still nothing.

"Great," said Sky. "Apparently you're just supposed to *tap* the Jumpers, not hold the button. Would've been good to know, eh, Errand? . . . Errand?"

Errand didn't answer.

"Errand, I'm sorry," said Sky. "I was just mad. You don't have to go away and stop bugging me. . . . Errand?"

Just then Sky heard glass break. He turned in time to see T-Bone leaping through a different ceiling window near the front of the store. A dozen flashlight beams from police officers swiveled, the light reflecting off the bits of falling glass, but the lights were too slow to spot T-Bone.

Sky was on his own and out of juice.

"Great."

Retracting his Pounder hand-cannon, he crept out of the

toy aisle and began working his way toward the back of the store, hoping he could slip out unnoticed.

Beams of light slid up and down the aisles as policemen patrolled. He dodged in and out of the shadows, narrowly avoiding detection.

Ahead he spotted the door that led to the warehouse and headed toward it, ducking behind a display of two-liter bottles of Coke as a patrolman passed by. He waited, holding his breath.

One . . .

Two . . .

As he began to step out, a light illuminated him from behind.

"Freeze!" yelled the officer. "Hands in the air where I can see them!"

Standing, Sky slowly turned around.

The officer was still several yards away, holding a flashlight in one hand and a Taser in the other.

"You're just a kid," said the officer as he caught a glimpse of Sky's darkened features beneath his hood. "Who are you?"

Sky rolled his eyes. He was really getting tired of that question.

"I'm your worst nightmare," said Sky, trying to make his voice sound deep and intimidating as he spit out the clichéd line that had appeared in every cop show, war movie, and adventure flick since 1982.

The officer drew back in surprise.

Sky dove to the ground, letting out a stream of billowing, sulfurous Fog.

The officer fired!

The Taser prongs missed Sky by inches, sticking into a

two-liter bottle of Coke, which promptly exploded, sending fountains of sugary unnatural flavor into the air. Sky put his shoulder against the display and sent it tumbling, scattering exploding Coke bottles everywhere.

And then he ran for it.

The store erupted in shouting voices and pounding feet. He sprang across an intersecting row and spotted Hands's dad staring at him in surprise, his eyes flashing in a way that made Sky every bit as frightened as when he'd faced the Gnomon, and then he was through the double doors.

"Lousy thief!" yelled Hands's dad. "I don't care if he is a boy! Shoot him!"

Sky wove his way between the pallets in the warehouse. He could hear the cops gaining on him, but he was almost to the back door now, moving faster and faster as escape beckoned him onward.

But even as he neared the door, and escape seemed inevitable, a shadow rose from a pallet of breakfast cereals to his right, and tackled him.

He wrestled the shadow, flailing and biting, but before he knew it, he was on his stomach, his hands wrenched painfully behind him, someone's knee pressed into his back. His hood dropped, and the shadow froze.

"Sky?" said Sheriff Beau.

"This isn't what it looks like, Sheriff," said Sky, struggling for breath. He decided to take a chance. "There was a monster."

The Sheriff was silent for a moment, and then . . . "Shhh," said Sheriff Beau. "Wait here."

The sheriff moved up the aisle, and Sky sat up, rubbing his wrist.

"Perp spotted heading east through canned goods.

All units report. Beau out," said Sheriff Beau into his walkie-talkie.

Sky watched as the flashlights that had been heading toward them suddenly turned and ran off to the east.

"Let's go," said Sheriff Beau, grabbing him by the arm and dragging him toward the back door.

As they popped through, the sheriff held him with one hand and pulled out a cell phone with the other. He began texting.

"Who are you texting?" asked Sky.

The sheriff finished and returned the phone to his pocket, ignoring Sky's question.

Sky glanced at the moon. It must have been past midnight.

"That was stupid, Sky. Very, very stupid."

"What was I supposed to do? Sit around and wait for the Arkhon to break free and kill everyone in town?"

The sheriff glanced at him.

"The Arkhon? And he was in there, was he? That's why you destroyed Vance Silverthorn's store?" said Sheriff Beau.

"Well, not him personally," said Sky.

The sheriff sighed. "Get in."

He motioned Sky toward the passenger door of his Blazer. Sky scrambled in, and the sheriff threw a big duffel bag at him. "Put that stuff in the bag. You look ridiculous."

Sheriff Beau started up the Blazer while Sky pulled off his robes and gear and shoved them into the bag.

The sheriff watched Sky for a moment, his eyes going wide as he saw the Pounder hand-cannon; the Core shoulder pads with all their buttons, wires, and rods that controlled everything; and the various containers of Fog (Cheez Whiz canisters), ICE (smashed ice cream buckets), and Jumper propellant (whipped topping cans).

"Where did you get that?"

"Er, I made it," said Sky, trying to cover for Crystal and the others. Even if they'd written him off, he wouldn't do the same to them.

"Sky, there aren't a lot of kids running around in black robes and cloaks these days, and there are even fewer capable of making equipment like *that*," said Sheriff Beau.

"But—"

"Don't worry," reassured the sheriff. "Your secret's safe with me. I know what it means to Phineas, and I won't mess up what he's done."

What he's done? And how did he know Phineas? This morning he'd tried to arrest Sky for breaking into Phineas's truck. Now he admitted that he knew him?

"You're a hunter, aren't you?" said Sky.

Sheriff Beau shook his head. "Don't call me that." He sounded almost angry.

"Why not?" asked Sky.

"There's no such thing as monsters," said Sheriff Beau.

Sky rolled his eyes. "I think it's a bit late for that. Denying they exist doesn't make them go away. My parents have been doing that most of my life—telling me it was just my imagination or the shadows. You can see how well it worked on me," said Sky. "Crystal came to you. She asked for your help! How could you just deny everything like that?"

"Sort of like what T-Bone did to Ren, you mean?" Sheriff Beau quipped. "Trust me. Crystal didn't come to me for help with monsters. The girl doesn't need it."

"What, then?" asked Sky. Crystal and Sheriff Beau had obviously talked, but why would she have gone to him if not for help with monsters?

"You'd have to ask her," said the Sheriff, skirting the issue. "But it near broke my heart watching Ren go through that."

"So why didn't you do something?" Sky demanded.

"What makes you think I didn't?" said Sheriff Beau. "Sky, sometimes the best thing you can do for a person is keep them ignorant. Ignorance is the gift the hunters have given the world for centuries. Can you imagine the reaction if people knew what was out there? It'd be the Dark Ages all over again!"

Sky remembered his own struggles with it—not believing in monsters, thinking that Phineas had pulled one over on him, promising to make his *gullible nephew* a hunter. But last night everything had changed.

Just as it must've changed for Ren when he'd fought the Gloom. And then to have everyone deny it . . .

"Now, you want to tell me what you were doing in that store and why I shouldn't take you straight to jail?" said Sheriff Beau.

"There was a monster," said Sky. "A Gnomon."

Sheriff Beau raised an eyebrow.

"I was trying to—er—*talk* to it," said Sky.

"I'll bet that was an interesting conversation," said Sheriff Beau.

"Very," said Sky.

The sheriff sighed and shook his head. "Sky, I owe Phineas a debt, and I mean to pay it, but you've got to stop putting yourself in danger like this. I might not be there next time, not to mention that the next time you might have more to worry about than just monsters and police."

"What? You mean Malvidia? The hunters?" Sky scoffed. "It sounds like they've already got it in for me! Mom thinks the only reason Malvidia let us come back to Exile in the first place was to lure in Phineas!"

"She told you that? Your mom?" prodded Sheriff Beau.

"Well . . . not directly, per se," Sky hedged, "but she did say it."

Sheriff Beau gave him a hard stare, and then shrugged. "Maybe she did. Everyone's got their reasons. Doesn't make them right, but there they are all the same."

Sky pondered the sheriff's aphorism—and couldn't understand a word of it. Absolute gibberish.

"Malvidia's relationship with your uncle was . . . uh . . . *complicated*," Sheriff Beau continued, smiling awkwardly. "It's hard to say what she really wants."

Sky didn't even want to think about what the sheriff was implying. He couldn't imagine Phineas being romantically involved with anyone, let alone a woman with a name like Malvidia.

"Well, she sounds horrible," said Sky.

"Trying to second-guess Malvidia won't get you anywhere," said Sheriff Beau. "Like it or not, she leads the few hunters that remain. She was the only hunter willing and strong enough to take over when your uncle fled."

"*Uncle Phineas* was head of the hunters?" Sky asked incredulously. "We're talking about Phineas T. Pimiscule, right? Drives a beat-up truck? Thinks long walks on the beach are best done *alone*?"

"That's him," said Sheriff Beau, smiling. "Ever the mysterious Hunter of Legend."

Sky's jaw dropped open. Hunter of Legend? Uncle Phineas?

"Best man I ever met," Sheriff Beau continued. "Just wish more hunters had thought so. Maybe he wouldn't be missing if they had."

"Wait a minute. Bat was supposedly a Hunter of Legend!"

Sky blurted, suddenly suspicious. "You think hunters were behind the attack?"

"You know Bat?" asked Sheriff Beau, looking confused. "Why would you think hunters were behind the attack? I saw blood by the truck, but—"

Right. Sheriff Beau didn't know.

"You're just going to have to believe me on this," Sky rushed. "Bat isn't who he says he is! He's a—"

"Get down!" Sheriff Beau cut in.

Up ahead Sky spotted a police barricade. He jumped into the backseat, dragging his bag with him.

"Any news?" asked the sheriff out the window as they rolled to a stop. The policeman shone his light around the car, forcing Sky to duck lower.

"Nope. Units are still inside. Larry says he saw some kid in a costume," said the officer.

"Kid in a costume?" said Sheriff Beau. "Sounds like Larry's been at the sauce again."

The officer laughed. "Maybe, maybe. But in this town nothin' would surprise me. The boys'll have a go at him over this, I can promise you that!"

"How'd Vance take it all?" asked Sheriff Beau.

"Not well," said the officer. "He's calling for a full investigation. Says he's going to get that wife of his involved—the *councilwoman*."

"That figures. Once Rachel's involved, we'll never get a rest," said Sheriff Beau.

"Wouldn't surprise me if it was that kid of theirs behind it all—lot of money, no supervision except for Osmer, who's not even around no more. I heard they shipped him off to an old folks home, and not even a nice one either. Sent him to that old place over on Riding and First, the place we nearly shut down last year because of rats. Bunch of wolves run the place if you ask me. Kid practically went ballistic when he found out about it. I just don't get it. All the money in the world, and you send your dad to a place like that. How much do you have to hate someone to do that kind of thing to 'em?"

"Everyone's got their reasons. Doesn't make them right, but there they are all the same," said Sheriff Beau.

Sky rolled his eyes. Absolute *gibberish*!

"Yeah. I guess you'd know that better than anyone, eh, Beau?" said the officer.

The sheriff grunted.

"I know vandalism ain't right, but if you ask me, old Vance had it coming—the way he treats that boy of his," said the officer, shaking his head. "Well, I'd best not keep you."

"Let me know if you find anything, Killjoy," said Sheriff Beau.

"Will do," said Officer Killjoy, and he waved them through.

CHAPTER 22

Shift-less

Sky waited until the flashing lights disappeared, and then he hopped back into the front seat. He didn't want to think about what Officer Killjoy had said about Hands and his family. Sky hoped Hands got away okay.

"Your uncle's notes are in the glove box," said the sheriff. "You should know that hunter's journals are private. It's considered bad etiquette to read one without permission unless the hunter is dead and gone, and then it usually passes to their next living relative. It's a hunter's obligation to make sure it does."

"So you didn't read it?" asked Sky, surprised, as he pulled the notes out of the glove box.

"Nope. You shouldn't either," said the Sheriff.

Sky looked up guiltily from the journal pages and shoved them into his pocket. He didn't think Phineas would mind, but he could wait until later when the sheriff wasn't around. Besides, he'd already read the important bits anyway.

"Of course, I know you'll look. You wouldn't be related to Phineas if you didn't. The man cheats at everything," said Sheriff Beau, smiling.

Sky inhaled. Could he really trust Sheriff Beau? The sheriff denied he was a hunter, but, then, who had he texted after he'd caught Sky? Not the police, certainly. Could it have been Malvidia? And if Sheriff Beau was working with the hunters, how much could Sky really tell him?

"Sheriff, I saw Phineas get attacked. Don't ask me how!" Sky spluttered before Sherriff Beau could open his mouth. "I just did. Bat isn't who he says he is. He's a Wargarou."

"That's quite an accusation, Sky. You can't just walk up to a Hunter of Legend and accuse him of being a monster. You're going to have to give me more than that." Sheriff Beau stared at him, waiting.

Sky ground his teeth. Puzzles. He definitely preferred puzzles.

"Look, I was edgewalking, okay."

"Edgewalking!"

"And I saw Ambrosia and Bat—"

"Did you say *Ambrosia*?" growled Sheriff Beau.

"Er, that's right," said Sky, beginning to feel frightened. "You know her, I take it?"

"Hmpf. You could say that," said Sheriff Beau, his voice even. "She was my sister-in-law."

Sky's mouth fell open. And then he remembered. He'd heard Beau's name before. And each time he'd heard it, he'd heard another name as well—*Ursula*.

"You married a Whisper?" Sky blurted before he could stop himself.

Beau smiled wryly. "So, you know about Whisper, you know about the Arkhon . . . Is there anything you *don't* know?"

"I don't know the atomic weight of boron," said Sky, trying to be funny.

"It's 10.81," said Beau without hesitating.

Sky's smile dropped.

"I was a metallurgy teacher," Beau explained, "taught hunters at Arkhon Academy before they all died. Boron's a nonmetal and not the most useful substance unless you want to bleach a monster's shirt. But a deficiency can keep some of the botanic monsters in check."

"Botany? Great," said Sky.

"That's what you get for talking to the former husband of the botany teacher," said Beau, a smile touching his lips, before melting away like a solitary snowflake at two degrees above freezing.

Ursula had been a monster, posing as a hunter, posing as a botany teacher! That was messed up!

"So . . . are you a . . . er . . . ," Sky stumbled, not quite sure how to say it.

Beau looked at him, brows creased, and then he understood. "A monster? A Whisper? No. Definitely not," said Beau. "But I almost wish I were. Maybe then she would've stayed."

Sky stared at the floor. The conversation had suddenly taken a rather uncomfortable turn.

"We loved each other, you know," said Beau, his eyes somewhere else. "We thought we'd have children together, grow old together, but when the hunters found out what she was . . ." Beau shook his head. "Phineas saved us that day, but we were outcasts. Ursula promised we could weather it, and then one day . . . she was gone. I looked everywhere for her. Even more than fourteen years later, I still look. Each time a shadow falls, each time someone I don't know smiles at me . . ."

Beau glanced at Sky, as if suddenly remembering he was there.

Sky grinned nervously. This was beyond him. Why Ursula had left, why she was back, but not telling—why Beau was telling him any of this at all!

"So, er," Sky muttered, trying to think of what Hannah would say at a moment like this. "*Ursula*. . . . Pretty name, huh?"

Man, he was lame! Taking inspiration from Hannah of all people! He definitely needed more role models in his life.

Beau smirked. "I suppose."

The sheriff pulled off to the side of the road a few houses up from Sky's. There weren't any lights on. Had they forgotten he was out? He really hoped so.

"Sky, I'm not a hunter anymore," said Beau solemnly. "Even when I was, I couldn't take on a Wargarou, let alone my deranged sister-in-law. Whisper by themselves aren't so bad, but give them a piece of something powerful, like a Wargarou, and watch out. If Bat really is a Wargarou like you say, Malvidia is the only one in town besides your uncle who can do something about it. But without solid proof . . ."

"She won't," said Sky bitterly, "especially to save Phineas."

Beau nodded. "I'll tell Malvidia, but don't get your hopes up. She's got her hands full with the Arkhon right now. But if you find anything I can take to her, or if you get in trouble, find me. Wargarou or not, I'll do what I can."

"Thanks," said Sky, trying to hide his disappointment. He knew the hunters didn't like Phineas, for whatever reason, but he thought for sure they'd do something about a child-eating monster hiding among them. Even without proof, it seemed like something worth looking into.

"You know, there aren't a lot of hunters who'd face down a Gnomon," said Beau. "Especially not to talk to it. Phineas would be proud."

Sky stared out the window, not sure what would come out of his mouth if he tried to speak.

He grabbed his bag of gear from the backseat and began to open the door, when a thought occurred to him. "Sheriff Beau . . ."

"Hmm?"

"The Arkhon is a shifter, right?" asked Sky, remembering the detail from Phineas's notes on Whisper.

Beau nodded.

"Is he bound to the moon like Whisper and Wargarou?" asked Sky.

"Are you wondering if he has weaknesses?" asked Beau.

"Sort of," said Sky.

"Then, the answer is no," said Beau. "The Arkhon is the father or grandfather of nearly all shifters—even the Whisper. He cursed his children, and *their* children, with weaknesses, but he doesn't have them himself."

"What about when he takes their forms?" asked Sky, but Beau was already shaking his head.

"I know what you're thinking, Sky," said Beau, "but it doesn't work—not well, anyway. The moment you exploit a weakness, he changes. Listen, the Arkhon once attacked a hunter stronghold in Bedlam Falls. He approached as a Darkhorn, attacking at twilight, when the Darkhorn's lances start their mesmerizing stirring. By the time the hunters had tracked down enough dog hairs to make a net, he'd shifted to a Harrow Knight and bloodied half the town. If not for a few lucky tricks and some foxglove to speed up the Arkhon's heart rate and oxidize the copper skin, the Arkhon would've destroyed the other half."

Sky absorbed this. "But by weakening his own children, he's weakened himself, right? I mean, so long as he shifts into one of their forms, he's got their weaknesses."

Beau nodded.

"That's one of the reasons why the manor prison is so important. Whatever his form, as long as he is within the prison walls, whether the prison's active or not, he can't shift. He's stuck as that monster until he crosses those walls," said Sheriff Beau.

"Wait. Whatever his form? You mean you don't even know what he looks like? How do you know he's even in there?" asked Sky, flabbergasted.

"Because Phineas said he was," said Beau. "Trust me, with the hunters dead, if the Arkhon were out, you'd know it. The whole *world* would know it."

Sky thought about this. "The Arkhon has to have a weakness," he said. "How else could they have trapped him?"

Beau shrugged. "No idea. Nobody understands that prison except for Phineas and Nikola. The wall, the manor, the keys—Phineas claimed they had to 'bottle the moon' to make it work."

Sky started to laugh—and then it hit him . . . Bottle the moon?

Had Phineas really given him a clue about the keys last night? And not just a clue—a key itself!

He reached into his pocket and pulled out the poem he'd kept from the journal pages he'd given the sheriff.

ENOF OD NABA BAN DO FONE

One key to set the time,
Two to see it right,
Three keys you wouldn't suspect,
To lock the prison tight.
Two, you wouldn't find
Without looking.
One you wouldn't find
Without watching. . . .

It was so simple! The answer had been right in front of him the whole time! One key to set the time . . . the key you wouldn't find without *watching*! His pocket watch ran by the phases of the moon, and Phineas had claimed that Solomon Rose had thought it worked the other way around, that the moon ran by the watch!

His pocket watch was one of the keys!

"What's that?" asked Sheriff Beau, looking at the wilted paper containing the poem.

"I . . . er . . . just remembered I have some homework due tomorrow," said Sky, shoving the paper back into his pocket.

Sheriff Beau nodded slowly, obviously not believing a word of it.

"Sheriff," said Sky, pausing, "I have a feeling tomorrow's going to be a busy night. If you've got any extra boron lying around, you might want to get it out. I think some monsters might need their shirts bleached."

Sheriff Beau stared at Sky for a moment, and then nodded. "With a criminal mind like yours, I'm bound to believe it. Best take care of yourself."

"You too. And thanks—you know, for not arresting me and stuff."

"Don't know what you're talking about," said Sheriff Beau, smiling.

A moment later the Blazer turned around and disappeared up the street.

Sky watched it go and then turned back toward his house, lugging his bag of gear. Even though Mom had let him go with Crystal to his "study group," he should have been home hours ago—especially since he was double grounded. As he walked, he wondered what crazy punishments Mom would come up with to top double grounding.

Unfortunately, he collapsed two steps later, never to find out.

CHAPTER 23

Taken

Sky stood and rubbed his head, feeling disoriented. What had happened to the sidewalk?

To his left he found bookshelves. To his right he found . . . nothing. The edges of the room just seemed to fade away like a memory he couldn't quite remember. Faint light slipped through the room's edges, casting the bookshelves in shadow.

"Next time could you give me a warning?" said Sky to the darkness. "Come on, Errand. I know it's you. I'm edgewalking again, right?"

Lightning flashed somewhere, painting the books around him in swirling colors. The room was circular, like a giant wheel with bookshelves running lengthwise toward the center of the room like spokes. Setting down his bag of gear somewhat reluctantly, Sky made his way along an aisle toward the center of the room.

He heard fighting somewhere far away, and thunder shook

the room like an earthquake every few minutes. But above the fighting and shaking, closer still, a baby cried.

"Errand, you're really freaking me out here."

At the inner edge of the bookshelves, near the center of the sizeable room, the floor sloped slightly downward, like a shallow bowl, and as he stepped out from behind the bookshelves, he noticed a giant pendulum hanging from a colored-glass dome several stories up. The pendulum swayed back and forth unnaturally, like the hand of a giant clock, leaping randomly each time it reached its outward peak, sometimes jumping a few inches forward, sometimes jumping several feet backward, but always unpredictable.

Lightning flashed through the colored-glass dome high above, and the room came alive with reds, blues, greens, and purples, lighting up almost a dozen hideous monsters lying around the edges of the pendulum's arc.

Sky leaped back behind the bookshelves, but the monsters didn't notice him. They were too busy being dead.

Sky exhaled slowly, feeling greatly relieved. And then he noticed a man standing near the center of the pendulum's bowl, looking quite unconcerned about the massive pendulum swinging unpredictably around him. The man wore a monocle on his eye, strangely similar to Phineas's, but whiter. He was clean-shaven, with cropped hair, and he wore black slacks, a white dress shirt unbuttoned at the top, and a long black trench coat that seemed entirely out of place with his other attire.

Strangest of all—stranger than the monocle, or the pendulum, or the dead monsters—was that in his arms he held a small, screaming black-haired infant.

"Shh," said the man, trying to calm the crying child. "It's all right. No more monsters. Phineas will be back soon. Just needs to make sure the prey is snared. Won't be gone long at all. Then we'll slip away."

The man glanced into the darkness, looking worried despite his assurances.

Sky glanced too, wondering what was going on. What was Phineas doing here? Who was the baby? Was this happening now, like when he saw Phineas attacked, or was he just wandering someone's dreams, like he had with the Gnomon. Sky wanted to step out and ask the man where he was, but if he was running around in someone's head, and they figured out he was there, he could die. He glanced nervously back at his bag of gear near the wall of darkness at the end of the aisle. He really wished he had it on.

"We won't let anything hurt you," the man continued, "not monsters, not hunters, not the Arkhon himself, no matter how badly he wants you. You just have to be here a little longer, just long enough to lure him in. Then we'll slip away and you'll be . . . well, not really safe, but, well, less *unsafe* anyway."

Sky balked. They were using the baby as bait for the Arkhon? Who would do such a thing? How could Phineas be involved with people who would do something like that? The Arkhon was locked up, which meant this probably wasn't happening in the present. A dream, then?

"You'll grow up with my son and the others," promised the man. "Even if we all have to leave this place, and we'll teach you how a hunter *should* act. All of us, we'll start aga—"

The man suddenly stopped, his eyes lifting.

From the corner of his eye, Sky saw a shadow slip forward, disappear like vapor, and then reappear behind the man.

"NO!" Sky screamed, but his voice echoed hollowly in the vast library.

The shadow raised his hand, and a silvery ring with a white Dovetail thorn on the end glittered in a lightning flash, driving into the man's neck.

The man slumped forward, and the shadow, clutching man and baby, laid them on the floor, the pendulum missing them by inches.

Sky rose from his hiding place as, with cruel efficiency, the shadowy man crossed the room and retrieved *another* infant from the shadows, laying him next to the first. The man watched the pendulum for a moment, his head bobbing as if counting, and then he adjusted the position of both children and dragged the guardian out of the way just as the pendulum swung past. He took the monocle from the guardian's eye before returning to the infants.

"What are you doing?" said Sky, his voice trembling, a horrible feeling coming over him.

The shadow didn't respond.

"I said, *what are you doing*?" Sky bellowed, dodging the swinging pendulum as he marched forward, determined to stop the man.

And then, as he got closer, Sky noticed something on the infants' palms. The first infant had the Hunter's Mark. The second infant, pulled from the shadows, had the trix.

Sky's mouth fell open.

From a small leather case the shadowy man withdrew a gnarled black claw and held it over the first infant.

"NO!" Sky screamed. He grabbed the shadowy man's shoulder, tugging at it, trying to drag him backward, but the man didn't even seem to notice. Letting go, Sky kicked him in the back; the man didn't sway, not even a bit. It was like kicking a rock.

The man pricked the Hunter's Mark, which promptly began to bleed faint white light and the child began screaming anew.

Returning the claw to his case, he picked up the white monocle, pressed the sides, moved a knob, and tapped top and then bottom. A tiny white needle suddenly popped out.

Sky paced, helpless to do anything.

Using the monocle needle, the man pricked the second infant's trix, which began to writhe and split open, trickling black blood, and darkness. The infant woke up and began screaming like the first.

The man tossed the monocle to the side and reached for both infants' hands.

A rope slipped around his neck.

Sky looked up, shocked.

The guardian jerked on the rope and dragged the man away from the children. "I won't let you hurt him!"

The man disappeared in a wisp of shadow, reappearing behind the guardian. But the guardian turned, and a long rusty metal knife, flecked with bits of silver, green, and gold, slid into his hand from his coat sleeve.

The shadow dodged the knife, coming in close. He punched the guardian in the stomach. The guardian swung again with the knife, and the shadowy man disappeared in a wisp and then reappeared in the same spot a second later, with another punch.

The two fought on, elbowing and punching, kneeing and stabbing, but it was obvious, even to Sky, that the guardian was outclassed and still woozy from the Dovetail.

Sky watched the fight nervously, glancing at the infants, both now screaming, the pendulum somehow missing them with each swing.

Just when Sky thought it was over, the guardian stepped to the side, and the pendulum swept past, blindsiding the shadowy man. He flew clear out of the bowl and slammed into a bookshelf, and then slumped to the ground.

The guardian, much more battered than he'd been moments before, twitched his shoulder, and the knife shot back up his sleeve. He retrieved his monocle and returned it to his eye as he crossed to the two infants.

"You have to let me finish it, Nikola," called the man from the bookshelves.

The guardian—Nikola—spun around.

"You must allow me to complete the process," the man continued, "or the Eye of Legend will kill them both."

"Who are you?" asked Nikola, looking wary. "Are you the Arkhon?"

"I never had the ambition," said the man, "and I'm no one of consequence. If you don't want the Arkhon to steal that Hunter's Mark and kill the boy, you'd best step aside."

Nikola's eyes flicked to the children and back. And in that moment the man slipped into shadow again, reappearing next to the children.

"NO!" screamed Nikola.

The shadowy man closed his eyes and pressed the infants' hands together, cupping them tightly in his own. The man's hands began to shake and tremble and shift from black to white and back again, throbbing and glowing as if he held a thunderstorm.

Nikola grabbed the man's hands to free the children.

The man's eyes shot open. "No!" His fingers parted just a fraction.

A stream of blinding white light shot out, flowing into the

monocle on Nikola's eye. The white stream suddenly shifted to black and veered away from Nikola, who fell to the ground, his eyes wide and staring, the white monocle smoking.

The ground shook. Books toppled from the shelves. Lightning crashed into the dome above again and again. The black stream plowed into the pendulum and its leaping, erratic swings lessened.

The man forced his fingers together, cutting off the stream. There was a bright flash, followed by total darkness.

When Sky's eyes adjusted, he saw a shadow slip out of the bowl, through the bookshelves, and into the darkness beyond. The man had fled and apparently taken one of the infants. The other, the black-haired boy the guardian had been protecting, lay screaming a few steps away.

The pendulum slowed. It didn't swing as strong or as far, and grew minutely weaker with each passing moment.

Sky crossed to Nikola, who stared at the ceiling and blinked on occasion but otherwise didn't move. As Sky hovered over him, Nikola smiled, and Sky had the eerie impression that he was smiling at him.

The sounds of fighting moved closer. A moment later Uncle Phineas burst into the room. His uncle was limping, covered in cuts and blood.

"HOLD THE DOOR!" Phineas bellowed. When he reached the edge of the bowl, Phineas took in the atmosphere with a glance. "Em, get in here! Your husband's down!"

Phineas ran for the screaming child.

A woman ran in. She wore a dark coat, like her husband, and her hair was long and as black as coal. She dropped beside Nikola, checking his pulse and looking for wounds, but Sky knew she wouldn't find any. "What's happened?"

Phineas scooped up the baby. "Shhh. It's okay. . . . It's all right now. . . . Shhh," Phineas comforted.

"Phineas!" Em barked, looking like she was on the verge of tears. *"What happened?"*

"I—," Phineas started, but his words cut off abruptly. He was staring at something—something on the child's hand. Sky moved around to get a better look.

And then he saw it too. A bleeding black trix. And within it a bleeding white Hunter's Mark. The Hunter's Mark and trix on the same baby.

"I—I," stuttered Phineas, at a loss for words.

"Phineas! Have you got them?" yelled a woman from the darkness. "Cass says the tunnel has collapsed. We're going to have to cut our way out the front!"

"One moment, Malvidia!" yelled Phineas.

Em's eyes locked on Phineas. She saw the bleeding trix.

"The Arkhon?" she asked in a low voice.

Phineas stared back at her. "The Arkhon is *in the yard*. I'd stake my life on it."

"You are," Em confirmed. "Nobody will believe the Arkhon didn't do this."

"I know," said Phineas.

A cold resolve slipped across his uncle's features as he drew a strangely colored long knife from his coat.

"Maybe you made a mistake," said Em.

"I didn't. The Arkhon is in the yard. Besides, he would have killed him after he took the Hunter's Mark," said Phineas. "It was not him."

"Who, then?" challenged Em.

Phineas looked over at Em, who was kneeling over her fallen husband.

"I don't know," said Phineas. "We need to find out who and why. We need answers."

"But if the other hunters see the mark," said Em, "they'll kill him."

"Nobody will touch Sky, so long as I live!" Phineas swore, holding the infant close. Sky's mouth fell open. This wasn't the present—not a dream; he was edgewalking through his *own memory*! That infant was him!

"I need time," said Phineas.

"You're going to run?" asked Em. "You're sure about this? They'll call you a traitor. They'll hunt you. The Hunters of Legend—Malvidia—they'll never let you return to Exile."

Phineas nodded wearily. "Maybe so. But Sky is not the Arkhon's pawn. He will decide his own fate. And maybe, when I have answers, or the hunters are in desperate need . . . Who knows what could happen?"

"How much time do you need to get away?" Em stood, took a deep breath, and picked Nikola up, throwing him over her shoulder in a fireman's carry. *Much stronger than she looks,* Sky thought numbly.

"Thank you, Em," said Phineas as he headed for the darkness, Em straining beside him carrying Nikola. "I'll set the gate for fifteen minutes. That should give you and Malvidia plenty of time to get out with Nikola. Nikola will be okay, Em. We'll find out what happened."

Sky gaped after them in silent disbelief as the room fell quiet once more.

"I can't help you anymore, Sky," said Errand.

Sky spun around, looking everywhere, but he couldn't see Errand.

"What? Why not?" asked Sky. "And who said you were helping me before?"

"He won't allow it," said Errand, his voice hollow—distant.

"Who?" asked Sky.

"My teacher," said Errand.

The world spun around Sky, darkness swallowed him, and suddenly he was back on the sidewalk, lying halfway on his neighbor's lawn, their pet poodle staring at him strangely.

"That better be slobber on my chin," said Sky, dragging himself to his feet.

ARF!

"Likely story," muttered Sky as he wandered off toward his house, wondering if his world would ever be the same again.

CHAPTER 24

Nackles

Peck, peck, peck.

Sky reached over to turn off the alarm clock.

Peck, peck, peck.

He reached farther . . . farther . . . fartherrr . . . CRASHING out of bed to the hardwood floor. He sat up. He *still* didn't own an alarm clock. Besides that, he couldn't have been asleep for more than a few hours. The moon was still up, for crying out loud!

He'd snuck in through the window after collapsing on his neighbor's lawn. For some reason, after the dream he just couldn't bring himself to face his parents, not until he sorted it all out.

Peck, peck, peck.

He threw open the window. "Read my lips: No. More. Crackers!"

The giant crow stared at him.

"CAW!"

It flapped its wings, landing on the tree branch a few feet away to gawk some more with the other crows.

"CAW!" they crowed.

He sighed. He'd planned to get up early anyway. Now was as good a time as any.

"Fine. Give me a minute," he said. He flipped on the gas lantern he'd found in the attic. He grabbed his yo-yo, his shoes, and his backpack. He shoved in the black light, a can of Fog, and a few other sundries before finally hefting the duffel bag with the monster hunter's gear. He hadn't bothered to change out of his clothes, so he was already dressed. He ran his hands through his hair, blew into his hand to check his breath, cringed, turned off the lantern, and climbed out the window.

"Here's the deal," he told the crows as he walked, lugging the duffel, his backpack over his shoulders. "You want more crackers, you're going to have to help me. Do you understand?"

He felt stupid talking to crows, but somehow he knew these weren't normal crows.

The crows stared at him as if he'd just issued a personal insult. Work for food? Was he serious?

"Okay, fine," said Sky. "You win."

He kicked up the leaves as he walked through the gate to Pimiscule Grounds, revealing a layer of fresh crackers the monster hunters must've put down the night before. The crows swooped down and began snatching up the crackers.

"Don't know why you need me anyway. Seems like you could move your own leaves."

The crows stopped eating and looked at him with their beaks held high, as if the very idea were preposterous.

"You know that phosphorus is from urine, don't you?"

"CAW!"

He shook his head and began walking up the trail, reaching the manor as the moon was setting.

"Ursula?" Sky whispered nervously, not sure he wanted an answer. "Are you there?"

He was sort of glad Ursula wasn't around. He'd waited until almost dawn in the hopes that she wouldn't be. He still hadn't digested everything he'd heard.

He wanted to be alone, to think and figure things out, but he didn't have any answers. Edgewalking through the memory of that night . . . Had Phineas really used him as bait to lure the Arkhon to Exile? Why would the Arkhon want him? And who was the man who'd marked Sky with the trix?

Sky strolled along the wall, running his hand along the perfectly smooth surface. The wall was back, along with the monsters, just as it had appeared two nights before. But not the day before. The wall and monsters appeared only under the full moon, and only recently—a sign, or a *fail-safe*, as his parents had called it, that the prison was about to open. That's why Crystal and the others didn't know about it; they spent their nights watching the town, not the manor, and even when they wandered the grounds at night, they didn't venture beyond the crossroads. They had no reason to come this far.

He continued along until he reached the crystalline gate.

In the middle of the gate he found what he was looking for; a small indentation about the size of his watch, set deep within the wall so the watch could connect with the inner workings.

There were no other grooves or blemishes of any kind.

In the memory Phineas had said he would set the gate for

fifteen minutes, which meant that the watch, as one of the keys, likely went here.

Was the prison as simple as that? Insert the watch and stand back? He didn't think so. For one thing he didn't see a pendulum in sight, and the "Enof Od Naba Ban Do Fone" poem specifically mentioned a pendulum. *With all three, on the pendulum bend, you might get lucky and lock the prison up again.*

Sky now knew where the pendulum was. He'd been bait for the Arkhon, and bait always went in the trap, which meant that the pendulum he'd seen must be inside the manor somewhere, likely hanging from the colored dome he could see bubbling from the manor top.

That meant there were at least two locks to the prison—one outside the manor on the gate, and one inside somehow linked to the pendulum.

Of course, the pendulum was only mentioned in relation to *locking* the prison up again, not opening it, so the watch alone might be enough to open it. That was a depressing thought. If Ambrosia or the Wargarou got the watch and figured out the poem, they could just open the gate and let the Arkhon stroll free. Fortunately, right now they didn't have the watch either, thanks to Crenshaw.

Sky stepped away from the gate and picked up a rock, throwing it at the closest monster. A Barrow Hag, by the looks of her (from the short story "Bag, the Barrow Hag of Hagerby"), with big froglike eyes and scaly skin. The rock sailed at the monster. There was a blue electric flash, and then the rock slowed to a stop in midair an inch from the monster's nose just as it crossed the outer part of the wall.

It looked almost like . . .

"A Shimmer. Hmmm," he mumbled, thinking of the blue nimbus that protected the monster hunters when they fell—the only piece of equipment Andrew hadn't built from scratch. What had he said? Something about diffusing energy through time and space?

Sky walked along the wall, throwing rock after rock at the monsters posed on top, all with the same effect—a blue flash followed by a slowing and then a stop until the rock hung in midair a few inches from the face, chest, or tentacles of the monster. He threw rocks as long as he could, until the sun began to rise.

And then, as the sun rose, the glass wall shimmered with electric light, until the wall and the hideous monsters disappeared, leaving the dilapidated manor behind.

He watched for a moment more, and then he turned and walked back toward the monster hunters' lair, the crows cawing as they followed.

As he drew closer to the lair, he heard the engines within kick on. He ducked into the trees, hiding, and Crystal emerged. She glanced around, but she seemed distracted, and then she disappeared down the trail heading for school.

Had she actually stayed there overnight? Wouldn't her family be worried? He should probably talk to her, but he wasn't quite ready to hand over the equipment just yet.

He listened for the others, but the engine had shut off. He scrambled out of the trees and entered the lair. He emerged some time later with a wheelbarrow full of Cheez Whiz canisters and wheeled it into the woods a short distance away, before disappearing into the lair again.

A short time after that, he came up with *another*

wheelbarrow—the same but for one notable difference. This time a frozen Gnomon (Nackles) rode on top of the mountain of Cheez Whiz canisters.

Sky wheeled Nackles deeper into the woods, away from the shack, parking her next to the first wheelbarrow.

He pulled her off, grunting with the effort. Then he pulled the Core shoulder pads from his duffel bag, swapped out his blue ICE freezing containers for red FIRE thawing containers, slipped the Core over his head, and strapped it on.

He hit a button on his chest, and the Pounder hand-cannon shot into his hand. He desperately hoped he'd assembled everything right.

"All right, here goes nothing."

Pulling the trigger, he launched a red globe of liquid that covered Nackles in a pile of goo that looked like bloody Jell-O.

He waited.

Waited some more.

Slowly he walked toward Nackles. When he was a few feet away, she leapt at him.

He hit his protective Shimmer, and she slowed and then slid to the ground.

Then she jumped to her feet, ready to pounce again.

"Nackles, stop!"

Nackles stopped when she heard her name.

He retracted his Pounder hand-cannon and stepped back, holding his hands in front of him to show he didn't mean any harm.

"Go. Take the wheelbarrows to your mom. She'll know what to do with them. Tell her I kept my promise. Now it's time to keep hers."

Nackles looked at the wheelbarrow like she expected it to

bite her, and then she gawped back at him in confusion, grunting and shrieking and popping in a way that almost made it sound like she was trying to talk.

"Errand, a little help here?" said Sky, waving his hand around.

Nackles looked at him like he was crazy.

He sighed. "Nackles, you." He pointed at her. "Take wheelbarrows." He pointed at the wheelbarrows. "To Rauschtlot. Ask Rauschtlot to please bury." He mimed digging. "Cheez Whiz." He held up a can of Cheese Whiz. "Under manor yard." He drew the shape of the manor with his fingers and then pointed northeast toward it. "And watch for signal." He pointed to his eyes, pointed at the sky, and then mimed an explosion with his hands.

She must've understood, because she issued several shrieks he could almost understand, before she smiled at him (he thought) and then grabbed a wheelbarrow in each hand, lifting them over her head without spilling a single canister, and then she ran off into the woods.

"CAW!" cawed the crows watching from the trees.

Sky pulled a package of crackers from his coat that he'd grabbed from his gear bag earlier, and tossed several crackers into the air.

The crows swooped down, gobbling them up.

"CAW!"

"Later," said Sky, shoving the rest of the crackers into his pocket. From a different pocket, he pulled out a small vial filled with a murky brown liquid.

"CAW?"

"You mess with the best, you get drawn and quartered like Aunt Tess," said Sky, smiling.

The crows flew off.

"No appreciation for genius," said Sky as he returned the vial to his pocket, removed his gear, hid his duffel in the woods, and headed for the trail.

Gym class was about to start, and today he was actually looking forward to it.

CHAPTER 25

I Love You with Love

It was after lunch, and gym class had already started by the time he arrived. He'd missed morning classes. Miss Hagfish would skin him alive later, but he had bigger concerns at the moment. He had less than one day (one day!) to get his watch back, locate the other two keys, and—most important—find his uncle.

He slipped into the locker room, changed into his gym clothes, and searched around until he found Crenshaw's locker. He emptied the locker, riffling through Crenshaw's clothes, books, knives (gulp). There was no sign of the watch, which meant that Crenshaw had it on him, probably so that he could taunt Sky with it.

He did manage to find a letter shoved into one of Crenshaw's shoes. He skimmed through it and started laughing. Then he slipped the murky vial and the letter into his gym shorts and left.

As he walked into the gym, he tried to catch Crystal's

eye. She glanced at him, her eyes went big with surprise (she must've thought he'd been caught!), and she looked relieved, then angry. Then she very deliberately spread out, taking up the open spot next to her. Andrew was wedged in between Marcus and a mousy kid named Federico. Andrew gave him a weak smile and then looked away. Marcus avoided looking at him altogether, which wasn't a big surprise, considering he'd beat Sky up the day before.

Marcus's response he could understand, but Crystal's and Andrew's?

His smile faded and he took a seat on the floor mat next to Felicity.

As he sat down, Crenshaw, who sat across from him, made a show of pulling out Sky's watch and checking the time.

"It's nice of you to join us, Sky. Had a busy morning, have we?" prodded Miss Terry.

"Er . . . sorry I'm late," said Sky, staring hard at Crenshaw. "I seem to have misplaced my *watch*."

Miss Terry glanced back and forth between Sky and Crenshaw, frowning. "I'm sorry to hear that." Crenshaw put the watch away, and Sky made sure to note the pocket.

He noticed something else as well—a rope directly behind Miss Terry. It hung from the ceiling several stories up.

His frown deepened.

He hated rope-climbing day. It was just another way to embarrass him in front of his peers.

"Marcus," said Miss Terry, turning from Sky, "I believe you were just explaining how you are unable to climb the rope today due to scurvy?"

"Oh, yeah," said Marcus, suddenly remembering that he was supposed to be sick. "I got the scurvy *real* bad."

"You realize scurvy is very uncommon unless you live in a third world country or you happen to be an eighteenth-century British sailor? You aren't an eighteenth-century British sailor, are you, Marcus?" asked Miss Terry.

The class chuckled.

"Here, I got a note from my doctor," said Marcus, handing a note to Miss Terry.

"Well, it's written on a doctor's prescription pad," said Miss Terry. "Very official."

Marcus smiled in triumph.

"Of course," said Miss Terry, "it seems like quite a coincidence that you *also* go to Crenshaw's father for medical advice. How many is that now? Four of you? Five? I believe I've lost count. And all of you with such uncommon diseases: malaria, polio, scarlet fever . . . the *bubonic plague*! My, my. You poor dears."

Miss Terry feigned concern.

"It's also quite remarkable," she continued, "that in all these years, I've never known 'scurvy' to be spelled with an *a* before. I've been pronouncing it all wrong! Maybe if I just added a little more *pirate* to it . . . Arrr, walk the plank, you *scarvy* dogs! There. That sounds better. Well done, Crenshaw. It looks like you spelled it correctly after all."

Crenshaw smiled proudly, and then frowned as he realized he'd been caught.

"Despite what some of you may think," said Miss Terry, "I am not a bumbling idiot. Now, Crenshaw, if that prescription pad doesn't miraculously find its way back to your father's office, I may be forced to call him for advice on how I can keep all of these very uncommon illnesses he's diagnosed from spreading to my other students. Do I make myself clear?"

"Yes," said Crenshaw.

"Excuse me?"

"Yes, ma'am," Crenshaw corrected.

"I'm glad we understand each other. Now, Marcus, if you'll kindly do the honors . . ."

As Marcus lumbered to his feet and headed for the rope, Sky leaned over to Felicity. "I need your help."

Felicity glanced at him. "Sorry. My dad's a plumber, not a doctor. You'll have to fake your own notes."

Sky blushed. "I don't need *that*."

Felicity smirked. "I know. You need a distraction, right? How much time do you need?"

"I—How did you—"

"That's your watch, right? You want it back. You've been holding your pocket in a vise grip since you walked in. You've either got something in there that'll help you get your watch back, or you're developing a severe case of the bubonic plague."

He stared at her. "You're amazing."

Felicity blushed.

He realized what he'd said, and *he* blushed right back at her.

"I can get you five minutes. Is that enough time?" asked Felicity.

He nodded. "Should be more than enough."

"Good. Now kiss me," said Felicity.

"What?"

Felicity sighed. "Boys."

She grabbed his head and kissed him full on the lips.

"Felicity Anne Finley!" snapped Miss Terry.

The whole class turned from watching Marcus struggle with the rope to watch Felicity and Sky kissing.

Felicity let go of him and looked at Miss Terry with innocent eyes. "Yes, Miss Terry?"

He was speechless. He was so speechless he couldn't speak. He was so speakless he couldn't speech. He'd *never* kissed a girl before—and, more important, a girl had never kissed him!

"Don't 'Yes, Miss Terry' me! The boy has been here two days! *Two* days! And already . . ." Miss Terry paused, glancing at him uncertainly, and then back at Felicity. "You were the instigator, weren't you?"

"We instigated each other," said Felicity sweetly, "but I did it first."

He stared at Felicity stupidly. She patted him on the cheek and then turned her attention to Miss Terry, all business.

"Well, then," said Miss Terry, "you come with me, young woman. I think your parents would be very interested in what's happened here today."

"Yes, Miss Terry." Felicity stood from the mat and followed after her. Before she left, Felicity turned, blowing him a kiss while Miss Terry wasn't watching. He caught it and stared at it in his hand with a blank expression.

And then he remembered where he was and why Felicity had kissed him.

He looked up and found the class watching him.

Crystal was glaring.

He cleared his throat and pulled the letter from his pocket as he stood.

"'My dearest most beloved Cordelia,'" he read. "'You spurn me, you spurn me, o' wretched spurning that spurns.'"

Cordelia sat up taller, her face going white.

Crenshaw's face darkened. "Where did you get that?"

"'It feels sharp,'" he continued, "'like in my stomach and stuff. My dad tells me it's indigestion, but I think it's love. Love for you, my love whom I love.'"

Crenshaw stood up. "Give it back, Sky!"

"'I love you, I love you, I love you with love! Like in my heart and stuff all scrunched into my aorta like a pack of fresh bologna! And I've gotta get it out! That's why I spurn others with my fists, because I've gotta get my love out. You say we're just friends and stuff, but someday . . .'" Sky lowered the letter, reciting the rest by memory as he stared at Crenshaw, "I'll be a doctor and everyone will have to love me then . . . even *you*. Your *eternal* love . . . Crenshaw."

The class busted up laughing.

With a roar Crenshaw rushed him.

He barely had time to pull the vial from his pocket before Crenshaw hit him and knocked him to the floor.

They wrestled around. Crenshaw fought like an animal, kicking and punching, until thick hands pulled him away.

"She's coming back, man. Let it go," said Marcus as he and Ren dragged Crenshaw toward his seat.

Sky sat up just as Miss Terry entered, Felicity in tow.

Felicity plopped down next to him. She looked him over, frowning as she spotted the blood and rapidly forming bruises on his face. "Maybe you should've let him keep the watch."

He smiled, his teeth red with blood.

Miss Terry looked back and forth between Crenshaw—who still hadn't taken his seat and looked as if he might rush Sky at any moment—and Sky, who was really quite content.

"Well, I assume you both got what was coming to you?" asked Miss Terry.

"Yes, Miss Terry," said Sky with a big smile.

Crenshaw watched him for a moment, looking confused.

And then he reached down to his pocket where the watch had been.

"You!" yelled Crenshaw.

Miss Terry stepped into his path. "Do you have a problem, Crenshaw?"

Crenshaw stopped. He eyed Miss Terry like he was trying to figure out whether he could get past her or not. He apparently decided *not*.

"He stole my watch," said Crenshaw.

Miss Terry turned to Sky. "Sky, is this true?"

"No, ma'am," he said innocently. "The only watch I have is this one here that my uncle gave me for my birthday."

"Good enough for me," said Miss Terry.

"B-but," sputtered Crenshaw.

"Sky has only *one* watch. You can't expect him to give you his only watch, now, can you?" asked Miss Terry.

Crenshaw sputtered some more and then finally got control of himself. "No. I suppose *not*."

"Good! Now why don't you take your seat," said Miss Terry.

Crenshaw clenched and unclenched his fists, and then he spun around and sat on the mat.

As he sat, there was a sound like the breaking of glass, and suddenly a putrid, sulfuric scent wafted upon the wind.

"Ewwww!" yelled several girls around Crenshaw as they scooted away.

"What?! I—It wasn't me!" yelled Crenshaw as he jumped up and examined the mat.

From where he was sitting, Sky could see a brown stain oozing through Crenshaw's back pocket, exactly where he'd placed the vial of murky brown putrid Fog solution.

Miss Terry quickly interjected herself, effectively blocking the view of the stain from the rest of the class, to Sky's immense disappointment.

"Renoir, Marcus, would you be so good as to escort your friend to the changing room? I fear our faithful janitor has been *cleaning* in here again," said Miss Terry, dismissing the smell.

Ren and Marcus stepped up next to Crenshaw, who, having not yet noticed the stain, looked confused. Miss Terry started them on their way, masterfully blocking the view of the stain until they disappeared from sight.

Sky was trying not to laugh. Miss Terry cast him a nasty look. She couldn't have known what he'd done, could she?

Crystal and Andrew were staring at him. Andrew grinned until he caught Crystal's frown, and then he frowned along, shaking his head in disapproval. But his eyes kept grinning.

"Well, I think we've done all the damage we can for one day," said Miss Terry, dismissing the class.

"Thanks for your help," said Sky to Felicity as he stood up, trying to breath through his mouth so he wouldn't have to smell the deeds of his own doing. "I hope I didn't get you in too much trouble."

"Nah," said Felicity. "We just stood in the hall."

"You did?"

"Yep. As soon as the door closed, she asked me how much time you needed. Then we just stood there," said Felicity.

"You mean *she knew*?" asked Sky in disbelief.

"Apparently. Maybe she noticed that you kiss like a dead fish, not realistic *at all*."

He looked back at Miss Terry as she ushered people out of the gym. "Unbelievable."

Felicity grabbed Sky's chin, turning his head back toward her.

"But if you ever need a diversion again"—she leaned forward like she was going to kiss him, and his heart stopped—"let me know."

At the last moment she turned his head, and kissed him on the cheek. With a laugh she set off for the girls' locker room.

He ogled after her, his mouth hanging open.

Crystal shoved past him without a second glance. Andrew looked back, shrugging his shoulders as he mouthed the word "Sorry."

"Wait! Crystal!" shouted Sky, but she just kept walking.

He took a step to catch up to her. He needed to talk to her about tonight—

"Sky, might I have a word with you?"

He stopped cold, cringing at the tone in Miss Terry's voice. He'd heard the same tone many times before from Mom.

He spun to face her. "Er . . ."

"You went too far today, Sky. Too far!" said Miss Terry.

He gave a nervous smile to two of his classmates—Federico and Sonya—as they passed by, leaving the gym empty except for him and Miss Terry.

"Er . . ."

"What were you trying to prove?" prodded Miss Terry.

"I wanted my watch back," said Sky defensively.

"Is that all? Because it looked to me like you wanted to humiliate Crenshaw beyond any hope of redemption," said Miss Terry.

"Not beyond *any* hope," said Sky, smiling slyly. She wasn't biting. "Fine. So what if I did? It's no worse than he did to me."

"Take care, Sky," said Miss Terry, "lest in fighting a monster, you *become one yourself*."

"Miss Terry?" said Sky, confused.

"That is all, Skyler," said Miss Terry, dismissing him.

CHAPTER 26

Fangs of Destiny

After he left the gym, he wandered the halls looking for Crystal. He knew he should be searching for the other two keys, but he couldn't concentrate. Miss Terry's words kept banging around in his head. Was what he'd done to Crenshaw really all that terrible? Crenshaw was a bully; he deserved what he got! So what if he'd wanted to humiliate Crenshaw? How did that make him the bad guy? Hadn't she even noticed that he was the one with the bloody lip?

"There you are, Sky. I've been looking all over for you."

He turned around and spotted Hannah moving briskly toward him, her eyes pleading. Tick followed a few steps behind like a lost puppy.

"Er, hello," said Sky.

"I was just telling Tick here about that thing we have to do right now. You know, that *thing* we do together during study hall—*alone*—just brother and sister."

"You mean bocce golf?" said Sky.

Hannah raised her eyebrows, giving him a look that said *Seriously, that's the best you can come up with?*

He smiled, but over her shoulder he spotted Crenshaw and his goons heading toward him.

"Yes," said Hannah, putting her arm around him in a hold somewhere between affection and a headlock, "bocce golf. Of course! We're going to play brother and sister *bocce golf,* just like we always do during study hall. So I'd love to see your truck, Tick, but, you know, little brother Sky here gets *craaazy* without his bocce golf." She mussed up his hair in a big-sisterly I'm-going-to-kill-you-later-while-you-sleep way.

Tick looked deflated.

At the end of the hall, Sky spotted Crenshaw moving closer. Sky had two options. He could hide behind Hannah and Tick until Crenshaw found something else to do, which could take a while, or he could escape before Crenshaw spotted him, and go find Crystal.

"Sorry, Hannah," said Sky, breaking Hannah's hold, his eyes locked on Crenshaw, who still hadn't spotted him. "You'll have to find another armada to run your blockade." He began backing away. "Take a rain check?"

"What?" exclaimed Hannah, gritting her teeth. "But, Sky, you know we play brother and sister bocce golf during study hall *every—single—day*. Same time. No outsies! What, I ask you, could be more important than *that*?"

Hannah's outburst drew Crenshaw's attention. He smiled, noticing Sky. Well, there was nothing for it. Sky was committed now.

"Survival," he offered as he spun around and started to run. "Sorry, Hannah. I owe you one!"

"You know that doesn't mean anything if you never *pay up*!" yelled Hannah after him.

"Armada? What is that guy, a ship or something?" asked Tick, laughing stupidly. Hannah didn't laugh. She didn't want to encourage him, but Tick wasn't the kind of guy who needed encouragement. "You like my jacket?" asked Tick. "It's a letterman's jacket. I'm captain of the football team, you know."

"I know, Tick! You told me that yesterday, like, three times!"

"Oh. It's made out of wool, like from sheep."

"Sheesh," said Hannah.

Sky turned another corner, and their voices disappeared behind him. He wasn't sure where he was going, but he was sure he'd rather be there than here.

Fast-moving footsteps echoed off the walls. They were gaining. Crenshaw had brought an armada of his own with him this time. There was Ren, Marcus, and Cordelia (who had her own personal vendetta to settle), as well as an older boy and girl Crenshaw had somehow bribed to follow him, the same ones who'd guarded the hallway the day before when Crenshaw had stolen his watch.

Around the next corner Sky spotted an OUT OF ORDER sign on the boys' bathroom. Without stopping he flung open the door and ducked inside. He caught sight of a trash can and began shuffling it toward the door.

That's when he noticed the janitor—long shaggy hair, janitor jumpsuit . . . something strangely familiar about him, though Sky couldn't place it.

The janitor was bent over a urinal, scrubbing at it with a filthy yellow-brown rag.

"Er, *hey*," said Sky, giving the janitor a nervous wave.

Without looking up from his task, the janitor reached into his pocket, pulled out a door key, and tossed it to him.

Sky stared at it for a moment. He glanced at the janitor scrubbing at a particularly awkward stain, and then Sky used the key to lock the bathroom door.

The janitor held up his hand, and Sky tossed the key back.

Without looking or slowing in his task, the janitor caught the key and put it back into his grimy blue jumpsuit.

Sky stared at him for a moment, unsure whether he should thank him or run for his life, but there was something so familiar about him . . .

And then Sky heard footsteps outside, and he turned back to the door, pressing his ear against it.

The footsteps slowed.

"He has to be around here somewhere. There's no way he could outrun us," said Crenshaw.

"Yeah. Did you see the size of his legs in those gym shorts? They were like little chicken legs," said Cordelia. "I'm surprised he could walk this far."

Sky glanced at his legs. They weren't that small, were they?

"I can't believe I actually felt sorry for that guy," Cordelia added.

"Maybe we should just leave him alone," said Marcus hesitantly. "He'll show up on his own eventually."

"We can't wait," said the older girl Sky didn't know.

"I don't get it. What's so important about Sky anyway?" asked Cordelia.

"It doesn't matter anymore," said Crenshaw. "Spread out and check the doors."

Sky stepped away from the door, holding his breath as the handle rattled. The footsteps moved away, and he exhaled.

He was safe for the moment.

He turned to thank the janitor for the key, but the words froze on his tongue as he watched the janitor take his dirty rag, dip it into the urinal water, and start on the mirrors—scrubbing with unholy vigor.

Sky cringed.

Urinal water ran down the mirror in streams, pushed onward by the demonic rag. *Pushed,* but not fast enough. Great waterfalls of fiendish sludge slipped by, falling in infernal torrents to pool on the unsuspecting counters below.

The janitor finished his diabolical job, unlocked the door, and stepped into Arkhon Academy's hallowed halls. But before he departed to perform his next nefarious deed, he turned to Sky.

"Urinal cakes aren't really cakes, you know."

And with that, he was gone.

Sky stared at the door in stunned silence, wondering if he'd been pricked by Dovetail again.

And then he heard a toilet flush, and he spun to face the bathroom. Someone else was in here?

A stall door opened.

Sky reached for the door handle, thought better of it, and let his hand hover a few inches away instead—ready to run at a moment's notice, but not so ready that he'd catch an infectious disease in the process.

Hands stepped out of the stall, a book under his arm.

Sky's hand dropped from the near proximity of the door handle. "Hands?"

This bathroom was getting weirder and weirder.

"Hey, Sky. Glad to see you're still alive. Thought we lost you for good last night."

Hands headed to the sink to wash up. He set his book on the counter and checked his reflection in the mirror.

"You are a beautiful thing, my man," Hands said to his reflection.

Leaning forward, Hands gave his reflection a *great—big—kiss*.

Sky cringed.

"What?" asked Hands.

"Er . . . nothing. What are you doing here? The bathroom's out of order," said Sky.

"The sign's mine," said Hands.

Sky stared.

"Don't look at me like that! I'm a man who values his privacy."

"Okay. Look, I need you to do something for me," said Sky.

"I've only got the one sign," said Hands.

"No, not that! You've got to convince the others to meet me by Emaline Livingstone's mausoleum right after school. Can you do that?" asked Sky.

"What for?"

"Just tell them I've got something they'll want to see." He peeked out the door, checking the halls.

"I'm not sure they'll go for it. No one's real happy with you at the moment," said Hands.

"I've noticed. Just make something up, okay? But you've got to get them there right after school. Got it?" said Sky.

Hands nodded slowly. "I'll see what I can do."

"Good," said Sky.

"Is everything all right?" asked Hands.

"Whoa! Ease up on the personal questions there, hombre,"

said Sky, smiling as he parroted Hands words from the night before. "You've gotta start light. Why don't you ask me about the weather."

Hands smirked. "All right. How's the weather, Sky Weathers?"

"There's too much of it, I'm afraid, with a high chance of gruesome death."

"Sounds like my kind of weather," said Hands.

Sky grinned . . . and then he noticed Hands's book.

The cover art portrayed a muscley man and a chesty woman locked in a passionate embrace, the man's razor-sharp canines inches from the woman's neck. Emblazoned across the top were the words "Embrace of the Vampire, Book 2: Fangs of Destiny."

"A romance novel?" Sky scoffed. "I thought that was a joke!"

"What? I've got to get my monster hunting techniques from somewhere," said Hands.

Sky snorted, and then he noticed something else. "Can I see your book?"

"Sure," said Hands, handing it to him. "Just don't ruin it. The librarian would kill me. Monsters are bad enough."

Sky examined the spine, staring at a small white tag at the bottom. "It's a Dewey decimal number."

"Yeah," said Hands, looking at him like he was crazy. "That's what they put on library books to keep track of them. Though on this one here, it's got the author's name seeing as it's a fiction book and all."

"No! 581.112! It's a Dewey decimal number!"

"If you say so," said Hands.

"Hands, if you hadn't just licked toilet water, I'd kiss you!"

"Licked what?"

"See you after school if I live that long!"

Sky rushed through the door and sprinted for the library.

CHAPTER 27
Special Collections

The Special Collections room at Arkhon Academy where, once upon a time, Beau and others had trained hunters, and where, Sky suspected, Phineas had hidden book 581.112, possibly when he had led the hunters, was located in the library's subbasement at the end of a darkened hallway lined with flickering lights and hastily filled storage rooms.

He followed the librarian through the subterranean labyrinth, glancing nervously into the shadows as their footsteps echoed down the empty halls.

"Lock up when you're done," said the librarian as she opened the last door on the left, turned, and began walking back down the hall.

He glanced into the room, which was filled, floor to ceiling, with boxes and stacks of books.

"But, where is it?" asked Sky, dismayed by the chaos before him.

"Your guess is as good as mine," called the librarian over her shoulder.

Gritting his teeth, he stepped into the room and shut the door behind him. A single bulbous light flickered fretfully overhead, like a sinking boat sending out its final Morse code. Many of the stacks leaned precariously, like a skinny man bending over to pick up a penny.

He slipped through the stacks of books, a rabbit in a forest of foxes.

In the center of the room, he found an old table and a few chairs in various stages of decay. He set his backpack on the table and looked around at the books.

"And she calls herself a librarian?" said Sky, shaking his head in disgust.

He started opening boxes at random. He pulled out a book, checked the number—295.023—put it back. Another box—876.03—put it back. Then 675.02, 229.567, 334.02, 783.421.

Pretty soon he realized that "Special Collections" at Arkhon Academy basically meant "place where we put all the books people don't like to read anymore." He also realized that while the librarians hadn't taken any time to organize the books, they had moved the books in clumps as they'd run out of space upstairs. So science books were usually together, English books went with English books, and books on vampire romances were nowhere to be found, since Hands had apparently checked them all out.

Based on this clumping, he realized that there was a pattern to the Dewey decimal numbers themselves—something he'd always assumed but never learned. The first number in the sequence—the five in 581.112—was linked to a specific area of knowledge. Zero was for computers and generalities, one was for philosophy, two for religion, and on and on, up to nine for history. Five was linked to the sciences. The succeeding numbers—those coming after the five—each got more and more specific as to the *type* of knowledge, with the last number representing the book itself.

So, based on the random books he'd viewed, he was able to figure out that 581.112 was likely some kind of science book on plants.

The other thing he noticed was that older books were piled in the back of the room, and newer books were closer to the front. This didn't help him that much until he realized that it wasn't the age of the book that affected their placement. It was the *date the book was last checked out*! And this information was stamped in the back of the older books!

He knew his uncle couldn't have checked 581.112 out more than eleven years ago, since, if it really held a key to the prison, he would've had it on him when he locked up the Arkhon. And he would have returned it before he went underground shortly thereafter, assuming Sky was even at the right library and that his uncle hadn't simply kept the book or put it somewhere else. In which case, he was toast, and not the delicious kind that Samuel the Simpleton made in *The Tourmaline of Foresight* either.

Assuming it was an unpopular book (which was likely, given that his uncle had been reading it and that it was botany based), the librarians probably would've left it on the shelf upstairs for maybe another year or two tops, which meant that the area where he would find 581.112 was somewhere . . . right around . . .

Here!

He held up the book in triumph. "Ha! Take *that,* librarians!"

He read the title. "'*A Botanist's Guide to Botany: Botany Through the Ages, Volume 2: The Seventeenth Century*. By Alexander Drake.'"

Sky stared at the book. "Drake. Wait a minute. I recognize this book! I *own* this book!"

He owned all these books, the entire twelve-volume set! He even owned a volume of Drake's journal!

He started flipping through the pages. Why would Phineas check out a book he must've already owned?

"Come on. There has to be something in here. Flora. . . . Effects on fauna. . . . The Great Fungus Fire of 1642. Pointless! No wonder I never made it past volume one!"

He paused, staring at the cover. "Wait! Encoding. There's got to be another encoded message in here!"

He flipped through the book again, looking for stained or wrinkled pages, marks along the spine, number sequences, anything!

But there was nothing there. "This can't be a coincidence."

"Ohhh, Sky-y-y. Come out, come out, wherever you are . . ."

He jerked his head around at the sound of Crenshaw's voice. How had he tracked him down here?

"We know you're in here!" yelled Crenshaw. "Come out, and maybe we won't burn the place to the ground!"

"We're not burning anything, Crenshaw," said the older girl Sky didn't know.

"Speak for yourself, Lucretia," said Crenshaw. "You and Lazar can leave if you don't want to dirty your hands."

Sky closed his book and began slinking forward.

"Crenshaw," said Lazar, the older boy he'd seen earlier,

"don't make it personal. That's what got you into this mess in the first place."

"*He* made it *personal*!" yelled Crenshaw. "Isn't that right, Sky?"

He could hear Crenshaw shuffling between piles of books near the door. Someone else was closer, off to Sky's right. Off to his left and further back, he could hear Marcus knocking over a pile of books and mumbling curses.

"You're late for detention, you know!" taunted Crenshaw.

He glanced at his watch. He'd been down here for *hours*. Not only was he late for detention (which he'd planned to dodge anyway), but he was late for his meeting with the monster hunters!

He mentally kicked himself. He'd wasted his whole afternoon and he had nothing to show for it. Worst of all, he was about to lose his last, best chance to regain the monster hunters' trust and stop the Arkhon from escaping.

"Miss Hagfish is *peeved*. I don't think she likes you very much," said Crenshaw.

Sky snuck toward the center of the room, moving deftly through the piles of books. If he could reach his bag . . .

He stopped. Ren and Lazar had just broken through to the center and found his bag. Great.

"We found his bag," called Lazar as he poured out the contents: books, pencils, a Rubik's Cube, a yo-yo, a canister of Fog.

"Kid doesn't have much of a life," said Lazar, tossing aside the Rubik's Cube.

Sky ground his teeth.

"Did you find anything?" asked Lucretia from somewhere ahead of Sky and to the right.

"No," said Lazar, holding up the Fog canister, his eyebrows knit as he, no doubt, tried to figure out why Sky carried such a thing. "No sign of the watch."

The watch? Why would they want the watch? He pulled the watch from his pocket. He knew it was a key to the prison, but did *they* know that?

And why would they care?

"Gotcha," whispered Cordelia by his ear, grabbing his arm.

He startled, toppling the stack of books next to him. The books fell, knocking them both to the ground. He scrambled to his feet, and lost *A Botanist's Guide to Botany*. He scanned the pile, but he didn't have time to look for it. His heart was racing. He was trapped, but he had one advantage. He'd spent the last several hours wandering through these books. He knew where he was going!

"Grab him!" yelled Lazar. "Get the watch!"

Sliding the ring at the end of the watch's retractable chain onto his finger, Sky darted to the left, jumping over Cordelia as she tried to dig her way out of the books. He pushed over stack after stack of books as he ran, disturbing the library's *One Hundred Years of Solitude* and *Finnegans Wake* as he crossed *Middlemarch* and plunged directly into the *Heart of Darkness*.

"Block the door!" yelled Lucretia as he passed by her, toppling a two-year-old clump of self-help books.

He careened onto the main path, sliding into a pile of English grammar books. He gave them an extra healthy kick—expelling years of pent-up animosity—and slipped beneath them as they fell like a surfer riding a wave. The door stood open before him, a beacon of hope, and in front of the door . . . Crenshaw.

"Game's up, Sky . . ."

Sky sprinted forward without slowing his pace. He could hear the others closing in behind. Twenty feet . . . fifteen feet . . . ten feet! He swung out, flinging the watch forward by its retractable chain! It sailed up, up, up, slamming into the lightbulb with a satisfying crunch. The front of the room plunged into darkness, momentarily blinding Crenshaw as Sky slid between his legs. The chain retracted and the watch sailed back into his hand, catching Crenshaw in his delicates along the way.

Crenshaw crumpled to the ground.

Jumping to his feet, Sky raced for the stairs. The long, dark hallway reached out to meet him. Storage rooms flew by. He was going to make it. He could see the stairs ahead.

And then suddenly something peeled from the shadows and bashed into him like a wrecking ball. He slid across the tiled floor and crashed into the wall. When his vision cleared, he saw . . .

"Principal Lem?"

Principal Lem stood, motionless, a few feet away, dressed in a stylish charcoal vested suit.

"I warned you, Mr. Weathers," said Principal Lem. "I warned you as clearly as I could. Leave it to the professionals."

Crenshaw, Cordelia, Marcus, Ren, Lucretia, and Lazar ran up.

"Lazar, Lucretia, would you please help Mr. Weathers to his feet? And if it wouldn't be too much of a bother, could you make sure he doesn't escape this time?"

"Hey, it wasn't our fault. Talk to your protégé there," said Lucretia, gesturing at Crenshaw.

"Don't blame me! If you two weren't total idiots, we would've had the other keys by now and none of this would've happened!" Crenshaw retorted.

"How were we supposed to know the old man would be so wily?" said Lazar defensively.

Old man? Did they mean Uncle Phineas?

"Yeah," said Lucretia, "it's not like he left a trail of bread crumbs for us to follow."

Trail of bread crumbs? Sky's heart leapt! Of course! Uncle Phineas had left a trail of breadcrumbs, a trail of breadcrumbs leading *home*! He knew where the second key was!

He quickly covered his smile, but they seemed too busy arguing to notice.

"And here I thought the two of you were supposed to be *hunters*," said Cordelia.

Sky frowned. Hunters?

"Yeah," added Crenshaw. "Malvidia said you were smart. How is it that you can't figure out a simple poem?"

If they were actually hunters, then the hunters' school at Arkhon Academy wasn't as dead as Sheriff Beau had led Sky to believe. Either that or the sheriff really didn't know about it.

And the poem . . .

"At least we didn't *lose* one of the keys!" said Lucretia.

"Yeah," taunted Lazar. "How's that relationship working out for you anyway, Crenshaw? Cordelia? Any wedding gift registries you'd like us to be aware of?"

"Enough!" shouted Principal Lem. "Normally I'd promote a healthy debate between my apprentices and Malvidia's—maybe even top it off with a little physical provocation—but it is *not the time*. Now, if you don't mind?" said Principal Lem, gesturing at Sky.

After a few mumbled curses Lazar and Lucretia dragged him to his feet.

"And the watch?" prompted Principal Lem.

Lazar forced Sky's hand open while Lucretia grabbed the watch, yanking the watch ring off his finger. Then they tied his hands behind his back for good measure, and handed the watch to Principal Lem.

"Excellent!" said Principal Lem, taking the watch. "Cordelia, have you suddenly taken an interest in your education? This is unprecedented!"

Sky looked over and saw that Cordelia had his backpack slung over her shoulder, a book under her arm.

"He had it with him—dropped it in the Special Collections room," said Cordelia, handing the book to Principal Lem.

"*A Botanist's Guide to Botany*. How interesting . . . and by Sir Alexander Drake, no less. A top-notch hunter!"

Sky groaned. She'd found it.

"Anything you'd like to tell us about this book, Mr. Weathers?" asked Principal Lem.

"I like the part where the purple orchid cross-pollinates with the yellow orchid. It's a little gratuitous, I guess, but you can skip those parts if you don't have the stomach," said Sky.

"Bon mot, Mr. Weathers! Well done! A bit *raunchy* for my tastes, really, but you continue to entertain! It almost makes me happy that we didn't kill you as a baby." Principal Lem smiled blandly, but Sky could see that the others looked surprised at the comment.

"You're Bat, aren't you?" said Sky, adding, "the Hunter of Legend who was supposed to meet with Uncle Phineas last night so he could come back and fix the prison?"

"Not in front of the *children*," said Principal Lem, gesturing at

Lazar and Lucretia, who were looking back at him suspiciously. Phineas had mentioned that Malvidia probably hadn't known about the meeting, and if Lucretia and Lazar were really her apprentice hunters, then the information would surprise them.

Bat was a Wargarou, which was something Lazar and Lucretia, in all likelihood, didn't know. But what about Crenshaw, Ren, Cordelia, and Marcus? Did they know? At a minimum Sky would put Lazar and Lucretia in danger if he pointed out that Bat was a Wargarou, and while he wasn't a big fan of them at the moment, he didn't want to see them hurt, especially since it wouldn't increase his chances of escape.

"Lazar, Lucretia, what do you make of this?" Principal Lem handed them the book.

"I don't know," said Lucretia hesitantly, not wanting to take her eyes off the principal. "There's nothing in it—nothing obvious."

"I don't see any stains or wrinkled pages," said Lazar, pulling a flashlight from his pocket. Black light spilled onto the pages as he flipped the flashlight on. "There's no residual information like there was when we found the poem residue on the truck's dashboard."

Sky's mouth dropped open. They'd pulled "Enof Od Naba Ban Do Fone" from the dashboard of Phineas's truck?

And then it occurred to him. He'd rubbed the page against the dash when he'd tried to heat up the paper! He must have left an imprint!

"Hmm. It looks like just a standard hunter's botany book," said Lucretia. "I've got the whole set if you want to borrow one."

Sky let out a sigh of relief. They hadn't spotted the number.

"That's quite all right, Lucretia," said Principal Lem. "Now if you'll just—"

"Hold on a minute," said Lazar, taking the book from Lucretia's hands. "The number on the spine. It's a Dewey decimal number!"

Sky groaned.

"Yes, library books do tend to have those, Lazar," said Principal Lem.

"No, not the book! Well, yes, the book too, but I'm talking about the number we found next to the poem! 581.112! It's right here on the book!" said Lazar.

Sky tried to slip away, but Lucretia tightened her grip.

"And you say these books are common?" asked Principal Lem.

"We all have them," said Cordelia, "even Marcus."

Marcus scowled at the jab, but he didn't say anything.

"So, what does this mean?" asked Principal Lem.

"No idea," said Lazar, "but it can't be a coincidence."

Principal Lem was silent for a moment. "You know what it means, don't you, Mr. Weathers?"

Sky didn't say anything, but he knew Principal Lem could tell he was hiding something.

"Yes. Indeed. This changes things. Crenshaw, Ren, take Mr. Weathers from our friends here."

"What? You can't do that!" Lucretia protested. "Malvidia told us not to come back without the watch."

"*And* Sky," added Lazar.

Crenshaw and Ren yanked Sky away from Lazar and Lucretia and wrenched his arms painfully behind him.

Lucretia and Lazar looked back and forth between Sky and Principal Lem nervously.

"Well, as you can see, I have Sky and the watch both well in hand," said Principal Lem as Cordelia and Marcus flanked the principal defensively, in a not-so-subtle manner. "I need you and Lucretia to take the book to Malvidia. See if you can figure out what it means."

Lazar and Lucretia still hesitated.

"Go, go! Off with you!" said Principal Lem, shooing them away with his hands.

Lazar and Lucretia glanced at Sky and then trotted off down a small hallway to his right.

"Finally," said Crenshaw as they disappeared. He spun, punching Sky in the stomach.

Sky sagged in Ren's hands, trying to catch his breath. He could feel his pulse racing. He waited for Errand to kick in, for the strength and speed he'd felt when Crenshaw had punched him the day before, but nothing came.

For whatever reason, Errand wasn't going to help him anymore. And Sky was beginning to find that he missed Errand's help. Strangely enough, he missed Errand too.

"Those two are such spoilsports," said Cordelia as she too punched Sky in the stomach. "That's for the letter." She punched him in his face, bloodying his lip again. "And that's for making me feel sorry for you."

"I couldn't agree more," said Principal Lem. "Marcus, are you okay? You look like you might throw up."

Marcus forced a smile. "Yeah, sure, it's just—what are we going to do with him? Sky, I mean?"

"We're just going on a little ride. Nothing to worry about, Marcus," said Principal Lem, flashing his teeth. "It's not like we're going to *eat* him."

Marcus chuckled nervously. "No, of course not."

"Can we get out of here already?" said Cordelia. "This place is *so boring*."

"Quite right, Cordelia," said Principal Lem, heading for the stairs. "This school just doesn't smell right."

"Shouldn't we take the tunnels?" asked Crenshaw.

"I'm afraid that won't be very safe for us in a few moments, once Lazar and Lucretia report to Malvidia. I suspect she might be displeased with me, and hunter-controlled tunnels are hardly the place to make a stand," said Principal Lem, "but it's good to see you finally using your brain."

Crenshaw smiled, propelling Sky forward as they headed up the stairs.

A rogue principal who was really a Wargarou, a humiliated classmate, a hunter's school that still trained killers. Sky was beginning to suspect that this might not end well for him. Not well at all.

CHAPTER 28

Maluidia

The hallways were empty as they passed through, except for a few random students involved in extracurricular activities. Principal Lem, Cordelia, and Marcus broke off just outside the library to attend to some "other business" while Crenshaw and Ren continued on, "escorting" Sky toward the main entrance, nearly running over Miss Terry as they turned a corner.

"It's nice to see you two have finally made up," said Miss Terry.

"I—," Sky started to say, but then he felt something sharp and pointy and *knifey* poke him in the back. "Uh, yeah. All made up and good as new. . . . Out for a little stroll with my new *BEAU*s here," he said, elbowing Crenshaw and Ren in the ribs not so playfully. "Not *SHER IF* I could get away if I *WANTED TO*." He finished, laughing nervously and gesturing at Crenshaw with his eyebrows.

"This guy," Crenshaw said, laughing and giving Sky a noogie as he strangled him. "I could just eat him up."

"I'm sure you could," said Miss Terry. "Well, don't let me

keep you. I hear it's going to be quite a night tonight—last night of the Hunter's Moon, you know. Don't stay out too late." With that, she turned and disappeared down the hall.

The sun was beginning to set by the time Crenshaw and Ren dragged him out of the school.

As they walked down the steps, he both hoped and feared that he'd find Mom waiting for him just as she'd threatened. He *hoped* to see her one last time, but at the same time, he *feared* that if she were here, she might try to stop Crenshaw and Ren from taking him, and he couldn't stand the thought of her getting hurt.

"Going somewhere?" a female voice purred behind him.

Sky cranked his head around, hoping for deliverance. Instead he found Miss Hagfish.

"Uh, nowhere in particular," said Crenshaw as he tightened his grip.

Ren stepped forward, putting himself between Sky and Miss Hagfish. "You shouldn't be here, Miss Hagfish," said Ren in a soft, menacing voice.

"Indeed?" said Miss Hagfish with an insipid raise of her right eyebrow.

Sky could see Ren slowly pulling something from underneath his coat.

"Don't even try it, Renoir. I trained your mother *and* your grandparents. I can certainly take care of *you*," said Miss Hagfish.

"You're Malvidia!" exclaimed Sky, comprehension dawning. "Leader of the hunters!"

"What's left of them," said Malvidia, smiling blandly.

Sky's eyes widened. Ren was pulling a knife! Was he seriously thinking of attacking a teacher with a knife?

"LOOK OUT!" Sky yelled.

Ren hesitated. And then, in one smooth motion, he pulled the knife and thrust forward.

Sky cringed, expecting to see the knife plunge into Malvidia's heart.

Almost casually Malvidia stepped to the side, catching Ren's knife arm under her own. In the same motion she put her hand on his bicep and twisted, throwing Ren to the ground. She grabbed his wrist as he fell, and, wrenching it behind his back, she came down on top of him.

She tightened her grip, and the knife fell from Ren's hand. She pulled some leaves and flowers from her pocket and pressed them against Ren's nose until his eyes slowly closed and he stopped struggling.

"Wolfsbane!" Sky gasped, recognizing the plant the shoe salesman had used to drive off the Shadow Wargs in Whimple. T-Bone was not going to be happy when he found out his brother was a Shadow Warg!

And if Ren was a Shadow Warg, chances were good that Crenshaw, Cordelia, and Marcus were as well. Bullet was frozen back at the lair, which meant that only three of the five Shadow Wargs were still in action, but one of them—the one that for some unknown reason hated Sky most of all—had a knife at his throat. Odds were not in his favor.

"Crenshaw, is there anything you'd like to add?" asked Malvidia, standing up from Ren's motionless body. "Or would you prefer to wait for more friends to show?"

Sky ran through the numbers frantically, trying to figure out how many "friends" were still unaccounted for. Cordelia and Marcus, definitely. Principal Lem, the Wargarou, would be along at any moment. And two Whisper: the Wargarou's accomplice, Ambrosia (bad), and Sheriff Beau's ex-wife, Ursula (probably good). Ambrosia and Ursula could change into almost anything under a full moon, they were sisters, daughters of the Arkhon and incredibly dangerous, but only Ambrosia was likely to help Principal Lem, and she hadn't shown her face since she'd attacked Phineas; where could she be?

Crenshaw started backing away, holding Sky in a headlock, a knife pressed against his back.

"How long have you known?" asked Crenshaw.

"I've known you were *stupid* for some time now," said Malvidia. "Why else would I allow my apprentices near you? But I didn't know how stupid until this moment, or possibly last night." Malvidia glanced at Sky, and Sky realized Sheriff Beau must've passed on his warning about Bat. "Out for a little revenge, are you?" she continued. "I understand the desire for revenge—believe me, I do—but becoming a Shadow Warg, Crenshaw? Really? Your father would be okay with it, I'm sure. He's a monster in his own right. But your mother must be rolling over in her grave."

"Yeah, well. My mother wouldn't *be* in a grave if it weren't for Sky and that old man you're always hunting!" said Crenshaw, lifting the knife to Sky's neck.

"What are you talking about, Crenshaw?" said Sky, honestly confused. "I don't even know your mom! And are you talking about Phineas?"

Sky knew Malvidia was after Phineas, that the whole move to Exile had been a well-constructed trap on her part to lure Phineas in and catch him, and probably so she could keep an eye on Sky. But why would Crenshaw think they had done something to his mom? Sky hadn't even known his mom was dead until now! How could Sky possibly have been responsible?

"He is indeed talking about your traitorous uncle, Mr. Weathers," said Malvidia, slowly moving toward Crenshaw, who—just as slowly—backed away, keeping the knife pressed against Sky's throat. "He's talking about how hunters, like his mother, were forced to fight and die after we had the Arkhon trapped, just so your uncle and I could save your worthless self."

"That's a lie," said Sky without thinking. "Phineas saved me. You and the other hunters wanted to kill me because you thought the Arkhon was behind whatever happened to me. You thought that he gave me the black mark on my hand eleven years ago, but you got it wrong. You should have listened to Phineas."

Malvidia raised an eyebrow. "You have an exceptional memory considering you were only a baby at the time. It almost makes one wonder."

Sky blanched. He'd been edgewalking when he'd seen that. He shouldn't have said anything. Phineas's journal entry had said that if the hunters saw Sky doing anything "abnormal" they would kill him, and he'd just given them a reason.

This day wasn't shaping up at all like he'd hoped.

"Nevertheless," continued Malvidia, "Crenshaw's point is valid. The Arkhon never would have come to Exile if not for you and that bothersome *Hunter's Mark*. Far more trouble than it's ever been worth, if you ask me." She spat in disgust. "But if the Arkhon had not come for it, Crenshaw's poor mother might still be alive."

Sky looked into Malvidia's maliciously twinkling eyes. She really did want him dead.

"But, *come on*! Crenshaw! I—I didn't do it on purpose!

Neither did Phineas! It's not like I lured the Arkhon here because I wanted your mom to die! I was bait—one year old, for crying out loud!" said Sky, feeling suddenly guilty for the death of Crenshaw's mom and all the other hunters, even though he knew it was absurd.

"You know," said Malvidia to Sky, "you really are a *slow* child for all the bluster Phineas made about you. I wonder if he ever regrets his decision to save you."

"I—what?" said Sky. "Why are you attacking *me* here? I'm the *victim*! Can you see the knife at my throat?"

"Phineas never should have let you live. You and those marks are a danger to us all," continued Malvidia. "Hunters are not trained to fight in open battles. We hunt alone, in the dark. Luring the Arkhon here was our death sentence. In a few hours the hunters that remain will be gathered, and the Arkhon will *feast*. Phineas has killed us all."

"Look," said Sky, "there seems to be a little bit of tension in the air—"

Crenshaw pushed the knife harder against his throat.

"But I'm sure if we just sit down over a nice, steamy cup of wolfbane-laced cocoa, we can work it all out."

"Just shut up, Sky!" yelled Crenshaw, shaking Sky dangerously, the knife flailing about. "You think the Arkhon is going to protect you now? You think you can kill me with those marks like you killed Alexis?"

"Who?" asked Sky, utterly dumbfounded.

Crenshaw let loose a feral scream that chilled Sky to the bone, and then Sky remembered Alexis, his missing classmate! She must have been Bullet!

Crenshaw thought he'd *killed* her? No wonder he was so ticked off.

Sky felt the knife quivering. He closed his eyes, waiting for the cut that would end his life.

"Well, go on. Kill him already! I haven't got all night!" said Malvidia.

Was she being serious?

"This has to be the worst rescue effort I've ever heard of," said Sky.

The knife nicked his skin as it shook in Crenshaw's hand, drawing a trickle of blood.

"You're a *monster,* Crenshaw," Malvidia jeered. "You can't fight what you are any more than the Arkhon could when he killed Solomon Rose. It's your nature. So, go on! Kill him! Avenge your mother!"

"Don't listen to her, Crenshaw," said Sky, his mind racing for a way out. "You're not a monster! You're not a killer! You're just, er, Wargily-challenged!"

Sky wanted to kick himself. Wargily-challenged? Seriously? His life was on the line and that was the best he could come up?

Malvidia laughed. "Oh, he's most definitely a killer; don't fool yourself into believing otherwise. His hesitation has nothing to do with compassion," said Malvidia, sneering. "He can't kill you, no matter how much you might deserve and need it. As long as you know something about the keys and the monsters don't, they'll keep you alive, especially since you're working for the same team, whether Phineas believes it or not. They might maim you horribly, sure, but not kill you. Crenshaw is bound to obey the Wargarou, who wants you alive. To disobey would mean his own death, and I'm not sure he hates you quite that much. Isn't that right, Crenshaw?"

"What do *you* know, Miss *Hagfish*? You think all monsters are evil, but it's you who's evil!" yelled Crenshaw.

Malvidia yawned, enraging Crenshaw even more.

Sky was going to die. Bound or not, Crenshaw was going to kill him. And Malvidia was going to drive him to it.

"You think you know everything!" screamed Crenshaw. "Well, I know something too! Lem told me what you and your fiancé did to his pack in Whimple!" Crenshaw smiled as Malvidia's eyes opened in surprise. "*And* he also told me what he did to your family afterward."

Whimple? But there was no way. *The Shadow Wargs of Whimple* was hundreds of years old! Older even than *The Evil Echo of Solomon Rose*! And Malvidia was the mayor's daughter, the real bride who'd survived Whimple's destruction, whose sister had been killed by the Wargarou. That would make Malvidia and the Wargarou more than four hundred years old! How was that even possible?! And in the story the mayor's daughter had been so . . . so . . . likable! Not . . . *this*.

"You claim to protect the innocent," continued Crenshaw, "you claim loyalty and pack, but all you really want is revenge. How is that any less evil than the Arkhon's thirst for power or the Wargarou's drive to protect his own?"

"While this academic discussion with you is entertaining, I do have a pressing engagement this evening," said Malvidia, her voice cold and empty. "So why don't you tell me where I can find Phineas so I can perhaps salvage something out of the mess he's made?"

"Oooh," muttered Crenshaw, shaking his head. "I'm sorry to disappoint you, Malvidia, but you can't kill the old man. He's already *dead*."

Sky jerked his head around, the blade cutting into his neck. "What?"

"Dead. D-E-D," spelled Crenshaw. "As in 'not living.' He's been dead for two days, or as good as."

"'As good as' isn't the same as dead," said Malvidia, studying Crenshaw. "You learned *nothing* from me. If you're going to go through the trouble of killing something, make sure it's dead. Do you have his body?"

Crenshaw's smile faltered. "No."

"Then he's not D-E-D," said Malvidia.

"We know where he is," said Crenshaw.

"If you know where he is and you think he's dead, but you still haven't bothered to collect his body, then *I* know where he is too," said Malvidia. "There are very few places a Whisper and a Wargarou would be afraid to go, and only one within walking distance for a horribly wounded hunter."

"He's still alive!" exclaimed Sky. "Malvidia—*Miss Hagfish*—if you know where he is, we can help him! He knows how to fix the trap! We can still stop the Arkhon from escaping!"

"We're doing just fine without him, thank you very much. But if your uncle's still alive," said Malvidia, "I will make him tell me how to fix the trap, purely out of curiosity, mind you, and then I will kill him. And this time I'll make *sure* he's dead."

Sky struggled against Crenshaw. "You're awful! How can you even say that? He was just trying to protect me! I was only a baby!"

"A baby whose very existence could destroy the world," said Malvidia.

Sky stared at her in shock.

"Ah, so now you begin to see my dilemma," she continued. “Save one hopeless child or save the entire helpless world. Phineas and I have both made our choices.”

“You’re completely mental,” Sky accused.

“This is growing tiresome. Crenshaw, tell me where I can find the Whisper Ambrosia and the Wargarou who ate Lem, and I might not kill you,” said Malvidia.

“You’d have to ask Lem where to find Ambrosia. She’s *in cogito*,” said Crenshaw.

“You think she’s in *what*?” asked Malvidia.

“Huh?” said Crenshaw, looking confused.

“You just said she was ‘in cogito,’ Latin for ‘I think in,’” said Malvidia. “So please tell me what you think she might be in.”

“I think he meant ‘incognito,’” supplied Sky. “You know, still posing as *someone else*.”

“Ah,” said Malvidia, “I see. In that case, where can I find the Wargarou who ate Principal Bartholomew ‘Bart’ Lem and took his place?”

“Behind you, actually,” said Crenshaw.

Malvidia spun with Ren’s knife, a silver stake flashing into her free hand from up her sleeve, but it was too late. Crenshaw had led her, unknowingly, into the shadow of a spruce, and Principal Lem flowed out of the shadows like a desolating plague, driving a knife into her stomach.

Principal Lem let go of the knife and stepped away with cool indifference, taking care to keep blood from spilling onto his suit.

The knife stuck out of Malvidia like a tombstone sticking out of dirt, and then—to Sky’s amazement—she wrapped her hands around the handle and slowly pulled it out.

She smiled grotesquely, blood soaking the front of her

black dress. "It'll take more than a knife to the stomach to take me down, *Wargarou*." She spun the knife in her hand and started advancing on Principal Lem.

"I remember," said Principal Lem, "that's why I coated the blade in Dovetail."

Malvidia's smile fell. She took a step forward and sank to her knees—the knife falling from her fingers.

"You hunters think you're so clever with your metals and your plants and your traps—exploiting our weaknesses like common *thugs*. Well, we can be clever too," said Principal Lem. "It was long ago, but I haven't forgotten Whimple."

"So it really is y-you. You're p-poisoning the meat. Aren't you g-g-going t-to eat me-e?" slurred Malvidia, trying to smile. "Like my s-s-sister . . . ?"

"Eat you? Your stringy principal was bad enough. If I hadn't needed his body, I wouldn't have bothered! I don't think I could stomach another of you Hunters of Legend!" The Wargarou laughed. "It'd be like eating old shoe leather. But eating your little sister . . . Well, I truly enjoyed that." Principal Lem licked his lips. "You know how much I like the young."

Rage swept across Malvidia's face. She struggled to her feet, took one more step, and then toppled to the ground.

CHAPTER 29

Wargarou!

Crenshaw tightened his grip.

"Marcus, if you'd be so good as to help Malvidia to the car," said Principal Lem.

Sky watched as Marcus somehow folded out of the shadows.

"Why bother with the old bat?" asked Crenshaw. "She's as good as dead."

Principal Lem rubbed something under Ren's nose, causing Ren to sit up swinging. "As Malvidia so astutely pointed out, 'as good as dead' *isn't* dead. Besides, her body might come in useful."

"You'd really eat *her*?" asked Crenshaw, disgusted.

"We still have a run-down old shoe salesman to find. Maybe he'll come out for his old flame," said Principal Lem.

Old shoe salesman? Sky's stomach dropped. Beau had told him that Phineas and Malvidia had a complicated history, but surely he couldn't have meant . . .

"Unless Phineas is already dead from the wound Ambrosia gave him. Nothing could've survived that," said Crenshaw. "*Nothing.*"

Sky felt sick. Uncle Phineas was the *shoe salesman* in Whimple! This just kept getting better and better! He knew Phineas was *old*—at least thirty—but hundreds of years old? And engaged to Malvidia, a woman who wanted to kill him? You'd think he might've mentioned that before!

"In which case you and Ren can fight the Jack for his body," said Principal Lem.

The Jack. Sky had heard that name before. Mom had warned Dad about the Jack when he went to Pimiscule Grounds, the night Crenshaw had first sought revenge as a Shadow Warg. But what was it?

"It's funny," said Principal Lem as he watched Marcus unsuccessfully manhandling Malvidia. "For almost four hundred years hunters have tried to imprison the Arkhon—trapping him in the earth, binding him at the bottom of the sea—but he always breaks free in the end, more powerful than before. Even now, time itself cannot hold him bound. The only thing that's ever really worked was feeding him to the Jack. Sure, he broke free *eventually*, but the Jack held him longer than any other. What a *marvelous* creature, the Jack . . ."

Crenshaw's smile fell.

"I'm not going in there again," said Ren quietly, his voice trembling. "Not with that *thing*."

"Yeah," added Crenshaw, "why don't you go in if you want the old man so bad."

Sky was surprised. They sounded terrified! They'd been cavorting with the Wargarou, frolicking with a Whisper, and they were Shadow Wargs themselves! What could be more frightening than that?

A long claw extended from Principal Lem's finger, and he pressed it against Crenshaw's throat. "Come, come. You'll hardly be the biggest threat as long as Phineas is in there. The Jack won't even notice you at all. *Me,* on the other hand. You won't catch me *dead* in that place. Is that reason enough for you, Crenshaw?"

Crenshaw gulped and nodded with the smallest possible shake to keep from impaling himself.

"Good," said Principal Lem, withdrawing the claw. "Use your mouth, Marcus."

Marcus was having a hard time lifting Malvidia, but whether he was having a hard time because he'd just contributed to the possible death of a teacher or because he was feeling awkward touching a girl, Sky couldn't tell.

"My mouth. Right. I knew that," said Marcus. As Sky watched, Marcus's body began to ripple and shift, sprouting tufts of thick, shadowy hair and an elongated though somewhat stubby snout, until Sky found himself looking at a rather pudgy Shadow Warg. One of the two Shadow Wargs that Sky hadn't named. Sky decided he'd call Marcus *Pudgy*. Or maybe Snouty. No, Pudgy was better. Ren was obviously Big, and Crenshaw was Vicious, Bullet (Alexis) was frozen. That left Cordelia, wherever she was. Thinking about her punch earlier, he decided he'd call her Dangerous.

Marcus bent down, grabbed Malvidia by the arm with his mouth, and dragged her toward the bus loop as a faded red 1957 Cadillac Eldorado Brougham pulled up—the same car that had followed his family into town two nights ago.

"Crenshaw, Ren, load Mr. Weath—" Principal Lem hesitated and turned toward Sky. "You know, we're such good friends now, would it bother you if I called you Sky?"

"I'd prefer you didn't call me *at all*," said Sky, "but I have your number. Maybe I'll look you up sometime."

"Bon mot, Sky! You are a clever boy!" Principal Lem complimented. He turned back to Ren and Crenshaw. "Put him in the car."

Sky looked around desperately for help, but the schoolyard and the parking lot were empty. He thought of running, but even if he managed to break free—which he doubted, he'd still have to outrun a pack of Shadow Wargs, something that hadn't ended too well for him the first time.

But still, he had to do something or Malvidia would die. As awful as she was, he couldn't let that happen.

He was on the verge of making a run for it when he saw the sheriff's Blazer appear at the bottom of the road. Hope surged through him.

Miss Terry had understood his message!

Principal Lem noticed the Blazer as well. He lifted his nose, sniffing the air.

"It looks like the good sheriff will be joining us in a moment. Cordelia, could you hold this for me, please?" Principal Lem handed her Sky's pocket watch. "Please ensure that this gets to Ambrosia as soon as possible should any unpleasantness happen."

"I guess," said Cordelia, taking the watch.

"Also, would you be so kind as to get out of the driver's seat and load the body so that Marcus can slip away? I'd hate for the sheriff to think we were up to something," said Principal Lem. "He and I are old friends after all . . ."

Cordelia slid across the seat, exiting from the passenger side. As the door opened, Sky spotted his backpack. Crenshaw and Ren shoved him into the backseat and, forcing him into the middle, assumed posts on either side.

Sky looked around the car, plotting his escape. Big on one side, Vicious on the other, locked doors, rolled-up windows, car in park and running, backpack on front seat.

"Done," said Cordelia a moment later, brushing her hands together as she crawled back in.

Marcus had disappeared.

Sky added *Dangerous in front seat* and *location of Pudgy unknown* to his list.

"A 1957 Cadillac Eldorado Brougham. A bit *obvious*, isn't it?" Sky prodded.

"Ambrosia likes obvious," said Cordelia. "She says it's the best way to hide."

Principal Lem tapped on the back window, and Crenshaw rolled it down.

"If he tries to escape or warn the sheriff, you have my permission to kill him. In fact, please do," said Principal Lem, giving Sky a toothy smile.

Sky gulped as Crenshaw returned the smile and started playing with his knife.

In the rearview mirror Sky could see Principal Lem walking toward Sheriff Beau's Blazer as it pulled to a stop.

"Sheriff! What a pleasant surprise," Sky heard Principal Lem say as he approached the Blazer's passenger side window.

Sky listened for sounds of movement from the trunk. He knew from experience that if Malvidia didn't get the crow's feet soon, she'd go to sleep and never wake up.

If the stomach wound didn't kill her first, that is.

He needed to escape, but his only hope for escape sat in the front seat.

"So you guys are Shadow Wargs, huh?" asked Sky, leaning forward to talk to Cordelia.

"Shut up," said Crenshaw as he tried to listen to the conversation between Principal Lem and Sheriff Beau.

"That must be something, being a *Shadow Warg*!" said Sky, feigning excitement.

"It's okay," said Cordelia, obviously bored with the notion.

"I've read about them before, you know. *The Shadow Wargs of Whimple*. Ever hear of it? It's in my backpack there, if you want to take a look."

"Hm," said Cordelia noncommittally.

"I know Crenshaw's heard all about it," said Sky, trying to catch her interest, "seeing as how it talks about your Wargarou pack leader and Malvidia and . . . and . . . *Phineas*, and all."

"Uh-huh," said Cordelia, who'd obviously never read it and, just as obviously, couldn't have cared less.

"It's got a great—er—*wedding* scene in it, " said Sky.

"Weddings are boring," said Cordelia.

"The bride nearly bites the groom's head off in the end," said Sky.

Cordelia sat up, suddenly interested. "Yeah?"

"Oh, yeah. There's lots of blood and stuff," said Sky.

Cordelia started rifling through his backpack looking for the book.

"Turns out she—er—*he*, Lem that is, was the Wargarou behind it all—ate the bride's sister, put on a veil, and took the bride's place at the wedding. Can you just imagine him in a wedding dress? It's right there, on the bottom," said Sky, peeking over the seat as Cordelia emptied the contents of his backpack. "He ends up destroying the town to get revenge on the shoe salesman who drove off his pack. Kills every one of them, except Malvidia, apparently . . . and . . . Phineas." He still couldn't imagine Phineas as a four-hundred-plus-year-old shoe salesman. "You see," Sky continued, "when the Shadow Wargs got far enough away from Lem, or Gourmand, as he was called in the story, he lost control of them and they were *free*. Well, at least until another Wargarou showed up and claimed the pack, but that's a different story."

Cordelia found the book and started leafing through it.

"I'm surprised you don't have it," said Sky. "I thought *The Shadow Wargs of Whimple* would be standard issue for hunters at Arkhon Academy."

"Hunters?" Cordelia chuckled. "There aren't any 'hunters' at Arkhon Academy. They're all dead except for a few old-timers who try to keep pointless traditions alive."

"So there's no school?" asked Sky.

"Oh, there's a school. You go to it, remember? There's just no 'hunters' school. It's all apprenticeship programs now. Each hunter takes on their own, and never more than a few at a time. Sometimes they swap, so one know-it-all can teach another's."

"Like with Lazar and Lucretia studying with Principal Lem. They're Malvidia's apprentices, right?" said Sky.

"Apprentices and *spies*," said Cordelia. "Malvidia's the biggest know-it-all of them all, and those two whelps of hers are almost as bad. Most hunters refuse to take on apprentices these days, or if they do, they don't tell anybody about it."

"Why's that?" asked Sky.

"Too many go bad, I guess," said Cordelia, showing her teeth.

"Would you two shut up?" said Crenshaw.

"He's quite the charmer, isn't he?" said Cordelia offhandedly.

"I can see why you fell for him," said Sky, smiling.

Cordelia started laughing, and for a moment he could see why Crenshaw had fallen for her. Not that dangerously bored girls who liked gore and could change into Shadow Wargs were his type, but he could see the appeal.

Crenshaw gritted his teeth and turned back to the window.

Sky glanced in the side mirror. It looked like Principal Lem and Sheriff Beau were wrapping things up. The sheriff knew Bat, the principal, was the Wargarou, because Sky had told him, but he also knew, as he'd told Sky, that he couldn't beat one. The only hunter in Exile besides Phineas who could was dying in the trunk.

Would Beau do anything?

Sky could imagine the conversation they must have been having.

"Nice weather today," Sheriff Beau would say.

"I couldn't agree more," Lem would say.

"Have you any boron?" Sheriff Beau would ask.

"These suits are dry-clean only," Lem would respond, and on and on, around and around they'd go. Neither would move until they'd sized up the other.

Sky just wished they'd hurry and get on with whatever they were going to do. Malvidia couldn't have much time left.

"I'm sorry I pulled you in on that whole letter thing," said Sky to Cordelia, trying to find an ally. "I wasn't trying to embarrass you."

"Collateral damage. It happens," said Cordelia.

"So, why did you do it? Become a Shadow Warg, I mean?"

"Just bored, I guess," said Cordelia. "It's nothing personal."

"Collateral damage, huh?" said Sky.

"Something like that," replied Cordelia.

Suddenly there was a gunshot, and everyone flipped around to see what'd happened.

In the mirror Sky saw Principal Lem dive out of the way, his skin rippling as he started to shift. It was the moment Sky had been waiting for.

Arms still tied behind his back, he dove over the front seat, ramming his head into the manual override button (the rigged spout) on the canister of Fog that Cordelia had emptied onto the seat from his backpack. Sulfuric Fog billowed out, filling the car within seconds.

He rolled over the seat, ramming his legs into the steering wheel. Muffling a yelp of pain, he scrambled around, grabbing on to the door handle with his teeth.

Cordelia grabbed his legs, yanking them out from under him.

Something slammed into the back of the car, flinging him into the driver's side door, which flipped open (pulled by his teeth). He then bounced into the dashboard and back onto the seat.

Shaken, he kicked out with a leg, connecting. Cordelia let go, and Sky caterpillared through the open door, trying to slide as much of the stuff from his backpack with him as he could, knowing he'd need it if he was going to stand any chance of escaping.

He tumbled out of the car, slamming his face into the ground. A few of his things cascaded around him, including his black light, which is what he'd been hoping for.

Moving his still bound arms under his legs to the front, he grabbed the black light the monster hunters had given him with the other gear, and he started running for the trees.

Over his shoulder, through the Fog billowing out of the

Cadillac, he spotted the Blazer, smashed into the back of the Brougham.

The Blazer rocked back and forth, and Sheriff Beau dove out the front door. There was a sudden grinding noise, and then the Blazer FLIPPED into the air, sailing just inches over Beau's head!

It continued to spin as it landed, crashing past Sky like a meteor, exploding in flame and light as it hit the forest he'd been racing toward. Afterimages, like ghosts, blinded him.

And then, through the Fog and through his fear, he saw it: Lem, the Wargarou, in its true form.

It resembled a Shadow Warg in the same way that a redwood resembles a pine. A pine might be impressive on its own, but when you put it next to a redwood, nobody in their right mind would say, "Wow! Look at that *pine*!"

It was shadowy and roughly wolf-shaped like a Shadow Warg, but there the resemblance ended. Long, thick tusks, like swords, stuck out from its chin and forehead, and shadowy hairs writhed all over its enormous body like worms, eating the light around it, the ends tipped with fire and shadow that shivered along the hairs' length.

Sky felt its blood-red eyes fall upon him. Its growl rumbled out like water breaking from a dam, and the wind it expelled caught Sky full on, flinging him into the air. He spun around and around, twisting and flipping, until he crashed into a tree at the forest's edge.

He crawled to his feet trying to shake off the blow. He saw the black light a few feet away, fallen from his fingers.

The Wargarou advanced, its movements like the swelling of a tide.

Frantically Sky scanned the surrounding forest, looking for

a way out, but he knew he couldn't outrun it, even if he *could* get his feet to move.

Shots rang out, and the Wargarou howled in pain. It turned away from him to face the sheriff, who was crouching, gun out, next to the Cadillac.

Sky raced to the black light.

"A cracker for you!" yelled Sky as he scooped up the black light, flipped the switch, and threw it into the air.

A mottled crow swooped out of the trees, snatching the light as it fell.

"CAW!"

"I know it's not a cracker, but I'll give you some later. I promise," said Sky. He knew these weren't normal birds, he could feel it, but were they smart enough to do what he wanted? Somehow he knew they understood him even if he couldn't really understand them, though he almost felt he was beginning to. "Just fly over the east cemetery! Near Rauschtlot and Emaline Livingstone's tomb! If Hands convinced them to show, they should be waiting for me! Bring them here, and hurry!"

Of course, this wasn't the triumphant moment he'd planned when he'd asked Hands to bring Crystal and the others to Andrew's mother's tomb to meet with Rauschtlot, but circumstances change.

"CAW!" cawed the crow, sounding very unhappy.

Other crows came out of the trees and, surrounding the first, they sailed higher and higher, the black light illuminating their bodies in dancing patterns of fluorescent light, like jellyfish floating through the sky, carried by the winds toward the cemetery.

"I owe you one!" yelled Sky.

It was a slim chance based on an even slimmer hope, but it was the only hope he had, and right now he'd take what he could get. Running was impossible. Fighting was suicidal. If he was going to make it, and Malvidia was going to survive, help would have to come to him.

He turned back around as a pudgy Shadow Warg—Marcus—slipped out of the woods and padded toward him, teeth barred.

Sky backed away.

"Hey, Marcus. Nice, er, *fur*," said Sky, kicking himself once again. He was *really* going to have to work on his compliments.

To his left the roof exploded off the Cadillac, and two more Shadow Wargs—Ren and Crenshaw—busted through. There was no sign of Cordelia. Had she already run off to deliver the watch to Ambrosia, as Lem had ordered? If so, he had almost no hope of getting it back since he still didn't know who she was.

"Easy there, Marcus. I can help you get out of this," said Sky, backing away. "We can take down the Wargarou and free you. Just walk away."

Marcus wasn't stopping.

"I know you don't want to be Crenshaw's stooge forever," said Sky.

Marcus growled, opening his mouth.

Sky raised his hand, willing the trix or the Hunter's Mark to put Marcus to sleep.

Marcus hesitated.

Nothing happened.

"Stupid trix! Stupid Hunter's Mark! Stupid Errand!"

As hope abandoned him, *yet another* Shadow Warg appeared, barreling out of the woods.

"What is it with this town?" exclaimed Sky.

The new Shadow Warg, not one of the original five, rammed Marcus in the side, sending him sliding across the road.

Without slowing, the Shadow Warg continued past Sky, racing for the Wargarou.

Sky watched, trying to figure out why the Shadow Warg looked so familiar, but something horrifying grabbed his attention . . .

Sheriff Beau.

The sheriff dragged a bum leg, his body coated in fresh blood from a number of gashes and gouges. He backed away toward the Cadillac, trapped between the Wargarou in front and Ren and Crenshaw to his sides.

As Sky watched, the Wargarou *lunged* forward, spearing Beau clean through with a tusk, pinning him against the Cadillac.

"No!" screamed Sky, rushing forward. He watched in horror, helpless, as the Wargarou backed away, Sherriff Beau hanging, limp and broken, from a bloody tusk, like a summer rose in autumn.

With the last pieces of his life, Sheriff Beau pumped bullet after bullet into the Wargarou, shooting again and again. The Wargarou howled, raising its writhing head to drive the broken sheriff into the ground.

That's when the Shadow Warg hit.

Since she'd emerged from the forest and barreled into Marcus, she hadn't stopped running. She sailed through the air, ramming her head into the Wargarou's side before it could complete its awful task.

The jolt threw the Wargarou off balance, and instead of slamming the Sheriff into the ground, it launched the sheriff into the air. He landed with a sickening crunch within the Fog spilling from the Cadillac.

The newest Shadow Warg snarled as she pressed her advantage, launching herself onto the Wargarou and gnawing its leg. Almost immediately—as the Wargarou's blood touched her lips—her body began to shift and ripple, growing bigger and stronger. She sprouted from a pine to a *redwood*.

And then Sky knew who she was.

"Ursula," he muttered in amazement.

The sheriff's wife had finally returned to him.

The two Wargarous circled each other, bashing and tearing. Lashes of fiery darkness, like whips, beat down, and streams of night swirled around them. They slipped in and out of shadow, appearing and disappearing and reappearing as they fought. They crashed into cars, knocked over telephone poles and trees, roaring and howling.

As the two monsters smashed together, a maelstrom of clashing tusks and flame and writhing darkness, Sky rushed forward, grabbed Sheriff Beau under the arms and dragged him deeper into the Fog.

The Fog dampened the sounds of the fighting Wargarou. Even so, their fury filled the night with eerie growls and ghostly snarls, like Wights waiting to capture the souls of the dead.

"Sky?" Sheriff Beau wheezed, not looking good at all.

"It's okay," muttered Sky as he knelt down, his eyes filling with tears. Why did everyone who tried to help him get hurt?

He felt around the sheriff's stomach until he found the wound. It was big and round and wet.

"You'll be okay," said Sky, tears rolling down his cheeks like desert rain. "It's not so bad—you should see Malvidia."

"Sky," wheezed the Sheriff, "get out of here."

Sky patted Beau's hand reassuringly like Mom had always done for him when he was sick.

And then, in the Fog, he saw what he'd been dreading: two sets of blood-red eyes. He stood, moving away from Beau.

Ren shot forward, batting Sky to the side with his head. Sky flew through the air, crashing hard several feet away. He climbed to his hands and knees, trying to get back to his feet. "You're not a killer, Ren. You couldn't be T-Bone's brother and be a killer."

Crenshaw rushed in from the other side and, picking Sky up in his jaws, threw him back toward Ren.

Sky tumbled through the air like a rag doll, sliding to a stop at Ren's feet. Sky's coat ripped to bits, and his face was covered in asphalt and road rash. He tried to roll over, to get to his feet again, but his body wouldn't respond.

"Ren, d-don't," spluttered Sky, looking up into Ren's shadowy face.

Ren snarled down at Sky . . . and then his expression seemed to change, as if he suddenly realized what he was about to do. He started biting at the air, waving his head around. He stepped backward, then forward, growling and whimpering in indecision.

Sky watched, a spectator, as Ren fought against himself for Sky's life.

This wasn't just playing anymore. This wasn't bullying, or wrestling, or roughing someone up. The Wargarou had *ordered* them to kill Sky if he tried to escape. Ren would forfeit his life if he disobeyed.

Sky watched the monster take hold of Ren, fighting down his better sense, and then Sky knew . . .

He was a dead man.

Ren gave one final snarl and then, with almost apologetic eyes, shot at Sky's neck with glistening fangs.

As Ren's head dropped, two metal gloves shimmering with electric light flew across Sky's body, latching on to the corners of Ren's open mouth.

T-Bone stepped across Sky, driving the monster back. In the darkening night high above, Sky could see scores of fluorescent blue dots circling in the heavens. The crows had done it; they'd found the monster hunters by the tomb and led them here. The monster hunters had spotted Sky's black light and followed, and Sky had held Ren and Crenshaw long enough to keep Beau alive. It had been a weak plan based on a weaker hope, but it had worked. The monster hunters hadn't abandoned him completely.

"T-Bone! It's Ren! Don't hurt him!" yelled Sky.

"What?" T-Bone faltered for a moment, and Ren nearly threw him, but T-Bone pressed down, forcing Ren to retreat.

Sky turned his head as Crenshaw howled, a glob of freezing ICE catching him in the side. A breath, and then two serrated prongs followed. Lightning shot along the wires joining Andrew's Taser-like Cross-Shocker to the prongs, freezing Crenshaw solid.

"Oooh, that thing is *so* going to feel that in the morning," said Hands as he helped Sky to his feet.

"The sheriff. We've got to help him!" said Sky, limping toward the spot where he'd left Sheriff Beau.

The spot was still there, but the sheriff wasn't.

"Where is he?" said Sky, realizing that the night had grown suddenly quiet. "Where are the Wargarous?"

A cracking noise broke the silence as the ice around

Crenshaw shattered. Howling, Crenshaw slipped away into the shadows, Ren fleeing at his heels a moment later.

Sky stumbled toward what was left of the Cadillac, which he could see clearly now that most of the Fog had lifted.

He forced open the trunk.

"Miss Hagfish?" said Hands, surprised.

"Malvidia," corrected Sky, glancing at T-Bone, who was still staring broodingly into the distance where Ren had disappeared. "Head of the hunters."

"The *hunters*?" said Andrew. "I thought they were dead."

"Not all of them," said Sky, "not yet anyway. She's still breathing, but she's been poisoned by Dovetail."

"And stabbed in the gut," said Hands.

Sky scanned the parking lot. There was no sign of the sheriff. Sky had to assume that whoever had won the fight (Lem or Ursula) had taken care of things—for better or worse.

The Piebalds dropped his black light. "Thanks." He scooped it up, spotted a pack of mostly whole crackers from his backpack, and tossed several to the Piebalds, before shoving the rest into a pocket. Everything else from his backpack had scattered; he'd have to come back for it later.

"I need to get the antidote. Phineas wouldn't want me to let her die, not when I can do something about it," said Sky as he stood and began walking toward the forest. "And I wouldn't want that either."

"What are we supposed to do with her?" asked Hands, sounding worried.

Sky picked up his pace, running toward the manor and the trail that would lead him home. "Make sure she doesn't die before I get back!"

CHAPTER 30

In the Ashes

Sky ran through his front door.

"Mom? Dad?"

It was time to talk to his parents. He knew they'd freak out—if they even believed him—but Malvidia would die if he didn't get help for her. And, there was still a chance Beau was dying out there somewhere.

He raced into the kitchen. "Mom?"

Empty.

He ran to the pantry and started searching through Mom's stash of dried plants. He found the crow's foot and shoved a few handfuls into a bag, and then, for good measure, he grabbed a few other plants and unidentifiable substances Mom had used on past injuries: Gilead root, rictus leaf, barrow weed, Jack seed . . . Jack seed? As in *the* Jack that everyone was afraid of? The same Jack that had once been used to imprison the Arkhon? Sky stared at the seeds, trying to unravel the puzzle he knew was here.

"Sky?" said a voice behind him.

He flipped around, spilling Jack seeds across the floor.

"Dad? Geez, you nearly scared me to death." He got on his knees, scrambling to gather up the Jack seeds.

"The feeling is mutual," said Dad. "What are you doing?"

He shoved the seeds into a bag, grabbed some extra wolfsbane, just in case, and turned for the door.

"Dad, I know you're not going to believe this, or maybe you already know and you'll deny it, but there are monsters in Exile," said Sky.

"Monsters?"

He pushed past Dad, heading for the stairs. He had one more thing to do.

"I know what you're going to say. It's just the shadows, just my imagination, but it's not! Sheriff Beau and Malvidia have been attacked! They might even be *dead*!" exclaimed Sky, taking the stairs two at a time, Dad a few steps behind.

"Sky, slow down. What's this all about?"

"No time!" said Sky, throwing open his bedroom door. He headed for his books. "I need you to trust me for once and stop lying! The manor is a trap. You know about it! I overheard you and Mom talking. It's why you brought us back here, isn't it?"

"Sky—," started Dad, but Sky cut him off.

"Phineas is in trouble. He's hurt, maybe even dead, and he's somewhere close! I know you and Mom aren't hunters, but we've got to find him and we've got to stop the trap from opening! He's the only one who knows how! But first we've got to get back to the school and help Sheriff Beau and Malvidia! Maybe if we split up . . ."

He scrolled through his books. *The Fantafstik Book of Myfical Mofnsters*, *Demon Wraiths of Windsor*, *Nonsensical*

Maps of Senseless Places You'd Rather Not Go . . . Ah! Here it is!

Sky pulled out *A Botanist's Guide to Botany: Botany Through the Ages, Volume 2: The Seventeenth Century*, by Alexander Drake.

The cover creaked from disuse as he opened it. Uncle Phineas knew he hated botany. The book would be the perfect place to hide something. And the clue leading to the book at the school library would have confused anyone but him. Nobody else knew that Phineas had given Sky a copy. Uncle Phineas had meant for *Sky* to find it, no one else.

He flipped through the pages.

And then he saw it. Hidden in the middle of the book—embedded in the pages like a diamond in a block of kimberlite—was the second key, a thick white monocle.

"Hah! Take that, Special Collections!" said Sky.

"What is that?" asked Dad as he crossed to the desk and turned on the gas lamp Sky had found in the attic.

"It's one of the two keys you won't find without 'looking,'" said Sky, pulling out the monocle.

It was nearly three centimeters deep, like a hockey puck, but not as broad. Various metals had been melded together to give the monocle a patchy blue-white hue like the color of the moon. As he looked closer, he noticed several latches and hinges jutting out, allowing him to open the various layers of the optics.

He clicked a small catch, and a wiry piece of white metal popped out, a hook on the end that could fit over the nose to keep the monocle in place. He pulled on the wire, watching it spool out and retract like his watch chain.

Despite the similarities, this wasn't his uncle's monocle. Phineas's monocle was much darker, more like the night enclosing the moon. But Sky had seen this monocle before.

He pressed the sides, moved a knob, and tapped top and then bottom, just like the man in his memory had on that night eleven years ago. A tiny white needle popped out. The needle that had pricked the other baby. The needle that had given Sky his trix.

"What is that?" asked Dad.

Sky pressed the sides, and the needle slipped back into the monocle. The trix . . . that night . . . not something he was ready to confront just yet (or had time to).

"A key," said Sky, glancing over his shoulder.

But if this was one of the two keys, and he knew that it was—then he also knew where to find the other. With Phineas. Two keys you wouldn't find without looking; the third key was Phineas's monocle.

"May I?" asked Dad, holding out his hand.

"Sure," said Sky, handing him the monocle.

Dad examined it.

"Now do you believe me?" asked Sky, crossing to the window to make sure he hadn't been followed. In the distance, high up on the hill west of Pimiscule Manor, he saw a thick haze rising into the night. "Is that smoke?"

"I don't think so," said Dad. "You said this was one of two keys you couldn't find without looking? Do you know where the other is?"

"Not exactly, but if we can find Uncle Phineas . . . I think that *is* smoke," said Sky, distracted, "but what could be burning? The only thing over there is . . ."

The gardener's shack.

Sky turned around and watched Dad walk over to look out the window, the floorboards bowing dangerously beneath him.

Words from Phineas's notes rang through Sky's mind . . . body density increases with age . . . shift into larger, heavier forms.

Heavier forms.

How could he have missed it? Hannah had even made fun of it just the other morning!

Ambrosia liked to hide in the open, Cordelia had said. The obvious place was the best place to hide! Could it really be true? Had she been in front of him the *whole time*?

Sky's stomach tightened to a knot as he casually stepped away from the window to give Dad room.

"That does look like fire," said Dad, glancing out without a hint of surprise. "Now, you were saying?"

"Er . . . Dad?" said Sky, continuing his discreet mosey toward the bedroom door. "Do you remember that time we went to Germany with Uncle Phineas and he bought you that lederhosen, but you refused to wear it because you thought it'd make your calves look fat?"

"Yeah? So? What does this have to do with the keys?" asked Dad.

"Nothing," said Sky, pretending to examine his ficus tree as he remembered that Whisper, like Wargarou, didn't get their victim's memories with their bodies. "It's just . . ."

He glanced at the door. It was only a few steps away now. "It's just—well . . . we've never *been* to Europe."

Dad's eyes went big, and Sky darted for the door.

Before he could reach it, Dad cut him off, wrapping his hand around the handle a split second before Sky.

"Sky," said Dad, grinning and shaking his head as Sky backed away. "You are a clever, clever boy—much too clever for your own good."

As Dad spoke, his skin started to ripple and pop, his bones

breaking and shifting, distorting horribly until a woman with mostly brown hair and piercing blue eyes, who didn't look terribly old, stood before him.

"I feel like we've gotten to know each other over the last two days while I've searched your house for those blasted keys, but perhaps it's time for me to formally introduce myself, even though your clever little mind has no doubt puzzled it out by now. . . . I am *Ambrosia*," said Ambrosia, displaying a captivating smile, black widow to the fly.

Sky didn't need an introduction. He'd seen this woman attack his uncle.

He backed away, slowly edging toward the window. He knew he couldn't get there before her, but he didn't know what else to do.

"Two nights ago, by the maze . . . that's when it happened, isn't it? Dad should've arrived at the manor before me, but he never made it," said Sky, putting it all together.

"Yes. He saw us chasing your uncle by the Dovetail. He distracted us long enough for Phineas to escape, though I don't think Phineas realized he was there," Ambrosia purred. "Phineas had already disappeared into the Dovetail by then. Pity for them, really. I don't think we could've taken both at once."

"You're the one who carried me home! It wasn't my dad at all!"

All this time, he'd thought Dad had rescued him.

"The Wargarou was trying to bring me here, wasn't he?" Sky continued. "He knew I'd figured out where the second key was, and he was going to make me tell you."

Ambrosia smiled.

"He did bring you here, just not the way I'd intended,

the cheeky boor. The worst part is that he destroyed my car! Failure is one thing, but the destruction of a classic? That is *unredeemable*. And I intend to make him pay for it when he finally shows his tusk-riddled face again. Mark my words," said Ambrosia, showing her teeth.

"Er . . . I will. I will mark your words. Consider them marked," said Sky, hoping he could talk his way out of this. "But have you ever considered maybe it was time for an upgrade to something better? Maybe it's . . . time for a change."

"Well, you'd definitely be the one to bring it," said Ambrosia, chuckling, though Sky couldn't figure out why. "You're more like us than you realize, Sky, as much as you deny it. But the thing your youthful mind can't understand is that things don't get better. They just get different."

"That's kind of bleak," said Sky.

"You've never had your car destroyed," said Ambrosia, "but soon enough . . ."

Worry caught hold of his heart. Last night he'd snuck in late. Mom had never checked on him; she always checked on him.

"What have you done with my parents?" he demanded.

A Whisper needed only a sample of the victim to change, but had she killed his parents anyway?

Ambrosia smiled. "They're safe enough. Dovetail is a plant with many uses, but it can be lethal if administered in too high a dose, as I'm sure you're aware. They're such *nice* parents. I would hate for you to become an orphan. There are far too many stories of orphans these days, don't you think?"

"Leave them out of this!" he yelled, feeling relieved that they were still alive, and furious that they were being treated like this. "They don't know anything!"

"I want the last key," said Ambrosia, casually pulling out Sky's pocket watch to check the time. Apparently Cordelia, at least, had found her. "Bring it to Pimiscule Manor by no later than eleven o'clock. It's a school night, and I'd like to have you home with your loving parents before it gets too late. You and your friends, if you still have any, will come unarmed. No fancy weapons, no defenses or cloaks to hide things beneath. No *tricks*. The shack was empty when I burned it. I don't want any surprises popping up."

The shack was empty? Hardly. She must not have found the lair underneath, which meant the spare gear was still intact.

"If you don't arrive by eleven," Ambrosia continued, "or you try to act *clever*, I will kill your parents, and I won't use peaceful Dovetail to do it. Do you understand what I am telling you, Sky?"

Sky looked out the window at the smoke rising from the gardener's shack in the distance. As he looked, an old truck rolled around the corner at a snail's pace, its engine rumbling like a thirty-year smoker.

Just ahead of the truck he could see Hannah walking on the sidewalk. She cut across their yard, and he could just hear her say, "No, Tick! I told you. I don't need a ride! My house is *right here*!" She vanished under the awning. The truck waited for a minute—trying to decide whether or not it should follow her into the house—and then it rumbled off.

"Sky, *do you understand*?" prompted Ambrosia.

A plan began to take shape in his mind.

"Perfectly," said Sky, turning from the window, "but I've got to know: Why do you want to free him so bad? The Arkhon doesn't sound like the kind of father who'd appreciate that kind of thing, or *anything* for that matter."

"I have been alive for centuries," said Ambrosia. "Nearly all of my kind are dead or Glooms. The young, like my sister Ursula, can remember only what our father is now, not what he once was."

"You mean he used to be different?" asked Sky. "Not . . . er . . . *evil*?"

"Long ago." Ambrosia gave him an insipid smile. "But now we're all monsters, aren't we? Tonight, Sky. Bring me the key, or . . . well . . ."

Sky nodded. He got it.

Outside his door he could hear Hannah tromping up the stairs.

"Oh, and one more thing," said Ambrosia, casually strolling toward the desk. "Those books of yours—very dangerous. We can't have them just lying around for anyone to see. People might get *ideas*."

She tapped the gas lamp, knocking it from the desk.

He jumped back as flames exploded across the desk and floor, consuming his books.

"ARE YOU NUTS!" he screamed as he grabbed his pillow and started beating at the flames.

Cackling, Ambrosia flung open the window and jumped out.

"Hey, twerp. Have you seen Mom and Da—," started Hannah, but as the door opened, the wind whipped the fire up onto the bed, setting the sheets ablaze. Hannah stopped.

"WHAT DID YOU DO?"

"I didn't do it!" he yelled as he threw the blankets from the bed and started jumping on them, trying to beat out the fire. He snatched the bag of plants from the desk, shoving it into his coat pocket. Then he started throwing books out the window.

"Sky, get out of there!" yelled Hannah. But he kept grabbing books, beating out the flames as he tossed them through. "Not yet!"

"Sky, come on!" Hannah grabbed his arm, dragging him away from the desk.

"Not yet!" he yelled, struggling against her. His books, all his precious books! Uncle Phineas had given them to him. He'd trusted Sky! He couldn't let him down!

"Sky!"

Suddenly the five-hundred-year-old floorboards began to creak and groan.

Hannah jerked him forward, and the two of them fell through the door just as the bedroom floor collapsed, raining fire and wood on the downstairs office.

"You are in sooo much trouble!" yelled Hannah as she pulled him to his feet.

It was gone. All his books . . . *gone*.

Hannah jerked him toward the stairs. "Look at my clothes! Do you see my clothes? Ugh. This will never come out!"

He glanced at her. Her cheerleading outfit did look a little worse for wear, but compared to the tragedy he'd just suffered, it didn't seem all that significant.

And then he remembered his parents. He'd almost just sacrificed them to save a few books.

Hannah stopped suddenly, her mouth a rictus of horror. "We're going to have to move again!" she cried.

He patted her on the back, not sure what else to do. She was obviously losing it.

"Hannah," he said softly, "we need to go."

His soft voice, offset against the sounds of burning around them, got her attention.

She nodded once, and they started moving, crouching to get below the thick gray smoke.

As they reached the top of the stairs, Hannah suddenly came alive.

"No! Wait! It can't burn!" Before he could stop her, Hannah turned and raced back down the hall, disappearing into the smoke. He had visions of her grabbing clothes, pom-poms, and cheerleading magazines. She was going to burn in this house over a few trifles. Not only was he going to be parentless, he was going to be sibling-less, too!

He pivoted and ran to catch her, but before he could take a step, he heard a loud cracking sound. He looked up just as a massive timber from the attic collapsed through the ceiling and swung toward him. He tried to jump out of the way, but he wasn't fast enough.

The beam sailed down, knocking him back, pinning the right half of his body against the wall from shoulder to pelvis. Fire and numbness flashed through his arm, chest, and leg, and he cried out in pain.

He was fully upright, and the smoke—combined with the weight of the timber on his chest—made it almost impossible to breath.

Fire spread along the wall, reaching for him with greedy, grasping tendrils.

"Errand, a little help here if it's not too much of a bother."

He felt his trix rip open, though he was so full of pains that he almost didn't notice, and then suddenly . . .

"Oh, look. A fire," said Errand drolly as he appeared next to Sky. "What a surprise. Our lives are on the line *again,* and you suddenly need me?"

"Errand! You came! I thought you weren't going to help me anymore?"

"I could leave," Errand offered.

"Look, I'm sorry! I didn't mean to hurt your feelings! When I said I never wanted to see you again after we left the Gnomon cave, I didn't mean *never*!" said Sky. "I'd just vomited on a stalagmite! You can't expect me to be pleasant after something like that!"

"It's always easy to revise history when you're about to die," said Errand, "but that's not why I stayed away. My life is on the line as much as yours here."

"Then, why?" asked Sky.

Errand sighed. "My teacher had one final lesson to give."

"Your teacher? You mean the same one that told you not to help me anymore? The same one that's going to get us both killed because you won't tell me anything?"

"The edgewalker who taught me how to reach you," said Errand, his hands passing through the timber as he tried to press against it. "He wasn't exactly happy about what I did in the store."

Sky looked around, even more worried. In the stories he'd read, Edgewalkers thrived by feasting on the dreams of others, leaving behind empty shells in place of people. And supposedly, according to *The Edge of Oblivion*, Solomon Rose had killed them all.

"You're right to be terrified, but he's not here," said Errand, his expression difficult to read. "I'd never let him come here."

"What was the lesson?"

"How to grow up," said Errand, smiling ruefully. His face was pale, his eyes sunken, and he looked completely worn out.

"What *are* you, Errand? You're not an Edgewalker. I've figured out that much," said Sky, struggling under the weight of the beam. "I've never heard of anything like you before."

"Like *us*," said Errand. "You've been searching for me your entire life. How can you not yet know who I am? After I showed you?"

"I know you think I should understand all this, but I don't," said Sky.

As he spoke, he heard another floor collapse. From the sound of it, he guessed it was Hannah's.

"Errand, pleeeaase. Hannah's down there. She might be dying!" He coughed. The smoke hung like a death shroud, thick and heavy. "You can't let her die."

Errand glanced back down the hall.

"Look," continued Sky, pleading, "can't you just use the trix or Hunter's Mark or something to make me strong, like you did against Crenshaw in the school?"

"You mean when I gave you the chance to fight back and you let him punch you and steal your watch instead?" replied Errand.

"I didn't know what was happening! I felt like I was going to kill him!" said Sky.

"You might have," said Errand. "My teacher says there's always a price for power." Errand dipped his finger into the blood oozing from Sky's trix, held it up for Sky to see, and then licked it off.

Sky grimaced. "So my blood is the price I pay for your help?"

"Just the opposite," said Errand. "*Eating* your blood is the price I pay for yours. And it's not really your blood. I'm in your head, remember? The Edgewalkers called this stuff Mindlife. Really, there's a lot to it, but I only know the basics."

Sky gave the beam a feeble push. His strength was failing. He had to get Errand to help him. Soon.

"Phineas never taught us any of the good stuff, you know," Errand continued, apparently too caught up in his own thoughts to notice Sky's struggles. "The real secrets are in journals, or learned from monsters, or passed down word of mouth, teacher to student. But the greatest secrets, the most powerful secrets are still hidden. My teacher means to find them, and he's promised we can help—you and me, Sky, both of us, together again, in the flesh, like we were eleven years ago. He'll tell us all the stuff Phineas never did, but first you have to find me."

"Find you? Where are you?" asked Sky, glancing distractedly down the hall. He pushed once again at the beam on his chest, but it wouldn't move. It was getting hard to breath. Hannah might be dying. . . .

"You need to get the last key," said Errand.

"I'm working on it, but what does that—" Sky stopped, finally realizing. "You're in the manor, aren't you?"

Errand nodded.

"That edgewalk. The memory you showed me. You're the other boy!" exclaimed Sky, the memory returning to him. Two boys. Both marked.

"The tunnels had collapsed," said Errand, sounding bitter. "When the man who took me found out, he left me behind."

"But, if I open the manor . . . ," started Sky.

"The Arkhon will get out," Errand confirmed, "but *so will I*."

Sky was so shocked that he almost forgot he had a huge timber pressing against his chest. He sagged in exhaustion, letting the timber and the wall hold him up. His breathing was shallow. He coughed, trying to clear his lungs, but the smoke rushed back in with each breath.

When he looked back up, Errand was gone.

The flame tendrils writhed ever closer. Only a few feet of wall separated him from their grasping pseudopodia, but he suspected the floor would give out long before the fire tendrils choked the last bit of breath from him.

His head drooped. He couldn't keep his eyes open anymore because of the stinging heat and smoke. He was going to die. He'd failed everyone—his sister, his parents, his uncle, the monster hunters.

If only he'd had one more day.

"I leave you for a minute, and look what happens, twerp," said Hannah, smiling and worried at the same time. She set down a package and examined the timber.

Bracing her shoulder against it, she pushed off the wall with her feet, straining against the weight. Never in his life had he been so glad that Hannah was a cheerleader—with big, beefy cheerleader legs!

The timber shifted, and he dropped to the floor, rolling to the side. Hannah gave one final push. The force sent the timber leaping from her shoulder a fraction of an inch. She stepped to the side, and the timber swung past her, crashing through the wall. At the same moment the clasps that had been holding the top portion gave way, sending the entire beam through the floor while Hannah and Sky scrambled away.

Fire raged all around them.

They descended amidst the vapors of smoke, the flickering

flames, and the falling debris. The threshold of the doorway crackled as they stepped off the porch, followed a moment later by more crackling as the porch steps caught fire.

"Wait!" yelled Sky, pulling Hannah toward the tree outside his window. Fire and bits of house fell around them. He sifted through the books, looking for one in particular.

"Sky, let it go!" Hannah yelled.

He found it and scooped up as many as he could carry, before Hannah dragged him away.

As they fled, he looked up in time to see the roof crumple and then collapse inward, sending splinters of wood and six centuries of dust hurling through the night sky. Air rushed in, and the flames jumped, shooting upward like comets.

As brother and sister reached the sidewalk in front of what used to be their home, Hannah, who'd been dragging Sky along, dropped him to the ground and collapsed next to him, struggling for air and clinging to the package she'd gone back for.

"That," she said between breaths, "was worse than cheerleading practice."

He chuckled, coughed, and then gave it up and smiled weakly.

The house was a total loss. The old wood burned like kindling doused with lighter fluid, drenched with gasoline, and coated in rocket fuel. It was hard to believe that only a few minutes had passed.

In the distance, Sky could hear sirens. Whatever passed for a fire department around here was on its way. Neighbors emerged from homes, throwing on bathrobes as they ogled the flames. In a few moments he and Hannah would be completely surrounded.

"Hannah, I need you to listen, and I don't have a lot of time to explain. We need to leave here *now*."

Hannah stared at him in shocked disbelief as he hobbled to his feet and held out his hand expectantly.

"Are you mad? We've just escaped from a burning house! A fire *you* started, by the way! What we need to do is wait for the fire department and for the ambulance and for *Mom and Dad* to tell them that *you* BURNED DOWN THEIR HOUSE! That's what we *need* to do!" said Hannah in a tirade. She paused for a moment, and then added, "You are in sooo much trouble!"

He glanced around nervously. As he did, a neighbor up the road spotted them and began marching over. Time was almost up.

"Hannah, listen. If these neighbors reach us—if the ambulance and the fire department find us and take us away—Mom and Dad will die, and so will a lot of other people!"

"What are you talking about?" said Hannah, narrowing her eyes.

"Hannah, we need to leave! You need to trust me!"

A small explosion rocked the house, sending kitchen appliances through the air. The neighbor that had been walking toward them suddenly found his way blocked by a smoldering black stove.

"Oh? Like I did that time in Gobbler's Falls when you claimed Egyptian gods were making crop circles on Mr. McPhain's lawn and it turned out to be the Parson bullies playing with a container of sea salt and an oversize novelty compass?" asked Hannah.

"I admit I sometimes overimagine, but I'm not overimagining this!"

Hannah's brow creased, and he feared he'd lost the fight—and then he recognized the package she held to her chest. It was a family picture book Mom had put together, wrapped in the sweater she'd been knitting for Hannah on the car ride to Exile. Of all the things Hannah could've saved, she'd chosen these two.

"Hannah, I know you're worried. None of this makes sense, and it's only going to get worse, but I promise—I'm not lying. I'm not making this up. Mom and Dad are in danger! If you don't come with me now, that album will be the only memory we have left of them. Come with me and I'll explain everything," he begged, holding out his hand. "*Please* just trust me."

Hannah stared at his hand for a moment and then took it, climbing to her feet.

Another explosion sounded, and soot and ash filled the air, providing them with cover as they made their escape.

CHAPTER 31
The Groundskeeper

Sky sat at the entrance to the Dovetail maze reading by moonlight as the monster hunters approached, hoods down. He'd retrieved his duffel from the woods by the burned-out lair and, like them, wore his gear.

"You're *reading*!" said T-Bone incredulously, stopping a few feet from him. "And in our loaner gear too?"

"Anything good?" asked Hands.

Andrew plopped down next to Sky, tilting the book cover so he could read it by the light of the moon. "Ooh, sorry, Hands. *The Journal of Alexander Drake*. No vampire romances for you."

Sky had stashed the few other books he'd saved, but this one he'd kept. The journal, apparently, was from Alexander's early years, back in the days of Solomon Rose. Alexander had been the hunter's foremost botany expert and had written the very boring botany series in which Sky had found the monocle. Sky had grabbed the journal before his house had exploded, hoping—as Errand had pointed out—that the journal might hold secrets left out of the stories. He hadn't been disappointed.

"Hey, you know I only read those for the hunting tips," said Hands.

"That's funny. I don't remember taking down a monster by 'wrapping it in a warm, sensuous embrace,'" said Andrew.

"You just wait. Someday when I try that, it will actually *work*. How stupid will you feel then, huh?" said Hands.

Sky knew Crystal was staring down at him, probably assuming he'd had a complete mental breakdown—if she hadn't assumed that long before now.

"Your sister gave us the message, Sky. We're here. Either tell us what you want or we're leaving," she said.

Sky had sent Hannah ahead with the antidote for Malvidia and a message for Crystal and the others to meet him here. Hannah had always been better at the botany stuff, anyway—just like she was at everything else—and he'd needed some time to think. He didn't want to pull her into all this and put her in danger—if things worked out the way he hoped, she *wouldn't* be—but Phineas had always taught him to never use a single vine when only a forest would do.

"Sky!" said Crystal in frustration.

"Hold on."

A second passed. Just as Crystal was getting ready to leave, he closed the book and started laughing.

"What's so funny?" asked T-Bone.

"Boron," said Sky, still laughing.

"Come on, guys," said Crystal, turning away.

"Okay, okay. Hold on," said Sky as he stood, his body crying murder from all the mistreatment he'd recently suffered. "I'm sorry. For everything. For going into the store and nearly getting you killed. For claiming to be a monster, which I'm *not*, by the way. For not returning your equipment. For pulling you into a fight with Shadow Wargs and then running off and leaving you with a dying teacher. For getting your shack burned down—"

"Getting our *what*?" exclaimed T-Bone.

"Look, let's not throw stones over who burned down whose shack. The point is: I need your help. For the last two days a monster named Ambrosia has been posing as my dad in the hopes of finding three keys to a prison holding the Arkhon, the most horrible monster that's ever lived. The Arkhon is also her dad. She's now taken both of my parents, and unless I get the last key to her by eleven o'clock—a key that lies with my uncle's possibly dead body in the center of this Dovetail—she's going to kill them."

He looked around at their solemn faces.

"There's nothing I could give you or tell you to get you to help me. You don't have any reason to trust me, and I wouldn't blame you if you turned around and left right now . . . but I *need* your help. Whatever's in there, monsters are afraid of, and since I'm afraid of them, I'm also afraid of what's in there."

"Huh?" said T-Bone.

"My point is," said Sky, "I can't do this on my own. I need you guys."

He looked at each of them, his eyes pleading.

Andrew glanced at Crystal, who was stone-faced, and then he stepped forward.

Sky had assumed that if any of them would help, it'd be Hands. Andrew was a bit of a surprise. Not as big a surprise as if T-Bone or Crystal had offered to help, but a surprise nonetheless.

"If your uncle Phineas is the same person as the old groundskeeper, Phineas *Smith*," said Andrew, "then I couldn't say no. He's the reason I'm a monster hunter."

"What?" exclaimed Sky and Crystal at the same time.

"When I was four, I used to sneak away at night to visit my . . . my mom—at her mausoleum—to, you know, just talk and stuff." Andrew rubbed at his eyes, and Sky looked away, giving him what little privacy he could.

"One night," continued Andrew, "I found him there—the groundskeeper—laying flowers on my mom's coffin. I ran when he spotted me, but he was there again the next night, and the next. Pretty soon he started bringing weird gadgets and toys, puzzles and games I'd never seen before. He'd set them on the ground when he saw me, and then he'd leave. Finally I talked to him, and he told me about faraway places and monsters and hunters, and about . . . about my mom. He said she'd been a great hunter, and my dad, too, and that I'd grow up to be like them. His visits got more sporadic the older I got. I haven't seen him in years, not since before Crystal and I started hunting, but if it's him . . . he's the *only one* who talked to me about my mom and dad. I'm in."

Sky was surprised, to say the least. He'd never imagined Uncle Phineas living as a groundskeeper, especially not on his own property! But somehow what he'd done for Andrew seemed to fit.

"I know this is going to sound weird," said Hands, "but I think I might know your uncle as well, if it's the same guy. My grandpa Osmer—he's the one who turned me on to vampire romances, by the way, if you want to blame somebody—he used to take me with him to visit different people in Exile before my dad kicked him out."

Hands ground his teeth, and then his face softened again. "Some nights we'd meet the groundskeeper. He and Grandpa would make me run laps or see how many falling leaves I could grab in a minute, while they shot the bull. The groundskeeper even sparred with me on occasion, using weird things like rakes and shovels. Told me I could never tell when a good shovel would come in handy. I've never thought much of it, because Grandpa introduced me to lots of crazies—it's one of the reasons Dad kicked him out—but I've always wondered what happened to the groundskeeper. I guess it's time to find out. Besides," added Hands, "peril, monsters—*certain death*? Sounds like my kind of thing. I'm definitely in."

Two of them knew Uncle Phineas? No, not two. *Three*. On their first meeting Crystal had told him that she knew Phineas the groundskeeper as well. What were the odds?

"Fine," said T-Bone. "I know him too."

Everyone looked at T-Bone.

"Don't tell me," said Hands. "He taught you how to split sandbags open with your head."

"No!" said T-Bone.

"What, then?" asked Andrew.

T-Bone sighed. "It's not a big deal."

"Then, stop making it a big deal and tell us," said Hands.

T-Bone glanced around. It was clear he felt awkward.

"Fine. He taught me how to paint," said T-Bone.

"But . . . your mom's a painter," said Andrew, confused.

"A painter with thirteen children," said Crystal. "It must be hard to get her time."

T-Bone shrugged. "I thought if I learned how to paint, well . . ."

"Maybe she'd notice you," finished Hands, smiling bitterly.

"The groundskeeper found me painting on one of the mausoleums. Instead of telling on me, he offered to teach me," said T-Bone. "I still don't trust you, Sky, but if your uncle Phineas is really the groundskeeper, then I owe him one."

Sky nodded.

"But, Sky," T-Bone added, "if the Arkhon is really as bad as you say, then I'm not going to give up the key. I'll help you get it and I'll help your parents, but I'll die before I give up the key. You should know where I stand."

"Fair enough," said Sky. "I don't want to give up the key either, but I won't watch my parents die when I can do something about it. You should know where *I* stand."

"Fair enough," said T-Bone.

Sky turned his attention to Crystal, the last holdout.

"You already know I know him," said Crystal, her expression cold. "If he's in there, I'll find him."

It wasn't the most heartfelt response, but it was good enough for him. The monster hunters were all in. His parents had a chance.

"All right. Thanks," said Sky, not sure what else to say.

"It looks like it was meant to be—the five of us," said Hands. "A destiny written in the stars."

"Or by my uncle," said Sky.

"It's nearly ten thirty," said Crystal. "How do you propose to get us through a maze we haven't managed to get through in years?"

"We follow the crackers," said Sky, pulling a cracker from his pocket.

He took a bite.

"Those crackers aren't from the lair, are they?" asked Andrew.

Sky gave Andrew a big smile and then tossed the cracker into the air.

CHAPTER 32

Dovetail and Jack

The night came alive around them. Sky flipped on his black light, illuminating hundreds of black-and-white crows with fluorescent blue skeletons as they took to the skies. The largest of the crows snatched the cracker out of the air before it could hit the ground.

"CAW!"

"Seriously, are those lair crackers?" asked Andrew.

Sky laughed and held the black light on the biggest crow as it flew upward.

"All right," said Sky, talking to the crows. "You know the deal. You want more, you lead us to the middle."

"You think they understand you?" asked T-Bone, eyeing the birds with suspicion.

"I know they do," said Sky, not sure how he knew. He glanced at his hand. The Hunter's Mark felt warm. Did that mean something?

They walked in silence for a while, taking in the sight of

the circling crows as the hunters followed the birds deeper and deeper into the ever-thickening Dovetail maze, the walls getting taller and more luscious as they moved along the downward sloping ground.

After a while Sky started talking. He told them about the Arkhon; and the hunters; and Malvidia and her trap; about Principal "Bat" Lem, the Wargarou; and Ambrosia the Whisper—about Ursula and Sheriff Beau. But mostly he told them about Phineas—how they used to trap each other in the woods, and how Phineas always cheated at everything, especially when he was winning. He told them about Phineas's love for salted meats and meat pies, and pies made of meat, and pies made without meat, and pies.

As they moved deeper in, the hedge started to shiver oddly around them, driving them closer together. Ahead, just out of sight, they heard something like running water, but every time they arrived at the spot where they expected to find water, they found their way blocked by Dovetail.

After the third or fourth time of this, Andrew said, "It's funny. I've never noticed a stream running in or out of the maze before."

"Me neither," said Crystal.

"That's because you're not hearing a stream," said Sky. "That's Dovetail."

"What?" said Crystal, sounding startled.

"It's the Dovetail. It's moving," said Sky, following the crows with his black light. He didn't really need the light to see the crows, but he suspected the others did.

"Plants don't move like that," said Andrew, looking around nervously.

"No, they don't," said Sky, "but Dovetail *isn't* a plant."

"What are you saying? You think it's a monster?" asked T-Bone, eyes flitting about nervously.

"Haven't you guys ever noticed how red the dirt is right around the Dovetail? How everything within a hundred feet is dead or dying?" asked Sky.

"I'd always blamed it on early deforestation," said Andrew.

"You would," prodded Hands, "Roving bands of the undead, that's what did it."

Crystal sighed.

"You're both horribly wrong," said Sky. "The Dovetail ate it. The only thing left in that dirt is iron. That's why it's red. According to *The Journal of Alexander Drake*, the book I was reading at the entrance, Dovetail doesn't like iron. It can grow around it if it has to, but not without loads of boron, levels so high that only a few small patches of Dovetail have ever been found. Nothing like this. I don't think it could've gotten this big on its own."

"You think someone grew it?" asked Hands. "Why would they do that?"

"To contain something *meaner*," said Crystal, staring forward as if her eyes could pierce the walls.

Sky glanced at her. He was beginning to get the feeling Crystal wasn't telling them something.

"But we're okay, right?" said Andrew, scowling at the Dovetail. "We've never had problems in here before. I mean, if the Dovetail can move, it would've eaten us by now if it wanted to."

"Not necessarily," said T-Bone. "There's more than two hundred times more *iron* in our bodies than boron. Like Sky said, it can get around it, but it takes time. That's what the thorns are for. Put a victim to sleep, then slowly devour them."

Everyone looked at T-Bone.

"What? I can't know something because I'm big?" said T-Bone defensively.

"T-Bone's right," said Sky, doing a double take. "We're not worth eating at the moment, not unless it comes to view us as a threat."

They finally came to a stop. Dovetail rose in front of them, thorny and treacherous. Sky ran his black light along the top, illuminating the crows as they came to a rest, landing on the Dovetail itself.

"Why doesn't it devour them?" asked Hands.

"Because," said Sky, "they're the antidote."

"Crows?" said T-Bone incredulously.

"Crow's feet—or *Piebald's* feet, more accurately," said Sky. "Here, have a look." He pulled out *The Journal of Alexander Drake* and handed it to T-Bone, flipping it open. "See, right there, along the top. Piebalds thrive on phosphorus, which is why they eat your pee crackers, and why they glow, but boron-deficient plants and monsters can't process phosphorus."

Sky turned back to get his bag of plants.

"They're monsters?" exclaimed T-Bone.

"CAW!" cried the Piebalds, flapping their wings.

"I don't think they like it when you call them that," said Sky.

"What? Monsters?" said T-Bone.

"CAW!"

The Piebalds jumped around, batting their wings in T-Bone's direction.

A putrid smell wafted over the group.

"Ah! What is that?" T-Bone exclaimed.

"I think they just flatulated at you," said Andrew.

"CAW!"

The Piebalds came to a rest, staring down at T-Bone with haughty eyes.

"So this is the center of the maze?" asked Hands, looking around curiously. "I expected it to be bigger."

"There's not a path to the center," said Sky.

He pulled out a handful of Jack seeds and stepped toward the Dovetail, which shivered as he approached.

"Then, how are we supposed to get through?" asked T-Bone, eyeing the Piebalds nervously.

"We make a path," said Sky, "by becoming a threat." Raising his hand, he threw the Jack seeds as hard as he could into the Dovetail.

The Jack seeds sailed through the boughs and thorns, spreading instant death.

The Dovetail shrieked in pain. Lines of black decay spread through the Dovetail, lancing in all directions as the Dovetail tried to pull back branches, feathers, and thorns to avoid the Jack seeds.

"Hurry!" yelled Sky, ushering everyone into the path of death. Crystal went first, and he handed her some Jack seeds. "Clear a path!" She ran, throwing seeds in front of her.

Sky went last. As he raced through, the lines of decay, racing across branches where the seeds had touched, began to slow . . . slow . . . slow. And then, with a whoosh like birds in flight, the Dovetail's gleaming black stalks began to close in on him faster than he could've imagined, consuming the dead material, snapping it off, regrowing around it. Pale white Dovetail leaves fluttered down like feathers from a down pillow.

Sky ducked his head, snapping through the branches and

thorns and vines made brittle from the Jack seed's touch, avoiding the new growth, his thick cloak blocking the poisonous bits of thorns. He stumbled, forcing his way through. Branches cracked and splintered, falling like broken glass all around him.

And still it went on.

He thrashed with his arms, kicked with his legs—a flailing, whirling blade of destruction. He could see the others ahead, could hear the encroaching black vines eating the dead. He could almost feel the vines' tantric vibrations swarming over him like bees at a picnic.

He slammed his protective Shimmer, the blue nimbus rose around him, and then he was through and falling into a pool of white-feathered leaves.

He could hear the others collapsing around him.

Over his shoulder he saw the final threads of Dovetail pinch closed. They'd made it through.

"Is everyone okay?" he asked as he stood. Crystal and T-Bone nodded.

"Present and accounted for," said Hands, brushing himself off.

"Accounted for? By whom?" asked Andrew. "Shouldn't you let Sky account for you before you make assumptions that you've been accounted for? He is the one doing the accounting, after all."

"Do you think he does taxes?" Hands queried.

"You could always ask," Andrew replied.

After ensuring that everyone was there, and clarifying that he didn't, in fact, do taxes, nor did he plan to start, Sky turned around to survey the center of the maze, surprised at its enormity and the strangeness of it all.

A no-man's-land stretched out before him, reaching gradually downward toward a thick forest of gargantuan stocks, green leaves, and snaking vines that connected hundreds upon hundreds of gourds of all sizes, from hold-in-your-hand small to is-that-thing-a-pumpkin-or-the-Mayflower! big.

A massive green-leafed canopy sat above it all, and far beyond, across the no-man's-land they stood upon, through bits of broken canopy and across the sprawling patch and another no-man's-land on the other side, Sky spotted the far side of the Dovetail, situated, by his estimates, close to the east cemetery.

"This is what all the monsters are afraid of? A giant pumpkin patch," said T-Bone. "This'll be fun." He stepped forward, raising his boot to punt a small pumpkin that had strayed into the no-man's-land.

"Don't!" yelled Sky, but he was too late. T-Bone kicked the pumpkin, his boot smashing through it. Bits of disgusting orange and white stuff flew everywhere.

The entire patch trembled.

The monster hunters froze, afraid to move. Vines shifted a hair's breadth. The ground shook. After a moment the trembling died down.

"And that's why you were a lineman," said Hands.

"Maybe we shouldn't antagonize the patch," Crystal added, her voice chastising.

"Agreed," said T-Bone.

Sky exhaled slowly. "It's the Jack," he said, staring at the sprawling patch and feeling very small. "It's the meaner thing that the Dovetail guards. They're poisonous to each other, but Dovetail defends the Jack because it produces boron."

Andrew laughed. "And the boron makes the Dovetail grow. The Jack built its own cage! That's ripe! You know . . . ripe? Ripe like a pumpkin."

"Lame, Andrew," said T-Bone.

"Totally," agreed Hands.

Andrew looked to Crystal for support, but she ignored him.

She was being strangely silent, and Sky wasn't sure why. Ever since she'd agreed to help him find Phineas, she'd been withdrawn. He watched her for a moment as her dark eyes took in the terrible patch. Was she just worried about their poor chances of making it out alive? Was there something more going on that she wasn't saying?

Sky sighed before continuing. "Ambrosia said Phineas escaped into the Dovetail, and Lem said he was going to make Crenshaw go into the Jack to retrieve Phineas's body. That, along with the boron thing, is how I knew the Jack must be in here, along with Phineas. The Jack's supposedly as old as dirt. Lem said hunters even fed the Arkhon to it once. The Arkhon was the one that had to escape."

"Any weaknesses?" asked T-Bone.

Sky shrugged. "According to *The Journal of Alexander Drake* each of the Jack's gourds has its own brain. A gourd can work independently, attack what it wants, but if the big brain gives a command, the thousands of little brains have to follow. Distract the big brain, and you distract the rest."

"And how do you do that?" asked Hands.

"First you have to get the big brain's attention—something you really don't want to do, by the sounds of it. But once you have it, the Jack will always attack the biggest threat first," said Sky. "So, two known weaknesses. First, attract the big brain and distract it with the biggest threat, and then, second, hit it with Dovetail, which might slow the Jack down, or just make it angrier—hard to say. But that's about it. *The Journal of Alexander Drake* said that the few hunters who faced the Jack didn't survive long enough to discover any other weaknesses."

"Well, that's hopeful," said Crystal.

"Phineas could be anywhere in there," Sky continued. "And what's more, I'm not even sure how he got in. According to Alexander's journal, the Jack sleeps most of the time, but it's a light sleeper. Fortunately, the only eyes are on the main head. Unfortunately, it has an incredibly strong sense of smell through glands on each of the gourds. And if it smells you and thinks you're a threat, it wakes up, and when it wakes up, it's nearly as bad as Hannah in the morning."

"We can't do anything about the eyes," said Crystal, "but we can do something about our smells."

Sky watched, disgusted, as she scooped some slimy Jack entrails from the gourd T-Bone had punted.

The substance was thick and stringy, like pumpkin guts, mixed with orange-whitish globules that looked like brain matter. And mixed in the matter itself were Jack seeds.

"We act like hunters," Crystal continued, smearing the Jack guts all over her. "We try to make it think we're friends . . . right up until we take what it loves and replace it with an immense sense of emptiness and disappointment."

Sky raised an eyebrow. Emptiness and disappointment? She was really starting to worry him.

"That's just foul," said Hands, his nose crinkled in distaste as Crystal smeared white matter through her hair.

The Piebalds swooped down, landing on top of various parts of the Jack, which rolled out in all directions.

"Lead on," said Sky to the largest of the Piebalds after he finished covering himself. He pocketed a few Jack seeds. And, for good measure, he had everyone grab some of the dead

Dovetail. The plan was to let the Jack sleep, but you could never be too careful.

The vines and leaves grew thick high overhead, growing thicker as the hunters moved on. The Piebalds refused to fly below the canopy roof, which was really annoying; Sky couldn't even entice them down with crackers.

Despite the infrequent sightings, he could hear the Piebalds cawing, and, he began to notice, he could almost feel where they were even when he couldn't see or hear them. At those times, his Hunter's Mark, warm and toasty, seemed to throb in time to the beating of his heart. He wasn't sure what it meant, but he found it comforting nonetheless, especially since his trix didn't split open when it happened.

Of course, in some ways, that made it even more confusing. His trix had always split open when Errand had helped him before, and Errand had claimed he wouldn't help him anymore. Errand had left him alone; he couldn't even feel him hiding in the back of his mind since the house had burned.

Errand's absence, the throbbing of the Hunter's Mark, and his newfound sense of the Piebalds. What did it all mean? Were these things connected somehow? Could he understand monsters without Errand? If he could, why hadn't he before?

As they walked, he was bewildered by the size of the gourds surrounding them. Some were nearly as big as his house, or at least the size his house had been before Ambrosia had burned it down. The thought was disheartening. If his family managed to survive the night, what would they do when this was all over? Where would they go?

"Maybe we should play a party game," suggested Andrew as they walked. "You know, to keep our mind off things."

Looking around, Sky realized how quiet it was—eerily so.

He couldn't even hear the Piebalds anymore, and the canopy was so dense that almost no moonlight broke through, forcing the monster hunters to pull out flashlights. Feeling the Piebalds swooping in the skies above had given him a certain level of comfort. He couldn't imagine how the others must feel without it.

"Party game?" T-Bone guffawed, as if he couldn't believe Andrew would suggest such a thing. "You mean like charades?"

"Or I Spy," said Andrew hopefully.

T-Bone stared at Andrew until he had the decency to act embarrassed.

"I Spy; I haven't played that since I was six!" said Crystal.

"Me neither," said Sky, smiling. "We always played Find the Hobo."

Crystal laughed.

"I spy," Hands began, to T-Bone's obvious chagrin, "with my little eye something . . . green!"

"The canopy!" yelled Andrew.

"That's it!" cried Hands, appearing excited beyond words.

T-Bone rolled his eyes.

"All right, all right. I spy with my little eye something . . . orange!" said Andrew.

"That gourd right there!" Hands pointed at a giant gourd.

"No."

"That one right there!" Hands cried, pointing at a different gourd.

"Right!"

"Would you two shut up?" said T-Bone. "You're not even doing it right!"

"Fine, Mr. Smarty Pants; you try," said Andrew.

"I will," T-Bone replied, sounding very superior. "I spy with my little eye something green."

"The canopy!" shouted Andrew.

"You idiot! You already did the canopy!" said T-Bone.

"Is it that large colored glass wall up ahead?" asked Sky, a sick feeling in his stomach.

"What glass wa . . . Oh. Right," said T-Bone, shining his flashlight up ahead.

Their game was over.

CHAPTER 33

Knick of Time

A few moments later they arrived at a stained-glass wall. The wall was circular and made up of three rings, turned horizontal, and stacked on top of one another—top, middle, and bottom. Additionally, each ring was made up of movable blocks. It looked similar to the wall that surrounded the manor at night, but for the rings, blocks, condition (more run-down), size (*much* smaller), and lack of monsters. But it had the same strangely colored glass, and the same weird innards—though these looked far more mechanical.

Bright, almost blinding, moonlight shone down through a giant hole in the canopy, and faint colors radiated out from the glass, lighting up the pumpkins around them and, within the wall, a cottage.

Sky picked up a rock and threw it over the wall; there was a bright flash, and the rock shot back at him, forcing him to dive out of the way.

Hands snickered.

"It's like the one in the lair," said Andrew, surveying the wall, "except the field seems distorted."

"What?" asked Sky, turning his full attention on Andrew.

Andrew looked nervously at Crystal and T-Bone.

Crystal sighed. "You might as well tell him now."

"Tell me what?" asked Sky.

"We, ah . . . that is . . . we have a model of a glass wall and your uncle's manor," Andrew sputtered. "We found it in the lair. It's where we got the Shimmer."

"Why didn't you guys tell me about this? You knew I was looking for it yesterday! I told you about the glass wall the first time we met, and you told me I was seeing things!" said Sky.

"We didn't trust you," said T-Bone simply.

"It's nothing personal, Sky," Hands explained. "We just didn't know you. Now that we do, we realize we should trust our instincts."

"So you're telling me that the Shimmer—that glowing blue nimbus that softens our landings—came from a model of a glass wall and Pimiscule Manor?" asked Sky. He'd suspected they might be similar, but he hadn't thought one had come from the other.

"A glass wall and a pendulum, actually. That's why we thought your poem was so interesting," said Hands.

"'Enof Od Naba Ban Do Fone,'" said Sky, quoting, "'with all three on the pendulum bend, you might get lucky and lock the prison up again.'"

"Exactly," said Hands.

"So you're saying that the pendulum and the glass wall around the manor somehow work together to create a Shimmer? And they what? Trap everything in time?"

"Something like that," said Andrew. "It's a bit complicated, really."

"Try me," said Sky.

"Okay . . . ," started Andrew hesitantly, looking at Crystal.

"Go ahead," said Crystal. "None of the rest of us understands it."

"All right," said Andrew. "Well, you see, the glass wall gets its color from various superconducting materials: lead, copper, ceramic—"

Sky was already tuning out.

"When the gate is activated by a key, chemicals in the wall are heated and turned into plasma, creating what quantum mechanists refer to as a 'plasma window.' When the temperature reaches 'critical,' superconductivity kicks in."

Sky's eyelids started to droop.

"The elements within the glass wall achieve an electrical resistance of zero and lose their interior magnetic fields—what's called the Meisner effect. For most purposes the conductivity of plasma is infinite. So while the moon's gravitational field drives the pendulum's swing, the superconductive materials in the glass siphon off the energy and—"

"Okay, okay, I get it," said Sky. "It's complicated. You could have just said it was 'magic.'"

Andrew grinned. "Don't worry. I haven't a clue how most of it works; I just stole a few pieces from the model. But, more simply put, once the trap's activated, whatever's in it becomes stuck in time, including the trap itself. It's ingenious, really, because if nothing can find the trap, nothing can open it."

"But if that's true," said Sky, "then why is the trap back?"

"I don't know." Andrew shrugged. "Maybe it's just broken."

Sky nodded, and then a horrible thought occurred to him. "If something happened to the pendulum—say some weird dark energy hit it and slowed it down," said Sky, "could that break the trap?"

"Oh, definitely," said Andrew, "but the pendulum has tapped into all kinds of powerful forces by the time it finds its rhythm. It's very unlikely anything could affect it. Why do you ask?"

Sky felt the bottom of his stomach drop out. When he'd gotten his trix, a stream of black light had crashed into the pendulum. And afterward the pendulum had slowed.

Crystal stared at him intently, and he realized he hadn't answered Andrew's question.

"Er . . . no reason," Sky muttered. "Just curious."

Crystal kept staring.

"The design of this wall looks older," said Hands, surveying the wall. To Sky's immense relief, Crystal left to join Hands, taking her suspicious eyes with her. "See the cracks and broken pieces?" Hands continued, "An early experiment, I'd bet—failed, by the looks of it."

"You think Phineas is in there?" asked T-Bone as the others wandered away.

"Could be," said Sky, trying to unravel the puzzle in front of him. "Looks like a good place to recover and hide, assuming nobody figured out the wall. The wall. That's why she needed me! They couldn't get through!"

"What's that?" said T-Bone.

"Phineas," said Sky, lowering his voice. "I think Ambrosia's using me to lure him out."

T-Bone glanced around, suddenly alert, his eyes scanning

the giant pumpkins all around. "You think they followed us in?" T-Bone whispered back.

"It's likely," said Sky.

Crystal, Andrew, and Hands had moved on, circling the wall as they examined it. Sky glanced nervously into the dark. If Ambrosia was hiding nearby, what would she do if Sky got past the wall? Or, maybe even worse, what would she do if Phineas came out? If Sky went in, she might wait to see what happened. But if Phineas came out, she would definitely attack.

"We have to find a way in," Sky whispered, "and we have to hope Phineas doesn't come out."

T-Bone nodded, apparently reaching the same conclusion.

But how were they supposed to get in? If Phineas was in there, he'd likely activated the wall from inside. Was there another way?

Sky moved closer, tracing his fingers along the colored glass.

Why was the wall separated into three rings? And why all the colored glass blocks, occasionally filled with strangely scattered gases, tubes, sprockets, and other inner watchlike workings?

The wall was clearly broken in places, as if something had tried to bash its way through; he even got a jolt when his hand slipped across a crack.

Farther on he came to a gap. He pushed up on a block directly below the gap, sliding it into the next ring.

"I think it's a puzzle," said Sky, letting the block fall back into place.

"That's what we think too," said Crystal as she approached

with Hands and Andrew. "You two should see this."

She led them to three rusted levers buried in the ground just next to the wall.

"What are those for?" asked T-Bone.

"The rings," Sky replied, "I'll bet they control the rings."

Crystal nodded. "My guess too. There's no opening in the wall, no way to get inside."

"So we have to make one," said Andrew.

"I get it," said Hands. "We have to move all the gaps together until we make a door."

"Right," said Sky, "but there's also probably a sequence or pattern to it. I had one like it once, from Uncle Phineas. 'This trap requires trial and error, serious reasoning, and patience to figure out,' he said. He called it the Engagement Ring, and thought it clever. It's based on color patterns. The levers should speed things up, letting us move entire rings to align gaps and get the right blocks on the right rings."

On the inside of the wall, closer to the cottage, Sky spotted three more ring controls, just like the ones in front of him. These control, he suspected, would spin the wall and close the door. Sky glanced at T-Bone, who nodded back. He'd spotted them too. They needed to get in and use those inside levers to shut the door as quickly as possible. Sky thought about warning the others of the plan, but the nearby shadows seemed a little too shifty.

"All right," said Crystal. "Hands, Andrew, T-Bone, and I will move the blocks. Sky, you move the rings and direct us."

"Me?" asked Sky, surprised.

"Who else?" said Crystal.

"Yeah," said Andrew. "You're apparently the puzzle master."

"I—," started Sky.

"It's settled, then," said Crystal, cutting him off. "Just make sure the door appears here."

"You guys can play blocks without me," said T-Bone. "I'm going to stay here and make sure Sky doesn't mess everything up."

"Good idea," said Sky. Once the door opened, T-Bone could rush in to operate the inner controls, allowing them to close the door as soon as everyone was through.

Crystal looked between them, harrumphed, and walked off with the others.

Ten minutes later, as the moon hung frightfully close to the eleven o'clock hour, they moved the last block into place. Phineas hadn't come out the whole time, and they'd seen no movement whatsoever within the house. Sky felt happy and disturbed by this—happy because they might just make it in without Ambrosia attacking, and disturbed because of what it could mean about Phineas.

T-Bone looked tense as well. He kept scanning the strange pumpkin forest and clenching and unclenching his fists, the metal-gloved Shockers sparkling with electricity each time he did.

As the last block clicked into place, the wall came to life. Gases churned, fires sprung up, and colors spilled out into the night. Sky watched as the heated gases sped up, changing into plasma. Filaments shot out like little threads of lightning.

T-Bone gave one last glance at the woods, nodded at Sky, and walked through the opening.

As Sky watched T-Bone stroll toward the inside levers, moving slowly so he wouldn't attract too much attention, Sky saw the wall flicker strangely. Before he could figure out the cause, he heard a terrible grinding and then an earsplitting whistle, growing in pitch.

He looked over and saw gases leaking through a section of wall.

"THE PLASMA!" Andrew screamed. "IT'S GOING TO BLO—"

A piercing wail struck his ears, sending Sky to his knees. The glass around the leaking gases shattered, sending shards like knives through the air. Flames jumped to the next plasma cylinder and the next. Glass and flame exploded out in all directions.

It cut, and cut again, before Sky had the presence of mind to activate the protective Shimmer around him.

From his knees he dove and rolled. The next blast hit him, sinking into the Shimmer. He had two seconds before the Shimmer dropped. Flames flew toward him. . . .

He dove under them and rolled again. The next blast hit. The Shimmer dropped.

With one final jump he dove behind a gourd as the walls closest to him shattered, driving glass shards and jets of flame into the pumpkins. The wailing died, and he scrambled to his feet, raced through the burning ring opening, and ran for T-Bone. Off in the distance a hideous roar sounded and the gourds and vines began to twitch and writhe.

T-Bone's robes were in smoldering tatters by the time Sky reached him; small gashes lined his hands and face, and a finger-size chunk of glass stuck out of his thigh. The robes must've been fire retardant, because his skin didn't look terribly burned. But he was unconscious.

"We've got to move him!" said Sky as the others ran up. "The Jack's waking up!"

The patch was coming to life, the huge gourds twitching and jerking, skin rippling, expanding, and contracting, as if breathing.

Within that writhing patch Sky saw shadows moving fast for the shattered wall opening.

"Go. We'll cover," said Crystal as she and Andrew stepped forward, weapons sliding into their hands.

Sky sprinted to the levers. Over his shoulder he saw car-size pumpkins coming over the wall—some flopping to the ground, severed by flames and sparking plasma; some flailing at Crystal and Andrew as they shot, the two hunters diving and rolling to stay alive.

The shadows reached the opening, and Sky yanked the levers. The flaming rings lurched and the opening disappeared, cutting off the Shadow Wargs, who promptly retreated from the flames.

Sky rushed back, and he and Hands dragged T-Bone around the piles of burning debris toward the cottage while Crystal and Andrew shot at stray vines and gourds that got too close.

Sky kicked junk out of the way as he went, making a path to the door, while Hands applied pressure to T-Bone's leg.

Blood oozed from wounds all over T-Bone's body, but none bled like the leg wound. If they couldn't get T-Bone to a doctor, he would die.

"Hello?" yelled Sky as he banged on the cottage door. "Phineas! ANYBODY?"

The door was locked.

Sky pushed on it, thumped it, kicked it, whacked it with debris, and railed on it. The thick wood seemed to push back at him, egging him on.

"What's taking you so long?" yelled Hands.

"IT WON'T OPEN!" Sky screamed in frustration.

Glancing over his shoulder, he spotted Crystal and Andrew

retreating, vines and gourds writhing and twisting after them in a delirium of frightful motion. The Jack roared again, and through the open canopy above the house, Sky saw flames shoot into the night still far in the distance.

"What is that?" mumbled Hands staring upward as the afterimages of the flame faded away.

Sky ripped his eyes away, searching for something he could use on the door.

Behind him he heard Hands curse. He spun, expecting to see Ambrosia or the Jack, but instead he saw something equally astounding: T-Bone was standing. His face was ashen, his teeth set against the pain.

He pushed Sky to the side, put his shoulder against the door, and heaved. The door shuddered, shuddered, and then cracked into splinters around the frame as it burst open.

T-Bone turned, smiled at Sky triumphantly, and collapsed to the ground.

Hands stepped up beside Sky and looked down at T-Bone. "Idiot."

CHAPTER 34

Botany Saved My Life

As Sky stepped through the door, someone put a knife to his throat.

"I've been stuck in here for two days since you cracked the wall—two days—and you figure it all out and decide to brave it now? Well, bully for you," said a gruff voice behind him. "Is that the Wargarou wedged in my door? He's big enough. . . . Blimey. What do you feed that monster?"

"Uncle Phineas!" yelled Sky, trying to turn, but Phineas pressed the knife against him. "Uncle Phineas, it's really me! Sky!"

"Likely story," muttered Phineas.

"Do you remember the time you took me hiking in the Superstition Mountains and we found those old lizard bones, but you convinced me it was a severed Gnomon thumb? Gnomons don't even *have* thumbs!" Sky exclaimed.

"Sky? It can't be," said Phineas, dropping the knife. He

wrapped Sky in his arms and held him tight. Sky hugged back every bit as tight. His uncle was okay. "What are you doing here?" Phineas exclaimed.

"I came looking for you! Ambrosia took Mom and Dad! She'll kill them if I don't bring the last key to the manor by eleven o'clock! It's your monocle, right?"

"Hmmm. That is a dilemma," said Phineas, and he collapsed to the floor.

"Uncle Phineas!" Sky dropped down next to his uncle. And then he noticed the blood—lots of it. "He's hurt!"

Outside, the Jack smashed things, but it sounded very far away at the moment.

"Get T-Bone inside!" said Sky as he pulled out his bag of plants and other miscellaneous substances and dumped it on the ground. He wished Mom were here. She'd know what to do. Even Hannah knew more about this kind of stuff than he did, but he'd sent her ahead to help Malvidia, and find Beau, and to do a number of other unpleasant tasks he was going to pay for later.

He crushed a pinch of barrow weed and held it under his uncle's nose while the others brought T-Bone in and slammed the door shut behind them. Phineas jolted awake and tried to sit up.

"It's okay. Give it a minute," said Sky, gently pressing Phineas back to the ground.

Hands and Crystal dragged T-Bone over, laying him next to Phineas.

Sky sorted through his plants and put together some pastes Mom had shown him. He put it on T-Bone's leg to stop the bleeding, and then turned back to Phineas while Hands began to apply pressure to T-Bone's wound.

Sky pulled open the tattered remains of his uncle's shirt. Beneath he found several gaping wounds, one of which was nearly the size of his palm, deep and burned and dark black around the edges. His mouth dropped open. He'd never seen anything so horrible before.

"How are you still alive?" Hands asked Phineas, watching over Sky's shoulder.

Phineas chuckled. "It takes more than a couple of flesh wounds to take down a *Hunter of Legend* like myself, but death takes us all in the end—usually quite painfully."

"You're not going to die! Look, I've still got plants," said Sky, desperately smashing up a Jack seed.

"Sky, I'm more Jack than hunter, I've got so many Jack seeds in me. But I've still got some fight left, and I think we'll all need it before the end comes. If you want to help, hold the Gilead root over me and crush it in your hand. See how the juices are red like blood? That's because it *is* blood. If you ever run into a Gilead, you thank it for me before it kills you. Now drip the blood into the wounds. That's it." The Gilead root fizzled as it hit the wound. "Good. Now pack it with the rictus leaf. Ahhhh! Bully that! How much barrow weed do you have left?"

Sky held out a small handful.

"That should be enough. Keep a little and put the rest in my hand." Phineas held out his hand, and Sky poured the barrow weed into it. "Usually I'd take this in hot water with a tub of honey at precisely midnight, but beggars and all that."

Phineas threw the barrow weed into his mouth and chewed it in disgust.

"I think T-Bone is ready. . . . Ah! I haven't seen that boy in so long. Too long . . . too long for all of you. I apologize for that, but running for your life does take *time*," said Phineas.

"You didn't want to make us targets by association," said Andrew. "We understand."

Everyone but Crystal nodded in agreement. Sky looked at her, wondering. She seemed distant, angry even. Her eyes locked on Phineas as if he were a heckler at a funeral.

"There was that as well," said Phineas, smiling through gritted teeth. "Unfortunately, you seem quite capable of becoming targets all on your own. Now rub the rest of the barrow weed under T-Bone's nose before he slips into a coma."

Sky did as instructed and then scooped the rest of the plants into his bag and returned the bag to his pocket.

A moment passed, and then . . .

T-Bones's eyes fluttered open, and he groaned. "Oooohhh. What smells like dead cat?"

"That's you," said Andrew.

"Did I call you a lineman before?" said Hands as he continued to press on T-Bone's leg. "You're not a lineman. You're the guy the coaches thought was too stupid to be a lineman."

T-Bone laughed, and then groaned again; he looked at Phineas. "So you really are the same guy. I'm afraid I left my brushes behind, Groundskeeper."

Phineas smiled. "Quite all right. I haven't the palette for it anyway."

T-Bone groaned. Even Andrew groaned. "And you guys thought I was bad."

Sky wanted to smile, but seeing his uncle and T-Bone like this hurt too much.

"They'll be here any minute. Help me up, will you?" said Phineas, offering his hand to Sky.

Sky bent to help him, and then stopped—

Crystal had a knife to Phineas's throat.

"Not just yet," said Crystal, her hands steady.

"Crystal? What are you doing? Are you nuts?" exclaimed Sky. As he looked around, he noticed that everyone else seemed as surprised as he was.

"You're one of them," muttered Sky, bewildered.

"No, Sky. She's not a shifter," said Phineas. "She's a hunter. One of the best students I ever had. Better than Malvidia, better even than her mother, Cassandra, whom I quite admire."

"Cassandra. Your mom is Cass?" said Sky. "She's the friend Mom grew up with but always clams up about, the one who wandered Pimiscule Grounds with her, searching for the northern boundary."

"I think you'll find many connections between *all* your parents," said Phineas, glancing at each of them. "And you've miraculously found one another far earlier than I'd anticipated."

"What? Are you saying you'd *planned* to bring us together?" asked Andrew, sounding amazed.

"A good trap is like a good story," said Sky, realizing what his uncle was saying, "hidden and leading toward one inevitable conclusion. It's the first and fourth rules of trap building."

Phineas smiled. "I suppose there was no way for five personalities such as yours to be in the same town and not find one another. It was always meant to be, but not like this."

"Where is she?" asked Crystal, her voice quiet, like morning frost.

"I don't know," said Phineas.

The earth shook around them as something moved in the yard.

"Where is she?" screamed Crystal. "You took her from me! You sent her away! It's been *three years*! WHERE IS SHE?"

"I know, I know. I did. It was wrong of me, a mistake," said Phineas. "One of many, I'm afraid."

"Crystal," said Sky as something thumped into the house. He could hear wood splintering upstairs.

"STAY OUT OF IT!" yelled Crystal, her hand shaking.

"I was selfish. I put my needs over those of a little girl who needed her mother. I didn't realize how much I'd asked, until she was gone. For the last few years I've been looking for her. A few days ago . . ." Phineas shook his head. "I have something for you, in my coat pocket."

Crystal reached into Phineas's frock coat and pulled out a small book and a bracelet with a charm on it that looked like half a strand of DNA.

"Her hunter's journal. Her bracelet," said Crystal, staring at the book. Tears began rolling down her cheeks. Her knife hand dropped away and the knife clattered to the floor.

She picked up the bracelet and snapped it to her own, the two pieces of DNA forming a single chain.

Phineas sat up, cringing against the pain in his side. He slipped both loops of the bracelet onto her wrist.

"I'm sorry, Crystal. I'm sorry I sent her. I'm sorry I wasn't here for you—for *any* of you. I know it hasn't been easy. The last entry was more than a month ago. I found the journal and bracelet in Skull Valley near Bedlam Falls, but that's as far as my skills could take me," said Phineas.

"What was she doing there?" asked Crystal, staring at the journal without really seeing it.

"She was searching for answers," said Phineas, glancing at Sky. Sky caught the look, and he remembered that night so long ago, when Phineas had picked him off the ground, promising the wife of Sky's fallen guardian that he'd return when he had answers . . . answers about *Sky*.

"Is she . . ." Crystal gulped, unable to finish.

"I don't believe so," said Phineas. The house started shaking violently. "But if we don't leave, you'll never have a chance to find out."

Crystal wiped away her tears and nodded. Phineas gave her shoulder a squeeze—his eyes filled with compassion, and then he turned to Sky.

"Sky, if you'd be so kind," said Phineas, holding out his hands for Sky to help him up.

"Are you going to be okay?" asked Sky.

Phineas put his arm around Sky and pulled him close, his smile sadder than ever. "Of course. But we should probably talk while we have a chance."

"Okay," said Sky hesitantly, glancing around at the others, who were busy ripping apart sheets and chairs to make bandages and splints for T-Bone, as the cottage continued to shake and groan. Was Phineas going to try to talk to him about that night? Sky would almost prefer for the cottage to collapse. He had enough horrible things to deal with right now. "Are you sure this can't wait?"

"Quite sure," said Phineas, leading Sky out of earshot. "I notice your trix has been bleeding."

"Er, yeah," said Sky, feeling embarrassed, and *really* not wanting to talk about this, "I must've cut it or something. It's fine now, though," he lied, trying to end the conversation.

"Hmpf," said Phineas, apparently not believing a word of it. "Sky, you know there's no such thing as magic, right?"

"Sure," said Sky, "just natural forces misunderstood."

"Precisely. Those marks on your hand—the Hunter's Mark and the trix, as you call it—are natural forces that are *very* misunderstood," said Phineas. "Fortunately, you have no idea what to do with them."

"What does that mean?" asked Sky. "And I thought you said the trix wasn't particularly special?"

"I said that because I'm a horrible liar—not bad at it, like you; I just do it quite often," said Phineas. "When did your trix start bleeding? Was it after you got here?"

"Yeah, I guess," Sky muttered. He *really* didn't want to talk about this. "Can we talk about this later?"

Phineas started pacing, cringed at the pain, apparently thought better of it, and leaned against a beat-up plaid couch instead. For a moment Sky thought Phineas might pass out, but then he took a deep breath and started in again.

"Sky, did you know that it can take a hunter a lifetime to learn a single monster language?" Phineas asked.

"Uh, no," said Sky, wondering what this had to do with anything.

"Even when a hunter learns to understand the language," said Phineas as the cottage shook some more and some pipes burst in the adjacent kitchen, spraying water everywhere, "many times they aren't physically capable of speaking it, and so most don't even bother anymore."

"That does sound frustrating," said Sky, wondering if his uncle had lost too much blood.

"It is. Long ago a hunter might have spent their life studying one monster, watching it, learning to talk to it, desperately hoping to learn a secret or two," said Phineas.

"A secret . . . like what?" asked Sky.

"Oh, it could be just about anything," said Phineas.

"Weaknesses, abilities, insights. For example, did you know that if you bury a rutabaga and the nose hair from a Barrow Hag under a harvest moon, you can grow a black rutabaga?"

"Er, no," said Sky.

"And if you eat that black rutabaga, you can leap as high as a Barrow Hag for a time," said Phineas.

"You can?" Sky exclaimed. "Why didn't you ever teach me any of *that*?"

Phineas smiled. "It's power, Sky, and power without understanding always leads to trouble. A black rutabaga has a cost, a mild cost relative to other things but a cost nonetheless."

"What's the cost?" asked Sky.

"Severe constipation and an inordinate amount of nose hair for a week," said Phineas.

Sky snickered.

"But the point is," Phineas continued, "that there's a natural force behind it all, a power we don't understand, a power outside the scope of our science. For a Barrow Hag, burying a nose hair and rutabaga under a harvest moon to make a black rutabaga is, for us, like rubbing two sticks together to make fire. Fire and friction we understand, but the force that creates a black rutabaga? Not so much. But Barrow Hags understand that force, and if a Barrow Hag trusts you, or fears you, it might tell you about black rutabagas—but first you have to be able to talk to it. You have to understand it. That's the First Secret buried in the Hunter's Mark."

"What? You're saying the Hunter's Mark lets me talk to monsters?" said Sky, feeling perplexed. "But if that's true, why haven't I been able to understand them? I mean, all the time?"

"It takes practice. You have to calm your mind like I taught you to, try to understand the thing—*see the now*," said Phineas.

"Only those with the Hunter's Mark can naturally talk to any monster. The rest of us have to learn the hard way."

"But the times I've understood, I haven't been calm at all!" said Sky.

"That's because you have yet to use it properly," said Phineas. "The Hunter's Mark draws on an attracting force. It unifies and binds. It traps things together. The languages, what's called the first secret, is a part of this. The trix draws on a repelling force—destructive, selfish, and hungry. *That's* what you've been using. Either you or something else has been using blood from the trix to force languages from the Hunter's Mark, with the cost—at least while it's open—of your emotional stability. There may be other costs. I'm not really sure, as no one has ever had both marks before."

"But I haven't—" Sky stopped. He hadn't been using his trix to force languages from the Hunter's Mark. He didn't even know he could do such a thing! But Errand, on the other hand . . . He had a teacher who had taught him to edgewalk. Surely he knew. And he had been there, ripping open Sky's trix, every time Sky had understood a monster.

"Despite how they may seem, neither of these forces is inherently evil. Both can be misused," Phineas continued, "but the trix more so."

"Why haven't you taught me this before?" asked Sky. "Why just teach me traps and puzzles?"

"To help you understand," said Phineas. "Power without understanding and self-mastery will always cost your humanity. Understanding must come first. It's the one lesson Solomon could never quite puzzle out. To use a force and not understand it is like walking into a trap and mistaking the noose for your favorite pillow. To understand the nature of a thing, you must walk in its shadow, suffer as it suffers, and find joy beside it. There is no understanding without struggle and sacrifice. There is no compassion without understanding. And power without compassion is the worst kind of evil there is."

Something smashed into the cottage, cracking a wall. Sky glanced about nervously.

"I believe our time has ended," said Phineas, a sad smile playing on his lips.

For the first time Phineas was giving him straight answers, and he didn't want it to end. Phineas put his arm around Sky, leaning on him for support as they walked back over to join the monster hunters.

Crystal and Hands had managed to rig splints for T-Bone. He could walk, but it wouldn't be fast.

Sky set Phineas against the wall. Phineas slumped down, closing his eyes, holding his side, and breathing in the same calming way he'd taught Sky.

"All right," said Sky, looking over the battered hunters. "So all we have to do is get past a fiery wall of plasma, slip through an oversize, very angry pumpkin patch, dodge a pack of juvenile Shadow Wargs with a personal vendetta, and escape through a poisonous flesh-eating maze, while carrying two very wounded people, all in the next fifteen minutes or so, or my parents die. Any ideas?"

The cottage shook again, pictures falling from the walls.

"Have a good cry, maybe?" Hands offered.

"You forgot to mention Lem and the Gnomon that's been trailing us since we first entered," said Crystal.

"Trailing us? A Gnomon? Jeez, Crystal. Any other gems you'd like to share?" asked T-Bone.

"She didn't share because she wasn't expecting to leave here alive," said Phineas without opening his eyes.

Crystal stared at the ground, pointedly not speaking. Sky didn't know what to think. Had she really meant to die here? He knew it was possible, but even so . . .

"It's not Lem," said Sky, refusing to acknowledge the possibility. "I saw only Shadow Wargs by the wall, and Lem said he wouldn't be caught dead in here." If Lem was still around, that meant Ursula had lost the fight at the school—even after changing into a Wargarou herself. And if Ursula had lost the fight, then the reason Sky hadn't been able to find Sheriff Beau's body was because Lem had eaten it (probably after Ursula's), and not because Ursula had taken her husband to safety.

And right now Sky just couldn't stomach the idea of losing two people who'd done so much to protect him.

"All right. Fine," said Crystal. "It's not Lem. Maybe it's Ambrosia and she just *looks* like Lem. I didn't see any traces of *her*. But whoever it is, the fact remains that there's only one way out of this: I distract the Jack and other *non-Lem* monsters by becoming the biggest threat, and you guys run. Got it?"

"Got it. Except for the part where I run," said Sky.

"Yeah," Andrew chimed in. "I'm not running either. The Jack would just follow me, anyway—biggest threat and all."

"You?" T-Bone laughed, hobbling to his feet. "None of you are up for this! It should be *me*. I'm obviously the biggest threat."

"What?" exclaimed Sky, Crystal, and Andrew at the same time.

"It's a nice plan, but it's not going to work," said Phineas.

"Why's that?" asked Sky.

"Because," said Hands, as he pivoted away from the window and raced for the door, "the biggest threat just *found us*!"

CHAPTER 35
Hunter of Legend

T-Bone and Hands threw their shoulders against the door, but it wasn't enough.

The Wargarou exploded through!

Large chunks of cottage fell all around, and everyone crashed to the floor.

The Wargarou snapped and clawed, fiery whips of darkness lashing out at dozens of entangling vines and gourds that held it tight.

As Sky met the Wargarou's eyes, a flicker of recognition passed between them, but before he could figure out what it meant, the Jack jerked the Wargarou back out the door.

Through the newly created break, Sky saw Crenshaw and the other Shadow Wargs fighting for their lives in the front yard, trying to break away from the Jack.

Sky scrambled to his feet, ejecting his Pounder hand-cannon, but before he could raise it, the cottage shook, and the walls suddenly tore apart around him.

Crystal pulled him out of the way as couch-size wedges of splintered wood and jagged metal rained down.

Above them a jack-o'-lantern head as big as the cottage stared down with burning green eyes. The Jack finished wrapping up the cottage in vines and lifted the cottage over its head.

Sky stared up into those gigantic fiery green eyes from the remains of the ruined foundation. He'd never seen anything so terrible. In the wildest fancies of his eldritch imagination, he'd never conjured up something so preposterously horrible.

The Jack roared as it threw the cottage to the side like a tin can. Through the hole in the canopy high above, Sky watched the cottage sail through the air, until, far, far away, it crashed into the Dovetail, and broke through row after row of the man-eating maze.

Crystal dragged him out of the foundation's wreckage. "Sky! Look!"

He came back to himself, spotting Phineas on the other side of the rubble. Phineas dodged and weaved through the Jack, spinning through the air in inhuman ways as he stabbed at the vines trying to drag T-Bone away, blood pouring from the wound on his side.

"We have to help them!" yelled Crystal, grabbing his hand and yanking him out of the shattered cottage.

Flaming plasma exploded from the last bits of wall, rising into the moonlit night like a desperate cry for help.

A vine latched on to Phineas's arm, and as Sky watched, he simply grabbed it and pulled. The whole patch around them seemed to sway with the force, and then the vine just popped out, flopping to the ground like a headless snake. Sky stared at his uncle as if he'd never really seen him before. Who was this man, and why hadn't he ever taught Sky how to do any of *that*?

Phineas cut through the last vine clinging to T-Bone and then, to Sky's further amazement, he knelt down and slung T-Bone over his shoulders in a fireman's carry. As Sky ran toward them, he noticed that the vines encasing the Wargarou and Shadow Wargs were loosening. Uncle Phineas had suddenly become the greatest threat, and for the first time in his life, Sky could see why.

He'd never thought of his uncle as a Hunter of Legend, despite what everyone said. To Sky, he'd always just been Phineas, his best friend, the person who understood him best, the person who watched out for him and listened to his complaints, the person who joked with him and treated him horribly and told him stories and wore a monocle and said "bully that" and made him eat brussels sprouts and goulash.

But in an instant the image he'd had of a quirky old man with a penchant for botany and overly complicated traps had disappeared, leaving behind a Hunter of Legend. A *monster hunter.* A hero, sacrificing himself for a boy who needed him.

Vines lashed at Phineas, binding his arms and legs, his body. He struck at them, cutting and slashing faster than humanly possible, but for every one he cut, five took its place. Vines pulled at T-Bone, trying to wrench him from Phineas's grip, but he wouldn't let go even to save himself.

And still Phineas pressed forward.

Gourds smashed at him, batting him in the head, in the back. He fell to one knee, and then struggled back to his feet. One step. Another. More and more vines appeared, wrapping around him like tentacles, until it looked like he was dragging the entire patch, and the whole world with it.

More vines and more, pulling him backward, dragging him down. Tens. Hundreds. *Thousands*. Wrapping around him.

His torso. His neck. His steps slowed . . . stopped. He stood, motionless, pressing against the weight and horror. Gourds pummeled him like fists, over and over, hitting him so hard they shattered from the impact. And still he stood, blood pouring from his side.

Sky struggled desperately to get through the maze of moving gourds and dangling vines separating them.

"PHINEAS!"

The Jack lowered its head, its eyes blazing. It *roared* in frustration, tugging against Phineas. And still he didn't move.

Phineas closed his eyes. When he opened them again, they blazed brighter than the Jack's fiery skull.

"AAAAAHHH!"

With a feral cry Phineas lunged forward, tearing through the vines and writhing terror that held T-Bone bound—throwing T-Bone toward Sky, throwing him to safety.

And then the earth seemed to grow strangely quiet as if all of creation held its breath. Phineas stood for a moment, pressing against the weight of the world, his body torn and broken . . . his side spilling terrible blood. His eyes locked on Sky, and a sad smile struggled to his lips. . . .

And then the Jack yanked him back and away, and Phineas disappeared beneath a mountain of vines and gourds and flaming green fire.

"PHINEAS! PHINEAS!" Sky screamed and screamed.

Someone pulled at him, dragging him away, but he fought them off, struggling to reach his uncle.

"PHINEAS!" screamed Sky, madly beating at the vines around him. "PHINEAS!"

People called his name, but he couldn't hear them. Tears streamed down his face. His uncle was gone. He was gone!

"Sky! We've got to go NOW! Your parents! We're almost out of time!"

His parents. Turning, Sky found Crystal next to him, pulling him forward. With his heart like ash in his mouth, he stumbled and started running on his own, each thumping footstep a death knell at his uncle's grave.

Sky raced on, following Crystal. Hands and Andrew dragged T-Bone between them as he struggled to keep up. They headed east toward the cottage remains, where the rings of Dovetail were narrowest and the cottage had cut a path. Behind him Sky heard terrible yells and roaring and when he glanced over his shoulder, he saw flashes of white light and flame bursting into the night.

And then the Jack *roared* again, the most terrifying sound Sky had ever heard because of what it meant, a sound full of outrage and triumph, and the patch began to writhe again. The Jack's gruesome work with Phineas done, it moved to find the next biggest threat. This time Sky passed the verge of tears, and they flowed, like a river feeding itself.

"We're almost there!" Andrew yelled.

Just ahead Sky spotted the no-man's-land, and beyond that the shattered remains of the cottage lying across the Dovetail.

But something horrible swept through the patch, parting the canopy high above. Before Sky could shout a warning, it was there, rising above him, eyes burning, filling him with a sense of dread that left him speechless.

Crystal opened fire with her Pounder hand-cannon, nailing the Jack in the mouth as it roared. The Jack's whirling boron-burning fire dimmed for a moment and then erupted like a volcano, shooting dark green flames from its face.

Sky regained his senses and dove to the side.

Crystal dodged the flames, running beneath the vines and gourds that were writhing from the Jack's body—slowly leading it away.

"NO!" Sky screamed. He couldn't stand to lose anyone else.

He opened fire with his own Pounder, drawing the Jack back toward him. Back and forth they went, Crystal shooting, then Sky shooting—keeping the Jack occupied while the others escaped.

And then something had his leg, and he tumbled forward, dropping his Pounder.

"SKY!" Hands yelled, letting go of T-Bone as he rushed for Sky, Andrew continuing to drag T-Bone toward the no-man's-land.

As the Jack jerked Sky into the air, he retracted his Pounder, reached into his pocket, and pulled out the Dovetail. The Jack held him aloft, staring at him with eyes that never closed.

Sky threw the Dovetail.

The Jack's green fire sputtered. It *roared* in pain, dropping him. As Sky fell, he hit his protective Shimmer. He took the impact hard, losing his wind and nearly blacking out.

Hands grabbed him, and let loose some Fog. And then they were running again, Sky's head spinning. The Fog flashed green again, again, and again. The Jack was blinded, its sense of smell blocked.

Sky couldn't think straight as the world pitched and shifted around him in the Fog and lights. They broke through the last bit of patch, entering the no-man's-land at the same time as Crystal, who dragged Andrew, apparently hurt and unconscious, behind her. Their robes and cloaks were scorched and torn, covered in Jack entrails.

They'd left T-Bone behind.

"No." Sky tried to turn around, nearly collapsing as the world spun, but Hands forced him onward to the Dovetail.

Bits of broken cottage littered the ground, and a gaping hole opened before them—a remnant of the cottage's passing that the Dovetail worked frantically to repair. Farther ahead Sky could see what was left of the cottage itself leaning against the outer walls of the Dovetail.

Hands set Sky down, nodded at Crystal, who was slapping Andrew awake, and ran back into the vines to get T-Bone, who was now fighting for his life.

Sky tried to stand, to help Hands, but he fell again, his head still spinning.

"Sorry I . . . ," said Sky, but the world swam around him, and he nearly passed out.

"It's okay, Sky. We'll get you out of here," said Crystal as the Pounder disappeared up her sleeve.

At that moment the Jack slipped through the Fog, its body writhing toward them across the no-man's-land, its eyes and mouth and vines dancing in dark green flames. It seemed to roll forward on thousands of massive gourds, like feet, shaking the earth with each step. From the front it was impossibly large, like the moon itself had popped by for a visit.

Within its writhing, horror-filled mass, Sky saw spots of electrical energy bouncing in chaotic arcs from Hands's Collapser staff and T-Bone's Shocker gloves, making the whole thing look surreal, like a malevolent botanical storm intent on their ruin.

Crystal grabbed him by the arm and dragged him through

the first gap in the Dovetail. He struggled to keep up. To his left he saw Andrew, now conscious, hobbling feebly, his face set in a grimace. They made it through the first gap . . . the second . . . the third.

The Jack reached the first gap and rushed through it like a fiery green flood.

Crystal gasped for breath as she dragged Sky forward. His senses were slowly returning. He held on to Crystal's hand like a drowning man.

The Jack flooded through the second gap . . . and then the third, shrieking in unholy triumph. The Dovetail struggled to reform, to block the rolling Jack, but the equilibrium had been broken and nothing could keep the menacing evil from its prey.

Crystal reached the remains of the house, dragging Sky and Andrew over the debris. Big chunks of timber and wall leaned against the outer walls of the Dovetail maze, like half a house still formed.

Sky scrambled through the hole where the foundation used to be, and then he ran up the walls, latching on to counters and shelving, picture frames, over random bits of furniture, through doorways, moving up, always up.

And then they reached the end. A long stretch of roof spread out before them, but there was nothing to grab on to.

He looked over his shoulder. The Dovetail had begun to recover. Branches, vines, and thorns shot through the Jack, entangling its gourds in silent death, but nothing seemed capable of stopping the horror from rolling onward, a fifty-foot wave in the midst of a hurricane of light and sound.

As Sky turned back around, Andrew suddenly rocketed past him. He stared after Andrew and then realized that Crystal was yelling something at him.

"Sky! Sky! Use your Jumpers! The Jumpers!" He stared at her blankly. He knew what she was saying should have made sense. He knew he should have understood it, but he didn't.

Without hesitating Crystal flipped him onto his back and jumped on top of him. "You might want to hold on," she said.

He wrapped his arms around her waist, staring up at her eyes. She really did have pretty eyes. She looked down at him, a funny look on her face, and then he realized that he'd said it out loud.

As the Jack's head popped through the closest gap, Crystal slapped a button on her Core chest plate, activating her jet-pack-like Jumpers. Hydrogen peroxide and steam shot out, propelling them upward. They shot diagonally up the chunk of roof, Sky's back sliding across the rough wood like cheese on a cheese grater. They sailed off the roof, hurtled through the air, and crashed onto the outer hedge wall, the Dovetail pricking him painfully.

He rolled to his side, his body as numb as his mind. Over his shoulder he saw the Jack rise up, its vines digging into the house, its gourds braced for support as it began to climb up the house's shattered remains.

From atop the wall of Dovetail, Sky saw Hands half-dragging T-Bone down below, within the writhing patch and Dovetail, dodging through the gaps, leaping over walls with their Jumpers . . . but they were too far back. He looked at Crystal; she wasn't moving.

Slowly he crawled toward her, dragging his body. The Dovetail flowed through his mind like cream, driving him to sleep, but he'd fought the Dovetail before. He pushed through it, focusing his mind on Crystal, on her freckled skin . . . on her red-brown hair like cinnamon . . . on her eyes . . .

He reached her just as the Jack eclipsed the top of the roof, bellowing in triumph; and then, as unstoppable as the tide, it opened its mouth and belched out a mountain of green flame and death.

With his last remaining strength Sky wrapped Crystal in his arms and rolled with her off the edge. Fire flashed above them, but they were already falling.

He slammed his Core, trying to activate his protective Shimmer, but he hit his Jumpers instead. Steam and hydrogen peroxide kicked in, and he spun. Steam sprayed off the hedge, sending him careening in the opposite direction. He spun again, bouncing and flopping, before finally getting his feet under him as he slammed into the ground.

No sooner had he landed than Andrew grabbed him by the wrist and dragged him away from the Dovetail, Crystal sliding along next to him. Up above, over the last wall, Hands and T-Bone sailed into view, crashing in a wave of shimmering energy. The Jack appeared behind them. It roared in rage, struggling forward, but the Dovetail finally had it. The two monsters clashed, vines and gourds and branches entwined in a maelstrom of movement and devastation.

Crawling, dragging, and shuffling, Sky and the monster hunters made their way up the steps and out of the valley of death, not stopping until they reached the east cemetery. Surrounded by the dead, they collapsed to the ground, panting. Wearily Andrew opened Sky's bag and gave them Crow Foot, antidote to Dovetail, before collapsing next to them.

They were wheezing, exhausted, and broken when Ambrosia stepped from the shadows. "All rested, then? Good. Let's see if we can end this, shall we?"

CHAPTER 36
The Crystalline Gate

As they moved away from the cemetery, Shadow Wargs stepped from hiding, corralling them toward the crystalline gate. Crenshaw—Vicious—bulky and powerful with a narrow face; Ren—Big—massive, broad, and brooding; Cordelia—Dangerous—full of subtle lines and sleek grace. Marcus—Pudgy—smaller than the rest with a portly belly and nervous prowl.

T-Bone glared at Ren, and Ren growled back.

"You're going to break Mom's heart," said T-Bone. "You know that, right?"

Ren snarled and then loped ahead.

In the copse of trees just below the manor, Ambrosia made Sky and the others ditch their equipment and what was left of their black robes and cloaks.

After Sky dropped his gear, he pulled a single cracker from his pocket, and tossed it into the air.

A Piebald swooped down and snatched it up, flapping its

wings in front of him until, hesitantly, Sky held out his arm so it could land.

"Thanks for your help," said Sky, watching the Piebald gobble up the cracker. "I never would've seen him again without you."

"CAW!" cawed the Piebald, but what Sky heard was, "Don't mention it." Sky's mouth fell open. He'd never understood them before! Not like this!

"Filthy birds," said Ambrosia as the Piebald snatched another cracker from Sky's pocket and flew away with its prize.

As they continued toward the manor, Sky realized that the Hunter's Mark felt warm—not spilling shadowy light, not covered in trix blood like when Errand was around—just *warm*.

The first secret—the ability to understand monsters, part of whatever strange attracting force powered the Hunter's Mark. He didn't understand it at all, no more than he understood black rutabagas (or normal rutabagas, for that matter), but this time, unlike times before with the trix, he didn't feel angry or scared—just *calm*.

The Wargarou waited for them at the gate, drawing Sky's attention. Even in human form Lem looked wolfish, his fine Italian suit in rags, his dark hair out of control, and he was covered in blood and what looked like liquid darkness—most of it probably *his*. The rest of it . . .

Ursula and Beau. Sky clenched his fists. Could they really both be dead? But if the Wargarou had eaten either one of them, or both of them, why did he still look like Lem? Why not shift?

Lem smiled at Sky as he approached, and Sky remembered that strange flicker of recognition Lem had given him right after he'd burst through the cottage door.

Sky hadn't had time to wonder as it happened (fleeing for his life as he had been), but now . . . What had it meant?

"Gourmand! Where have you been?" Ambrosia demanded. "Crenshaw informed me that you sent them into the Jack alone!"

"I was otherwise engaged," said Lem, examining his nails. "I showed up to the château when I could. Lovely place. Horrible wreck now, of course. I wouldn't even take my *sister* there, and you know how I feel about *her*."

"You don't even have a sister," Ambrosia countered.

"All the more reason not to take her." Lem continued examining his nails, and Ambrosia just shook her head, turning back to Sky, who did his best to hide his shock. Lem might not have had a sister, but Sky knew someone who did.

"Never partner with an insane Wargarou," said Ambrosia. "Let that be a lesson to you, Sky."

Sky looked around for his parents. "Where are they? You said they'd be here!"

"Soon enough, soon enough!" said Ambrosia. "I believe there was a certain *key* involved in the exchange?"

A sinking horror swept through Sky. He'd forgotten all about the key! He'd never gotten it from Phineas! And now . . .

"I—I . . . My parents first," Sky demanded. "Then the key."

Ambrosia watched him hawkishly. "You don't have it, do you? Your deceased uncle never gave it to you, and now it's rotting in the Jack! Why, *that's just terrible*!"

Sky clenched his jaw. "Please."

"Ah, but it's after eleven, Sky!" Ambrosia cooed. "I was so willing to forgive and forget, but now that you don't even have the key? You remember our arrangement. don't you?"

Sky's stomach dropped. *"Please,"* he begged.

Lem stopped looking at his nails. "I could go back in and get it if you'd like, Ambrosia."

"Why, Gourmand. I haven't heard you offer to do anything in almost two hundred years! You must've really taken a liking to this boy," said Ambrosia.

Lem glanced at Sky, shaking his head, and Sky realized that without the key, there was no way of knowing where Ambrosia had put his parents, and no way to make her tell.

"No. That won't be necessary, Gourmand. By all accounts the trap will open soon enough on its own," Ambrosia continued, pulling out Sky's pocket watch and checking the time. "It's too bad, really, Sky. Your parents must have a good thirty minutes of life remaining."

"It won't open on its own," Sky bluffed.

"Excuse me."

"It won't," said Sky, making it up as he went. "You don't think Phineas would've built this trap without some kind of backup in place, do you?"

For the first time Ambrosia looked doubtful.

"It's true," Crystal chimed in. "That's why we have the poem."

Sky glanced at Crystal and felt an overwhelming desire to hug her. He was a *horrible* liar; he could use all the support he could get.

"What? That gibberish?" Ambrosia scoffed. "That just told us where the keys were and where to put them!"

"Only if you don't read between the lines!" said Andrew.

Sky nodded. "Phineas never let a poem mean one thing when it could mean two. You're just not seeing it right. Listen:

ENOF OD NABA BAN DO FONE

One key to set the time,
Two to see it right,
Three keys you wouldn't suspect,
To lock the prison tight.
Two, you wouldn't find
Without looking.
One you wouldn't find
Without watching.
With all three,
On the pendulum bend,
You might get lucky
And lock the prison
Up again.
But then again, maybe,
Just maybe,
You'll kill everyone
You've ever loved
And find a pain-filled end.

"Still an atrocious poem," said Ambrosia. "Gibberish!"

"That's because you're missing it," said T-Bone, hobbling up next to Sky. Sky glanced at T-Bone, began to turn back to Ambrosia—paused—and then looked back at T-Bone. Why was he walking so strangely? Hobbling like that, scratching at his makeshift splint?

"Totally missing the point," said Hands, drawing Sky's attention. "The poem says you *might* lock the prison up again, but it also says you might find a pain-filled end! It's obviously a warning."

And then Sky realized . . . Hands was right! It was a warning, and he'd missed it! But what did it mean? And were there more clues hiding in the poem somewhere?

"Would you like a powder, or maybe a refreshing ointment?" said Ambrosia, sounding very smarmy.

Confused, Sky glanced over and spotted T-Bone itching vigorously at his thigh.

"It's just . . . ," said T-Bone, digging at his brace. "There's something . . . chaffing . . . something . . . just . . . got it!" T-Bone suddenly held up Phineas's monocle, looking as surprised as everyone else.

"How did you get that?" Sky exclaimed.

"Phineas must've slipped it into the brace!" said T-Bone. He held on to it for a moment, looking up at the manor, and Sky remembered the promise T-Bone had made outside the Dovetail, that he'd rather die than give up the key and free the Arkhon . . . even if it meant the life of Sky's parents.

T-Bone looked at him, weighing the monocle in his hand, and then he handed it to Sky without a word.

"That's all three keys, Ambrosia," said Sky, holding it in front of him. "Two monocles, one watch. Now, if you want *this*"—he waved the monocle—"tell me where they are."

"I don't know, Sky," said Ambrosia hesitantly. "There's still the matter of your tardiness to consider. And it would hardly be a fair trade. A key I don't really need for parents you do? How about this . . . How about if you go open the trap and I'll give you a *clue*, a riddle if you like, and you can figure it out along the way. You like riddles, don't you, Sky?"

Sky glared at her. Frankly he was growing tired of riddles. "And what if we don't figure it out?"

"I think your parents must have twenty-seven minutes of

life remaining at least. That should be plenty of time for someone of your obvious genius to figure out a simple riddle."

Sky glanced at Lem. It was the best deal he was going to get.

"Don't look at Gourmand," said Ambrosia. "I seriously doubt he'll give you a better offer. He *eats* little children, remember? Besides, I'm still not sure I believe your story. You're lucky I'm offering you anything at all."

"Fine," said Sky, "but we'll need the keys."

"Excellent!" Ambrosia handed him the other two keys, and he tucked them away. He had all three keys and no idea what he was going to do with them.

He'd do anything to save his parents and, as annoying as he could be at times, even Errand. But if he opened the trap for Ambrosia in order to free them, he would free the Arkhon as well, who would then kill them and everyone else.

Open the trap and kill everyone; lock it again and kill only those he cared about most. No matter what he did, he would lose.

"Ready for the riddle?" asked Ambrosia.

Sky nodded.

"Good," said Ambrosia. "Here it is, then:

> I always hold you no matter what; you always
>   treat me as I am.
> I'm overhead and underfoot, but only when in
>   no-man's-land.
> I'd wait for you, if wait I could, but if you see
>   me under sky,
> Then you'll know, what I do hold; I do not
>   wait, I merely lie.

"Got it?" asked Ambrosia.

Sky nodded. He'd remember.

"Good," said Ambrosia. "Now you're all set. You'd best run along. Off you go, then! Scoot, scoot!" She waved them toward the gate.

Sky stepped forward, huddling with the others. "Any ideas?"

They all shook their heads.

"All right," said Sky. He'd hoped for more, but his mind was so frazzled that he hadn't come up with any answers to the riddle either. He thought about fighting, but even if they managed to beat Ambrosia, which wasn't likely, they didn't have time to force out the information. He'd have to hold that as his last resort, which meant that until he knew what he needed to know, he couldn't afford to let anything happen to her. His best hope was solving the riddle.

Feeling disheartened, he moved on. "I'm pretty sure the watch will open the gate, but I'm not convinced, like I once was, that it will awaken the monsters. The trick is the pendulum, and if the trick's there, then so's the trap."

"Are you certain?" asked Crystal.

Sky flipped over the watch, looking at the etching of the Hunter's Mark on the back. His uncle had told him that the Mark had been etched long before Sky was ever born—that the Mark itself hadn't been seen since Solomon Rose almost four hundred years ago.

He thought over all the oddities—the way the normally precise watch had been off the morning after he'd visited the manor, the warning in the poem, the way his uncle always did things in the most complicated, backward way possible.

"Certain enough," said Sky.

He approached the gate, looking nervously up at the monsters. If this went wrong, those monsters would break free, and any hope he had of fixing the prison and saving Errand and his parents would disappear.

He placed the watch into the indentation in the middle of the gate, and several wires grabbed hold, pulling it in, a pane of glass sliding over the top of it. The strange innards of the wall began moving, and hundreds of cylindrical pockets along its length filled with gaseous plasma alive with writhing electric filaments.

The hair on his arms stood on end and the air around him sizzled. Strangely colored storm clouds began to form spontaneously overhead, building in power.

Just when he thought he'd blown it, a thunderous ring of energy swept out of the manor knocking him to the ground.

As he climbed back to his feet, the glass that had encased the watch slid open. He grabbed the watch, and the gate opened with a rumble.

"Twenty-three minutes, Sky. I'd recommend you hurry," said Ambrosia.

CHAPTER 37
Lost and Not Found

There are so *many*," said Hands, looking at the monsters, hiding in the trees covered in fall leaves, fallen in the rich gardens, and drowning in the bubbling streams.

As the hunters got closer to the manor, Sky began to recognize a few of the monsters—froglike Barrow Hags and shadowy Umberlings, formless Seeping Creepers, leather-skinned Satyrns, and many-legged Erabin, towering Marrowicks with waxlike skin that would melt in the sun, and the Echo he'd spotted on his first day with its pupil-less white eyes, but for every monster he recognized, there were a dozen he didn't.

"What's that one there?" asked T-Bone, pointing to a large human-shaped blob as they ran past.

"That's a Humanatee," said Sky.

"A humanity?" said T-Bone.

"No. A Hu-man-a-tee—half man, half manatee. Very rare," said Sky.

"You made that up," said Hands.

"Bully that," said Sky. "It's from the story *Oh! The Humanatee!*"

"You made that up too," said Hands.

"I'll loan you the book if we ever make it out alive," said Sky, and then he remembered with a pang that all his books had burned. "Scratch that. I'll *tell* you the story."

"So which one of these is the Arkhon, do you think?" asked Crystal.

He glanced at her. "I don't really know. He's a shifter. He could be any of them, I guess."

"Weaknesses?" asked T-Bone.

"None that I know of," said Sky. "Our only advantage is that as long as he's within these walls, he can't shift."

"At all? Even if the prison is open?" asked Andrew.

"At all, opened or closed," said Sky. "That's what Sheriff Beau said. Once the Arkhon gets outside, though, we've lost him. We've got to keep him within these walls no matter what."

"But that's only if we're stupid enough to open the prison in the first place," said T-Bone, wheezing dreadfully as he ran. "I gave you the key because I hoped to buy us time to save your parents. But if we open the prison, your parents are dead either way, and so are mine and so are everyone else's."

Sky gritted his teeth. T-Bone was probably right, but how could Sky just abandon his parents? Not to mention Errand.

"My mom is already dead," said Andrew, cutting in. "She died eleven years ago, probably right here. Her crypt is empty. Did you know that? Phineas told me. We could be walking right by her body and I'd never know. If opening the prison has any chance of saving your parents, Sky, I say take it."

Sky nodded, feeling horrible and grateful all at once. How would Andrew feel when he found out that the Arkhon had come to Exile for Sky? Would he react like Crenshaw and blame Sky for his mother's death?

Hands and Crystal looked troubled, and Sky wondered how they felt about it all. He hadn't told any of them about Errand, or the trap he'd set with Rauschtlot in case the prison opened, mainly because he hadn't had time to explain it all, but also because, with Errand especially, he didn't know where to begin.

"Sky," said Crystal, "with all these monsters around, and the Arkhon being a shifter and all, how did the hunters know he was in here?"

"Because Phineas said he was," Sky answered.

"And how did *he* know?" pressed Crystal.

"I—I don't really know," said Sky, suddenly wondering.

"Well, I don't know what he is," said Hands, "but he's obviously hiding, and if he's hiding, then he's afraid, and if he's afraid, then he's not invincible, and he knows it. All these monsters, they're just Fog."

"But Phineas saw through it," said Andrew. "Based on the number of monsters the Arkhon brought with him, the Arkhon must've suspected a trap, but he came anyway, which means he *really* wanted the bait, whatever it was."

Sky had reached the same conclusion. What's more, he knew the bait personally, and, with Hannah, he'd figured it into his trap.

"If the Arkhon is afraid," said Crystal, looking thoughtful, "he's likely hiding in a form capable of blending in but big enough and strong enough to get out in a hurry."

"So we're looking for something big, sneaky, and dangerous," said Hands. "T-Bone, I'm sorry to say this, but we're going to have to freeze you now."

"Ha, ha," said T-Bone, his breathing labored. Sky could see fresh blood spilling through T-Bone's pant leg. "But seriously, that could be *any* of these monsters. And it doesn't matter because we're not opening the prison anyway."

"It's not *any* of them," said Crystal. "It's just *one* of them. Phineas knew something; he understood the Arkhon well enough to predict his form. We just have to figure out what he knew that allowed him to know. If the prison opens, whether we want it to or not, we'll have to know what he knew."

That almost made sense, but before Sky could figure out whether it really did or not, they reached the manor.

Sky led them through the broken front door and into a large entry room filled with a staircase, dusty chandeliers, and a whole mess of dead and dying monsters that were (thankfully) still sleeping, or frozen in time, or whatever it was that was happening to them.

Hands flipped on the light, but nothing happened. "All that power out there and they couldn't even route a light."

"They probably had more pressing priorities at the time," said Andrew.

"So how do we find the pendulum?" asked T-Bone.

"We follow the bodies," Sky pointed out, indicating the path of fallen monsters running up the stairs and down the hall—a path, he knew, Phineas and the other hunters had created on their way out after the tunnels had collapsed.

"If we could see the bodies," added Hands. "We ditched our flashlights with our gear, remember?"

"I can see them," Sky admitted, who could see perfectly.

"How can *you* see them?" asked Crystal.

"Right now I think you'd rather not know," said Sky, suspecting his freakish vision could have something to do with his marks, and fearing how they'd react, and knowing he didn't have time to explain it all, "but later, I promise, I'll tell you guys everything. All right?"

They didn't seem happy, but they agreed.

He led them through the old manor, always following the trail of bodies. Occasionally, there were splotches of moonlight, or light from strange clouds above, but mostly it was just dark. As they ran, he called out directions—"Body on your left," "Right turn," "Watch out for the mirror," and on and on as he led them into the heart of Pimiscule Manor.

Monster bodies sat thick around the door when he finally reached the pendulum room, but the door was open a crack, so he slipped through, leading them in. Inside he found the circular room just as he remembered it, but older, more run-down.

Bookshelves, dusty and empty of books, spun out around him in the wheel and spoke pattern, leading inward toward the gradually sloping bowl in the center. The walls looked substantial, not weirdly black like they had while he'd edgewalked here, and no lightning flashed or thunder rolled just yet, but as he moved toward the center, he noticed angry storm clouds swirling through the colored glass dome.

The pendulum hung from the dome, also like he remembered, but its erratic swinging had nearly come to an end, replaced instead by a lurching hesitancy—like a boy after a first date, waiting for a kiss.

Almost a dozen monsters covered the floor of the library—massive creatures of hair and fang, rock and earth, shadow and flame . . . all dead.

"What happened in here?" whispered Crystal as the others slipped into the room to join him.

"Later," said Sky, moving toward the pendulum. Whatever he was going to do, he had to do it quickly.

"Did hunters kill all these? Phineas maybe?" asked Hands, sounding impressed as he surveyed the terrible monsters scattered around the room.

"It wasn't Phineas," said Sky, remembering Nikola, his guardian—a man who, according to Phineas's journal notes, had gone insane. "At least, I don't think it was—not all of them anyway. It was another man. He got . . . er . . . injured when the pendulum was damaged." Injured. That was one way to put it.

"How do you know all this?" asked Crystal.

The pendulum swung, slowly, slowly, its arc no longer than a handbreadth across.

"Someone told me," said Sky, sighing in exasperation, "and I *promise* I'll tell you all about it later, but right now we've got to figure out how to work this thing. Any ideas?"

"Can't we just push on it or something?" asked T-Bone.

"The pendulum's entangled with the moon's gravitational fields," said Andrew, "fields powerful enough to create waves in the ocean. I don't think a little *kick's* going to do it."

"The answer's in the poem," said Sky, watching the pendulum arc slowly diminish. He pulled out the poem and began to examine it.

"Well, you'd better hurry and figure it out. My guess is that we have less than a minute," said Andrew.

"With all three on the pendulum bend," said Crystal, circling the pendulum, "we can lock the prison up again."

She bent down, probing the pendulum as it swung. "There's a hole here, in the ground, and another two on the pendulum itself—bottom and side. Side for the watch, bottom and ground for the monocles—looks about the right size."

"So it's easy," said Hands. "We stick the keys in the holes, and voila, it's locked."

"I don't think so," said Sky, shaking his head.

"That's because you don't *want* to think so," said T-Bone, sounding peevish.

Sky looked around at the others. Only Andrew would meet his eyes.

"That's not why it won't work," said Sky, feeling horrible. "I think Hands was right. I think the last few lines of the poem are a warning."

"A warning about what?" asked Andrew.

"I don't know," said Sky, "but something bad."

The pendulum ticked down, slower and slower, precious seconds drifting by, and Sky watched each and every one slip away. Every second brought his parents closer to freedom, and every second brought them all closer to death.

"Has anyone figured out Ambrosia's riddle?" asked Crystal, looking very serious.

No one spoke up.

"Does anyone think the monsters will stay asleep if this pendulum stops?" asked Crystal.

Still no one spoke.

"Sky, as much as I'd like to support you on this, what's right is right," said Hands, "There's no warning in the poem. I was just making stuff up."

"I don't think you were," said Sky, "even if you thought you were. The poem is warning us of something."

"But it could be warning us of anything!" said T-Bone. "Don't stay up past eight, make sure to feed the fish—"

"Don't distill your own urine," added Hands.

"Exactly," said T-Bone. "Who knows? If we let the pendulum

stop, we *know* the prison will open. And if it opens, we can't relock it completely and put the monsters back to sleep until we're outside the gate with the watch!"

"Which means we need to do it now, Sky. We have to lock it; we can't let the monsters wake up," said Crystal. "I'm sorry," she added quietly.

"I—it's just . . . no . . . something's not right," said Sky. Something was wrong with the solution; he could feel it.

"Sky, Ambrosia's not going to let your parents go if we open the prison!" said T-Bone. "We fix this, we go out there, we figure out the riddle, and we save them. Opening the prison gets us nothing!"

"It gets us more time," said Andrew, "maybe enough to save his parents."

"You don't know that!" T-Bone yelled.

"Something's off," said Sky, shaking his head stubbornly.

"We don't have time to second-guess this solution," said Crystal. "The delay could be costing your parents their lives! Don't get so caught up in an imaginary puzzle that you let your parents die!"

"That's not why I'm saying this!" Sky exclaimed. "I know what Ambrosia will do! It's just . . . just . . ." He thought of Errand, locked away. Was he looking for something to be wrong with the solution so he could free Errand? So he wouldn't have to feel bad about freeing the Arkhon in the process and maybe getting lots of people killed? And what about his parents? Would he be condemning them in the very act of saving Errand?

"Just give me the keys. I'll do it!" said Crystal, holding out her hand.

Sky shook his head. "It just doesn't *feel* right."

"*Doesn't feel right* isn't good enough, Sky!" yelled T-Bone, hovering over Sky threateningly. "Give her the keys!"

Sky stared at the keys in his hand. "No."

T-Bone made a grab for the keys, but Andrew pushed him away. "Back off, T-Bone! Do you really want to be the one responsible for killing his parents?"

T-Bone pushed back, and Andrew toppled to the ground. "You want to be responsible for killing mine?"

Andrew jumped to his feet, planting himself in front of Sky. This was all getting way out of hand.

"Sky!" yelled Crystal, continuing to hold out her hand. *"Please!"*

Patience. . . . He needed to *see* what was in front of him now.

"I—I can't. It's not right. . . . We're missing something," said Sky, thinking furiously. "There's a piece missing."

Crystal hung her head. The others stared at him, their faces angry, resigned, and disappointed. He felt miserable, but he had to trust his instinct; the heart could puzzle out things the mind couldn't. It saw the now when the mind could only see the *next*.

As he thought and wrestled for an answer, the pendulum slowed.

"Last chance to do the right thing," said T-Bone.

Slowed . . .

"I . . . ," said Sky, his mind racing. The piece. Something was missing . . . and even if it wasn't, he realized, he couldn't condemn Errand.

Slowed . . .

T-Bone dove past Andrew, grabbing Sky. Sky fell to the floor and scrambled to get away. . . .

Stopped.

Lightning struck the glass dome above, exciting the plasma, which began to swirl with a smoky, shadowy charged light.

A concussive wave rippled from the pendulum, stirring up dust, barreling out like a gale. Sky could hear it growing in power as it ripped through the house and crashed toward the glass wall and beyond.

"The time streams have collapsed. The prison's open," said Andrew.

"We've failed," said Crystal.

CHAPTER 38
The Solution

At that moment the solution occurred to Sky. "It *is* a warning!"

"No, Sky, I'm pretty sure we're beyond *that*," said Crystal bitterly.

"No. The poem! 'Enof Od Naba Ban Do Fone'! The second part is a warning like Hands said!" Sky exclaimed. He scrambled out from under T-Bone, found the spot in the poem, and began to read:

"With all three,
On the pendulum bend,
You might get lucky
And lock the prison
Up again.
But then again, maybe,
Just maybe,
You'll kill everyone
You've ever loved
And find a pain-filled end."

"Phineas never let a poem mean just one thing when it could mean *two*," said Sky. "He used bad poetry to point out when something was important. Like here. It doesn't say that putting the keys on the pendulum will lock the prison. It says it *might* lock the prison, but it also says you're just as likely to kill everyone you've ever loved and find a pain-filled end."

"It doesn't matter anymore, Sky. The prison's open," said Hands.

Outside, in the hallways, Sky could hear monsters waking up—roaring, snarling, howls of pain and anger.

"It was *supposed* to open!" said Sky. "Phineas could have fixed the prison any night since it appeared. Why wait until the last possible minute? *And,* right after the pendulum was damaged, he saw that it slowed. He had all the keys, but he didn't fix it! Why would he wait if the pendulum wasn't supposed to stop first?"

T-Bone scoffed. Sky waited for him to say "And how do you know that," but Crystal jumped in before he could.

"No . . . Sky's right," said Crystal, frowning. "It *is* a warning. I missed it."

"Rule number four: A trap, like a good story, pretends to be something it's not until the very end," said Sky. "I almost missed it too. If we'd put the keys on while the pendulum still moved, something bad would've happened—an explosion, an implosion, monsters falling from the ceiling. I don't know, but something bad! It was a trap to stop hunters and monsters from messing with the trap—a double whatsit topped only by the triple trolley (or troll snatcher) and the mother of them all, the quadruple quandary! But the point is, now that it has stopped, we can fix it. It's not too late!"

"Well, let's pop those keys onto the pendulum and get out of here!" Hands exclaimed.

"I still don't think that will work," said Sky. "We're still missing something. The answer is *in* the poem."

"What about your parents and the riddle? What about the Arkhon and the monsters? Who's going to keep them in the prison while we figure out the poem?" asked Andrew as a visceral shriek reverberated through the halls.

"The Arkhon came here looking for something. I suspect he won't leave until he finds it or figures out it's not here," said Sky, shivering. It was the part of the plan none of them would like, and that's why he couldn't tell them. "We've got to keep as many monsters within the walls as possible. But, more importantly we've got to figure out what the Arkhon is."

"Hands and I can take care of that," said T-Bone.

Hands smiled. "Finally! My years of tireless study are going to pay off—the Arkhon is going to get sooo hugged. How you like my romance books now, Andrew?"

Andrew rolled his eyes.

"Just don't fight him! Find me at the gate!" said Sky. Hands almost looked disappointed. "Hannah should be retrieving our gear as we speak"—assuming she'd done what he'd asked—"and she'll bring it to the gate. I suspect the monsters will be disoriented for a time. Eleven years is a long nap, and they may not even realize what's happened to them. So just keep running until you reach the gate, and you should be okay."

"And then what?" asked T-Bone.

"After that, we'll see." After that, he'd search for Errand, and bait the Arkhon, but he wasn't going to mention that just yet either.

"And your parents?" asked Crystal.

"I'll handle that," said Sky, "before Hands and T-Bone arrive."

"What about fixing the prison?" asked Andrew.

"You and Crystal can figure it out," said Sky. "There's a number next to the poem: 581.112."

"A Dewey decimal number," said Crystal without hesitation.

He scowled. It'd taken him more than a day to figure that out.

"Right," said Sky, "but if you add up the numbers—"

"You get eighteen," said Andrew.

"And there are eighteen lines in 'Enof Od Naba Ban Do Fone,'" added Crystal, nodding. "The number is a map to the poem."

"Exactly," said Sky, still mildly irked at how quickly they'd worked it out. "As soon as you figure out what the poem means, take the keys and get out of here as fast as you can. I'll leave marks on the wall for you to follow. No matter what happens—whether the three of us are there or not—use the watch to close the gate."

Crystal nodded. "Good luck."

"You too," said Sky.

He slipped out the door, checking the hall. A few bodies were missing from the pile of monsters outside the door, but he didn't see them.

"Clear," said Sky.

As Hands stepped through the door, something grabbed Sky's leg, and he yelped.

"What? What is it?" yelled Hands.

Claws sank into Sky's ankle, and something growled deep

and low. He struggled, trying to yank his leg from the monster's grasp.

"Sky? What's happening?" Hands tumbled into him, knocking him to the ground.

Sky kicked at the clawed hand until it let go, the already injured monster dying with a final groan.

"Are you two okay?" yelled T-Bone, stepping through the door.

"Yeah, we're fine," Sky replied, helping Hands to his feet. "Just a little scare." He spotted a candelabra on a table a short distance down the hall. If it was silver, it could make a weapon, if it wasn't, it could make a completely worthless candleholder.

"You two wait here. I'm going to see if I can find some weapons."

He could search faster without them.

"It's pitch black past the door, Sky. I don't get how you can see *anything*," said Hands, "let alone find weapons."

Sky reached the table he'd spotted and picked up the candelabra, weighing it in his hands. It wasn't great, but it *was* silver. Silver didn't work against everything (most things, really), but he felt better with it than without.

He'd started to turn back, when he heard something . . . a whimper a few doors down. It almost sounded like . . .

Crying.

A chill ran down his spine. It was a baby.

"What is that?" called Hands. "I think I hear crying."

"Hold on a minute," Sky yelled back. He moved farther down the hall toward the sound. A doorway on his right. He stepped into a small bedroom, moonlight trickling through the window, lightning flashing.

Déjà vu washed over him . . . but it couldn't be . . . It couldn't possibly be . . .

Holding the candelabra high, he walked over and stared down at the black-haired baby crying in the crib. He looked so familiar.

And then he saw the child's palm—a white eye with a larger black eye encircling it. The Hunter's Mark and the trix.

"Errand . . ."

The baby looked up at him and smiled. And then, as Sky watched, the baby started to change, growing older before his eyes.

As the baby got older, his crying turned to howling, and then his howling turned to laughing. And in a moment eleven years of life held in check by a prison locked in time crept back, and Errand struggled to his feet, standing on real legs for the first time in his life.

"Sky. You found me!" Errand started crying.

"Errand? But—but . . . ," stuttered Sky. "Am I edgewalking? Dreaming?"

He looked around, expecting at any moment to hear his uncle's voice in the hall, or to see him step out of the shadows.

"For the first time in my life, this isn't a dream, Sky!" Errand stumbled around the room, touching stuff like a little kid.

"I don't understand," said Sky, unable to take it all in. "You've been a baby this whole time? Why do you still look just like me?"

"Because of the change," said Errand as he stared out the window with his *real* eyes, trying, Sky assumed, to see past the thick trees blocking his view.

"The change?" Sky muttered.

"From Phineas's journal notes," said Errand. "Whatever they were before, they're both the same after."

Sky stared at Errand, still not comprehending. "What does that have to do with—" And then Sky finally understood. Two baby boys, one a hunter, one a monster, their blood mingled under the birth moon, both exactly alike thereafter, unable to merge and change with another hunter or monster until one killed the other . . . their lives swapped, traded, one taking the place of the other fully, completely. "I'm—I'm a Changeling," said Sky. The realization crashed down upon him with the weight of a lifetime of lost dreams.

All these years, living a life he'd thought was his, with parents who'd thought he was theirs. How could he not have seen it? The way he'd never really fit in, how Hannah had been so much better at everything, and Phineas . . . Had he known? Had he suspected? Why else would he have the notes on Changelings in his journal if he hadn't suspected? What must Phineas have thought of him?

Sky was nothing but a thief, a monster who'd stolen another boy's life.

And then another thought occurred to him, a memory of that night. The room had gone dark. He couldn't see. The shadowy man had run off with one of the children, but which one? He saw Errand watching him, waiting for him to reach the inevitable conclusion.

"It could be either of us," said Sky.

Errand nodded. "Our memories, our bodies, our marks—everything became the same the moment the shadowy man put our hands together and mingled our blood. For all intents and purposes, we're both hunters—and we're *both* monsters. It's either of us and both of us. We're both Changed. We're both *Changelings*," said Errand, picking up an unlit candle from the dresser and sniffing it. "And we're something else, too—not normal at all. Something odd. The cuts and mixed blood under a birth moon—or *birthday* moon—made us Changelings; the marks made us something else."

"But, which one *am* I?" asked Sky.

"You mean which one *were* you," said Errand. "We're both Changelings now."

"But, which one *was* I?" asked Sky, a haze clouding his mind like smoke in the dying embers of a campfire. He had to have been the hunter. He just had to be! If he'd been the monster, what had happened to that family? Were they out there somewhere wondering what had happened to their little boy? Had they given their son away willingly, or had he been snatched from them? And what kind of monsters were they? The only requirement he knew of for a monster to become a Changeling was that it had to have shifter blood, but beyond that, he had no idea.

"I've asked myself the same question," said Errand, distracted by a small rattle he'd picked up from the crib. "Which one was I? Eleven years of watching you live a life that might have been mine, of hiding in the back of your head while you played games with Phineas and went to school. Watching helplessly while bullies beat you up and classmates made fun of you, while you wandered the dark, searching for something you couldn't find. Watching while you searched for *me,* unable to say a word, to make you *hear* me, unable to do more than push you to keep looking. Believe me, I've *asked* the question."

Sky felt horrible. All these years . . . He couldn't imagine.

"I'm sorry, Errand," said Sky, feeling truly awful. "I had no idea . . ."

"I *know*," said Errand, a brittle smile on his lips. "That was always the problem, wasn't it? Until my teacher found me and taught me, I couldn't help you. I couldn't make you know I was there. I don't know who was the monster and who was the hunter in the beginning. Only one person does."

"The shadowy man," said Sky.

Errand nodded. "The shadowy man. I mean to find him. And when I do, he will *pay*."

"Sky?" He could hear Hands and T-Bone calling for him, inching their way down the hall. Sky was running out of time. His parents must have only minutes left. How much time did he have?

"Errand, come with us. We can set things right! You can live with us. I know my parents will take you in!" said Sky, suddenly feeling guilty as he noticed the flash of pain in Errand's eyes. Were they really *his* parents? He'd spent his life with them, but was he nothing more than a thief?

"I've lived through you my entire life," said Errand, "but it's time I lived through myself. My teacher is here somewhere. He told me to find him when I woke up. He said he'd wait for me. He knows who did this to us."

"Your teacher? He's here?" said Sky.

"Of course. How else could I have talked to him? You're the only reason I could edgewalk outside these walls. He's had nobody at all. Just lives in the forest between the manor and the cornfield near the east wall. We always met there in his dreams, and I only ever heard his voice," said Errand. "It was the only way we could meet."

"Errand, Edgewalkers are *extinct*," said Sky, beginning to get a bad feeling about all this. "Whatever wants you to find it, it's *not* an Edgewalker."

"I know, Sky. And you're right, he's not really an Edgewalker. He's the one who killed them all," Errand bragged.

Sky's mouth fell open. "You're telling me that Solomon Rose is your *teacher*? He's even deader than the Edgewalkers! I hate to break it to you, but the dead are very poor conversationalists."

"Believe what you want, Sky; I know it's him," said Errand.

"Just think about it for a minute—," Sky started.

"You don't have to worry about me annoying you anymore, Sky," said Errand, setting down an old feather pen he'd been playing with, his back to Sky. "If I find out anything, I'll let you know."

"Errand, you've got to come with us! We're going to lock the prison again! *You have to get out*!" exclaimed Sky. "Look, after you find your teacher, meet me at the gate. Promise?"

The door crashed open. "Sky? Are you in here? Are you all right?"

"Take care, Sky—I'll—I'll miss you," said Errand, staring at the ground, apparently embarrassed by his admission, and then he spun and ran through the door, barreling past T-Bone and Hands as lightning flashed outside and the rain and wind pounded against the window like lost footsteps in an empty house.

"Errand, wait!" yelled Sky.

But Errand was already gone.

CHAPTER 39
Treat Me as I Am

Sky, did you just run past me?" asked Hands.

"Still here. We need to get outside," said Sky, storming out. Hands and T-Bone trailed behind, bumping into things.

Sky was mad and ashamed and adrift. It was like a part of him had been ripped out. All those nights he'd searched in the woods and deserts, all those times he'd felt alone, only to find that what he'd been looking for had been with him the whole time!

He swept through the manor ignoring the monstrous sounds echoing all around, monsters scrambling to escape, hunting, *dying*.

"Sky, slow down!" yelled Hands as he slammed into an end table Sky had forgotten to warn them about.

Sky paused, allowing them to catch up as he gathered his thoughts. All he wanted to do was hurt something—to rush through the halls swinging his candelabra, to strike out blindly and carelessly at the lie he'd been living—but his parents were still out there.

Even if they might not really be *his*.

He focused on the riddle, running through it over and over, each line, each word. *Always hold you no matter what . . . always treat me as I am . . . as I am . . .*

They reached the front door, and Sky threw it open. A scene of horror and chaos like nothing he'd ever known or imagined confronted him, a sudden riptide dragging his sanity out to sea.

Everywhere he looked, monsters were waking up, starting closest to the manor and moving outward. Shrieking and howling, they limped and slithered as they came back to themselves, returning from whatever strange places their minds had wandered.

In the night sky above, lightning danced like a ballerina at her first recital, bumbling and falling without regard to the people watching. It lit up the night with rolling blue and red light as it moved around the plasma cloud above the manor, spilling across the yard, making the field below come alive with shadow and blood.

"Monsters closest to the manor are waking first," said Sky. "Those that can't fly, burrow, or jump will funnel toward the gate once they're oriented. We'll need to hold them. The rest we'll deal with later. If you find anything that might be the Arkhon—something big, strong, and sneaky that could get away fast but isn't getting away—get back to the gate and let me know. Be back in ten minutes, whether you've found anything or not. Crystal and Andrew shouldn't be long."

"What could be easier?" said T-Bone, laughing. "Three unarmed teenagers against scores of bloodthirsty monsters!"

"You think we should make it fairer for them?" said Hands.

"Just get your *hugs* ready," said Sky, smiling. "And trust me—it's not as hopeless as it looks. It's much, much *worse*. Ready?"

T-Bone popped his neck, tightened the bandage on his leg. Hands stretched his hamstrings, bent to the left, arm overhead, to the right, jogged in place, nodded.

Sky shook his head, grinning. In all likelihood they were about to die, and yet Hands was still messing around. But in the face of terrible things—things they'd all had to face—what else could you do? Sometimes, you just had to laugh, because if you didn't, you might go insane.

"See you at the gate," said Sky.

He took off, heading for the gate, while T-Bone and Hands circled the manor, heading northwest toward the back wall.

Monsters came awake around him, bawling and howling as he ran, but he ignored them, focusing instead on the riddle, muttering under his breath.

"'I always hold you no matter what; you always treat me as I am. I'm overhead and underfoot, but only when in no-man's-land. I'd wait for you, if wait I could, but if you see me under sky, then you'll know, what I do hold; I do not wait, I merely lie.' Lie but not wait . . . Always hold . . . Always treat me . . . No-man's-land . . . No-man's-land . . . Gnomon's land! Dirt! It holds us and we treat it like dirt! They're buried!"

He picked up his pace, sprinting as fast as he could. How much time? Minutes? Seconds? Was he too late?

Ambrosia's eyes grew big as he rounded a small grove and came into view, reaching the gate a moment later. Obviously she hadn't expected to see him again.

"Sky! What a pleasant surprise!" Ambrosia exclaimed.

"You buried them!" Sky screamed.

Lem jumped to his feet.

"Where are they?" Sky demanded.

"That wasn't our arrangement," said Ambrosia, practically purring. "You have all the clues you need. Maybe my taking your parents will help you understand what you *hunters* did to mine."

"I'm not a hunter!" Sky snarled. "Not like *them*. I want to help you, not hurt you!"

"Tick tock, Sky," said Ambrosia. "Time is up."

Lem pounced on Ambrosia, grabbing her from behind. "TELL HIM WHERE THEY ARE!"

"Ursula, it's taken you long enough," said Ambrosia. "We could have reminisced about the good old days if you'd only dropped the charade sooner."

Lem changed before their eyes, shifting into Ursula.

"What? How did you—" Ursula started.

"Oh, please! You don't think I'd recognize my own *sister*? Making eyes at Sky? Offering to go into the Jack to get a key? Honestly! Gourmand would never have sat on the ground or been seen like *that*!"

"Tell him where they are," Ursula growled.

"I don't think so," said Ambrosia. "Shadow Wargs, if you would please . . ."

The Shadow Wargs charged.

"No. I drove Lem off! Stay back!" Ursula cried, but the Shadow Wargs didn't listen.

"He turned them, but you don't really think I would've let *Gourmand* control the pack, do you? Please," Ambrosia scoffed. "Give me more credit than that."

Ursula shifted into a Wargarou, bands of writhing darkness, like fiery whips, flipping out of her skin.

"I appreciate the help, Sky," said Ambrosia. "I never could have done it all without you!"

Ambrosia in turn shifted into a Gnomon, broke free, and dove into the ground, disappearing from sight before Sky could move, backfilling behind her.

"NO!" Sky yelled, rushing to find her, clawing at the dirt.

As the Shadow Wargs crashed into Ursula, fiery whips of darkness rose from her body and latched on to them, tossing them to the side.

Ursula let out a snarl, growling and biting at the air, the shadows swirling around her.

Sky gave up his digging. He focused on Ursula's shadows, watching them . . . trying to understand.

His Hunter's Mark warmed, and then he saw what she was saying.

"*—bind you to me in blood and fire and maybe free you—more than you deserve I might add—but for now you'll fight. In darkness and shadow you are mine!*" Ursula cried.

Bright streams of flame burst from her body, flashing into the Shadow Wargs. Blinded, Sky looked away. When he looked back, he saw Crenshaw and the others collapse on the ground in their normal bodies.

"Where are my parents?" Sky demanded as Crenshaw climbed to his feet.

"I wouldn't tell you if I knew!" spat Crenshaw.

"We don't know, Sky," said Cordelia. "She did it while we were in the Jack. I'm . . . sorry." And she actually sounded like she was.

Sky paced.

"Calm down, Sky," said Ursula, shifting back. "Think. Ambrosia said you have all the clues."

Sky stopped pacing. He stared at the ground, trying to focus. *Think. Think. Think.*

Dirt . . . Always treat me . . . Gnomon's land . . . wait for you, wait if I could, but if you see me under sky, then you'll know, what I do hold . . . Under sky . . . I do hold . . . Under sky . . . Under SKY!

"They're right here!" he screamed, rushing to the place he'd been standing when Ambrosia had given the riddle; she'd buried them right under his feet!

He started digging with his hands. Ursula joined him. So did Cordelia, then Marcus, and finally even Ren.

Sky kept digging and digging, getting more and more frustrated.

And then he felt a hesitant and thumbless hand on his shoulder. For a moment he feared Ambrosia had returned. But turning, he found Nackles. She gestured at the ground and then gestured for them all to stand back.

She dove in. Seconds passed by. Minutes. It felt like an eternity. Just when he was about to give up hope, Nackles burst out of the ground a few feet away, pulling Sky's parents up behind her.

"Mom! Dad!" Sky ran to them, helping them to their feet as they coughed up dirt. Through the hole, Sky could see a small hollowed-out pit far below, just big enough to hold his parents and a small amount of oxygen.

They hugged him fiercely.

"Oh, Sky!" Mom cried, holding him close. She looked him over, fretting all the more. "My poor baby!"

"I'm okay, Mom," said Sky, feeling suddenly uncomfortable. "You're the one we had to dig up, remember?"

My poor baby . . . but was he?

"Ursula? Can you hold the gate?" asked Sky, pulling away from Mom. His parents looked startled when they heard Ursula's name, and then, turning, noticed her for the first time.

Ursula nodded.

"Mom, Dad, you need to find the hunters if there are any left," said Sky. "Tell them it's an emergency!"

Thunder cracked overhead.

They looked at each other.

"Please," Sky begged, "I'll be fine here! The faster you go, the finer I'll be! Trust me for once! I have a plan!"

This made his parents look even *more* hesitant. They glanced at Ursula nervously.

"She's fine!" Sky declared, feeling exasperated. "If she'd wanted to hurt me, she could have long before now! She saved my life. She saved *your* lives!"

"All right," said Mom, giving him a hug. "Stay out here—by *her*." Mom glared at Ursula, and Sky had to wonder: Was this about Beau or something more? Did Mom really just not like monsters? If so, how would she feel when she found out he was one? "Just . . . just don't do anything . . . ," Mom continued. "Just don't do anything you'd normally do. All right?"

Sky nodded, feeling numb. He had to find out—*had* to know what he was.

Dad gave him a hug, and then his parents ran off.

The strange storm raged on the other side of the wall, and it looked like it was growing. Surely ten minutes had passed? Monsters would begin to arrive any moment. Where were the monster hunters? And where was Hannah?

Sky scooped up his candelabra.

"What's that for?" asked Ursula.

"To light the way," said Sky, "or to hit monsters. It doesn't appear to do either thing very well."

Ursula raised an eyebrow. "It seems to have gotten you this far."

Sky shrugged. "Ursula, do you know about . . . about that night? When your dad was captured?"

"I know enough," she answered, sounding cautious.

"You know why he came?" asked Sky, gulping. Why was this so hard? Why was he so afraid of the answer? "You know what happened to me?"

"I have my guesses," Ursula hedged.

"And they are?"

"The Arkhon wanted the Hunter's Mark. I suspect the person behind what happened to you didn't want him to have it," said Ursula.

"But why did he want me? What could my Hunter's Mark possibly give him that he doesn't already have?"

"You misunderstand, Sky," said Ursula. "He didn't want *your* Hunter's Mark. He wanted *the* Hunter's Mark, without you. For himself. For the power it holds. He believes it can protect him."

"From what?" asked Sky.

"From others like him who know what he seeks," said Ursula, "The Arkhon wants an ancient power, a power that nearly destroyed the world."

"What power?" asked Sky.

"It's not my place to say," said Ursula, "but your friends seem to be very late, and I've got monsters to stop."

Looking over, Sky noticed the first monsters approaching—

just a few, but the rest were sure to come soon enough. Where were the monster hunters? Where was Hannah? If she didn't show, his whole plan would fall apart!

And what about Errand? Where was he? Would he listen to Sky? Would he come to the gate?

And then, a terrible thought occurred to him.

"The Arkhon wasn't after me. He was after the Hunter's Mark! And even if he was after me, I might not even have been me anyway!"

Ursula, who'd been calmly crossing to join the Shadow Wargs as they readied for the gathering monsters, turned around. "I'm sorry. I missed that."

"You said whoever did this to me wanted to stop the Arkhon from taking the Hunter's Mark. What would happen now if the Arkhon tried? Could he take it?" asked Sky.

"Possibly. With the right tools, under the right *circumstances*, it could happen. But as it stands now, without those things it wouldn't work," said Ursula.

Sky gave one final glance down the cobblestone road, looking for Hannah. He ground his teeth.

"I've got to go," said Sky, marching toward the gate. Nackles stood by the gate, watching him. "Thank you, Nackles, for saving my parents."

Nackles barked out a few guttural sounds. Sky focused, calming his mind, trying to understand. The Hunter's Mark warmed. "Mother keepsss her promissse," hissed Nackles.

"Thank you," said Sky, his throat feeling weird. "I'll signal when it's time." Nackles smiled.

"Where are you going?" said Ursula, wrenching her eyes away from Sky—apparently surprised he could speak Gnomon. She sounded worried. "You've got to stay here, where I can protect you. Once those monsters reach this gate, it'll be plugged. There'll be no way out."

"Then we're all in for it anyway. Crystal and Andrew have the keys, and they're inside," said Sky. "If Hannah shows up, tell her I'll stick to the wall as long as I can, heading east. Tell her to hurry."

Sky slipped through the gate, running.

Ursula began to object, but by then enough monsters had gathered that they apparently felt brave enough for a charge. As Ursula shifted and Crenshaw and the other Shadow Wargs (now bound to obey Ursula) crashed into the approaching monsters, Sky had the distinct impression that the charging monsters wouldn't live to regret their hastiness.

Sky raced along, wondering what had happened to the monster hunters. Crystal and Andrew should've figured out the pendulum by now, and T-Bone and Hands should've given up the search. So where were they?

He shook it off. There was nothing he could do for them at the moment. They could take care of themselves. Errand, on the other hand . . . stumbling around the room touching things like a little kid . . . the way he'd cried when Sky had found him . . . and seriously believing his teacher was the very dead Solomon Rose? Errand's teacher was more likely to be the Arkhon than Solomon Rose! That was a scary thought, and also quite possible. What would Errand do when he found out? What would Sky do, for that matter, especially without his gear?

Sky stuck to the wall, running east, hoping Hannah would find him.

Monsters hung in trees, swinging from vines, caught in pits or in quicksand. He raced past them, the terrible storm above casting lightning bolts down every ten seconds or so, the thunder becoming almost a constant rumble. If Sky couldn't find Errand and the others and get out of here soon, monsters would be the least of their worries.

As Sky ran, he began to realize that Phineas had designed the rambling landscape around the manor as one elaborate trap—easy to get into and impossible to get out of, except through the gate.

Sky ducked from cover to cover, frantically scrambling to stay ahead of the monsters that had begun chasing him.

Phineas had taught him everything he knew about traps. Sky watched for stinging Lizzies and double bogies, steering clear of an upsy daisy and a screaming wedgie as he wove between Montezuma's revenge, and finally skipped across a Bob's your uncle.

He swung the candelabra with his left hand, driving a monster back.

Monsters howled and bellowed, leaping after him. Stones littered the ground, surrounding woozy monsters clambering to their feet, heads covered with horrible knots.

Sky grinned. Throwing rocks earlier had been petty, but worth it.

He raced through bushes, plowed through gardens, pushed through dense copses.

"Come on, Hannah." Sky struggled to see through the colorful, swirling wall for signs of her, his night vision blinded. And then he realized that even if she was out there, she likely couldn't see him through the wall. It was far too bright!

Ahead, monsters, fallen from the wall, climbed to their feet, blocking the way. Sky spun left—more monsters. And behind—

He was trapped.

Sky looked down at his candelabra. A horrible weapon, but maybe as a light . . .

He threw it into the air!

It flipped end over end, catching the flickering glow of the lightning and the color-stained light from the swirling glass wall, the silver flashing. He had one hope.

"*See it* . . . Come on. "

He backed toward the wall, watching as the candelabra fell to the ground. Monsters closed in.

"Anytime now, Hannah."

As he spoke, four cloaked figures leapt from the wall and crashed to the ground in shimmering light, rolling about like really, really *awkward* turtles on their backs, as they tried to regain their feet.

The first rose shakily, shooting the Taser-like Cross-Shocker at a toadlike Barrow Hag that jumped at Sky—knocking it from the air.

"Bull's-eye! Did you see that, Squid? Did you *see* that? That's why *I'm* captain of the football team!" yelled Tick.

"That thing did all the work; that's hardly fair!" said Squid.

"Yeah, why didn't I get the shootie thing. All I got is these gloves—owww!" said Lazy Eye as he accidently shocked himself.

"Would you three shut up and electrocute something? Jeez," said Hannah as she turned the Pounder on a charging monster with too many teeth, and pulled the trigger.

"Keep moving!" yelled Sky, dodging a tentacle as he picked up his candelabra and started running again, heading through the opening Hannah had created.

As they ran, Sky noticed that Squid and Lazy Eye each carried two bags of gear, one slung over each shoulder.

"What took you so long?" said Sky as he ran next to Hannah. "You were supposed to give Malvidia the antidote, make sure she was okay, and get the stuff I asked for—not nurse her back to health for six months!"

"Oh, I'm sorry, but I was busy wandering the sewers with captain letterman here, looking for this . . . this . . . *junk* in your burned-down lair! At *your request,* I might add! And do you have any idea how hard this garbage dump refuse is to put on by yourself?" said Hannah, shooting another monster. "Not to mention that it's a complete fashion disaster!"

"I offered to help you put on the suit, Hannah," said Tick, taking aim at a scaly thing that got too close.

"Oh, you would have liked that, wouldn't you!" said Hannah accusingly as Lazy Eye flew past screaming. He landed a few feet ahead of Sky and sat up, spitting out dirt. Sky ran past, but over his shoulder he saw Lazy Eye jump to his feet, racing to catch up with them before the monsters caught up with him.

"Um, no?" said Tick, guessing, as he pulled the trigger. The electrified prongs from the Cross-Shocker sailed into the scaly thing seconds after Hannah hit it with an ICE glob. Sky watched as the scaly thing froze solid.

"You wouldn't have?" asked Hannah, outraged. "Oh, do I disgust you? Am I not good enough for the *captain of the football team*?"

"Wait, wait! I meant yes!" said Tick as he launched more prongs from the Cross-Shocker.

"Boys!" said Hannah.

A loud *BOOM* rolled overhead. As Sky looked up, he saw a colossal funnel forming in the plasma storm. It reached down, touching the glass dome covering the pendulum room.

The monsters, apparently afraid of the sound and the

weapons now, began to fall back, giving the group some breathing room, but as Sky passed through a grove of trees, he found another problem facing him: a hunter.

She stood in the grove watching them, her bowstring pulled back, arrow pointed at Sky's face.

Sky stopped in his tracks, and she lowered the bow. The hunter looked at him, surprise and confusion on her face, her long dark hair blowing in the wind, hair the color of charcoal. "What's happening?" asked the hunter. "Did we catch him? Did Malvidia make it out?"

The hunter looked familiar, but Sky couldn't place her.

"Malvidia? She's hurt, but . . . You've been locked in," he said, realization dawning on him.

The hunter frowned. "Locked in? How long?"

"Eleven years," said Sky. Monsters were closing in behind. They had to get moving again.

The hunter looked stunned. "Eleven years? My son . . ."

Sky didn't know what to say to her, but, more important, he didn't have time to say it.

"I'm sorry, but you need to get outside the wall now . . . to the gate. There's a Wargarou, Shadow Wargs, and a Gnomon there—allies. Can you make it?" asked Sky.

The hunter's eyes flashed. "There may be others." She turned and sprinted away, disappearing into the dark. Others? It had never occurred to him that he might find live hunters in here. Did Malvidia know? Had Phineas?

"Sky, we've got to move!" yelled Hannah, urging him forward.

The monsters hovered back, snarling and enraged but wary.

"Hannah! Did you bring it?" asked Sky.

"You owe me big-time," said Hannah as she tossed him a backpack filled with things that she'd collected from the totaled Cadillac.

He riffled through it as he ran, making sure she'd collected everything he'd asked her to, especially the modified car battery from the lair. His plan wouldn't work without it. "You guys should get out of here now."

"No worries," said Tick as he barreled past a hairy monster Sky didn't recognize. "These monsters are no bigger than Quindlemore linebackers, and we *killed* Quindlemore. Ain't that right, Squid?"

"Sure did."

Sky found the battery and finally found what he was looking for—a flare gun.

"The sheriff's not going to be happy that I stole that from his Blazer—totaled or not," said Hannah. "If he gets upset, this is all on *you,* Sky. Just like the house!"

"I didn't burn down the house!"

"Tell it to Mom and Dad. You are in sooo much trouble!"

He started to respond, but he noticed something in his backpack . . . a book. His *favorite* book: *The Evil Echo of Solomon Rose*.

The Echo. Solomon had gouged out their eyes, but the Echo locked in here had *eyes*—pupil-less white eyes! It was big, strong, stealthy, and could make a quick escape with its giant black leathery wings!

"I know who the Arkhon is!" Sky declared.

"What?" said Hannah.

"Hannah, you need to get outside the wall!" yelled Sky, hopping past a clawed hand as it swiped at him. "Tell the monsters guarding the gate to watch for an Echo!"

"A what?"

"A big treelike thing with black wings!" Sky exclaimed.

Lazy Eye barreled into a monster, providing a solid block for Sky.

Sky glanced back, watching as monsters clambered over the dimming wall, which had, he'd noticed, been dimming ever since the boom and the funnel had first appeared over the manor. The dimming made it easier now to see through the wall. As he watched, a monster suddenly fell, a knife in its chest. On top of the wall, he saw Lazar and Lucretia. Lucretia fired a bow, hitting a Barrow Hag, while Lazar threw knife after knife, some of which found their targets.

Below Lazar and Lucretia he saw Malvidia, just outside the wall, a silver stake in one hand, a knife in the other, her black mourning dress whirling as she took down monster after monster. And beyond her, more shadows—hunters—moving through the trees.

As the monsters around Malvidia fell, she took a step, leaping into the air to land on top of the wall. She cringed, holding her side as she ran along the top toward Lazar and Lucretia.

"Run, stupid!" yelled Hannah, pushing Sky forward.

He realized he'd stopped, his mouth hanging open. Black rutabaga. He laughed despite himself. "She's going to be constipated for a *week*! I can't wait to see the nose hairs!"

"What? What nose hairs?" asked Hannah, sounding horrified. She crossed her eyes and crinkled her nose, apparently trying to see if she'd suddenly sprouted nose hairs.

"Never mind. Hannah, you've got to get over the wall!" said Sky as he started running again. "Take this extra flare gun." He shoved it into her hand. "When Crystal, Andrew, T-Bone, and Hands make it to the gate, shoot it into the air! I also need you to send Nackles to find me. The Echo is rootless! I think I know how to take it down! When you see my flare, if Nackles isn't back, I'll need you to spring the trap! Give me thirty seconds after you spring it, and then lock the gate!"

"What's a Nackles? And where are you going?" bellowed Hannah, shooting a leathery, shrieking Satyrn as it got too close.

"I need to find Errand!" yelled Sky.

"What's an Errand?" Hannah kept running next to him.

"Just go!" Sky yelled.

"Whatever. I'm not leaving you, not here!" said Hannah, shooting a scaly thing with not enough arms as she kept pace with Sky, refusing to let him out of her sight. "Mom and Dad would be *ticked*."

"What?"

"Not *you*, Tick!"

"Oh."

"I'll be okay, Hannah. I know you're worried even if you don't want to admit it, but honestly—I'll be okay," said Sky, suspecting that he'd be anything *but* okay.

"Don't be *stupid*," said Hannah, refusing to look at him.

"Hannah," said Sky, grabbing her hand as they ran. "I'll be okay. Trust me."

Hannah finally looked at him, tears in her eyes. "Just don't die, okay?"

He nodded. "I—"

"Hey," said Tick, interrupting them as he ran up from behind. "I know this probably isn't the best time, but would it bother you if I dated your sister?"

"Not now, Tick!" yelled Hannah.

Sky smiled. Those two were *perfect* for each other. "Thanks, Hannah. I owe you one!"

"Stop saying that!" yelled Hannah, opening up in frustration on a hideously deformed Seeping Creeper.

"Lazy Eye! Squid! Toss the bags into the cornfield there!" yelled Sky.

"Sure thing!" They launched the gear into the cornfield, throwing it farther than he'd expected. As they continued running for the eastern wall, Sky slipped off, into the cornfields, hiding until the monsters passed.

Then he gathered up the bags. Four bags. One for each of the monster hunters. He hadn't counted on Errand needing a way out. And he hadn't counted on needing one himself. He was the bait, after all, and bait stayed in the trap until it was snatched up.

He waited a moment more, making sure Hannah and the others made it safely over the wall. He watched as unseen hunters kept the monsters at bay—and then, after hiding the bags, he started running again, breaking through the cornstalks as he raced deeper into the heart of the storm.

CHAPTER 40

The Evil Echo of Solomon Rose

Sky popped out of the cornfield, continuing north toward the grove where he'd first spotted the Echo, the grove where Errand was supposed to meet his teacher—a teacher, Sky now felt certain, who was the Arkhon himself.

In the distance, closer to the manor, massive funnels from the plasma clouds overhead reached down like pilfering hands, and as they touched, they broke from the storm—tornados of color and filaments, whirling and sparking as they burgled the earth.

Monsters fled everywhere, running for their lives.

As Sky raced toward the grove of linden trees, he struggled to ignore the chaos, to focus on the monster he hunted. How had Phineas known the Arkhon was an Echo? Had he noticed the same thing Sky had—that the Echo had eyes? Or had it been something more? And why would the Arkhon appear as an Echo in the first place?

The Echo was a fearsome monster, sure—one of the most horrible walking the earth—but why not a bronze-skinned Harrow Knight like at Bedlam Falls, or one of the ocean-dwelling Morospawn giants that walked unfathomable crevices in search of light, or the earth eater, Paragoth of the Deep, or even the hideous Nithok with its fiery wings and gruesome features that could drive a person mad if they looked at it?

As his eyes drifted across the landscape, he spotted the grove of linden trees, standing almost motionless as the storm raged around it.

And within that grove he saw Errand, standing just as motionless, as if waiting for him.

Sky slowed down as he approached, searching the trees for signs of the Echo. "Errand?"

"I'm sorry, Sky," Errand muttered, looking embarrassed.

Where was Errand's teacher?

"Why are you just standing here? You need to get out! We need to—"

He almost missed it—a giant black splotch in the night, taller than the linden trees it resembled. Its enormous leathery wings were folded to blend in, its tentacle-like branches creaking and groaning as it stood up behind Errand.

"Errand, run!" screamed Sky, but before he could get away, a tentacle-like branch wrapped around him, picking him up.

He pounded against it, striving to break free. The Echo lifted him into the air and gently set him on his feet next to Errand.

"Calm down, Sky! He's not going to hurt you. He promised," said Errand, grabbing Sky's arm before he could run again. "That's my teacher. He explained everything to me! That's Solomon Rose!"

"That's the Arkhon, Errand! The Arkhon. Do you understand?!"

"He knows who I am, Sky," said the Arkhon. "The question is, how do you?"

Sky turned to face the colossal Echo towering over him.

"Solomon Rose gouged out the Echo's eyes, but you still have yours," said Sky, shaking loose of Errand—not on purpose either. His knees were simply shaking so badly that he just kind of drifted away.

"Yes, I suppose I did," rumbled the Arkhon, his voice rattling Sky to the bone, "and I suppose I do."

"What do you mean . . . ," started Sky, and then it hit him.

Edgewalkers, Echo, and the Arkhon. There was a common link between all three: Solomon Rose.

The greatest hunter of all time. The last bearer of the Hunter's Mark.

Solomon Rose. The man who'd driven the Edgewalkers to extinction, who'd edgewalked through the Echo's dreams before gouging out their eyes—the act that had started him on the fast track to power, the path of destruction he'd walked the rest of his life.

Solomon Rose . . . the man who'd supposedly been killed by the Arkhon.

Solomon Rose . . . the man who would remember fondly the days he'd spent among the Echo, before he'd punished them, the days when, according to *The Evil Echo of Solomon Rose*, he'd fallen in love with a woman named Lenore and walked with her among the old forests of the earth. These memories would be so fond that he'd be very likely to pick the Echo as his form when he, somehow, developed the ability to shift into anything he wanted.

Phineas hadn't spotted the Echo because it had eyes. He'd spotted it because he'd understood Solomon Rose!

"You're Solomon Rose," said Sky, stunned. "You're *actually* him."

Errand began to recite:

The evil echo came, a gloaming in the dark,
'pon belly bowering and crawing for the Mark,
to Solomon Rose the same, who sang the
names of yore,
and with it brought his evil forth, a gibbering
from the moor.
My branches shook and writhed, and standing
did I shriek,
"Why callest thou me, thou thawing thorn?
What sorrows dost thou seek?"
Old Solomon shook and shivered, but
dreaming of Lenore,
'pon his evil he shed his mind, and cast it in
the gore.
"I'm Solomon," he said, "and my servants you
shall be,
till earth and sky begin to shake,
and the sieves of time begin to seep."
Then he found us, and bound us,
and sent us off to dream,
till finally watchful waiting, our senses fading,
his evil echo slithered off to sleep.

Errand finished, and a silence settled even as the plasma storm seethed outside the grove.

"Lenore, my beloved," whispered Solomon. "I remember. The Echo knew what I was going to do even before I did, the power I sought, what I meant to do to the Arkhon, where it would lead me. I couldn't hide it from them, nor Lenore."

"You're Solomon Rose!" said Sky. "One of the greatest hunters who's ever lived! I can sort of see why you'd pose as an Echo—fond memories and all before you gouged out their eyes—but how can *you* be the Arkhon?!"

Solomon started laughing, low in the chest at first, and then rising up like a geyser.

"It's a good joke, a joke few know, and none have the humor to appreciate it," Solomon rumbled. "Especially you. Someday, if you survive, maybe I will share the joke with you. For now know that I am not truly the Arkhon, but this is his body. As you'll soon discover, the right monster can teach you amazing things."

Solomon smiled down at Errand, who smiled back, though not nearly as big, and Sky suddenly had a very sick feeling in his belly.

"Ambrosia . . . She said you changed centuries ago," said Sky.

"She doesn't know who I am or what we did with her father; very, very few know. It's a dangerous secret for all." Solomon spoke with a note as final as the sunset.

Sky gulped.

"When you took the Arkhon's body from him—however you did it—you lost your Hunter's Mark," said Sky, his mind racing. "That's why you want ours, isn't it?"

Solomon smiled darkly, his head dropping to look at Sky, his eyes several times larger than Sky's whole body.

"The Hunter's Mark was stolen from me," Solomon rumbled,

the earth shaking with his bitterness, "but look what I *gained*." A branch suddenly snapped around Sky's ankle and hoisted him into the air. Solomon opened his mouth—a mouth wide and terrible, full of unending darkness and pinpricks like stars, and carved in the center of it all, a darkness darker than the rest: the trix.

Solomon laughed, dropping Sky roughly back to the ground.

"I have stolen the body of one of Legend's own sons! And now I will get what I came for," Solomon threatened, his rattling boom a promise of horrors to come.

"But . . . but you can't! You don't have the right tools, or the right . . . er . . . circumstance!" Sky yelled, trying to remember what Ursula had said. "The marks protect us somehow. That's why you want it, right? To protect yourself from others like you?"

"There are no others like me!" Solomon roared, shaking the trees around them, "and I create my own circumstances."

Branches fell from the night, and hanging from them, tangled among them—branches shoved into mouths like gags, tightened around necks and limbs—were the monster hunters. Crystal. Andrew. T-Bone. Hands.

"No," Sky muttered.

They hung, struggling, staring down at Sky, eyes wide with horror . . . except for T-Bone. His eyes stayed shut, his head hung limply, and his pants were red with blood. He didn't struggle at all.

Rage boiled up in Sky, clawing to get out. He spun on Errand.

"Yes," said Solomon. "Your suspicions are correct. Errand was instrumental in gathering your friends for me. Only Crystal had the presence of mind to question him and he answered as you would have, of course, having been trapped in your mind for eleven years, watching as you stole his life."

Errand had betrayed him; he'd betrayed them all.

"Errand . . . why?" asked Sky. If Sky had trusted them—if he'd had time—if he'd told them about Errand . . .

"He knows who did this to us, Sky!" Errand shouted. "He promised to tell if I helped him! He promised he wouldn't hurt you if I did what he said!"

Sky clenched his hands, trying to keep himself from charging Errand. How could Errand have been so blind? Errand knew what Crystal and the others meant to him. How could he not see that Solomon had set a snare for them all—even Errand?

Solomon let out a rumbling chuckle. "A hunter always keeps his promises. That's why I'm going to let *you* hurt him, Errand."

"What?" Errand cried.

But it was nothing less than what Sky had expected.

"One of you has what I need. The other is redundant," said Solomon, his voice booming through the grove.

"B-but," stuttered Errand.

"There's always a price," Solomon rumbled. "If you want to know who took you—if you want your life back—you must take it. Sky is not going to give it to you."

Always a price. But making them fight this way . . . What did he gain? Why not just kill one of them and be done with it?

"And if we refuse to fight?" asked Sky.

Solomon tightened his branches around the monster hunters until they grimaced in pain. "And why would you do that?"

Sky clenched his fists.

For eleven years Errand had lived in the back of his mind;

eleven years of poking and prodding and getting him into trouble. Eleven years of pain and anger and grounding.

And . . . eleven years of wanting to defend him from bullies, of feeling his loneliness and pain, of trying to comfort him when he was down. Eleven years of always being there, warning him of danger, encouraging him to push on when all he wanted was to give up.

Eleven years . . .

"Errand," rumbled Solomon, "when you finish him, we will walk the Way of Secrets together, like father and son. We will find the man who harmed you and make him pay. We can have our revenge just like I promised."

Errand stared at the ground, avoiding Sky's gaze. More than anything, Errand looked lonely and desperate, like a boy who had no idea how to survive on his own in a world where almost nobody knew what he was, or even that he existed.

Sky knew that Solomon had just offered Errand exactly what he wanted: safety, a father, revenge, power, a life of his own. What could Sky possibly offer Errand if they got out of this alive? A shared life? Suspicion?

Crystal's eyes screamed at him to run for it. But there was no escape. Kill the monster hunters, or kill his best friend. He wouldn't let himself get trapped like this.

He dropped his candelabra.

"Errand, we don't have to do this," said Sky.

Solomon growled, low and deep.

"Sorry, Sky," Errand picked up a sharp rock and dragged it across his trix. As Errand's trix split open, Sky felt his own grow cold, on the verge of splitting open itself, but surprisingly it didn't. And then Sky realized, those other times, when Errand had opened his trix and Sky's had opened too, they had been in Sky's head. Errand must've been opening Sky's.

Sky caught movement out of the corner of his eye. He spotted Nackles hiding in the woods. Sky gestured at Solomon and pointed at the ground. When he glanced back, Nackles was gone.

"Errand, he *wants* us to fight each other!" said Sky, hoping Nackles understood. "If he wants it, there's a reason. There's always a reason! Why not kill one of us himself? Just think about it for a minute!"

Errand crossed to Solomon. Solomon bent down, opening his mouth. Errand stepped toward Solomon's mouth, almost into it, raising his trix.

"Errand?" Sky muttered, growing even more worried. Solomon had been Errand's teacher. What else besides edge-walking had he taught him?

Solomon seemed to breathe upon Errand, and then a stream of darkness shot out of Solomon's mouth. At the same moment, darkness shot out of Errand's trix. The two forces connected and repelled each other. Errand flew backward, and back again, crashing into a tree.

"Errand!" Sky ran to help him, but before he could get there, Errand stood up. His eyes had lost their color, becoming pupil-less and white, like an Echo's.

Errand put one hand against the tree behind him, pointing the other, trix out, at Sky.

Sharp roots, like spears, shot out of Errand's palm.

Sky dropped to the ground. The roots sailed over his head, driving into the tree behind him. Errand looked stuck, one hand on the tree, the other connected to the roots he'd just shot out.

With a jerk Errand snapped the roots from his palm and pulled away from the tree. As he did, Sky noticed that the tree had turned gray and dead. It snapped, crashing to the forest floor.

"Whoa," Sky muttered, rolling to his feet.

Errand raced to the next tree, inhumanly fast. He pressed his hand against it, pointing the other at Sky.

Sky dove over a fallen trunk, running, scrambling for cover as more roots shot over his head, and more roots, and more, driving into the trunk, shooting into the ground next to him, dead tree after dead tree falling with a thump.

He dove to avoid falling trees, dodged to avoid flying roots, finally jumping over a massive trunk and taking cover as more roots hit, trees slamming into the trunk he hid behind, nearly hitting him.

Crouching further, Sky scrambled along behind the trunk, trying to get closer to Solomon.

He waited for a thump, and then snuck a peek, watching Errand disentangle himself—dead trees lying all around him.

"Errand, do you remember the time we crashed through the ice at Puddle's Pond looking for freezing Erkbacks?" Sky yelled.

Errand stopped for a moment, his hands still attached to the last tree he'd killed and the roots he'd shot trying to kill Sky.

"Mom grounded us for a month," said Errand, snapping free. "She said it would give us time to *chill out*." Peeking over the trunk, Sky noticed a small smile on Errand's lips, but then his smile faded. "But that was *you*, Sky! It wasn't me!"

"It was *both* of us—together!" Sky exclaimed.

Roots started flying again. Sky reached a clearing and raced across, trees falling and dirt exploding around him. Reaching the other side, he dove into some bushes, scrambled under a broken tree, and combat-crawled to the next patch of cover.

Solomon rumbled with laughter. "*This* is the boy Errand has been bragging about! The great *Sky Weathers*, who faced down a Wargarou and escaped the Jack? My old teacher must have grown senile in his old age! He forgot to teach you how to fight!"

Snarling, Sky picked up a rock and threw it at Errand. Errand batted it to the side, and Sky used the distraction to circle Solomon, putting the giant Echo between them.

"Errand! Listen! How long have we known each other? Hm?" Sky shuffled around Solomon, keeping him in the middle. "A long time, right?"

Errand found another tree and raised his hand. Snaking roots shot out, branching around Solomon to get to Sky. Sky dove out of the way just as the roots ripped into the ground, sending chunks of dirt scattering everywhere.

"Errand, you made a mistake, but it's not too late to change! Crystal, Andrew, T-Bone, Hands—they're still alive!" Sky glanced up at T-Bone's sagging body desperately hoping it was true. "We can fix this, but you need to trust me!"

"Not everything broken can be fixed," said Errand, sending more roots Sky's way. Sky dove.

"We don't have to fix everything!" Sky yelled, scuttling to keep Solomon between them, Solomon rumbling with laughter as he looked down at them. "Don't you see? Take care of the now and the future will work out as it should! That's what Phineas was trying to teach us!"

"You mean trying to teach you," Errand spat, shooting more roots at Sky.

Sky dove again, moving to keep Solomon between them, making sure to position himself so that Errand shot lengthwise across Solomon's wings.

"All right! All right! He didn't know about you, but I did," said Sky. "I've always known you were there. I never understood you—I'm not sure I understand you now—but you don't have to do what this monster tells you. If he could kill us, he would! He wouldn't go through the trouble of setting up this elaborate trap!"

And then, finally, Sky understood what Solomon wanted. "Errand, just think about it for a minute. There's only one way either of us can ever Change again and join with another person. One of us has to kill the other with our own hands! Blood has to return to blood. That's what Phineas's notes said! The Changeling shift—the permanence—is something he can't replicate, even as the Arkhon! Solomon wants the Hunter's Mark. The only way he can get it is the same way we got it—by becoming a Changeling, but one of us has to kill the other before he can! We're the only ones who can give him what he wants!"

"Errand, this is growing tiresome," rumbled Solomon. "Claim your prize and I will teach you all the things I have held back. End his life, and you will have power to rival my own."

Errand shot another tangle of roots, blocking off Sky's retreat, penning him in. One more shot. Sky needed Errand to shoot vines at him just one more time. Sky circled Solomon, positioning himself. He was almost completely penned in behind Solomon now.

"Look," said Sky, "everything has a price. That's what you said. The price of power without understanding is your *humanity*. That's what Solomon still can't puzzle out. You can't expect to walk the same path he's walked and end up somewhere else! It doesn't work like that! You step on his path, and you'll wind up just like him—friendless, scared, and trapped!"

This time the roots spread out, striking the ground to his left, right, above, below, clipping his shoulder, piercing his hand. Sky cried out in pain.

Errand snapped the roots from his hands, crossing to stare down at him as he struggled within his rooty tomb. Errand jerked a spiked root from the ground, one of the walls of Sky's very own prison.

"Eleven years I spent like *that*," Errand barked, looking down at him through the gaps in his prison wall. "Watching, wondering . . . *trapped*."

Errand raised the spiked root, holding it over Sky.

"But you had me," said Sky. "What will you have now?"

Errand hesitated.

"Do it, Errand," Solomon commanded. *"Take back what is yours."*

With a feral scream Errand drove the root into the ground next to Sky.

CHAPTER 41

The Quadruple Quandary

Solomon smashed Errand across the face with a branch, sending him tumbling through the air.

Sky slipped through the opening Errand had made when he broke off his spear. Sky turned to run, but Solomon grabbed him by the ankle, jerking him upward.

As he flew toward Solomon's mouth, Sky concentrated, thought of Nackles, and began to shriek hideously, almost as if he were trying to talk.

The ground suddenly opened up beneath Solomon, sucking him down into Nackles's trap.

As he fell, Solomon flung Sky and the monster hunters to the side, reaching out with his branches to slow his fall. He moved to spread his wings, but they were penned in by the roots Errand had shot at Sky, just as Sky had intended.

Sky hit the ground hard, rolling. He stumbled to his feet, grabbing Errand.

"How did you . . . ?" Errand started, watching Solomon struggle in the pit.

"Nackles dug it," said Sky, dragging Errand behind him as he searched for the fallen monster hunters. "Without roots, Echo fly high, but they also fall far."

He found T-Bone, and Errand hoisted him onto his shoulders.

"You've really got to show me how to do that sometime," said Sky.

"Later," said Errand.

They scrambled around, looking for the others. The once quiet grove was sputtering with cries and shrieks, the storm touching down to join Solomon's terrible rumbling.

"The trap won't hold long enough!" said Errand. "I caused this. It's my fault! Take the monster hunters and go! I'll keep him in here!"

"You're insane!" exclaimed Sky.

"And I'm really enjoying it!" said Errand, laughing. "I can keep him distracted long enough for you guys to get out. He trained me. I have the best chance."

"You'll get yourself killed is all!" said Sky. "And even if you managed to distract him, you'd be stuck again."

"If you don't get T-Bone out of here, he's going to die! You don't want that kind of thing on your conscience, do you?" said Errand.

Sky ground his teeth. He needed to get them out, but he wasn't leaving. Not by a long shot.

"Good-bye, Sky," said Errand. He set down T-Bone as the other monster hunters came into view. "I'll let you know if I survive."

"Errand! Wait!" yelled Sky as Errand disappeared back into the trees.

Hands and Andrew helped manhandle T-Bone through the grove.

"Did you figure out the poem?" asked Sky.

"Yes!" yelled Andrew above the tempest. Lightning flashed everywhere, lighting up the night.

"And the keys? The watch?" asked Sky.

"Right here," said Crystal, showing him the watch.

"Good."

They raced through the trees and burst out of the grove, the cornfield a short sprint away. Behind them Solomon bellowed and roared, wrestling to get out of the hole.

"Hurry! Get to the gate! Hannah knows what to do! Tell her thirty seconds from my flare no matter what! Your bags of gear are on the edge of the cornfield to the south!" Sky yelled above the howling.

"What about you?" asked Hands.

"We can't let Solomon escape! I have to help Errand!" said Sky.

"What makes you think you can stop Solomon?" asked Andrew.

"Because I'm the bait!" said Sky, giving them a broad grin.

"Well, don't let him hug you!" said Hands. "It's not all it's cracked up to be!"

"Not at all!" said Andrew, agreeing.

Crystal stared at him for a moment, opened her mouth to speak, closed it, and then turned and walked away. Eyebrows raised, Hands and Andrew followed.

"Don't get caught," yelled Hands as they stepped into the cornfield. "You still owe us a story!"

Sky had started to return to the grove, when to his right he spotted the group of monsters that had been chasing him earlier. A thought occurred to him, and he veered toward them. "I am such an idiot. Hey, guys! Over here!"

The monsters looked up at the words and began running toward him.

"The Arkhon is ahead!" yelled Sky, hoping the Arkhon's descendents, and any other monsters wandering around, hated him as much as Ambrosia had led him to believe. "He can't shift! Now's your chance to tell him how you feel!"

As he spoke, he could feel his tongue moving in strange ways, his throat expanding and constricting, his Hunter's Mark burning hot. But it was no good. He couldn't talk to them all at once. Instead he focused on one kind of monster, then the next, and the next, calling out the same message, trying to figure out how it might communicate—speech, shadows, something else—and once he spotted that, all it took was some concentration. Then the Hunter's Mark would warm. He couldn't always tell, but enough seemed to understand.

As Solomon came into sight, Sky's breath caught in his throat.

Solomon had managed to free himself from the trap and he stood solidly on the ground, his branches flailing madly. Errand raced through Solomon's branches, dodging and jumping like a crazy person—dancing and falling and spinning with inhuman speed, smashing Solomon's branchy arms with Sky's candelabra.

Solomon screeched with each hit—his sensitive branchlike arms vulnerable while he stayed on the ground.

Sky rushed between Solomon's thrashing branches, leading the Arkhon's monstrous children back to him.

"Errand, get out of there!"

Scores of monsters leapt and clawed and gouged, attacking. Ambrosia had been right; they really did hate him.

Sky raced around Solomon, dodging between stray branches as Solomon fought off his attackers, shrieking and roaring in rage.

Sky ducked behind a linden tree, catching his breath. He ripped off his backpack, searching through it for something he could use to get Errand away from here.

Solomon roared in pain.

As the giant Echo turned to face him, Sky saw Errand leaping across Solomon's face to shove the candelabra into Solomon's other eye, sliding downward as he ripped it open from top to bottom. For one insane moment Sky envisioned a young Solomon Rose gouging out the Echo's eyes, the atrocious act setting his feet on a path of destruction that had changed his life forever.

"No. Oh, no, Errand," Sky mumbled, a grim terror taking hold as he watched the blood and gore drip from Solomon's gouged-out eyes. "What have you done?"

Monsters lay dead, smashed and broken around the woods.

As Errand hit the ground, Solomon stepped forward, shaking the earth. For a brief moment Errand lost his balance, and then Solomon had him. Branches groping, wrapping, entangling, Solomon squeezed the life out of Errand.

Solomon bellowed, his voice cracked and broken, a lonely rock tumbling down a forgotten hill.

Errand—shattered and unconscious—dangled in front of Solomon's cavernous mouth. And then he was dropping.

Sky stepped out from hiding. "STOP!"

Solomon turned to face him, white sludge streaming from his eyes.

Sky raised his flare gun.

"You think you can kill me with a gun?" rumbled Solomon, his voice an agony to hear. "You think you can steal my power?"

"I'm not trying to kill you, and you can *keep* your power," said Sky, deciding to bluff, hoping to give Crystal and the others time to reach the wall. "In less than a minute my friends will lock the gate . . . unless I shoot this first."

That wasn't *really* the plan, but he couldn't shoot the flare yet, not until he saw the flare telling him they'd reached the gate. He also knew that the longer he stood here, the more likely it would be for Solomon to snatch the gun from him, and if Solomon did, he'd discover that Sky had set a trap of his own.

Sky pointed the flare gun at the ground, deciding to give the bluff some extra credibility. "If you try to take it, I'll shoot it into the ground."

"Your friends wouldn't lock the gate with you inside," said Solomon.

"You don't know my friends," said Sky.

"What do you want from me, *boy*?" Solomon rumbled.

"Let Errand go. We're not going to kill each other. You can't get what you want."

"You're *right*," said Solomon. With a flick of a branch he tossed Errand over the wall.

"ERRAND!" yelled Sky.

In two quick steps that cracked the earth, Solomon closed the space between them. An arm—branchy like a branch, slimy like a tentacle, and as flexible as a vine—wrapped around Sky's ankle and hoisted him into the air again.

He dangled in front of Solomon's barky face, Solomon's pupil-less white Echo eyes running down his cheeks like tears in the rain, his body cut and torn, branches broken.

Sky stared into Solomon's cavernous mouth as it opened, mesmerized by the vast chasm of darkness and sparkling lights, the dark trix staring back, as if Solomon had swallowed the moon and the stars and the night itself.

The vine holding him swung out and away from Solomon's mouth. And for a moment, he feared Solomon would swing the vine back and *eat him*, but then the vine stopped.

"You're clever, boy. Like Phineas," wheezed Solomon as a branch pried the flare gun from Sky's hand. "But you know, over the years, I've discovered that *clever* tastes exactly the same as *stupid*."

"If you kill me, you'll never get the Hunter's Mark," said Sky.

Please . . . please . . . please be out.

"The easy way didn't work, but there's always the hard way, and for that I need only one of you," hissed Solomon. "Errand will help me before the end. But you are dangerous."

"I feel sorry for you," said Sky. "You must be the most miserable creature alive."

"For now, but in a moment—that will be *you*," said Solomon.

Solomon fired the flare gun, fooled by Sky's bluff into thinking the flare would keep the prison open, when in fact the opposite was true. The flare sailed up, up, up, bursting into the night.

A moment later explosions shook the ground everywhere,

starting near the gate and spreading outward. Nackles or Hannah had gotten the message.

"What was that?" Solomon rumbled, sounding scared.

"Distilled urine—very dangerous—highly explosive," said Sky, counting down the seconds. Twenty-nine . . . Twenty-eight . . . Twenty-seven . . .

Fog suddenly erupted from craters all over the sprawling yard, spilling forth like a volcano from the Cheez Whiz canisters Rauschtlot had buried beneath the yard, coating the landscape in a thick bluish haze.

"Fog won't hide you from *me*, boy," Solomon rumbled.

"It's a good thing it's not fog, then," said Sky. He calmed his mind. He focused, reaching for the warmth.

"Another trick?"

"Not a trick. A trap and a poem," said Sky. "My *uncle Phineas* taught it to me."

Solomon's body went rigid again.

"A grape might become a raisin," said Sky, pulling a cracker out of his pocket, "and taste the sweeter for it, but even a raisin will rot on the vine, if you do nothing for it."

Twenty-three . . . Twenty-two . . . Twenty-one . . .

"Hideous! What is it supposed to mean?" rumbled Solomon, his black mouth opening. Darkness spilled out as Sky was slowly lowered toward it.

"Unlike you, my friends don't want to forget me. CAW!" he croaked, tossing the cracker into the air! In English it sounded horrible, but, he knew, in Piebald it was really quite beautiful and rather complex. It meant something like "When the western wind doth blow, fly to me, my feathered friend, and cackling and cawing we will go, till you fly me home again. . . . Oh, and by the way, there's a cracker in it for you.'"

Before the cracker could hit the ground, a Piebald swooped out of nowhere and scooped it up. Sky had felt them circling, watching for him.

Scores of monstrous Piebalds followed, falling from the welkin to lodge in Solomon's broken branches, pecking and clawing and cawing and yammering.

"No!" Solomon cried out, lashing at them, but he was too big and they were too many. Solomon squirmed and writhed, trying to shake the Piebalds off.

Nineteen . . . Eighteen . . .

The arm holding Sky suddenly let go.

He fell!

As the ground rushed toward him, the Piebalds scooped him up like a giant cracker, latching on to his hair, his clothes, his skin, dragging him upward.

And at that moment, Sky saw a flare go off by the gate; the monster hunters had made it out.

Solomon shrieked, opening his wings.

As Sky rose above the mist, Solomon shot after him, grasping . . . writhing . . . branches flapping . . . mouth opening . . . darkness undulating like chimney smoke . . . wings spreading . . . eyes *dripping* . . .

Sky slapped his backpack and dropped it into the mists below.

Ten . . . Nine . . . Eight . . .

Electricity shot from the backpack, frying it to pieces, revealing the modified car battery Hannah had concealed within.

"I told you it's not fog," said Sky as the mist started to crystallize around Solomon. "It's ICE."

Solomon shrieked as he froze. Thick fingers of ICE slithered around him, wrapping him up, embracing him, before solidifying and dragging him down, down into the swirling vortex below.

"Quadruple quandary," said Sky as the Piebalds carried him closer and closer to the wall—so close now . . .

Four . . .

Solomon gave a shriek, breaking free of the ICE.

Three . . .

Plasma sparked in the glass, and the storm churned, swirling inward toward the massive funnel over the pendulum room.

Two . . .

Solomon reached for Sky, branches shooting forward.

One . . .

A concussive wave rippled out of the manor, knocking the Piebalds from the air.

Sky fell, twisting and spinning—*CRACK* against the wall—tumbling just to the outer side. He caught a glimpse of Solomon—thrashing, caught in a riptide of chaos, jerked spinning toward the manor, along with the wall, and the storm above, twisting into nothing under the watchful eye of the Hunter's Moon.

And then, as the wind spun Sky around, he saw dozens of small children streaming from the copse of trees to the south, laughing and skipping.

Rauschtlot kept her promise. His last thought.

Like a worried mother, the ground rose to meet Sky.

And then everything went black.

CHAPTER 42
Last Will and Testament

His nonexistent alarm clock beeped at him. He rolled over in bed, swatting at it.

He opened his eyes, pulling his hand away from the EKG machine he'd been swatting. He was in a hospital . . . *alive*, as far as he could tell.

"Mom? Dad?"

"Oh, Sky!" Mom cried, jumping up from a nearby chair and wrapping him in her arms.

"It's okay, Sky. You're in a hospital. You're safe," said Dad.

"Crystal? Hands? T-Bone? Andrew? They're okay?" asked Sky. "Hannah? What about Hannah? Is she all right?"

"I'm fine, squirt. Glad to see you kept your promise for once," said Hannah, stepping up next to his hospital bed to ruffle his hair. "Your friends are around here *somewhere*. The nurses threw them out after Hands made a pass at one of them."

"Like with a football?" asked Sky.

"Like with a bad pickup line," said Hannah. "Total *cheese*."

He laughed. "How did Tick fair?"

"He lived," said Hannah with a scowl. "We have a date next Friday."

Dad's ears perked up. "A date?"

"Dad! I had to! It was the only way I could get him to help!"

Dad's ever-present smile twitched, almost falling. He had a strict policy on dating . . . not before you were forty-two.

A hand pushed the curtain aside.

"Hey, roomie. Finally awake, I see . . ."

"Sheriff Beau!" exclaimed Sky.

"You can drop the 'sheriff' part. People who save my life get to call me Beau," said Beau from the hospital bed next to him.

Beau didn't look so good, wrapped in braces and slings and gauze. But as Sky looked himself over—the bruises, the scabs, the claw marks on his arms where the Piebalds had latched on to him—he realized he probably didn't look any better.

"That goes for you too, Hannah," continued Beau. "I don't care how modest you are . . ."

Modest? Hannah?

"Claiming you weren't the one who called the ambulance . . ." Beau shook his head. "If you hadn't called and given me the Jack seeds, I'd be a corpse right now. Of course, there's still the issue of some missing flare guns."

Hannah's face turned pale. "But, Sheriff, I'm too *pretty* to go to jail! And you have no idea what prison lights would do to my complexion!"

Beau started chuckling. "I was going to say I could make you some better ones if you'd like." Beau looked at Sky. "I could help you build all sorts of things."

"Oh. Uh, thanks, I guess," said Hannah.

Sky smiled. Beau had been the hunters' metallurgy teacher before they'd kicked him out. Having him help build things would be perfect! They might even be able to use *real materials* instead of garbage! Of course, Sky was assuming Crystal and the others would forgive him for everything.

There was a commotion in the hall.

"Whatd'ya mean it's from a catheter? I thought you said it was apple juice, Hands!"

He could hear Hands and Andrew snickering.

"Relax, T-Bone," said Crystal. "They're just messing with you. You are messing with him, right? Please tell me you were messing with him."

Hands and Andrew snickered more loudly.

"Relax? I almost gave that to my little brother!" yelled T-Bone.

Hands and Andrew were still snickering when they entered Sky's room. Hands had his arm around a young boy of no more than five whom Sky'd never seen before. The boy looked scared, unsure—smiling shyly.

"I'm sure *Dickens* could tell the difference," said Andrew.

"Yeah," said Hands. "Apple juice has less of a *uriny* flavor."

As T-Bone and Crystal entered, T-Bone dropped a cup full of yellow liquid into the trash can.

"Hey! I was going to use that!" said Andrew.

The young boy—Dickens—broke away from Hands and crossed to Sky.

"Nobody's stopping you. Look, it didn't even tip over," said T-Bone.

Andrew dove for the trash. "What? Let me see! . . . Amazing.

A perfect landing. There's a little bit of sloshing, but nothing terrible."

Dickens edged past Sky's parents and stared at Sky.

Sky stared back.

"Rauscht-lot says th-thank you," said Dickens, his voice awkward, halting. There was something wild about him, a *hunted* look to his eyes. But then, Sky guessed, living with monsters after being declared legally dead could do that to you.

"He's awake!" yelled Hands before Sky could respond to Dickens.

Sky's mom patted him on the hand, and Dad squeezed his shoulder before stepping back so his friends could gather around. As his parents stepped away, Sky watched them, searching for something—anger, fear . . . maybe even hesitation—but all he saw was the same thing he always saw. Love . . . and maybe a little indigestion.

Did they know what he was?

"How's the mighty monster hunter of Pimiscule Grounds?" asked Hands.

"I've gotta admit—I've felt better," said Sky. "Something gave me a *nasty* hug."

"Did you hug it back?" asked Hands.

"My hug was like a raging storm, I hugged it so good," said Sky.

Hands smiled. "See? Supernatural romances never lie."

"You look *terrible*," said Crystal, taking his hand.

"You should see how I *feel*," said Sky, the words not coming out quite right.

He smiled. Her hand was so soft . . . so warm . . . and then he glanced at Dad, who was almost frowning, his lip quivering with restraint. Crystal must've noticed too, because she pulled her hand away, leaving Sky cold again.

T-Bone stood over him, his hands resting on Dickens's shoulders protectively. His leg was bandaged, but since he was still in street clothes, it looked like the hospital doctors hadn't been able to make him stay. As T-Bone stared down at Sky, his eyes brimmed with tears.

"How did you know?" T-Bone choked out, his hands tightening on Dickens's shoulders.

"Rauschtlot confirmed my suspicions at the store," said Sky, "but I suspected it before then. The story of the night you guys met—hearing Dickens in the cemetery by the crypt of Andrew's mom, the body, the timing of the Gloom's appearance at the manor, knowing a child-eating Wargarou was in town—and then capturing Nackles around the time Dickens turned up missing . . . The pieces just didn't fit," said Sky.

"That's why you wanted me to bring everyone to Emaline's crypt—not so you could send glowing Piebalds to fetch us to save you from Shadow Wargs," said Hands. "You were going to show us the children."

"All twenty of them," said Crystal, smiling a smile bigger than he'd ever seen her smile before.

Sky nodded. "I had to improvise, and then things moved so quickly that I didn't have time to show you, and I knew you wouldn't believe me if I told you. Rauschtlot did her part in the plan by burying the canisters. She waited until it was relatively safe, and then she kept her promise and brought the missing children to the manor. I saw them as I fell, but even I was surprised at the number of children she'd saved."

"Twenty. That's a lot of mouths to feed!" said T-Bone,

shaking his head. "And to think I nearly froze her at the store while she was getting food and toys for them."

"But I still don't get it," said Andrew. "Why take the kids in the first place? Was it revenge for us taking Nackles? Was Rauschtlot just lonely?"

"She was lonely," said Sky, "but that's not why she took them. She took them to protect them—"

"From the Wargarou," cut in Beau, who'd been quiet since the monster hunters had entered. "She knew he was hunting children at the school—some to add to the pack, some to *eat*. He'd been hiding in the north cemetery for years before he'd killed Lem, and he had a personal vendetta against Phineas and Malvidia. I should've seen it."

"The Wargarou had very specific tastes," said Sky. "It preferred the young. Rauschtlot figured it out, and anytime she got wind that the Wargarou was hunting, she'd swoop in and snatch the child away before he could get to it. She wanted to return the children, but there was no one she could go to—no one she could tell, because nobody could understand her. Not to mention that the hunters would kill her on sight."

"But what about the DNA? I ran the tests myself. It was *Dickens*, T-Bone's little brother here," said Beau, smiling at Dickens.

"It was the Gloom, the fallen Whisper that can't control its shifting," said Sky. "Rauschtlot knew that if you found Dickens, it'd just be a matter of time before the Wargarou got him, so she lured the Gloom to the manor, took some of Dickens's saliva, and fed it to the Gloom to throw you off the trail. The mindless Gloom took the saliva, made a lifeless copy of Dickens, and spit it out. Rauschtlot's been taking care of Dickens and the rest of the children ever since."

T-Bone patted Dickens's head. "Hands and Andrew rushed me here, but Crystal stayed behind. When she found the kids wandering the yard after the wall disappeared, they refused to come with her unless we promised to keep Rauschtlot and Nackles safe."

"*And* promised that they could go back for visits and baseball games," said Hands, hitting Dickens playfully in the arm. "What? Are we mere humans not good enough for you anymore, Mogli?"

Dickens smiled.

"So, what happens now, Sky?" asked Crystal.

"Yeah. We heard about how you burned your house down," said T-Bone.

Sky looked at Hannah.

"What? I didn't say anything! It was Tick!" Hannah protested.

"Sure," said Hands. "Blame it on the captain of the football team. You know he's captain of the football team, right?"

Hannah scowled at Hands.

"I don't know what's next," said Sky, looking at Mom and Dad.

"We're staying in a hotel for the moment," said Mom.

"And when the moment's over?" asked Sky.

Mom and Dad looked at each other.

"Oh, great! This has to be a new record or something!" exclaimed Hannah, "Less than a week, and we're already moving."

"Deal with it, Hannah," said Mom. "We lost our house!"

"We'd always anticipated that the move here would be temporary," said Dad. "We just didn't know how temporary."

"I still remember when my first house burned down," said

Beau, his eyes going distant—whether from memories or morphine, Sky couldn't tell. "Ursula and I thought we'd be there forever."

"I'm sure she loved you, Beau," said Mom. "Loves you *still*."

Beau shrugged. "Yeah, well, she's got a funny way of showing it if she does."

Mom frowned. Sky remembered what she'd said about Ursula the night he'd followed Dad into the cemetery and had seen his first monster (Ursula *herself*, as it had turned out). Mom had said that she didn't trust Ursula. But he remembered Dad's response. Dad had told her to trust *Phineas*. It was just like his uncle to give Ursula a chance, even knowing what she was.

Phineas didn't give up on people . . . even in the end.

Beau didn't know that Ursula had been in Exile, and, Sky suspected, Ursula didn't want him to know.

"You're welcome to stay with me until you find a new place," said Beau. "It's not big, but what it lacks in size, it makes up for in *mildew*."

"We appreciate that, Beau," said Dad, smiling. "It looks bad for us now, but I'm sure things will work out."

"I couldn't agree more," said Malvidia from the doorway. "Phineas wasn't the type of man to leave loose ends."

Sky turned, along with everyone else, to stare at her. He had no idea how long she'd been there, but as far as he was concerned, any length of time was too long.

She'd cleaned up since he'd last seen her—which wasn't hard, considering she'd been covered in blood—but her clothes were still black and out-of-date. But what really drew the eye were her nose hairs. Dozens of them, long and black, dangling from her nose. Leftovers, Sky assumed, from the black rutabaga. She'd obviously tried to trim them, but they looked fairly stubborn.

He stifled a laugh, and he could see the monster hunters doing the same.

In her hands Malvidia held a big cooking pot with a folded paper on top. Was she really bringing him food?

"Don't worry," continued Malvidia, "I'm not here to spoil your party . . . as scintillating as that is—but I always pay my debts."

She set the pot on the table with the folded paper next to it.

"Er, thank you?" said Sky, eyeing the pan.

"Is that a question?" asked Malvidia.

"Is what a question?" said Sky.

Malvidia narrowed her eyes, her nose hairs waving at him. "Don't *inflect* with me, young man, or I'll have you in detention so fast that the *gale force winds* will make your hollow head ring like a bell."

"But you've already given me detention," said Sky. "For the next week."

"Then, I'll give you even more!" said Malvidia, flustered.

Hands snickered.

"Mr. Silverthorn, you need a haircut," said Malvidia.

"Yes, ma'am," said Hands, his smile fading.

"You saved my life, Mr. Weathers," said Malvidia. "It almost makes me happy that I didn't k—"

"Kill me as a child," said Sky. "I know. I get that a lot." He could see Dad's arm wrapped tightly around Mom, keeping her from dismantling Malvidia limb from limb.

"You swore you'd protect him!" exclaimed Mom.

"No," said Malvidia. "I promised you I wouldn't *harm*

him. There is a difference. Despite what you may think, I had no idea a Wargarou was lurking in the dingy halls of Arkhon Academy—especially *that* Wargarou," she spat. "Let alone that it had eaten and replaced Principal Bartholomew 'the Bat' Goethe Lem and turned his apprentices into Shadow Wargs. Though, looking back on it now, perhaps I should've been suspicious when he started bathing."

"You've never forgiven Phineas for leaving you," said Mom. "This has never been about the Arkhon and what you think happened to Sky."

Nobody besides the monster hunters knew about Errand. They probably didn't know anything about Changelings, and he wondered how they'd react when he explained it all, but more than that, he wondered how much his parents knew. And when they found out more, what would they do?

"This has always been about the danger Sky poses, despite what you believe," said Malvidia, glancing pointedly at his hand, "but perhaps you're right. Perhaps it's time to forgive Phineas for costing the lives of countless hunters to save this one boy. I'm curious, Mr. Livingstone. Did you know your family was torn apart to save this little monster here? Did you know that he is the reason the Arkhon came to Exile in the first place? What are your thoughts on the matter? Should we forgive the boy responsible for your family's destruction?"

Malvidia glanced at Andrew . . . and then she noticed the cup he was holding, the one he'd retrieved from the garbage can, full of yellow liquid.

"It's for phosphorus," said Andrew, looking sheepish.

"I'm sure it is," said Malvidia, her lip curling. "Perhaps we should ask you then, Mr. Silverthorn. Didn't your grandmother die eleven years ago, leaving your grandpa Osmer a widower? Quite a coincidence that it happened to be about the time Phineas set his trap, don't you think?"

Hands frowned at Sky. Hands had never mentioned his grandma's death before. Hands had been only three when it had happened, Sky guessed, and chances were, he didn't know the details. But Sky could see that Malvidia wanted to make sure Hands knew all about it now and, more important, who'd caused it. Not Phineas, who was dead and out of reach, but *Sky*, who was quite alive and an arm's length away.

"Mr. Bullneck, you've had one brother miraculously raised from the dead, as it were, but it makes you wonder. Would he ever have been taken in the first place if Phineas hadn't allowed the Wargarou to escape from the prison in Phineas's attempts to save Sky?"

T-Bone scowled.

She was methodically pounding a wedge between them and Sky and defacing Phineas's legacy in the process. She was taking everything they'd won over the last few days and turning it to ash in their mouths, a defeat in the face of victory.

"And finally, Miss Bittlesworth. Your mother has been missing for an *awfully* long time. It almost makes you wonder what on earth could be so important that a loving mother would leave her little girl behind with a shiftless father to face poverty and despair alone. What in the world could she possibly be looking for?" Malvidia glanced at Sky, smiling viciously.

Answers. That's what Crystal's mother was looking for. Answers about Sky. Phineas never knew about Errand, and for some reason Cassandra's search had taken her to Skull Valley, where she'd disappeared. Sky hadn't had a chance to tell Crystal yet, but Malvidia knew what Cassandra had been looking for, and Malvidia was using it to drive another wedge between them.

"So," said Malvidia, turning back to face Mom, "maybe you're right, Helen. Maybe it is time to forgive Phineas for his past transgressions. No harm done, right?"

She looked them all over, and he felt like crawling into Rauschtlot's cave and never coming out.

"You know, Sky," said Crystal, pulling the two monocles and the watch from her pocket as she ignored Malvidia. "I never told you the solution to the final puzzle, did I?"

Malvidia's eyes went big at the sight of the keys.

"Er, *no*," said Sky. "I think I was in a coma at the time."

"It was really quite complicated at first—even with Sky's insight that the number pointed to the poem," said Crystal, fiddling with the keys. "We tried having numbers represent lines in the poem, and then words in the poem, and then *letters* in the poem. None of it worked. We would've been there all night if Andrew hadn't spotted it."

"I thought it was a silly title," said Andrew. "Who ever heard of 'Enof Od Naba Ban Do Fone'?"

"I assumed it was a place-name that really referred to someplace else," said Crystal.

"Like the Ingubriate Ocean really being the Atlantic Ocean in *The Tourmaline of Foresight*. That's what I thought too. . . . *Wait a minute*," said Sky, suddenly realizing what he'd missed. "I know what it is! It's not a place at all. It's a *palindrome*!"

"A palin what?" said T-Bone.

"A palindrome, Mr. Bullneck," said Malvidia, frowning. "A word or sentence that reads the same backward and forward, like . . . like . . ."

"Like 'bird rib,'" said Andrew.

"Or 'Bob,'" said Sky.

"Or 'live, party, trap evil,'" added Hands.

"Yes," said Malvidia, her lip curling, "precisely."

"'Enof Od Naba Ban Do Fone,'" said Crystal. "A Band of One."

Crystal held up the keys she'd been fiddling with. They were connected together. The two monocles joined in the middle, by the nosepieces, forming a single pair of glasses. The pocket watch, in turn, hung down from the nosepiece by its chain.

Crystal turned to Malvidia. "So that was the solution to the final puzzle, Miss Hagfish. Don't you find that interesting?"

Malvidia stared down her nose at Crystal, her eyes full of disdain.

"Well, *I* find it interesting," said Mom. "I think that solution may even deserve some extra credit, Malvidia."

"I expect to see you in class on Monday, Mr. Weathers," said Malvidia. "A wound like this should be *nothing* to a mighty hunter such as yourself."

"But our arrangement with you and the other hunters allowed us to stay only until the crisis was over," said Dad. "Does this mean you're extending it?"

"I *always* pay my debts," she said without turning from Sky. "Now, if you'll excuse me, I have several traumatized hunters to attend to. Eleven years stuck in a time prison, with only your thoughts for company, is a long time."

She stared at him for a moment longer—her eyes narrowing—and then she turned and started for the door.

"Wait!" said Andrew. "You found hunters alive?"

Malvidia stopped for a moment, her back to them.

"I'm sorry, Andrew," said Malvidia, her voice soft. "Your mother was not among them."

"Oh. Right," said Andrew, sounding heartbroken.

Malvidia swept out the door.

"Thanks for the letter and . . . er . . . food!" Sky called after her, eyeing the pan on the table.

"It's not from me," replied Malvidia without slowing as she disappeared into the hospital to torment some other poor souls.

Hands walked over to the table and lifted the lid on the pot. "What a *witch*. Worst teacher I ever had! It wouldn't surprise me if this soup were made from the tears of drowned puppies and the broken dreams of little children."

"What is it?" asked Andrew, peeking into the pot, his hand held over his cup to keep the yellow liquid from spilling in.

Hands dipped his finger into the pot and took a taste. His face contorted in a grimace.

"Hands! Are you okay? Is it poison?" cried Crystal.

"N-no," spluttered Hands, trying to speak through the grimace. "I think it's *goulash*."

"Tears and broken dreams it is, then," said Andrew.

Sky perked up, his mind wandering back from the dark places Malvidia's words had driven it.

"Goulash!" screamed Sky. "Let me see that!"

Hands held the pot for him. Sky looked in, spotting unnameable meats and horror-laden vegetables drowning in an unholy tide of grotesque pasta and brown-red soup from the horrid waters of the lowest regions of the stygian abyss.

He took a bite and his face contorted. "It *is* goulash!"

"Sky, you should read this," said T-Bone, frowning. He held out the paper that'd come with the monstrous goulash.

Sky took it, his smile disappearing as he read.

LAST WILL AND TESTAMENT OF

PHINEAS T. PIMISCULE

By now Malvidia has received this, my last will and testament, and delivered it to you, Sky, along with a most delectable mess of goulash—which she will (no doubt) have the good graces to prepare upon completion of this letter. She has always been a magnificent hunter, a stupendous cook, a passable fiancé, and an irreplaceable friend. . . . I hope you find as much joy in eating the goulash as she (almost certainly) found in preparing it. It should serve as the perfect side dish to your words.

Sky smiled. He'd told Phineas on his birthday that if botany ever saved his life, he'd eat a whole *pot* of goulash. It was a good thing he was already in the hospital.

Sky, I hereby bequeath Pimiscule Manor and the surrounding grounds (and all hideous atrocities therewith) to you, my friend and heir.

Sky stared at the letter, dumbfounded. The manor was *his*?

It's a perfectly appalling tenement on a hideous hillside replete with nightmarish visions of revulsion and despair. I put it all in your highly capable hands. It has always been horrid, but at one point it was livable, and if the trap has been reset, it should be livable again, with some work.

But one thing of interest I will point out: If you go to the far room on the second floor—the one beyond the painting of the woman with the face of a camel (your great-great-aunt Tess, I might mention, before she was drawn and quartered)—you'll find a hidden panel and, behind the hidden panel, a small study with a somewhat extraordinary and highly macabre collection of books . . . some of which you might recognize.

The books, he realized. All the books that'd burned in the fire . . . Phineas must've had backup copies!

This collection—while not as grand as the former collection in the pendulum room, which I bequeathed to Arkhon Academy after my flight—should keep you bored for many years to come. I expect you to take good care of them.

Sky, I wish I could be there with you, with all of you. You've no doubt learned about the Eye of Legend by now (what you call the trix) and what happened that night eleven years ago—why we were forced to leave so abruptly. Over the years, I've found few answers about what happened that night. I have suspicions, but I can't discuss them openly. Stay watchful; I won't leave you clueless.

Tell the others they can expect to receive more personalized deliveries over the coming weeks. I haven't forgotten them, but I assumed your need would be more urgent. Goulash waits for no man.

Finally, since a letter would be unlikely to find her, please give my regards to Ursula. You'll find she's a real mystery, but I promise you, she's worth the effort.

Eventually all paths cross again.

With Love,
Uncle Phineas T. Pimiscule

He looked up from the letter, silent.

"So what does it say?" prodded Hannah.

"It says we don't have to move again," said Sky.

CHAPTER 43

A Mystery Solved

A few days later they let Sky out of the hospital. The doctors were amazed at how quickly he'd healed, but Mom just smiled. She'd secretly been feeding him all kinds of weird stuff while Hands had (unsuccessfully) distracted the nurses.

He and Hannah stayed with Beau for a few days while his parents made some "minor" repairs to the house, which landed them back in the hospital a few days later while Dad recovered from a freak miming accident—incurred when Mom tried to show him how to properly use a hammer and hit him in the groin instead. At least it wasn't his fault this time.

Sky spent most of his time with Crystal and the others. When they entered the hunters' lair for the first time since Sky's hospitalization—through the tunnels in the sewers because the shack had burned to the ground (NOT his fault!)—they found Alexis, the former classmate/Shadow Warg they'd captured, gibbering in the dark. Apparently she'd become human again when Ursula freed the others and the ICE encasing her had broken apart. With the primary exit blocked by debris from the fire, she'd wandered the tunnels, lost, before finally hunkering down in a mad-eyed stupor—surviving on cave water and Cheez Whiz until they found her.

They blindfolded her so she couldn't find her way back, and took her home to her parents.

He still had detention to make up for, and Malvidia made it as unbearable as possible. He had to scrub chalkboards, stack and unstack desks for no reason, read Jane Austen with Andrew's sisters. . . . She even made him help the janitor clean the bathrooms of all their unholy filth and muck.

As it turns out, urinal cakes really *aren't* cakes.

When he wasn't in detention, or with his friends, or visiting a family member at the hospital, or feeding the Piebalds crackers (Andrew and Hands made an extra large batch of phosphorus especially for them), he wandered the manor.

The glass wall and the pendulum were gone, along with Solomon and his monsters—trapped somewhere in the slipstreams of time. The only things left were the run-down manor and yard, which, as Phineas had said, needed a lot of work; but at least they had a place to live. Sky had no idea what would happen if the Arkhon's and the wall prison returned while they were inside the manor, but he couldn't imagine Phineas saying the place was livable unless he'd built in some kind of fail-safe, or warning system, to protect them if such a thing happened.

As Sky walked the empty halls, he thought about Errand. The trix on Sky's hand had finally healed fully but somehow, Sky still seemed to bleed.

At nights he lay awake, waiting for Errand to reach out to him again—to appear by his side and make fun of him and terrorize him and tell him he forgave him. Had Errand really died out there? Had he gone off in search of the shadowy man, looking for answers? Sky hadn't found Errand's body despite numerous searches, but plenty of hungry monsters had roamed free that night.

And night after night his dreams remained dark and empty, like an undeveloped picture too soon exposed to the light.

He still couldn't bring himself to go into the small study mentioned in his uncle's will. Somehow the thought of seeing all those books returned to life—while the giver himself rotted in the Jack—brought back memories more than he could bear.

A few days later—in an attempt to avoid his dark and often confusing thoughts—he decided it was time to complete another task that Phineas had given him in his will.

"Yes, Sky?"

"I just wanted to thank you, Miss Terry," said Sky, watching to make sure none of the other students were close enough to hear as they exited gym class.

"Whatever for?"

He squirmed. "For, you know . . . your *help* the other night."

"Don't mention it," said Miss Terry. "I would've called Sheriff Beau for any of my students accosted by bullies."

"That's not what I mean," said Sky.

"Oh?"

"No, that *is* what I mean. Thank you for that, too. But I meant the . . . *other* stuff. My parents and stuff." He dropped his voice for a moment, waiting for some students to pass. One of them, Felicity, winked at him, causing him to blush.

Miss Terry raised an eyebrow.

"Er, what I mean to say is, *my uncle Phineas sends his regards*."

Miss Terry's eyebrow went even higher.

"It was in his will. He wanted me to tell you that," said Sky, adding, more quietly, "Ursula."

Miss Terry was quiet for a moment. "What gave me away?"

"Your name," said Sky. "In the will Phineas said you were a *mystery* worth the effort. '*Mystery*' . . . '*Miss Terry*.' Your name is a play on words."

"Very clever of you," said Miss Terry, smiling, "and very *reckless* of your uncle. I'd appreciate it if we kept this between us."

"I understand," said Sky, going quiet again as Alexis passed by, her eyes darting about nervously. She had yet to recover from her ordeal in the lair.

Crenshaw, Ren, Marcus, and Cordelia passed by a moment later. Crenshaw scowled at him, while Marcus avoided eye contact entirely.

Cordelia faced him head-on, giving him a little wink and a nod. They weren't friends or anything, but at least they weren't enemies. She'd forgiven him for embarrassing her in gym, and he'd forgiven her for trying to rip out his throat and for losing his copy of *The Shadow Wargs of Whimple*, which she claimed had been destroyed with the Cadillac. He had his doubts.

Ren was the last in line, giving him a terse nod. Ren had never really thanked him for finding Dickens, but he *had* stopped beating him up. As far as Sky was concerned, that was thanks enough.

"What'll happen to them?" asked Sky after they left the gym.

"They're unbound now. I had to give them up at sunrise to retake this form," said Miss Terry.

Sky hadn't thought about it before, but now he wondered.

"Is there a *real* Miss Terry out there?" he asked. "I know

you don't have to . . . you know . . . kill stuff and eat it to take its form like a Wargarou, but . . ."

"I'm not sure a Wargarou does either," said Miss Terry. "I think they may just *like* to. But no, there's not a real Miss Terry out there. Older Whisper, like myself, don't need to copy exactly; we can make small changes—hair color, eyes, size of nose, that sort of thing—just enough to make us distinct."

Sky nodded. "So Crenshaw, the others? Unbound? What does that mean exactly?"

"Turning the pack and then handing it off to my sister wasn't smart of the Wargarou," said Ursula. "To make a pack, a Wargarou must give up part of itself. Ambrosia controlled them, but the Wargarou bound them. When I freed his pack, they became unbound and the Wargarou lost that part of itself. It weakened him. It would surprise me if he even has the ability to take a new form anymore. So much of his power is now latent in Crenshaw and the others, waiting to be awoken or reclaimed. But as long as the Wargarou stays away, there'll be no more Shadow Wargs in Exile. Malvidia will see to it."

He nodded. "And if he comes back, you can always bite him again."

"There's that as well," said Miss Terry, smiling, "but I shudder at the thought. Hairy Wargarou tastes just awful."

He laughed. "You should try goulash. I ate a whole pot full the other day. The rigor mortis was terrible."

"Why in the world would you do such a thing?" asked Miss Terry, flabbergasted.

"Because," said Sky, "botany saved my life."

Miss Terry shook her head, confused, but he didn't elaborate. He'd made a promise to his uncle, and he'd kept it.

Besides, it turned out that goulash really was the perfect side dish to eating his words.

"I see," said Miss Terry. "You know, your uncle was a good man, Sky; his death is a loss to us all. You remind me a lot of him."

"How so?"

"Well . . . ," said Miss Terry, "your uncle never tried to do things because he thought he could succeed. He tried because it was the *right thing to do*."

Sky fidgeted, feeling awkward. "Er, there's still something I don't understand."

"What's that?" asked Miss Terry.

"Well, you're a *monster*, right? A Whisper?" said Sky.

"I am," said Miss Terry.

"So when we first met," continued Sky, "you told me you were there to help me."

"I did."

"And when I found out about your history with Beau, I thought I understood why. I thought you were, you know, trying to fix past mistakes and stuff."

Miss Terry raised an eyebrow.

"What I mean to say," Sky said in a rush, "is that I thought you'd come back for *him*. That you were hoping Phineas would patch things up or something. But after the Wargarou attack, when he was injured, you came to help me instead of going with Beau to the hospital. Why?"

"I made sure he was taken care of," said Miss Terry.

"That's not my point," said Sky.

"I know." She sighed. "We all have our secrets."

⌑ ⌑ ⌑

Later that evening he decided it was finally time. The halls were dark, dusty, and quiet—the electricity yet to be turned on. He'd retrieved the candelabra he'd lost in his mad flight through the yard, and he carried it with him, lit this time, its candles flickering and sparkling with hazy light as they drove the darkness before him. He could see in the dark, it was true, but he could see better in the light.

He passed the picture of his great-great-aunt Tess (who really did look like a camel) and briefly wondered if his uncle had been right in saying the painting had been done *before* she'd been drawn and quartered.

He spotted a length of slightly discolored wall, and as he approached the secret door leading to the study, he crouched low, hearing muffled sounds from within—yapping and howling and shrieking. He pushed the door open, raising the candelabra high overhead to defend himself.

"About time you showed up," said T-Bone from a comfy-looking leather recliner as the laughter of a moment before died down.

"How did you . . ."

"We've been here every night waiting for *you*," said Crystal, setting down the book she'd been reading.

As he looked around, he realized the walls were covered with books from floor to ceiling. There were rolling ladders, couches, chairs, tables and desks, a loft, and even a large, roaring fireplace lighting the room.

"We had to clean it up a bit," said Andrew, glancing up from the card game he was playing with T-Bone and Hands, "but not much. Someone has kept things pretty well preserved."

Sky nodded, taking it all in.

"So . . . are you going to put that thing down, or are you determined to burn down another house?" Hands prodded.

"I didn't burn down—" He stopped as Hands started laughing. Sky smiled too. He crossed the room and set the candelabra on a table. Then he wandered about, looking at all the books.

"*Shammy the Shameless Charlatan*, *The Feather Out of Time*, *Demon Wraiths of Windsor*, *Reaper Keeper*, *The Edge of Oblivion*, *The Tourmaline of Foresight*, even *The Shadow Wargs of Whimple*!" exclaimed Sky. "They're all here!"

"And then some," said Andrew.

The room, the warm fire, his friends, all the books—it was almost too much to take in. Sky took a deep breath, preparing himself. It was time to come clean.

"I haven't been completely honest with you guys," said Sky, walking over to the coffee table so he could face them directly.

"What is it now?" said T-Bone.

Sky decided to start with something easy, something they probably already knew.

"You've probably already figured it out, but I wanted you to hear it from me. I'm the reason the Arkhon came to Exile," said Sky, turning to Andrew. "I was the bait that drew him here, that got all those hunters killed . . . including your mom."

Andrew nodded. "I don't blame you, Sky, if that's what you think. We heard enough through the branches in our ears to figure things out. You're as much a victim as any of us—maybe more so."

"Still, I'm sorry," said Sky.

Andrew shrugged, staring at the floor.

"So," said Hands, "we get that Solomon came for the Mark on your hand, but why?"

"I don't really know," Sky admitted. "According to Ursula, he thinks the Hunter's Mark can somehow protect him from others like him while he searches for an ancient power that nearly destroyed the world."

"Destroyed the world . . . and this guy was one of your heroes?" asked T-Bone.

"Not the best role model now, I'll admit," said Sky, "but once upon a time Solomon Rose was pretty amazing. I don't know exactly how or why he went bad and became the Arkhon, but it would be a pretty big blow to hunters if they found out about it—not to mention how monsters would react. Maybe that's why Phineas never said anything."

"So, let me see if I understand this," said Hands. "Solomon Rose took the Arkhon's body four hundred years ago after, apparently, faking his own death. This is a dangerous fact known by nobody but us, Phineas, and maybe a few others. Since then, Solomon, posing as the Arkhon, either has been imprisoned or has been searching for some ancient power that nearly destroyed the world. Eleven years ago he came to Exile, shifted into an Echo, decimated the hunters, and stepped into a trap while looking for the Hunter's Mark, a mark he still doesn't have, thanks to us, but still desperately wants. Is that about right?" asked Hands.

"More or less," said Sky.

"That's messed up," said Hands.

"But what about the real Arkhon?" asked Crystal. "What happened to him?"

Sky shrugged. "Who knows? Maybe his consciousness or whatever died when Solomon took his body? Maybe he's still alive somewhere, trapped in some other body, or hiding in Solomon's head? Solomon wanted the Arkhon's body so he could get the trix, but in the process he lost the Hunter's Mark. He claims it was stolen from him. He must've had some kind of plan in place to get both, but something went wrong. Maybe the Arkhon messed up his plans."

"Or someone else. He could've had an accomplice," said T-Bone.

"True," said Sky, taking a deep breath. Now for the hard part.

"There's something else I need to tell you—about Errand . . . what he really is . . . what *I* really am," said Sky.

"Is this about the Changeling thing? We know all about that," said Hands.

"What? How do you know?" exclaimed Sky. "I mean, I know you must've heard me talking to Errand while we fought, but—"

"Phineas mentioned it in the letters he sent us," Andrew cut in, "and there are a lot of books in this study—even books on Changelings. You gave us plenty of time to study up."

Each of them had received a letter and a gift of one kind or another—strange knives, puzzles, books, art supplies. None but *him* had received goulash.

"B-but why didn't you say something before?" Sky sputtered, feeling relieved.

"Phineas said to wait for you here in the evenings. He said you'd come when you were ready," said Crystal.

Sky shook his head. He'd been sweating over this for days. He hadn't even talked to his *parents* yet, a conversation he didn't know how to begin. "So Mom and Dad," he'd start, "how's the weather? Oh? That's splendid. Did you know that you may have raised a Changeling instead of your real child? No? Yes? Well . . . er . . . funny thing, huh? Shall I pack my bags, or would you prefer to do it for me?"

"It's okay, Sky," said Andrew. "It's water under the bridge—*all* of it."

"We've had a change of heart where monsters are concerned," said Crystal. "Rauschtlot, the Piebalds, Ursula—you were right. They're not all bad."

"Besides," said T-Bone, "we all agree. You're one of us now, no matter what else you might be."

The others nodded in agreement.

"Er, *thanks*," said Sky, not sure he could say more.

"It's amazing. The poor guy," said Hands. "Trapped in here the whole time."

"Yeah. I wish I had— Wait. I don't remember saying anything about him being stuck in here," said Sky, perking up. "How did you know that?"

"What do you mean? It was in the letter," said Crystal, staring at him curiously.

Sky fell back, slapping his head. Luckily there was a seat behind him.

"What's wrong?" asked Crystal, beginning to look worried.

The others set down their cards.

"He's not dead," said Sky.

"What?" said Crystal.

"Phineas. He's not dead. He had notes on Changelings. Maybe he could've guessed about that, but he didn't even know Errand existed!" said Sky. "Crystal, Phineas asked your mom to find answers about *me*. That's why she was in Skull Valley!"

Crystal nodded as if she already knew as much.

"But Phineas never found the answers. He didn't *know*!" Sky continued. "The Jack took Phineas *before* I found Errand in the manor! Phineas never knew he was in here, which means he wrote the letters *afterward*!"

"I don't know, Sky," said Crystal. "He could have found out before we found him in the maze. Maybe Errand reached out to him like he did to you."

Sky shook his head. "He didn't. He would've said something. One of them would have."

"It was a clue," said Hands, "like he said he'd leave us in his will. Phineas wanted us to know he was still alive—that he was still out there somewhere . . . alone . . . ragged . . . fighting the good fight . . . alone."

"This is all fine and dandy," said T-Bone, "but if Phineas isn't dead, where is he?"

Sky didn't have an answer.

"Hey," said Crystal, patting herself down, "has anyone seen a monocle? I swear I had it on me before I came here."

Sky glanced at Hands.

"What? Don't look at me!" Hands exclaimed defensively.

Everyone looked around nervously, eyeing the shadows.

"I can't believe you lost it," said Andrew. "We never would've made it out of the manor without the monocles."

"I forgot to mark the walls!" Sky exclaimed, remembering. He'd been so caught up with Errand.

"That was the least of our worries," said Crystal, "Besides, it turns out that the monocles let you see in the dark. Go figure."

"Ooo-wee-oooh," said Andrew.

"What is that? Like a sneeze or something?" said Hands.

"It's a horror riff," said Andrew, "signifying the mysterious and unexplained."

"It sounded more like a barfing frog," said Hands. "Speaking of which, I believe you owe me a story, Sky . . ."

"What? Seriously? Now?" said Sky.

Hands stared at him expectantly, his knuckles planted beneath his chin, his elbows resting on the coffee table. As Sky looked around at the others, he saw the same dopey expressions on their faces as they stared back, waiting.

"Hhhh. *Fine*. Once upon a time," he started, snuggling down into the recliner he'd fallen into, "there was a *Humanatee* . . ."

EPILOGUE
The Fifth Rule

Phineas T. Pimiscule fidgeted with his monocle, very glad to have found it, hiding as it had been, in Crystal's pocket. He watched the figures moving in the manor window from a cornfield a short distance away. He watched and watched, and watched again, and then watched some more, until the light dimmed, and the shadows gathered, and the darkness crept in like a widow approaching her husband's casket, wondering what tomorrow would bring.

Swinging the cane from under his arm, he turned away, smiling, as he hobbled back toward the east cemetery, cringing with each step as tremors moved through the still-healing wound on his side.

The gibbous moon shone brightly overhead, and the stars were full and dazzling in the night sky, like millions of sugar grains swirling in a fish bowl moments before dissolving.

As he walked, a woman stepped out of the trees, falling

into step next to him. She was tall, with thick black hair like charcoal.

"You really think I'll be able to find her?" said the woman.

"Somebody has to. We need to *know*, Em," said Phineas.

Em looked back at the manor.

"I'm sorry. It's not a choice I'd ever wish for you," said Phineas, noticing.

As he spoke, two Gnomon, Rauschtlot and Nackles, stepped out of the crypt he'd been heading toward, causing Em to jump and reach into her coat.

"It's okay. They won't harm you," said Phineas.

The woman dropped her hand but continued to watch the Gnomon. Rauschtlot made several shrieking and popping sounds, and Phineas replied in kind.

"Rauschtlot says that she and Nackles will take care of you for as long as you'd like to stay. The place is *yours*, after all," said Phineas.

Em stared at the crypt, her face unreadable.

"I can't recommend their services highly enough," Phineas continued. "If it weren't for them, and a few well-placed Gnomon holes, I'd be bubbling in the belly of a Jack at the moment."

"You can talk to them?" Em asked.

"Even better than that," said Phineas. "I can *listen*. It's amazing what you can pick up with a little effort and a few centuries."

"Or what you can lose in a *moment*," Em replied, her eyes going distant again as she glanced back at the manor. "Eleven years . . . when those kids found me . . ." She shook her head.

"It's your decision," Phineas said softly. "I can't make it for you, nor would I want to. Your husband is *mad*, but he's still alive. Malvidia found him a job at the school that he rather likes. And your son is taken care of, but a boy always needs his mother. If you decide to go back to Malvidia and let her know you survived, I won't blame you. She could use the help, and nobody would have to know one way or the other. In her own way she can be as discreet as I can."

"But you need me?" asked Em.

"Desperately," said Phineas. "I'm dead, remember?"

"Aren't we all?" replied Em, smiling sadly as she stared at her own crypt, her son's initials on the coffin hidden inside: "With Love Forever, ANL." "And you really believe this will help them—that it will help your nephew, that it will help my son?"

"The future of the world rests on their shoulders," said Phineas.

"Aren't you afraid of what could happen if the Hunters of Legend find out?" asked Em.

"Bully that! It's the fifth rule of trap building," said Phineas. "A trap, like a good story, always leaves them hanging. Besides, there's a reason I'm playing dead. It makes everything much easier . . . especially where the Hunters of Legend are concerned. I need time to find answers."

Em was silent a moment. "Skull Valley." She shook her head as if she couldn't believe the words were coming out of her mouth. "I just don't know, Phineas. I was never as good as Cass."

"You may fare better than you think. Bedlam isn't like his brother," said Phineas. "If you weren't determined to stay dead, I'd never ask it of you, but we need to know what *happened.* Everything could depend on it."

Em looked back up at the manor. "I'll think about it. But

what about you? Where will you go now that you're dead?"

"All these years, I didn't know what had happened, but now . . ." He shook his head. "There's a boy whom I owe a terrible debt; he also needs to be prepared."

"Prepared for what?" Em asked.

"For the horrors to come."

HUNTER'S JOURNAL ADDENDUM, SKY WEATHERS

For reference, I've compiled some notes on a few of the monsters I've come across, read about, or heard about so far.

While I've included a few survival tips, your first, and best course of action is always to RUN. I mean it. Flee. Vamoose. Hotfoot it out. Shake a rug. Just get out of there. If that doesn't work, try a friendly "hello"; it won't help at all, but at least you won't die impolite.

SHADOW WARGS:

Shadow Wargs are hunters who have made a pact with a Wargarou: the hunter agrees to become the Wargarou's minion and, in exchange, the hunter gains the ability to shift into a Shadow Warg. Shadow Wargs are Clydesdale-size, wolf-like, and very annoying. They are made of darkness, can slip between shadows without being seen, and are practically invulnerable.

HOW TO SURVIVE AN ENCOUNTER:
The Shadow Wargs of Whimple mentions three weaknesses: silver, fire, and wolfsbane.

WARGAROU:

Wargarous are vicious, vaguely wolf-like, and impossible to kill. They can change shape over the three days of a full moon by eating the body of the victim they wish to change into, and they keep that shape until they eat another, or revert to their *true* form—a terrible monster of darkness and fire.

Wargarous can flit through shadows, disappearing and reappearing like knives in a sheath. They can create Shadow Wargs and, if they find Shadow Wargs that other Wargarous have created, they can bind them. Once bound, the Shadow Warg is bound for life unless the Wargarou frees it, has its pack taken from it (usually after losing a fight to another Wargarou), or dies.

Wargarous seem to have a love for fine things and eating small children. Usually, they keep a low profile, hiding in wait, but when they change into their fiery form—look out.

HOW TO SURVIVE AN ENCOUNTER:
According to *Wicked, Wicked Wargarou*, water and cold can sometimes quench a Wargarou's fire, but it won't stop it. Driving off a Wargarou's pack will weaken it. And, supposedly, a "hunter's blade" can kill it—whatever that is.

Also, being able to change into a Wargarou yourself doesn't hurt.

GNOMON:

"Four to the foot,
larger than man,
long of the arm,
and not very tan,
they look like gnomes,
with less-pointy hats,
and if you find one,
you better skee-dats . . . tle."

—Taken from *The Tourmaline of Foresight*

*Note: Gnomon are *nothing* like gnomes! They are monstrously tall with large, black eyes, nose-less, wrinkled faces, and pale, white-gray translucent skin that pulses with red and blue and black veins (*Blue as it stills, Black as it flies, Red as it kills*—a description of their color-changing skin from *Much Ado About Gnomon*). They wear caps over their heads to hide dozens of tiny mouths, all of which are lipless and full of razor sharp teeth, which they use for tunneling. Few things can match a Gnomon's strength. Some stories claim that Gnomon may even be descended from Paragoth of the Deep, the Earth Eater.

HOW TO SURVIVE AN ENCOUNTER:
Gnomon don't have opposable thumbs.

WHISPER:

These sneaky creatures are masters of infiltration. In my experience, they prefer human form, and even their true form seems human. But don't let that fool you: Whisper can change into almost anything (even Shadow Wargs and Wargarou as I found out the hard way). Their body densities increase with age so they can shift into larger forms, so watch for sudden weight changes in those around you. Unlike their father, the Arkhon, Whisper can only shift over the three days of the full moon—not all the time. And, Whisper need a fresh biological sample of the creature they want to change into (though older Whisper have some limited control of their features without a sample). Whisper feel a consuming urge to shift all the time, but if they shift outside of a full moon, their bodies become increasingly chaotic until they lose control completely and become Glooms—fallen Whisper.

HOW TO SURVIVE AN ENCOUNTER:
NEVER hunt a Whisper under a full moon (you might as well be hunting the Arkhon; seriously, they're just as bad).

ECHO:

The Evil Echo of Solomon Rose describes Echo as vaguely treelike, with large black leathery wings that fold out of their trunkish bodies. Their branchy arms can be inflexible as iron one moment, and slithery as tentacles the next, and when the wings spread out, the branches sweep downward into a rickety, protective shell. Or, if they choose, outward like writhing spears to flay and terrify those below—a tree one instant, a nightmare with wings the next.

Great pupil-less white eyes run half the length of the trunk—or at least, they did until Solomon Rose gouged them out, one by one, when the Echo refused to follow him against a monster he claimed would destroy the world. Robbed of their sight, Echo began to "see" through highly sensitive organs in their branches and mouth—tasting the scents, and sights, and emotions around them.

Echo keep to themselves, hiding in the old, dark forests of the world. Tangled roots spread deep, deep beneath them, clinging to the roots of other Echo like children holding hands, and they spend days and nights lost in a haunting sort of collective dream.

According to the Echo narrator of *The Evil Echo of Solomon Rose*, breaking an Echo from its roots ends the dream, effectively exiling the Echo, and is one of the cruelest things that can happen; it is also one of the best, because a rooted Echo can't fly, and flying, as the narrator claims, is a dream worth waking up for.

HOW TO SURVIVE AN ENCOUNTER:
Echo have highly sensitive sensory organs all along their limbs. So long as the limbs are flexible (i.e., not in protective mode), they can be attacked. At best, this will temporarily "blind" the Echo, giving you time to run.

PIEBALDS:

Mottled black-and-white crows. If you shine a black light on them, their skeletons will glow. Piebalds thrive on high levels of phosphorus and the scales from their feet can drive away some types of poison (like Dovetail).

HOW TO SURVIVE AN ENCOUNTER:
Don't give a Piebald crackers (especially phosphorus-laced crackers) and it will leave you alone.

THE JACK:

The Jack is a sprawling, living, fire-breathing pumpkin patch. According to *The Journal of Alexander Drake*, each of the Jack's gourds (some of which are the size of houses) has its own brain. A gourd can work independently, attack what it wants, but if the big brain gives a command, the thousands of little brains have to follow. Distract the big brain and you distract the rest.

The Jack sleeps most the time, but it's a light sleeper. Fortunately, the only eyes are on the main head. Unfortunately, it has an incredibly strong sense of smell through glands on each of the gourds. And if it smells you and thinks you're a threat, it wakes up, and when it wakes up, it's nearly as bad as Hannah in the morning.

Jack Seeds, from the gourds, can accelerate healing. They are also poisonous to DoveTail.

HOW TO SURVIVE AN ENCOUNTER:
Two known weaknesses: attract the big brain and distract it with the biggest threat, and then, second, hit it with DoveTail, which might slow it down or just make it angrier. *The Journal of Alexander Drake* says that hunters who faced the Jack didn't survive long enough to discover any other weaknesses. Based on my own experiences, I can attest to this.

DOVETAIL:

A giant, boron-eating hedge maze. White leaves, like feathers, cover thick black branches. Red and black budding flowers on the DoveTail are strangely inviting (just watch out for the poisonous thorns!).

The earth around DoveTail is usually red and barren, due to the fact that the DoveTail has eaten most everything else.

HOW TO SURVIVE AN ENCOUNTER:
DoveTail moves slowly, unless it views you as a real threat. Don't threaten it, and you should be fine. If it does decide to attack you, make sure you have Jack Seeds and Crow's Feet on hand. Whatever you do, DON'T FALL ASLEEP!

THE ARKHON:

Terror of The Night, Bringer of The Dark, One of Three, The Immortal, The Blood Thief, The Wasting Hunger, The Shifting Horror, The Moon Goblin, The Night. The Arkhon is The ultimate shifter, The father of most other shifters. He can change into anything so long as he has tasted it before.

The Arkhon is ancient and not all he seems . . .
AVOID AT ALL COSTS!

HOW TO SURVIVE AN ENCOUNTER:
While he's in a form, he acquires The form's weaknesses, but The second you try to corner him, he shifts. The only way to stop him is to stop his shifting.

GLOOMS:

According to *The Fantafstik Book of Myfical Mofnsters*, Glooms are "Fallen Whisper"—Whisper who couldn't resist the urge to shift outside of a full moon and lost control. Like Whisper, Glooms take on forms by ingesting biological samples, but unlike Whisper, Glooms can't sustain those forms and will frequently spin them off, leaving behind a fleshy mess. They are like "rolling chaos," "unpredictable," and "insane"—"forever lost in madness."

HOW TO SURVIVE AN ENCOUNTER:
Glooms hibernate in winter. Cold and cement slow them.

CHANGELINGS:

Changelings are not born; they are made. You start with two of any number of creatures, but at least on of them must be a shifter with "old blood" (blood of the Arkhon, I'm guessing). Blood is traded with blood under a birth moon. From then on, no matter what they were before, both are Changelings thereafter, becoming alike in every way, and permanently linked from then on. The Change is complete and total in a way that no other shifter or creature, no matter how powerful, can ever achieve. To Change again, and link with another, a Changeling must kill its counterpart. Blood must return to blood, and the murder must be by its own hand.

HOW TO SURVIVE AN ENCOUNTER:
Depends on what form it takes. But usually, they're easy to kill (far *too* easy if you ask me).

EDGEWALKERS:

Before they became extinct, Edgewalkers could travel through people's minds, leaving their own hideous bodies behind. They were dream-stealers, gorging on a person's hopes and fears until there was nothing left—feeding a wasting hunger they could never satisfy.

In *The Edge of Oblivion*, Solomon Rose led a group of hunters against the Edgewalkers. They found the Edgewalker's wasted bodies, one by one, and killed them while they slept—leading to the monster's complete and total extinction, if the story is to be believed.

Before their extinction, when an Edgewalker entered

a mind or a dream, all they had with them was what they took from the waking world: their self-image and the things on their own sleeping bodies. Once inside a mind, they could use what they found there to get out again (if they wanted to). Edgewalkers (and those trained in edgewalking) could slip from one mind to another undetected, but once detected, they became stuck in the hosts mind until: 1. The host let them out. 2. They drove the host insane and took control. 3. They died.

HOW TO SURVIVE AN ENCOUNTER:
Edgewalkers are, by all accounts, extinct. But, if you happen across one (and I really hope you don't), don't let it drink your blood; this is how they strengthen their bond with you and gain power in your mind. If you find yourself stalked by a persistent and pernicious Edgewalker, your best bet is to find its body and destroy it; if you try to take it on, head-to-head, in your mind, you are very likely to lose.

DARKHORN:

A hairy black horse the size of a Wargarou, with a lance of darkness protruding from its forehead, and a glowing esca dangling from the lance. The lance and esca apparently perform some kind of "mesmerizing stirring" on those who see it, putting them to sleep.

Sheriff Beau once told me that the Arkhon approached an old hunter stronghold—Bedlam Falls—disguised as a Darkhorn. Before they could stop him, the Arkhon shifted into a Harrow Knight and destroyed half the town.

HOW TO SURVIVE AN ENCOUNTER:
Can be captured with a dog-hair net.

HARROW KNIGHT:

Giants with some limited shifting abilities (enough to blend in with their surroundings, look like rocks, etc.). The oldest ones are rumored to be the size of small hills, and spend their time sleeping, but most are smaller—a mere fifteen to twenty feet tall.

When they get aggravated, their blood boils and their skin catches on fire. A burning, copper-like substance oozes through their skin, covering them from head to toe in a flexible, though impenetrable, coppery armor. As they cool down, usually after everything around them is dead, the coppery substance hardens and breaks off, revealing a fresh layer of skin beneath.

HOW TO SURVIVE AN ENCOUNTER:
Foxglove will speed up their heart rate and cause the copper to oxidize (rust). This exposes their skin and makes them more vulnerable.

HARROW WIGHT:

Like Harrow Knights, but human-size and human-looking. Harrow Wights spend a lot more time around humans than Harrow Knights and, as a consequence, are nearly all insane (if your skin was always catching on fire and going all coppery, you would be too!). Like the Whisper, they are master infiltrators.

HOW TO SURVIVE AN ENCOUNTER:
Foxglove and kind words.

GILEADS:

Botanical monster. The main part of a Gilead's body is made up of snaking roots that rest underground. It can have any number of appendages aboveground, and these appendages shift into a variety of plants and trees to fit in; but according to *The Journal of Alexander Drake*, Gilead appendages usually appear as Dragon Trees.

Gilead Roots provide a burst of adrenaline and can accelerate healing.

HOW TO SURVIVE AN ENCOUNTER:
No idea.

BARROW HAGS:

Barrow Hags have big, frog-like eyes and scaly skin and can jump enormous distances.

Apparently, if you wrap the nose hair of a Barrow Hag around a rutabaga and bury it under a full moon, you will get a Black Rutabaga. If you eat the Black Rutabaga, you can jump like a Barrow Hag (just watch out for the side effects!).

HOW TO SURVIVE AN ENCOUNTER:
Can be frozen with the right gear.

HUMANATEES:

Half man, half manatee. Need I say more?

HOW TO SURVIVE AN ENCOUNTER:
Humanatees are notoriously docile; don't get it angry and you should be fine.

UMBERLINGS:

Umberlings mimic the shadows of creatures around them. They are hard to spot, and even harder to stop.

HOW TO SURVIVE AN ENCOUNTER:
No idea.

SEEPING CREEPERS:

Formless. Seeping Creepers appear as lumps of dirt, metal, water, or sludge. They are incredibly poisonous and hard to predict.

HOW TO SURVIVE AN ENCOUNTER:
No idea. Maybe you can freeze it, or use cement mix?

SATYRNS:

Satyrns have night-black, leathery skin that can stretch and shift. Most of the time, they appear as half one creature, and half another. Animals, monsters, people—nothing is off limits. The only thing that never shifts is their thick skin, which (by all accounts) moves disturbingly as their innards reorganize themselves.

HOW TO SURVIVE AN ENCOUNTER:
No idea. Let me know if you find out.

ERABIN:

Erabin are massive, Wargarou-size creatures that are somewhere between a scarab and a spider. They can spin webs like a spider and dig underground like a scarab and their bite is poisonous.

HOW TO SURVIVE AN ENCOUNTER:
No idea.

MARROWICKS:

Towering, with waxlike skin that melts in the sun. Waxy wings rise from its back and the Marrowick uses these wings like extra legs. The Marrowick will frequently try to mimic the appearance of hunters it encounters.

The Journal of Alexander Drake claims that hunters used to make equipment out of Marrowick wax—though I have no idea how or why.

HOW TO SURVIVE AN ENCOUNTER:
No idea.

MOROSPAWN:

Ocean-dwelling giants. Morospawn wander the unfathomable crevices of the ocean in search of light.

HOW TO SURVIVE AN ENCOUNTER:
No idea. I've never encountered one and I hope I never will.

PARAGOTH OF THE DEEP:

The Earth Eater. Paragoth lives deep underground, in the hard-to-reach places of the earth. I've never read a first-hand account of an encounter with Paragoth, but rumors say that Paragoth is like a rolling ball covered with thousands of silent mouths snapping and chewing.

HOW TO SURVIVE AN ENCOUNTER:
Feed it and beg for mercy.

NITHOK:

Hideous, with fiery wings and gruesome features that will drive a person mad just by looking at it.

HOW TO SURVIVE AN ENCOUNTER:
Don't look at it.

ACKNOWLEDGMENTS

Naming all the people who helped make this book would, in fact, require the making of another book. Since nobody would read a book filled with the names of people they don't know, unless they were looking for a phone number, a dead ancestor, or possibly the suspect in a horrible crime, I will try to keep it short.

First, I'd like to thank my editor, Courtney Bongiolatti, and my publisher, Justin Chanda. You propelled this book to heights I never could have imagined. Courtney, your insights made everything so much better. I owe you both the world.

Steven Malk, my agent, you made everything possible. You saw this book's potential even when I could not. I owe you two worlds, or at least a world and a small moon.

John Rocco, the artist, and Laurent Linn, the designer, your vision gave us all the gift of sight. Everyone else at S&S who has been involved with this book whose names I have yet to hear and whose faces I have yet to see, I thank you.

Brandon Mull, for your expertise, your character, and your willingness to share both.

My friends and early readers, Dave Butler, Matt Butler, Sam Butler, Georgianne Dalzen, and Platte Clark—the discussions I had with you were priceless. Ellen, my niece, you read versions of this book long before it was worth reading.

Heather, my sister, for the parrot and frantic late night reads. Tyler and Todd, my brothers, for inspiring me as you battle your own monsters. My parents, for birthing me. My in-laws, for birthing my wife.

Katie, my wife, you read this book far more times than any sane person should. Jordon, Lucas, and Connor, my children, you have yet to read this book, but the monsters you've drawn on the backs of old printings—especially the Freegee—inspired my own monsters.

Finally, my future readers, may you find as much pleasure in reading this book as I found in finishing it.